Deep in the Heart

Staci Stallings

Spirit Light Publishing

Deep in the Heart

Cover Design: Allan Kristopher Palor
Contact info: allan.palor@yahoo.com
Interior Formatting: Ellen C. Maze, The Author's Mentor,
 www.theauthorsmentor.com
Author Website: http://www.stacistallings.com

ISBN-13: 978-0615647234 (Spirit Light Publishing)
ISBN-10: 0615647235
Also available in eBook publication

Spirit Light Publishing

PRINTED IN THE UNITED STATES OF AMERICA

For all the children of the world:
May we realize they are each precious
in the eyes of their Father.

One

"Please, baby, please, just get me through these gates and up to that front door," Maggie Montgomery pleaded with her '77 Chevette even as her gaze took in the enormous circle drive that led its winding way up a hill to the cream mansion with the stately pillars beyond. "Oh, Lord, what am I doing here? This has got to be the craziest thing I've ever gotten myself into."

Trying not to think about how her beat-up navy blue two-door looked on the grounds that were perfectly manicured right down to the yellow and red rosebushes, Maggie steered the car around the concrete that was edged with white stones the size of her dresser back in her dorm room. At the apex of the circle, she put the car in park and heaved a sigh that might well be her last.

With a push she resettled her glasses on her nose, grabbed her two-page resume and shouldered the door open. "Just breathe," she told herself as she stood on legs wobbly from the three-hour car drive. Pine Hill, Texas and the Ayer Mansion seemed a million miles from Gold Dust Drive in Del Rio. It was still Texas, but the similarities stopped there.

Of course, she was in her best dress, a floral print that was a size too big. That was better than the heels, which were at least two sizes too big. They were the best Mrs. Malinowski could do on ten minutes' notice. The grace of God alone had gotten Maggie this far, and truth be told, she wasn't at all sure how much longer His patience with her would hold out.

"Listen, Holy Spirit, I know I'm probably over my quota by now, but please... Please, let me get this. I don't know what I'll do if I don't." The remaining two dollars in her purse crossed her mind, pulling her spirit down. Defiantly she squared her shoulders and pulled herself to her full five feet, seven inches.

Every step was pushed on by a prayer. The six wide steps up to the front door nearly did her in, but finally, after 17 years of struggling just to survive, she was here—one knock away from something more than a minute-by-minute existence.

She reached up and rang the doorbell. The wait was worse than the walk. Nervousness raked her hand up her purse strap. Seconds slid by, but nothing happened. What now? Should she ring it again? She looked back at her car and fought the fear and desperation rising in her.

Just before she bolted from the whole idea outright, the door clicked and then opened. On the other side stood a small, Hispanic woman dressed head-to-toe in white.

"Hello," Maggie said, corralling her purse strap even as she held out her other hand. "I'm here about the nanny position."

"Doesn't anyone know how to follow a simple order anymore?" the bellowing, jowl-ridden, over-paunched, balding man at the desk fumed, shaking his head even as he continued to make notes. "I built a whole company, put in oil wells across this state—Midland, West Texas, South Texas—even three in the Gulf, and now my own son can't get one simple solitary task carried out without messing it up."

"Dad, it's not that big of a deal. Q-Main and Transistor will be ready for the track in two weeks. We just need a little more time with Dragnet. He's not where he needs to be yet." Keith Ayers fought the urge to shift in his chair. Laid back and nonchalant was by far his best bet with his father. That much he had learned so long ago, he couldn't clearly remember when it had happened.

One-on-one, head-to-head confrontation had never gotten them anywhere. He clasped his dirt-stained hands in front of him and set his stubble-strewn jaw. His dad was tough, but horses weren't his specialty. They were Keith's.

Racing a thoroughbred, especially one with as much promise as Dragnet before it was ready was the best way he knew to ruin one permanently. No amount of blustering changed the fact that Dragnet simply wasn't ready. "I talked to Ike this morning. He's thinking we can bring Dragnet up for a real race sometime in July."

His father exhaled hard, clearly not pleased with the assessment. "I paid $250,000 for that animal, and I don't like watching my investments sit around eating me out of house and home."

The fact that house and home weren't exactly in jeopardy crossed Keith's mind, but he wisely chose not to say that. "Would you prefer to sink a $250,000 investment by racing him too soon? Trust me on this one, Dad, a little patience now could hold out big rewards later."

His father scowled, his expression sinking into his jowls. "I didn't build a billion dollar empire on patience." Then he nodded. "You've got two months."

May? That was too soon, but it was all Keith would get, and he knew it. "I'll tell Ike." He started to stand and felt his father stand as well. Never. Never a good sign. "Uh, I know my way out."

"Yes, but you also know your way back in. That's what concerns me." The laugh that accompanied the statement tried to pass it off as a joke, but it felt more like a knife to Keith.

His father followed him right to the door and out. "So, have you heard from Dallas? How's she doing at Yale? Law school going okay?"

In the hallway Keith replaced his beat up, loose straw cowboy hat back over the blue bandana stretched across his head. "Good," Keith answered with the obligatory nod. "She should be back for Spring Break. Graduation's in May. Hayden & Elliott after she passes the bar."

"To infinity and beyond. I like that," his father said with the first smile Keith had seen from him all afternoon. At the staircase that wound to the upper floors, his father stopped, looked up it, and smiled. "Well. Well."

Keith's gaze followed his father's up the carpeted-just-so steps, and although he first noticed his stepmother next to the railing, he stopped dead when he saw the young lady descending between her and the wall.

"Of course you will get time off occasionally," his stepmother, Vivian, said. Her suit dress was perfectly pressed all the way up to the ruffled collar that ringed her neck like a flower. That was Vivian, always impeccable lest anyone see she wasn't perfect. "However, I need you to realize that this is basically a 24 hour, seven day a week job."

3

"Oh, yes, Ma'am. That's not a problem," the young lady with the mesmerizing head of chestnut brown hair which was falling out of the clip she had in the back of her head said. She pulled the strap of her purse up onto her shoulder. She was coming down, trying to keep her gaze on Vivian out of respect and attention, but she clearly could've used the banister Vivian was using as her own. The descent was anything but graceful, more halting and awkward. In fact, she was having so much trouble keeping up with everything that it was two steps from the bottom before the young lady with the dark glasses and cascading tresses even noticed there were others watching her descent. Her glance from Vivian to the two men standing at the bottom threw her attention from the concentration she was obviously exerting to get down the stairs for one moment too long.

As Keith watched, one step from the bottom, disaster struck. He saw it as it happened, but it was like it was in slow motion. She stepped down with her left foot, but her shoe planted awkwardly in the plush carpet. Her ankle turned, and like a puppet falling to the stage, her body pitched forward with a jerk.

"Ahh!" Her scream lasted all of two seconds—the exact amount of time it took for him to realize what was happening and reach out to snag her downward motion, which would've pitched her unceremoniously to the hardwood floor of the entryway had he not stepped between her and certain humiliation.

"Oh, watch...!" It was all he got out before she thwacked into him. "Ugh!" The impact of her body on his didn't so much as move him although it was significant enough to jar her glasses askew. It was only the clasp of his hands on her arms that kept her from bouncing off of him and ending her descent on the floor next to him anyway. When her unscheduled tumble came to a complete stop, she was sprawled across him from his shoulder to his arms, which supported her without effort. In fact it felt more like holding a weightless butterfly than anything.

"Oh! Oh my gosh! I'm sorry. I'm so sorry." Mortified, she yanked herself upright away from him although she looked as unhinged from the encounter as he felt. His insides were dancing with amusement and fascination as he watched her disentangle herself from him and wobble on the uncooperative shoe once more.

"I'm sorry. I'm so sorry." She was standing, readjusting her dress, her glasses, herself. "I don't know why I'm so clumsy today. I…"

"Are you all right?" Keith asked, gazing at her as if he'd just fallen under an angel's spell. His hands stayed out to catch her again if need be.

"Yeah… Yes. I'm fine." Perturbed with herself, the young lady shook her head quickly and resumed her attempt to look like she belonged there, which she didn't. At all. And somehow, he kind of liked that.

He smiled at her, but she was clearly doing her best not to look at him. "You sure?" But she had resumed her concentration on Vivian.

"Conrad," Vivian said with no small amount of a frown at the ineptitude of her current interviewee, "this is the young lady I told you about. Maggie Montgomery. She's come about the nanny position."

"Oh, yes," Keith's father said. He extended his hand to her, which she shook even as she continued to fight to get herself under control. "It's nice to meet you Ms. Montgomery."

"I have explained to Maggie," Vivian continued, "that she is on a six month probation period. Anything not up to our standards during that time will be cause for immediate termination."

Maggie's gaze fell to the stairs, but she pulled her head up and looked right at Mr. Ayer with a forced smile.

"And that's acceptable to you?" his father asked.

"Yes, sir. It is." She looked like a proud filly with her chin up and her hazel eyes flashing determination.

"I suppose you will need two weeks to let your current employer know you are leaving," Vivian said with a sigh, and Keith couldn't help but notice the dramatics. She should've been an actress.

"Oh," Maggie said, and he heard the note of concern. "No, Ma'am. I can start as soon as you need me to." She pulled her fingers up through her purse strap. "I can start now… if that works for you."

"Wonderful," Mr. Ayer said. "That's what I like. Someone who can make decisions."

"You don't mind starting today?" Vivian couldn't hide the pitch of excitement.

Maggie turned to her. "Right now is fine if that's what you

need."

She was intriguing, mesmerizing, captivating. And yet just why that was, Keith couldn't accurately tell. She was nothing like the girls he'd been out with. They with their debutant good looks and impeccable manners. No, this one, this Maggie Montgomery, looked more like a nervous, high-strung pony. Proud and strong, and determined not to be broken by anyone.

"Well, then," Vivian said smartly. "Let's go meet the children."

"Good luck, Ms. Montgomery," his father said, extending his hand to help her down the last step. "It's nice to have you."

All the air had gone right out of the room as Keith's gaze followed her down the hallway and out of sight in the direction of the children's wing of the estate.

"What're you still doing here?" his father asked, surveying him. "I thought you had horses to train."

"I'm on it." With that, he exited the main house and descended the front steps. There in the driveway sat a car that Keith couldn't even be sure still ran. It looked like it would be a better fit for a junkyard than in front of his parents' house. As he started past it, the thought occurred to him that it belonged to her. Her. Maggie Montgomery.

"Well, it will be an interesting two weeks anyway." With a knowing smile, he strode on. He shook his head at his own joke. They never lasted more than two weeks. Never.

In fact, he wouldn't have lasted more than two weeks but for the simple fact that they couldn't get rid of him. He was a member of the family—whether they liked it or not.

"This is Peter," Mrs. Ayer said, indicating the small boy with the blond hair, sitting at the table coloring slowly. "And this is Isabella." She picked the little girl with the bright blond curls up into her arms.

"Hello, little one." Maggie reached a hand out to the soft little face. "You are a sweetie-pie."

Mrs. Ayer slid the little girl back to the ground and planted her hands on her hips. "Dinner is promptly at 6 p.m. They are to be dressed and ready no later than 5:30. Inez will be able to fill you in on the rest of their schedules."

Maggie nodded, taking in the information with the sense that even perfection wouldn't be good enough.

"If you'd like some time to get settled, I can get Inez to watch the children for a few more minutes."

"Oh, no. I think I'm fine." Then she remembered. "But I do need to move my car. It's still out front."

Mrs. Ayer sighed with disapproval. "Very well. You may park it over at the guesthouse. It's just through the back, down the lane, and off to the right."

"It'll only take me a few minutes," Maggie said, trying to assure her new employer that she was competent enough to handle all of this.

"You may as well bring your suitcases in as well. Your room will be at the top of these stairs, right next to the children's rooms."

"I'm sure I can find it."

"Inez!" Mrs. Ayer called out the door.

"Yes, Ma'am."

Maggie couldn't clearly tell how the maid had been able to answer so quickly. It was as if she had materialized there from thin air.

"Please watch the children while Ms. Montgomery gets her things settled."

Inez bowed slightly. "Very good, Ma'am."

Once more Mrs. Ayer surveyed Maggie, and the fact that she didn't believe this would ever work traced through Maggie's consciousness. "If you need anything else, let Inez know."

"Yes, Ma'am."

"And now you'd better get that car moved before Jeffrey has a cardiac."

"Yes, Ma'am." Something told her she would be saying that a lot now. Pleading with her heels to cooperate long enough to get her back to the car and then back here, Maggie hurried out. The early afternoon Texas sun beat down on the outside surroundings. After having been in the comfort of the mansion's air conditioning, the combination of humidity and heat hit Maggie like two fists.

She got in the car and took her first real breath. "Oh, thank You, Jesus." Except for the unceremonious stumble into the hired hand, the interview had gone as well as she could've hoped for.

"Ugh. How clumsy can you be, Maggie? That was a good one." Forcing herself not to think about it, she pumped the accelerator and twisted the key to get the little car started. Then she carefully backed up so she could go down the back drive as Mrs. Ayer had instructed.

With a frustrated swipe, Maggie pushed the trail of loose strands of hair from her face and then blew them back up when they didn't stay. Carefully she drove around the house, which was enormous no matter which angle it was seen from. Her heart pounded in her ears as the car slipped into the grove of hulking trees. Trees seemed to be everywhere. Somehow she had expected them to dissipate beyond the mansion, but if anything, they got more massive and thicker the farther she drove.

"Did she say right or left?" Intensely Maggie scanned the areas on either side of the driveway that had narrowed to a trail. "This is great. I get lost on my first day."

Then just ahead, off to the right, through the knot of trees, she caught sight of the place. When she got closer, Maggie sucked in a gasp of air. If this was the guesthouse, they certainly treated their guests very, very well. Sporting orange-tan brick with blue-gray accents, the house had a bevy of inlets and cutouts. There were enormous windows, and wraparound accents at the corners, and an inlet door that looked like it alone cost half the national debt. "Wow."

Wide-eyed in awe but trying to keep her mind on her present mission, Maggie surveyed the small hill of a lawn, the flowerbeds, and every inlet for some clue as to where she was supposed to park. She turned her gaze up the trail. Surely there was a garage somewhere. "Oh, Jesus. Help." The trail dovetailed with a small perpendicular drive just beyond the house, and carefully she turned there, hoping maybe this was right. In fact, there was a garage, but the moment she pulled up to it, she had second thoughts. What if someone needed in or out of that garage? If she was parked in the way, that would be a problem.

Twisting her mouth as she tried to find an answer to this dilemma, her heart jumped into her throat when her gaze caught movement in her driver's side mirror. Fear jerked her head around just in time for her to see the hired hand with the blue bandana sticking out from under the ratty cowboy hat come striding up the side of her car. For a moment she felt better, but it was only for a moment because the reality of being out here alone with no knowledge of the terrain if trouble struck with a guy who felt like the Rock of Gibraltar did nothing to calm her nerves.

She swallowed hard. Very cautiously she reached up and locked her door, praying the others were already locked.

"Hey," he said when he got to her window. His easy smile spread across his face as she rolled down her window just far enough not to be rude. "Fancy meeting you here."

It was impossible not to notice his biceps, which looked like massive tree trunks streaming down from the ripped-off sleeves of his denim shirt. In a fight, she would lose without him even trying.

"Hi." Panic smashed into her, and her lungs constricted around it. "Umm... Mrs. Ayer said I could park here, but I'm not sure where she meant." Anxiety had never meant what it did at that moment.

"Oh, she did. Did she? Well, that figures." He laughed, which threw her incomprehension devices into full-throttle. "Na. It's okay. Swing around back here. We can put it in the barn."

Maggie nodded although no real signals were getting to her brain. She rolled up the window and backed onto the driveway so she could follow him down the increasingly narrow trail. From behind, he was all denim, save for the bent, straw cowboy hat and those arms. "Oh, dear God, I don't know about this. Please tell me if I should be doing this." But as far as she could tell, God was not giving her any other options.

At the end of the drive, mercifully, the trees broke their hold on the surroundings, and she drove out into a clearing and down a gravel road over to the building he had called a barn, but like everything else here, 'barn' didn't quite do it justice. He swung the two doors open and stepped back so she could drive in.

Crossing from outside to in, the darkness enveloped her eyes so that it took her longer than it would've seemed necessary to make it safely into the building. Once inside, she shoved the car into park and then had to corral her fear to gather enough courage to open the door. "Oh, God, be with me. I'm asking here." Busying herself, lest he see just how scared she was, Maggie got out, went to the back, and unlocked the trunk. With a heave she pulled her lone suitcase out, praying it wouldn't fall apart at her feet.

"Oh, here. Let me get that for you." He reached out for it

even as he stood at the door that stood open.

"No. I can get it." She tried to swing it out of his reach, but with a soft smile and a wink he took it anyway.

"It's half a mile back to the house," he said. "In this heat you'll be French fried by the time you carry this thing all the way back."

Her heart was beating so loudly, her brain didn't have a chance to put up a logical argument, so she nodded, ducked her head, and stepped past him. The bright sunshine beyond the door attacked her eyes, and she squinted as he closed the barn door behind them. Everything in her wanted to take that suitcase back and run, but barring humiliating herself against his strength again, she saw no way to do that. The gravel at her feet was playing havoc with her heels, and she fought to keep her balance and stay up with his strides as they started up the incline to the guesthouse.

He wasn't tall exactly. Maybe a couple inches taller than her but no more than that. But the solidity of everything about him swept the air from her lungs just the same.

"So, you work here?" she asked, willing her voice to stay steady even as her shoes threatened to pitch her into the sharp white rocks at her feet just as they had pitched her into him at the mansion. The thought made her ears burn.

"Yeah. As little as possible." There was that smile again, and if she hadn't been so nervous, it might have had a chance to do serious work on her insides. "I run the stable operation up the way."

"Stable?" Her brain was having trouble processing anything.

"Horses."

"Oh."

They made it back up to the trees, and uneasiness pushed into her consciousness again. She looked around, and the trees seemed thicker now, closing in on her, blocking all escape routes.

"I hear you're gonna be on the pay roll too," he said.

"Oh, yeah. Yeah, I am."

"Well, you must be downright impressive. Most of the time they won't let anyone within shooting distance of this place that doesn't have security clearance from the Pentagon."

They had made it to the main road and headed back to the mansion. Crossing in front of it now, the guesthouse was even more impressive going by slowly—if that was possible. Maggie fought not to gawk at it, but it wasn't easy. "I passed my background check, and I had a personal reference from the Dean of Early Childhood Development at A&M Kingsville." She sounded like she was defending herself, and she hated that.

"Impressive." And he actually sounded impressed. "So, you're from Kingsville then?"

"Del Rio." Her heel picked that moment to twist out from under her. "Ugh." Thankfully, she caught her own balance this time, but it was a close save. "These stupid shoes."

Skeptically he surveyed her feet. "They don't make walking look all that easy or that safe."

"Tell me about it." She continued walking although he had slowed down in deference to her struggle.

Shaking his head, he pressed his lips together in earnest concern. "Why don't you take them off? You're gonna kill yourself on that last quarter up the hill."

"Oh, yeah. Like I'm going to walk into the Ayer mansion barefoot. That should make a really great first impression." Sarcasm dripped from her spirit. Who would even make such a dumb suggestion?

He glanced behind them. "Well, nobody comes down this road but me. They ain't gonna see you anyway, and besides, I'll warn you before we get too close."

Maggie still wasn't so sure, but her ankles were starting to protest rather loudly. "Okay, fine." She reached down for one shoe but had to scoot her other foot around to keep her balance. She reached out for something solid and met his arm coming the other way.

Smooth skin under her palm ripped sanity away from her. How in the world had she gotten here? Sweat beaded out of her back, and she was quite sure it had nothing to do with the humidity. Quickly she removed first one shoe and then the other. When they were off and she was once again on solid footing, she had to admit it was a good idea, even if her breathing was no longer working properly.

"You got it?" he asked, eyeing her seriously.

"Yeah." She forced a knot of a smile on her face and started walking. The pavement would've been burning hot had it not been shaded by the millions of leaves above them. Just then a breeze swept through the branches and right over them. "Ah." The sigh of relief was automatic.

"So, you're an early childhood education major?" he asked as they made their way back up the road. It didn't take long to understand what he meant about that last quarter of a hill. If it was any steeper than this part, she was in trouble.

"Yeah. I graduated in December. This is the first permanent thing I found."

"Well, we're glad to have you. I'm sure Pete and Izzy will keep you on your toes."

The question of how familiar he seemed in referring to the children traced through her, but before she could voice that thought, he looked at her, and that scattered her thoughts like the pieces of a shattering window.

"So, are you up for the 24-hour thing? Most people hear that and go running for the exits."

She shrugged, and it took a solid breath to beat the sadness in her chest down. "I like the idea of having a roof over my head. It's worth a little work to have that."

He nodded, head down, concentrating on walking. When she looked over at him, she fought not to notice how rugged and tanned his face was. In fact, with that face and that body, he looked like he belonged nowhere else other than out in nature, taming some wild beast. His whiskers were more than a five o'clock shadow. They were a dark emphasis to the sheer masculinity of the rest of him. With a glance he caught her looking at him and smiled. Lines of amusement appeared on either side of his face. "What?"

"Oh. Nothing." She ripped her gaze away from him. "I just hope I don't do anything to mess this up."

When he looked at her again, the smile that was already beginning to get to her was a soft and encouraging. "I think you'll be just fine."

Two

"Schedules are to be followed not questioned," Inez said with no small amount of seriousness. "I will have Patty Ann put a full schedule for the children's next week on the desk in your room."

"Umm, Patty Ann?" Maggie asked, wanting not to miss even the smallest detail.

"Mrs. Ayer's personal secretary. She handles all of Mrs. Ayer's personal affairs including children issues."

Children issues? They sounded like line items on a checklist.

"For tonight's purposes, baths are at 7:30 sharp. Bedtime is eight. It would be best if you stayed in your room or at least in the children's wing during your time here. I do not recommend going anywhere else other than down these stairs to the kitchen or the entryway stairs to the outside if need be. The last nanny was fired for being where she wasn't supposed to be."

Fear pounced on her, but she yanked it back. "Oh, that shouldn't be a problem."

"Good. Well, unless there are any questions, it's time for me to start dinner."

The United States Navy couldn't have sounded any more regimented.

"I think I'll be fine."

Like a drill sergeant Inez turned on her heel and started down the stairs that led right into the kitchen. With a sigh of exasperated relief, Maggie turned the other direction. "Welcome to the life of the rich and famous." She went into the playroom. Peter was now sitting quietly on the floor, playing with the blocks. Isabella was lying on the little couch sucking her thumb. Big brown eyes stared at Maggie, wary but hopeful.

"Ah, sweetie-girl, are you tired?" Maggie walked over and picked her up, soft pink ruffled dress and all. "What do you say we sit here in the chair and read a book? How would that be?" She carried the child to the wooden rocking chair and sat down.

Reaching to the side, she pulled up the first book she came to. *Sleeping Beauty*. With the barest of pushes of her toe, she started the chair rocking gently. Isabella tucked her head closer to Maggie who wrapped her spirit around the baby in her lap. "Once upon a time..."

Calling Dallas wasn't all that unusual for Keith. In fact, he usually found some excuse to bridge the gap between them at least three or four times during the week. So why placing that call on Thursday night felt so strange, he couldn't exactly tell. She would be back home in a couple of weeks, and in truth he was looking forward to seeing her again.

When her phone clicked, he smiled as he always did when they stole a few minutes away from life to be together. He settled deeper into the soft cream couch. "Hey, babe. How's it going?"

Dinner had been interesting. Baths weren't much better. Not because the children were bad or hard to manage. Much the opposite. As Maggie sat on her massive, preternaturally high, four-poster queen bed, she leaned her head first one way, then the other to work out the kinks. It wasn't something she could put into actual words, but both children did not seem so much children as miniature adults.

They were quiet. Very quiet. Especially Peter. He seemed so circumspect about every move he made. Like when they entered the formal dining room and he had walked first to his mother to give her a kiss on the cheek and then to his father whom he shook hands with. It was like watching someone meet the queen.

Isabella was more demonstrative but measurably so. Maggie wrapped her arms around her knees as she thought about holding the little girl while they rocked, read, and then took a nap together. Here there was no yelling, no danger of physical harm, and yet, there was no joy either.

Even at Mrs. Malowinski's, there were always ropes to jump and games to play. Here, games seemed to be relegated to Peter being one-on-one with a few blocks in the corner. Maggie shook her head and pursed her lips together. Pulling the heavy deep red comforter dotted with thousands of tiny white flowers entwined with green vine from her legs, she slid off the bed and onto her knees. The plush cream carpeting felt like clouds. Propping her hands on the edge of the bed, she bent her head and let the words in her heart become wings of prayer.

"Dear Lord, I know these kids have everything. Everything except what they really need. Please give me the strength and the wisdom to bring Your joy and love into their lives. Bind Satan from this house and let him not get a foothold here. Cast him out into the darkness, and fill this house with Your light, Your love, Your grace, and Your peace. Amen. Oh, and keep Mrs. Mal and all her kids safe for me. Rain Your saving love into the hearts of every child who is alone, afraid, or in need tonight. I ask all these things in Your Name. Amen."

When she stood, she considered getting into bed but thought better of it. Instead she padded quietly to the door. She cracked it open and checked both ways. Slipping into the hallway, she tiptoed to the door next to hers—Isabella's.

As it had the first time, the sheer size of the room brought a shake of her head. She walked silently to the baby bed wrapped in big, pink ruffles and peered over the side. Peaceful and soft, Isabella lay, sucking her thumb, eyes closed, and cooing softly. "Good night, little one. God bless you." Maggie laid her hand on the little curls and said a quick prayer. Then she turned and tiptoed out into the nightlight-illuminated hallway and to the room across the way.

In the junior bed with the ball and bat wallpaper ringing the room around him lay Peter. He seemed at first to be sleeping, but then she noticed his little eyes twitching ever-so-slightly. Puzzled, she bent closer to him and watched carefully. It took several seconds, but his eyes became slits.

"Peter," she said softly in case he really was asleep. At that he came full awake. "Hey, sweetheart. You're not asleep yet?"

Solemnly he shook his head, his soft brown eyes pleading with her not to be mad. She smiled gently. "Tell you what. Why don't we say our prayers together? Maybe that will help." Kneeling next to his bed, she took hold of his little hand and closed her eyes. "Dear Jesus, be with Peter tonight. Give him peace. Help him to fall asleep. Send Your saints and angels to guard him through the night until the dawning of the morning light. This we ask in Your Name. Amen."

A grateful smile traced through Peter's eyes and across his face.

"Better?" she asked, gazing at him seriously.

Up and down went the little head.

"Good." She pulled the covers around him and tucked them in. When she stood, she ran her hand over his blond hair. "Now you get some sleep and let Jesus take care of everything else. K?"

"K."

"I'm right down the hall if you need anything."

He nodded. His eyes already starting to look heavy and laden with sleep.

"Good night, sweet prince," she said, and with one more brush of his hair, she left him to his dreams.

As stupid as it sounded, Keith wondered the next day how Maggie was getting by. He checked on her car on his way to work, and it was indeed still in the barn. Impressive, crossed his mind. Of course, it couldn't last. Vivian was impossible with the help, and his father was more apt to fire than to listen. Trying to dismiss her from his thoughts, Keith entered the stables and strode to the office in the back. "Morning."

Ike Jones, the trainer, looked up, and his face fell in concern. "You're up early. You feeling okay?"

"I'm fine. I just figured if we've only got 'til May to get Dragnet going, we'd better get to work."

"Hodges called about the feed," Ike said. "It should be here tomorrow. Something about hauling regs upstate."

"We got enough to cover it?"

"Yeah, but we need to keep a watch on them. They did this last minute thing to us two months ago. I don't want to make a habit out of cutting it this close."

"Got it." Keith yanked on his work gloves. "Did you get that fence fixed yesterday?"

"Fence?" Ike asked incredulously. "I've been buried here under this mountain of paperwork for a week. What do you think?"

Keith smiled with a slight tease on the edges. "I'll let you worry about the paperwork. Leave the real work to me."

"Ha. Ha." But Ike didn't really protest. "Don't hurt yourself getting your head through the door."

This time Keith laughed out right. "No worries there. That's why they made the barn doors so wide."

Ike too joined in the laughter. Then his gaze fell to the desk. "Oh, and sometime today you need to take these invoices up to the main house. Your dad needs them for the accountants."

"Invoices? Be still my beating heart."

"Yeah. Yours or mine," Ike said with more seriousness this time. "And with all due respect, I'd rather it be yours."

Keith yanked the nail bags from the sidewall. "Such loyalty. You won't take a bullet for me?"

"A bullet yes. Your father on the other hand..."

With a shake of his head, Keith attached the belt to his waist. "You're the definition of bravery, Ike."

"Bravery around here gets people killed or fired... Neither of which I really need right now."

Keith started toward the door and was halfway out of it when Ike yelled.

"Hey! Invoices."

Some excitement in life just couldn't be avoided. He stepped back to the trainer's desk and took the stack of papers. "Okay, but if I don't come back, it's your fault."

"Better my fault than my head."

And Keith ducked out. His father was bad. There was no doubt about it. Everyone knew it, and they all lived life in barely disguised fear. But really he wasn't all that bad. At least he hadn't been when Keith's mother was still alive. The sadness that always accompanied thoughts of her drifted over him. Pushing it back, he loaded the tools he needed into the bright red, Dodge extended cab and climbed in. That was the one lesson he had learned with precision from his father—the great therapeutic benefits of good, old-fashioned hard work.

It had taken her most of the morning to find it, but with careful examination, Maggie had indeed carved out one whole hour in which nothing else was planned for the children. In the morning it was dance class for Isabella and art for Peter. Then lunch in the breakfast nook. Even that detail was noted on the schedule. In fact, everything was noted down to the minute, including the ten minutes of walking in the garden from one o'clock to ten after.

However, after the walk and before naptime, which was also clearly spelled out, there it was—a whole blessed hour with not one thing scheduled. She had seen the enormous redwood playhouse in the backyard from the window in the playroom. Bending down to their level, she let her eyes go wide. "What do you say before naptime we go out in the playhouse and read some stories?"

"Stowies!" Isabella squealed excitedly.

"Shh!" Peter immediately warned, and the fear was evident.

"No, it's okay, Peter," Maggie said, taking his hand. "Isabella's just happy. Aren't you happy?"

"I don't want to go." Sullen and afraid, he looked like a trapped animal.

"Really? Why not?"

His gaze dropped to the carpet. "I don't want to get dirty. We'll get dirty if we go outside."

"Oh." She sounded like she understood although she really didn't. "Well, I'll tell you what. We'll find some clothes that we don't have to worry about a little dirt. How would that be?"

Peter still didn't look convinced, but Maggie started about finding the clothes despite his reluctance. It took fifteen minutes of their precious hour, but she got them ready, and with Isabella in one arm and Peter's hand tucked securely in her other hand, they went out to the playhouse in the backyard.

"Crud." The invoices still lay on the seat. Really and truly Keith didn't have time for this, but he knew it was time that had to be made. Turning the pickup up the side road, he bypassed the stables and headed to the main house. Jeffrey was out front mowing, and Keith waved at him with a lift of his hand. "Just get this done and get back to work."

He climbed the front steps two at a time and entered without announcing his presence. Everything was quiet. Not a sound anywhere. He wondered for a moment where Maggie and the kids were. Probably at some lesson of some kind. There was never a shortage of lessons with Vivian at the helm. Quietly he made his way down to his father's office at the end of the hallway. He was one second from knocking when he heard the voices from beyond the door, which was open a fraction of an inch.

It took him a minute of listening to decide who was in there and whether or not he should knock. By the time he decided, knocking was obviously less than prudent.

"I can't believe you didn't notice this on her records," his father said. "That's not inconsequential you know."

"I know, Conrad. Believe me. I know. If I would've noticed it, I would never have even called her in the first place, but you know how desperate I've been for someone. I thought Alicia was the answer, but then she quit before she ever showed up. This was the only application I had left."

"You should know better, Viv. We can't have just anybody coming in this house. There are records and information—not to mention the money and the jewelry. Someone with her background... You just never know. How can we trust someone like that?"

"I get it, Conrad. Really I do, but we're leaving Monday. We've had this cruise scheduled for six months. If I fire her now, there's no way I'll have someone else by then. I don't want to miss this trip. We haven't been anywhere just the two of us since Izzy was born."

"I don't know. Leaving her here for a whole week with no one to look after the place? I don't like the sound of that."

As if he hadn't been standing there for five minutes, Keith knocked on the door. "Dad?" He pushed the door open, and his father and Vivian both looked up like they had been caught. "Oh, sorry, Vivian. I didn't realize you were here." He held up the receipts. "I just needed to drop these off."

Nonchalantly he stepped into the room and handed the receipts over to his father. Then he turned to go but stopped. "Oh.

We're keeping an eye on Hodges. They've been jerking us around on the feed supply. Just so you know."

"Okay."

Keith could feel the intense conversation going on between the two of them without hearing any of it. "Well, that's it. I'll just get…"

"You know, Keith." His father stood, still looking at Vivian. Finally he put his full gaze on his son. "We're going on vacation come Monday, and we're needing someone to keep watch over things here while we're gone."

"Oh, sure thing." He nodded. "I'll make sure everything stays on an even keel just like always." Once again, he turned for the door, and this time he had his hand actually on the knob.

"Uh, no," his father said, stopping him. "I don't think you understand." When Keith turned, his father was looking at Vivian, obviously trying to get her to give up the crazy idea. Finally his father relented and stepped around the desk. "We want you to stay up here, in the main house and keep an eye on Peter and Isabella."

"Pete and Izzy? Isn't that why you hired Maggie?"

"Well, yes." The battle to figure out a plausible lie was clear. "But she doesn't even know her way around yet. I'd hate to dump all of this on her and take off."

Keith considered this a moment and then shrugged. "Well, I don't mind if you don't."

Anger flashed to the surface of his father's demeanor. "Of course I don't mind. What's that supposed to mean?"

"It was a joke, Dad. You know a joke. Ha. Ha." But no one was laughing.

Vivian turned to him. "But you'll do it then?"

Again Keith shrugged. "What the heck. Sure."

"Careful down. Careful down." Maggie stood at the foot of the ladder that stretched up into the playhouse above. Reading was fun, but their hour was gone. She was going to have to hurry to get them down for naps. Already Isabella was huddled into Maggie's shoulder, sucking her thumb. Helping Peter down the last two steps, Maggie took his hand, and they started for the house.

That house had a way of getting bigger every time she looked at it. She wondered how many rooms there actually were. Many more than she would ever be privy to visiting she was sure. She pushed those thoughts to the back of her mind and stepped up to the door, which she opened and held for Peter.

"Come on. We'd better get your sister down for her nap." They crossed through the living room and were two steps into the entryway when from the other hallway the hired hand who seemed to be following her around met them at the stairs.

"Well, hey there," he said, and his easy smile was never far behind.

"Hi." She could feel her glasses sliding down on her nose, but she didn't have enough hands to push them back up.

He stepped over to her and ran his hand down Isabella's back. "Tired little girl."

"We went in the playhouse," Peter said at Maggie's knee, and she looked down at him in surprise.

The hired hand sat down on his heel so he was on Peter's level. "I bet that was lots of fun. You being a good boy for Maggie?"

Peter nodded, and Maggie fought not to notice the strength in the hand the guy reached out to ruffle Peter's hair.

"Good deal. Keep it up, sport."

Noise from down the hallway brought him to his feet, and Maggie's attention snapped that direction. Side-by-side Mr. and Mrs. Ayer walked in.

"Oh, Maggie. Good I'm glad we caught you," Mrs. Ayer said.

As Maggie turned to them, she felt Peter cowering behind her knee. Balance was a challenge what with Isabella now breathing softly on her chest and Peter's arm wrapped around her leg. However, she anchored herself to the floor to keep from being buffeted by the two little ones.

"We're going out of town next week," Mrs. Ayer said. "We've asked Keith to keep an eye on the place."

For a split second Maggie had the name with a question mark after it on her tongue, but before she could ask, the hired hand smiled at her. Her brain surged into gear. "Oh." She fought to smile as six thousand different emotions cracked over her. "Great."

"I promise I won't be too much of a pain," he said, and when he smiled at her, she couldn't stop her own from coming for real.

Her gaze fell to the side. When she brought it up again, it was to look at Mrs. Ayer. "Just give Patty Ann the schedule you want for the kids. I'm sure we'll be fine." She wanted to say more. Her heart was jumping all over until in the swirl of emotions, she thought she might do something really stupid. "Well, I'd better get these two upstairs for their nap. We're late."

Turning for the stairs carefully, she took hold of Peter's hand. "Come on, Peter. You can help me put Baby Bella down."

Keith couldn't help but watch the three of them all the way up the stairs. She was such a natural with the kids—not demanding or overbearing like the last three nannies they'd suffered through. No, Maggie had a genuine caring in her eyes. It was clear this wasn't just a job for her. Depression tamped down over his heart when he remembered it couldn't last. Certainly not with her less-than-perfect clothes and manner, and definitely not now that they had found whatever they'd found in her background. He wondered about that as she disappeared around the curve of the staircase to the level above.

"Well, then it's settled," his father said, dragging Keith's attention back to reality. "We leave for Miami Monday morning, and we'll be back... when?"

"The next Tuesday," Vivian said as she folded her arms across her chest. She stared up the steps. "I hate to leave her alone like this."

"Don't worry about it, Viv," Keith said confidently. "I've got it covered."

Three

"Ms. Montgomery," Patty Ann, the prim, middle-aged lady with the stern face and the voice of stone said, stopping Maggie ten steps from the dining room that evening.

Children dangled from her hip and her hand. "Oh. Yes, Ma'am."

"You're late, Ms. Montgomery."

"Late?" Maggie pulled Peter's hand up with her watch. "It's two minutes 'til."

"Yes. *Dinner* is at six. *Arrival* is prior to that so that dinner can be served promptly on time. You must understand. Mrs. Ayer is very particular about the timing of the day, and Mr. Ayer is a very busy man."

Maggie fought the urge to curtsey. "Yes, Ma'am. I understand. I'm sorry. It won't happen again."

There was disapproval all the way down to the tip of the long nose. "Make sure that it doesn't."

That night, Maggie put the kids to bed right on schedule, then went to her own room to get herself ready for bed. However, before she could completely settle down for the night, she made one last little pilgrimage back to their rooms to check on them. It was a ritual she could get used to.

Isabella was asleep, and Peter was waiting.

"You're supposed to be asleep, little prince," she said as she knelt next to his bed.

He rubbed his eye with a pudgy hand. "But we didn't say our prayers yet."

His simple trust drilled through her heart. "Okay. Then we'd better get cracking, huh?"

He closed his eyes, and she bent her head over his hand clasped in her two. "Dear Jesus, please be with us tonight. Keep us safe and give us good rest so we can have a great day tomorrow. Amen."

"Amen." There was no stopping the bright smile he beamed at her. "'Night, Maggie."

"Good night, sweet prince." She stood and ran her hand over his hair, gazing at him for one more moment. With a sigh she turned for the door. Quietly she let herself out of the room and slipped back across the hallway.

At her own bed, she knelt down and let her head fall forward as her eyes fell closed. "God, I know today's Sunday. I'm sorry I missed church. I just don't think right now asking for time off is such a good idea. Maybe next week… when they're gone." Anxiety pinged into her heart, but she breathed it down. "Please be with us this week. Be with the kids, and be with me. Thank You, Father, for every good thing in our lives. Keep all the children in Your embrace, hold them, and wipe all tears from their eyes. Amen."

After she climbed in the bed and shut off the light, Maggie sank into the soft cotton sheets. When she closed her eyes, his smile drifted through her thoughts. Him. Keith. It wasn't fair to a girl's heart for a guy to look that good.

Frustrated with herself, she flipped over the other way. "Stop it, Maggie. Stay focused on what's important here." However, no lecture in the world could keep him from her dreams.

Four days and she was out of everything. Blouses, pants, dresses, even underwear. Monday morning Maggie stood in her room looking into her empty suitcase wishing she had thought to ask Inez where to wash things. "Great. This is just wonderful."

She pushed her hair out of her face, bent and picked up the blouse she had worn the day before. "Well, at least they're gone. Maybe I won't get crucified this time." Dressing quickly lest she let her spirit dive too far, her thoughts went to today and all the terror it held. "God, I'm asking here. Help me out, okay? I can't make an idiot of myself when he's around. Please."

Keith waited until eight o'clock to make his way up to the house. It wasn't that he wanted to wait, but it was safer. This way his father and Vivian would be long gone, and the only two she-wolves he would have to contend with were Inez and Patty Ann. They were bad enough to make him question his sanity in going. Nonetheless the chance that he might get to see Maggie if he stopped in pulled courage into him.

He went in the front door without knocking nor ringing the bell. Down the hallway he could hear voices in the kitchen, and he angled his steps that direction. As he broke into the sunshine streaming into the breakfast nook, his heart swelled. He was glad he'd come. "Good morning."

Isabella took one look up and slung her arms out toward him. "Keef!"

"Hey, Izzy. Well, look how cute you are with this Cheerio stuck to your chin." He reached down and wiped it away with his thumb. Normally he wouldn't have had the guts to pick her up out of the high chair, but today, things were different. Today only Maggie was here, and in his heart he knew she wouldn't mind. Carefully he slid the tray forward and pulled Izzy up into his arms.

Like the angel she was, she wrapped her little arms all the way around his neck. He squeezed her, closing his eyes to breathe in her love. When the hug broke, he pulled back to look at her. "You are the cutest little thing I've ever seen." He put her back into the high chair and slid the tray back into place.

Turning to Peter he put a hand in the air. "And you, my man. What are you up to this morning?"

"I petted the cat yesterday."

Surprise jumped through Keith. "No kidding? Wow. That's awesome." Then his gaze settled where it had wanted to since he'd first taken in the scene. She had a way of looking unkempt and completely beautiful at the same time. The clip in her hair only held half of it, and the other half was streaming down around her head and shoulders, shining in the sunlight at her back. "Morning, Maggie."

"Morning." She seemed to shrink back into the window seat where she sat. "Umm... Inez went into town for groceries. I haven't seen Patty Ann yet. I think Jeffrey is supposed to be working on the front flower beds, but I haven't seen him yet either."

"Oh, cool." Keith took a handful of Cheerios from the box and tossed them in his mouth. "You got lots planned today?"

Trepidation trounced across her features. "Piano for Peter, and baby and mom gymnastics for Is."

"Baby and mom? Isn't that gonna be a little hard considering mom is in Miami?" He sat down in one of the chairs between Peter and Isabella. Leaning back, he watched Maggie intently.

"Well, I guess I'm kind of filling in."

That was one way of putting it. He took another handful of Cheerios. "So, you get all settled in and everything?"

She nodded. "I think I'm good."

"Good deal. Glad to hear it." On his belt his small cell phone beeped. In one motion he pulled it up and turned it on. "This is Keith."

Maggie had the distinct impression she was going to suffocate. His presence seemed to fill the whole room. He was talking on the phone. Somebody named Ike although she was trying not to listen. When he beeped the phone off, he stood.

"Time to get to work."

"Oh." She looked up and had to readjust her glasses which she was sure were cockeyed. "Well, don't worry about us. We'll be fine."

His gaze narrowed on her, and concern slammed into her.

"Tell you what," he said. He turned for the kitchen, rummaged through one drawer and came back with a pencil and a piece of paper. "Here's my number. If you need anything, you let me know."

"Oh." Surprised, she fought to recover enough sanity to sound semi-intelligent. "Okay." He handed it over to her with that smile, and her head spun on the lack of air. "Thanks."

"No problem." On his heel he turned back for the kids. "Give me five, slugger." Peter did as instructed. Keith stepped over to Isabella. "You be a good girl for Maggie. Hear me?"

"Keef!" Isabella squealed.

"Yeah, Keef." He laughed and ruffled her hair. "Well, take it easy. I'll be back for dinner tonight unless I hear from you before that."

"We'll be fine," Maggie said, willing her voice not to crack.

"Good to know. See ya."

"Yeah," she said when he was gone. "See ya."

"Ugh. Must you wear that dirty thing in the mansion?" Patty Ann asked as Keith got to the front door.

Getting away that easy was too good to be true. He knew it, and yet he had hoped... Slowly he turned, his hand still on the doorknob. "You have a problem with my hat?"

"Yes. I have a problem with it." She looked like a withered principal about to pronounce punishment on him. "Dirt has no place in the mansion."

Keith shook his head without really shaking it. "Now, now, Patty Ann, there's no need to get personal."

The tailored, black suit, the haughty, condescending face, the click of her tongue to emphasize her disapproval of him—they all added up to one thing in Keith, resolve not to hear another thing from her.

"Mr. Ayer," she said with all the self-importance of a dictator.

Keith held up his hand. "Wait. Stop. Right there." He waited a beat to make sure she had stopped, then he wound his finger as if rewinding a tape. "Say that part again."

Her eyes narrowed into little slits. "What *part?*"

"You know. The part about Mr. Ayer." The arrow went right through her puffed up pride. "Yeah. Uh-huh." He had lived life for five years under her shoe, but that was then, and then was gone. "Let's get one thing straight, shall we? I am not someone you can boss around just because you think you own this place. You don't. If it were up to me, your bags would already be packed and on that front step—or better yet in the driveway.

"Now you may think you can run my father and Vivian, and maybe you do. But you do not run me, so while I'm here, while I'm in charge, I think it's in your best interest to lay low and stay as far out of sight as possible." His thoughts traveled down the hallway to an innocent bystander who was about to get run over.

"And, let me make this very clear. You are not to go near Maggie or the kids this week. They are off-limits."

"Mr. Ay…"

"No." The stone-hardness of the word slammed her protest into a brick wall and smashed it into a thousand pieces. "I'm watching, and I'm listening, and if you so much as breathe on them wrong, you will be toast the minute Dad and Vivian step back through this door." He let those words sink in. "Are we clear on that?"

It took her an eternity of seconds, but finally, angrily, she nodded.

"Good." He reached up and tipped his hat. "Then have a nice day, Patty Ann."

Somehow Maggie made it through the rest of the day without thinking about him too much. At least that's what she would've told anyone who had asked. The truth was, every sound she heard in the house brought the anxious excitement that had come to punctuate every encounter she'd had with him.

At six o'clock sharp she set the children in the formal dining room, napkins and three forks all in place.

Inez stepped in. "Do you want to go ahead or should we wait, Ma'am?"

Ma'am. The word cracked Maggie backward. "I think we'll just go ahead. He might have decided not to come after all."

When Inez nodded and turned back for the kitchen, Maggie wondered which would be worse—if he didn't show up or if he did. They'd made it through the day with no mishap major enough to warrant hailing him on the cell phone. That was a good thing. At least he wouldn't think she was completely incompetent.

"Sorry. Sorry. I didn't realize it was so late." Keith made his entrance without really making it. One minute he wasn't there. The next minute he was.

"Keef!" Isabella said excitedly.

"Hey, baby girl." He took the seat across from Maggie, right next to Peter.

Inez followed him in, holding the serving platter. She set it on the table.

"It looks wonderful," Keith said.

"Will there be anything else?"

"Looks great."

Inez bowed and walked out.

"Well." Keith breathed the word as if he had been running a marathon right up to the moment he sat down. He reached for the serving spoon, and Maggie gasped softly. His gaze jumped to her. "What?"

She fought with her emotions to get a smile on her face. "Shouldn't we say grace first?"

"Oh, of course." His hand fell back to his lap, and he bent his head obediently.

"Father, bless this food and all those gathered here. Please keep Peter and Isabella's mommy and daddy safe on their trip, and let them come back soon. Amen."

"Amen." His gaze slid up to hers, and she couldn't read what was written there. In the next breath he was serving everyone as Maggie passed him Isabella's plate and then worked to cut up the food for Isabella.

She did her level best not to stare at him. He looked wholly out-of-place in this room. Somehow the chandelier and the bandana didn't scream complementary. As they ate, she kept her gaze on her plate or helped Isabella.

"So, how was piano?" Keith finally asked Peter.

"Hard."

"Yeah, well nothing worthwhile is easy."

Once again, Maggie marveled at his easy way with the kids. He didn't seem intimidated nor apprehensive around them at all.

"How was work?" Maggie asked him just so there was something more than silence in the room.

The question took him off-guard. "Oh, it was good. Ike thinks Q-Main has a great chance at Grand Prairie this weekend."

"Q-Main?" She needed more information to formulate a response.

"Our best thoroughbred. Ike and Tanner are heading out Wednesday morning."

"To Grand Prairie?"

"Yeah. It's not too bad. Just upstate."

"And you're not going?"

The smile only lifted halfway. "No, I'm babysitting,

remember?"

The reply rumbled over her, and Maggie dropped her gaze. "We'd be fine. Really. We hate to keep you."

He shook his head, and his smile was full now. "Na, I was kidding. I only go to the big ones anyway. Too much work to get done around here to be off partying at the races."

"Ho'sies," Isabella said, and a light went on behind Keith's eyes.

"That's right. Horses. Good girl." He started to take a bite and then let the fork drop down. "Hey, you know, you guys haven't been out to the stables in a while. Why don't you come out tomorrow? I could come get you after lunch if you want."

The no jumped into Maggie's consciousness. "Oh, I don't..."

"Really?" Peter's eyes widened to saucer-size. Then he seemed to remember where he was, and his gaze slid to Maggie's just before it fell to the table. "No, we better not."

That pushed Keith backward in his chair. A concerned scowl dropped across his features. "Why not? You love the horses."

Peter never lifted his gaze. "We might get dirty."

Disappointment slid over Keith's features. "Oh."

Maggie heard the hurt in that single syllable. She knew it was taking her life in her hands, but nobody would ever know anyway. "Well, I think it sounds like lots of fun. We'll put it on the schedule and call it a field trip."

The smile was back. She was beginning to love that smile.

Keith made sure to call Dallas from the main house that night. It was good to hear her voice, to hear about her day, to hear about how things were going with the law clerking she was doing. It sounded so perfectly Dallas, he was happy for her. When he hung up, his thoughts traveled through the house to the other side. The kids' wing. He considered going over to make sure everything was all right, but sanity stopped him from doing that. She would think he was checking up on her, and he didn't want that.

Besides, he needed sleep. Tomorrow was a big day. They were coming to the stables.

Maggie was crazy enough to try this little diversion, but she hadn't completely lost her mind. "Car seats," she said as she stood on the mansion's top step overlooking the driveway, two car seats flanking her stance. As always Isabella was snuggled in her arms and Peter was hovering not too far away.

"Can't be too safe." Keith yanked the two seats from the top step and descended as if he was carrying a glass of water rather than two awkward, heavy objects.

Maggie followed him to the pickup and waited while he fought to get the first seat in and secure. When Isabella's was ready, Maggie stepped forward and settled her in. From the other side of the pickup, Keith opened the driver door and then the back. Once again, he went to work, getting the second seat in place and ready.

"You didn't know it was going to take an Act of Congress, huh?" Maggie asked, teasing him.

"Na, it's just a bill," he replied.

She laughed as he lifted Peter into the seat. A click and Keith slammed the door. She followed suit before climbing in front. "So, how far is this anyway?"

"Mile and a half. We'll be there before you know it."

For as dusty and dirty as Keith always was, the pickup was remarkably clean. In fact, the dark gray seats looked as if they could have just rolled off the lot. The air conditioner was on, not hard and high, but light and gentle. On the stereo, George Strait sang a waltz, and Maggie glanced at the read out, which showed Track 9. Not just some country station. He had the CD. That must mean he listened to Strait. That was a good sign. He had good taste.

They skirted the main gate and went down a side road practically hidden in the crush of trees. Up a hill and down another stretch of road, and then a full racetrack came into view. "Wow. When you said racing, I had no idea."

"If you're going to do it, you might as well do it right," Keith said with a glance at her.

"I guess so."

At the track they turned to the left, down another little road until they stopped at the barn.

"Do we get to ride too?" Peter asked from the back.

31

"You still remember how, don't you?" Keith got out, and Maggie followed his lead.

"Yes."

"Cool. Then we get to ride."

Keith had purposely "forgotten" to tell Ike about this little outing. It wasn't that Ike would be mad. On the contrary, he was forever hinting at his concern for the kids with little off-handed comments. Still, something in Keith didn't want to tip Ike off about things that weren't happening anyway. It was better that way.

"Hey," Keith said, ducking into the trainer's office. "We're gonna take Buck and Nell out for a spin. Just so you know."

However, Ike's glance up snagged on Peter standing at Keith's knee. "Ok... Peter. Well. Well. Look at you. Aren't you getting to be the big boy?"

Great. There was no going back now. Ike stood and strode to the door. His sharply pressed jeans made their customary swishing sound. Those things must stand up in the corner by themselves. Unfortunately Ike's approach pushed Keith back into the barn's breezeway where Maggie stood, holding Isabella. The second Ike stepped out of the office nervous awkwardness snaked through Keith.

"Oh, well, who do we have here?" Ike asked.

"Maggie Montgomery." She held out her hand, which Ike took like the true gentleman he was. "I'm the new nanny."

"Well, Ms. Montgomery, may I say you are a welcome addition to the outfit."

"Thank you," she said and ducked with a half step back.

"Like I said." Keith whacked a hand into Ike's chest. "We're going to take Buck and Nell out for a while."

The glint in Ike's eyes told him he would never hear the end of this one. "Okay, but don't get lost."

One ride on a pony at the county fair when she was five didn't exactly give Maggie immense experience in the art of horseback riding. However, Isabella couldn't ride by herself. So, praying like she'd never prayed before, she mounted the reddish mare that Keith swore was the tamest on the place.

Once she was on, Keith handed her Isabella. It took a little effort to get her situated between the saddle horn and Maggie, but when she was finally there, she felt made for that space.

"Got it?" Keith asked, gazing up at her from his stance on the ground.

"Yeah. We're good."

"Cool. Now for you little man." With seemingly no effort at all, Keith swung Peter onto the other mount, a gray-speckled but otherwise dirty-beige-colored horse. There was no pause as Keith mounted behind Peter. "We set?"

"Set," Maggie affirmed.

Keith turned his horse down onto the little trail, and with a deep breath, Maggie followed. The horses took a steady but slow pace as they passed through a knot of trees that Maggie had to duck underneath. There was a short span that the trees gave them breathing room, one more set of extra close ones and then they broke out onto the open plain beyond.

"Oh, wow," Maggie gasped before she could stop herself.

He looked over his shoulder. "Nice, huh?"

"It's beautiful." The field stretching to the horizon was awash in bluebonnets and orange paintbrushes. Spring had definitely arrived. A cool breeze brushed through her hair, sending it streaming behind her. It felt so good in so many ways she couldn't catalog them all. The breeze was great. The day was beautiful. The landscape was perfect.

Even the movement of the red mare was lulling and rhythmic. Staying right here forever sounded like the best idea she had ever heard. How far they went, she didn't know, but suddenly she became aware of the heaviness of the child in front of her. Not wanting to bother Keith with slowing down, Maggie twisted her head around until she could see that yes, in fact, Isabella was asleep.

She didn't blame the little girl. Had she not known she was on an animal that could be unpredictable, she too would've fallen asleep. This was more perfection than anyone should have the right to enjoy. Her thoughts drifted to the kids at Mrs. Malinowski's. They had no idea these kinds of places even existed. They had no idea of the possibilities in life. She wondered if she had ever known the possibilities in this life until this very afternoon.

Determination to do something to show them drifted into her spirit. Someday. When she wasn't worried about how to pay for tomorrow, she would step into Mrs. Malowinski's shoes and do for others what that woman in her faith had done for her.

"How ya doing?" Keith asked from ahead of her.

"Great."

He spun slightly in his saddle to look at her. "Oh, she's out."

"Yeah. She didn't last long."

"Maybe we should go back."

"No. It's okay." Maggie shook her head, feeling the hair dance in the freedom of the breeze. "Let's keep going a little longer. We can be a little late for naptime."

Four

There was no question by the time dinner was finished that she was going to be sore tomorrow. Maggie stood from the table and swallowed the groan of pain that attacked her.

Keith looked up from his spot by Peter. "So, how was riding?"

"Fun!" Peter said before Maggie had the chance.

"Ho'sies!" Isabella said as Maggie took her plate and set it to the side.

"You, little missy need a good scrubbing." Maggie picked the little girl out of the high chair, the evidence of the mashed potatoes smeared all across her face. "Goodness. You even smell like those ho'sies."

"Ho'sies!" Isabella said again, swinging her little feet into Maggie's thigh.

"Maybe some other time. Right now, it's bath time."

Without being told, Peter stood from his place, stacked his silverware on his plate, and took it to the kitchen. Maggie sighed in spite of herself. He was much too old for four. "Well, we'll see you in the morning."

"Yeah. Have a good night."

"We will." She took Peter's hand. "Come on, buster. I'll let you play with the Ernie boat."

It was stupid. Keith knew it, but the quieter the house got, the more he wanted to check, just one time. They were already in bed, probably asleep, and yet, he wanted to make sure of that. Finally, unable to talk himself out of it, he quietly exited his room on the far opposite side of the mansion. He shook his head as he crossed past the master suite. How very far it seemed from the kids' rooms.

Not for the first time ever, he wondered why they bothered to have Pete and Izzy in the first place. Little trophies. That's all they had ever really been. It was just like Ike said. Kids were meant to live with their parents, not be put on display to make the parents look good. Shaking his head to clear it of the disturbing thoughts, Keith made his way to the three doors at the far end of the hall.

He noticed without really looking that the light was on under her door. She was probably reading or getting ready for bed. He'd have to be extra quiet. On his way to Isabella's door, however, he noticed the white door on the opposite side cracked open. That was strange. Curious, he stepped over to it and peeked inside. The scene beyond knocked sanity and air from him simultaneously.

There, on her knees, next to Peter's bed knelt Maggie. He couldn't see her face, but her back was arched. She was huddled in the protectiveness of her shoulders. Next to her, Peter lay, eyes closed, but turned toward her.

"And help Mommy and Daddy come home safely. Thank You for today, God. Give us good sleep tonight, and let us have a great day tomorrow. Amen."

Unbidden tears sprang into Keith's heart as he watched.

"Amen." Peter's eyes opened, and he smiled at Maggie. Just then he glanced up, and Keith knew he was busted. He sniffed self-consciously.

In the next heartbeat Maggie whirled around, fear and determination met in her face right up until she figured out who he was standing there. She stumbled to her feet. "Keith. I didn't hear you there."

The A-lined white cotton shirt set off her curves as did the oversized tan pants. They were very loose and too short to be called pants. He was having trouble getting a full thought through his head. "I... I'm sorry. I was just checking everything before I turned in."

"Oh." Her hand slid to the back of her shirt, which she pulled down. Then she brought her hand back around her middle and scratched the inside of her other forearm. "Everything locked down tight?"

"Seems to be."

"Oh. Good."

If he hadn't been thrown so hard off-track, he might have noticed how much trouble she was having to not fidget right off the planet. She wrapped her arms in front of her and scratched behind her ear. "We were…" Her gaze fell to Peter. "… just…"

Compassion for her came over him. "No, hey. No need to explain. I talk to Him sometimes too."

"Oh." She seemed rooted to the spot. "Well… I guess I should be getting to bed." Her smile became gentle as she glanced back at Peter. "You, mister, have a good night. Okay? I'll see you in the morning."

"Okay."

The quiet peace of the scene traced over Keith as he watched her tuck the covers in around Pete. She was going to make a marvelous mother someday.

"Good night, sweet prince." She kissed the tips of two of her fingers and pressed them onto Peter's forehead. "Now go to sleep." Gently she drifted her fingers over his face and down the sides of his nose. With a sigh, he settled down and soft peace came over his little face.

Maggie turned back to the door and walked all the way to it and through it without stopping. Keith let her pass and then closed the door and stood watching her in the hallway.

"That was nice."

She had made it to her door obviously not planning to stop and talk to him. Her gaze was down when she turned to him. "Peter has a tough time getting to sleep. It seems to help."

Tenderness touched his heart. "So, you do that every night… pray with him?"

It took her a long moment before she nodded. "It always helps me, so I figured it couldn't hurt with him."

True admiration for her tilted his head to the side. "They're lucky to have you."

She tried to meet his gaze but couldn't hold it. "I wish I could do more. They're great kids."

If he could've thought of something to say that would've kept her there, he would've said it. However, for some reason his brain wasn't cooperating with his mouth.

"Well, 'night." She turned, opened her door, and stepped inside.

"Yeah, 'night."

And then she was gone. Keith closed his eyes and shook his head. Why she had this effect on him, he couldn't clearly tell. This was completely crazy. He was, after all, engaged to be married. Engaged. That meant you weren't up at all hours of the night, standing in darkened hallways with some woman in her pajamas. He needed to call Dallas if for no other reason than to douse the guilt slashing its way through him.

Okay, there are certain things in this life a girl just shouldn't have to deal with. Changing flat tires for instance. Radiators overheating, yes. A busted pipe. Programming the remote control. But being blindsided like that wasn't fair at all. When the door closed between them, Maggie forced herself to breathe in a deep inhale. It did nothing at all to stop the swimming of her thoughts or the racing of her heart, but at that point anything was worth a try.

Showing up in the kitchen at breakfast for no reason was one thing. Showing up when she was in her oldest pajamas with the rip on one side was quite another. Her hand went up to her hair, and she raked her fingers through it extra hard. There was no telling how she looked, but how he looked? Wow, was he easy on the eyes. Not to even mention how heart-stoppingly handsome he was minus the hat and the bandana. Dark hair, cropped extra short, and that face, and that smile. Ugh. It just wasn't fair.

She rolled her eyes so she was looking up at the ceiling in desperation. "God, listen to me. I do not need to fall for this guy. I don't need him to keep showing up like this. Please. Please. I'm asking You…"

"Good morning," Keith said brightly the very next morning as he strode into the kitchen, bandana on, and hat in hand. Apparently her prayers all night long had had no effect.

Maggie sighed in consternation and planted a patient smile on her face. "Morning. There's Cheerios."

"Cool." He sat down between the two kids and grabbed the box and a bowl from the middle of the table. Maggie had been wondering why Inez had set an extra one out. Now she knew.

"Did you sleep well?" he asked.

"Good. You?"

"I'm going to have to go get my own pillow from my place. These extra fluffy things are about to do me in." He leaned his head first one way then the other.

"Ike's heading out this morning?" she asked, pulling her shoulders up to her ears as wrists to elbows she straightened on the little window seat.

"Ten. I've got to get over there as soon as I can. They're gonna be wondering where I am." He ate a bite and then looked over at her, which did nothing to calm her stomach. "You don't eat breakfast?"

"Oh. I had a muffin earlier."

"A muffin." He lifted his chin skeptically. "Well, that's one plus in your favor. Helga got canned because she ate too much."

Maggie swallowed at the implication. "Helga?"

"She was the nanny... what? A year. Year and a half ago. Something like that."

If he was trying to make her feel better, it wasn't working. "So, they go through a lot of nannies. Huh?"

Keith shrugged as he finished off his Cheerios. "About one every couple months or so."

"Oh." It was all she could get out.

"Well, I'm off to the races." He stood and grabbed his hat from the table. When it was on his head, Maggie had to force herself to think. Then he smiled and all the remaining thoughts scattered along with their counterparts. "Or to get 'em ready for the races anyway. Y'all have a good day."

"'Bye, Keef," Isabella said through her mouthful of food.

"'Bye, baby doll." Keith bent and kissed her forehead. "See ya, slugger." He waved at Peter, and with that he strode out of the kitchen.

The air she hadn't realized she wasn't breathing escaped in a rush. He had to quit doing that. He was going to kill her before they had a chance to fire her.

Keith felt bad about mentioning the nanny situation, but it was only fair to warn her. More to the point, every time he saw her, he had to remind himself that this couldn't last. She would be gone by the end of the month if she lasted that long. He had a life. His own life. And it did not include Maggie Montgomery.

"So, you decided to grace us with your presence this morning?" Ike asked when Keith stalked into the barn.

"I'm early."

"And happy about it, I see." Ike was busy loading the horse equipment into the trailer. When he hopped from the trailer's running board, his cowboy boots kicked up a puff of dust. "You see Maggie this morning?"

He didn't want to answer that question. It did funny things to his heart. "Yeah. She was at breakfast."

The trainer's motion slowed to a stop, and he exhaled hard. "Listen, Keith. This is none of my business."

Keith looked up at him and steeled himself. There was a challenge in his eyes and his voice. "But…?"

Ike shook his head slowly. "Look, I don't have to tell you the score. You know it better than I do. But a spring fling with someone who will almost surely be gone before anyone knows she's here is not worth risking what you have with Dallas. As good as it looks, as easy as it looks, it's not worth it."

Anger and embarrassment cracked into Keith. "Come on, Ike. I'm not that stupid. Besides, you know that's not my style anymore. Maggie's a friend, and not even that."

"Yeah, well." Ike stopped toe-to-toe with Keith, his faded gray eyes as serious as Keith had ever seen them. "Keep it that way, okay?"

"Dallas! Hey. How's it going?" Keith put his elbow over the soft tan couch cushion as he sat back that night. He was safe and secure, locked in his own bedroom, far across the mansion from the kids' wing.

"Ugh. I'm about two seconds from cracking somebody's skull against a wall," Dallas said in typical, Dallas fashion.

"Oh, why's that?"

"What's it always? Studying as usual." Her voice softened. "It's good to hear your voice though. I need some sanity."

"Now I'm sanity?" He laughed. "That's scary."

"Tell me about it. I'm so ready to get out of here, I could scream."

"Two weeks you'll be back here, with me. No books. No studying." He closed his eyes and could almost catch the feeling of her being right there with him.

"Can I come now?"

His laugh was a breath. "'Fraid not. But I'll tell you what. You buckle down and stick with it, and when you get here, we'll throw you a big party."

"Ugh. Don't remind me."

"What? You having second thoughts?"

"No." The sigh was soft, barely there. "But the planning and the parties and the crowds? Can't we just elope?"

"Oh, your dad would love that."

"Don't remind me. Mom called today. They're coming up for a visit. Well, it's actually for a fundraiser, but that's as close as I get to a real visit these days."

"The junior senator from Texas has higher ambitions?" Keith asked, amused.

"Always. Him. Me. It runs in the family."

"Well, I can't speak for him, but I'm very proud of you."

"Thanks. I needed to hear that." She sighed, and he felt it run him through. "I'm so ready to see you."

"Me too." Then he stopped himself. "I mean I can't wait to see you. I see myself every morning."

"You're crazy."

"Yeah, about you."

They talked awhile longer, and when he hung up, Keith felt better. Ike was right. Being around Maggie was playing with fire, and he didn't need that in his life. He'd done that enough and had been burned, repeatedly. No. In four days his parents would be back, she would probably be gone for reasons he still didn't know. What he did know was that at some point things would go back to normal, and normal did not include Maggie Montgomery. Hanging onto that thought, he dug himself in the pillows and forced himself to stay there.

By the next morning Keith had come up with a solid plan. He wouldn't go anywhere near her unless absolutely necessary. For breakfast he grabbed a Dr. Pepper out of Ike's stash in the barn. If all went well, he would have lunch at his place and call to let Inez know he was going to be late for dinner tonight. He could show up after they had gone to bed. It was a great plan.

The fact that Keith hadn't been around didn't stop Maggie's heart from jumping every time there was a noise at a door. She had never felt so scattered or so flightly. The kids were great as usual. Through the soccer lesson and lunch, they were angels. For that Maggie was grateful because she was having a really hard time concentrating on anything other than when he might show up again.

Trying to come up with anything that might stave off insanity, she had a thought after lunch. "Hey, you two. What do you say we make smoothies and take them out to the playhouse?"

"What's a smoothie?" Peter asked.

"Come on. I'll show you." She took them both to the kitchen, knowing Inez had gone into town to do errands and Patty Ann wasn't due back until at least four. Careful to anchor her, Maggie set Isabella on the counter. With only two cabinet openings, she found the blender. From his spot on the floor, Peter watched her. "Here." She stood him up on the chair. "You watch your sister."

Obediently Peter put his hands on Isabella. Maggie went to the refrigerator and got out a few things. They wouldn't be the most elaborate smoothies in the world, but she didn't think the kids would care anyway. "This is going to be fun."

She plugged the blender in and put several ingredients in—the strawberry yogurt, the bananas, the raspberries, and the ice. "Oh, milk." In five steps, the refrigerator door was open in her hand. It was then that she heard the scream.

"Izzy! No!"

On one whirl she was around, and her own scream joined Peter's. "Izzy, no!"

The growl of the blender was cacophonous—like a jackhammer on concrete. Crushing, crunching, screeching—the blender flung the pink concoction in every conceivable direction.

Who was screaming what, Maggie had no idea. All she knew was that by the time she got the blender shut off, there were pink splotches all over the kids, all over her, and most distressingly all over the kitchen. Pink was dripping down the white glass cabinets, off the white and navy curtains, and all over the grouted, gray tile floor. "Oh, my… No." She put her head back to keep from crying. "No. No. No. No."

Pulling patience to her with all her strength, she looked at the two children. Isabella was in the throes of an all-out panic attack, and Peter was cowering away from her like he was about to be beaten.

She fought back her own distress and took a breath to try to calm herself. Carefully, gently, Maggie took Isabella into her arms and sat down on the chair next to Peter, oblivious to the pink squish underneath her. "It's okay, baby. I shouldn't have let you that close." In her arms, Maggie rocked the inconsolable child slowly until her wails became whimpers. "My fault. That was all my fault."

Peter's sniff behind her brought her attention to him, and with tears crowding her own eyes, Maggie reached back for him. "It's okay, Peter. It's okay." Her tenderness wrenched sobs of fear and guilt free from the little boy, and his wails replaced Isabella's. "I shouldn't have left you there like that. I shouldn't have. It was stupid, but it was my stupid not yours. That wasn't your fault. It wasn't."

Peter looked around the kitchen and shrank into the slats of the chair. "Inez will be mad."

It was true. Maggie knew it in her bones as she looked around the yogurt-splattered kitchen. This could well come at the cost of her job. "Well, you let me worry about Inez."

"What? Did the Pepto-Bismol explode?"

Maggie spun so fast, she nearly sent all three of them crashing off the chair. He stood in the kitchen doorway, hands on hips, surveying the mess.

"Keith."

He'd only been by to talk to Jeffrey about the yard for the engagement party. He hadn't even intended to stop in and say hi, but when screams erupt and you're the one in charge, you come running. Behind him, he heard Jeffrey's hard, disgusted sigh. However, whether she was thinking when she did it or not didn't matter at the moment. What mattered was that all three of them looked like they were about to be thrown out permanently, and they knew it. They shrunk backward away from his presence. He stepped farther into the kitchen, toward the counter and shook his head in consternation. "What happened?"

"It was my fault." Maggie stood shakily, placing herself between him and the children. "We were going to make smoothies. I left them over here, and the blender got turned on. It's my fault. I should've been watching them closer."

Smoothie-splatters streaked down her blue blouse, across her hair, and down her face. In fact, it was everywhere.

Things happened. Keith knew that as well as anybody. However, he also knew there were people on this place who wouldn't take that for a reason. "Okay. Why don't you take the kids upstairs? Hose them off. Get them into clean clothes. Whatever it takes. Jeffrey and I will get this mess cleaned up."

He heard Jeffrey's grunt of disapproval, but with one glance backward, he silenced any protest.

Twisting, Maggie picked Isabella up even as she kept her gaze on Keith. "Are you sure? I don't want to get you into trouble."

"Let me worry about that. You take care of them."

A wary nod, and Maggie herded the children out and up the stairs. Keith turned to Jeffrey who looked positively mortified. "Come on. We'd better get this place cleaned up before the she-wolves get back."

Upstairs Maggie did her best to calm the children down. Isabella was the easiest. With a quick slide through the bathtub, clean clothes, and her bed coupled with the intense crying of earlier, the little girl was asleep in no time. Peter, on the other hand, was a different story. He watched her carefully. Every move she made, he seemed to cringe back from her in fear.

In the bath when she went to put the soap on him, he backed away a full inch before she caught hold of him. "Hey, hey, Peter-boy. Where're you going? It's okay. I'm not going to hurt you. See, we're just going to wash all this icky old yogurt off so you're all nice and clean." She kept talking in that singsong voice that kids melted into. It didn't help him, but it sure helped her.

When Peter made it out of the tub and dressed, Maggie took him in the rocking chair, wondering about what was going on downstairs. However, as deadly to her job as that sounded, she had to trust that they would do the best they could. Whatever happened after that would happen.

"What in the wide world?" Inez stopped cold in the doorway to the kitchen.

Keith held up his hand that sported the little rope around his wrist as he stood on the chair, wiping yogurt from the ceiling. "I can explain."

Inez swung the bags onto the counter. "Well, somebody better. Look at this mess."

He surveyed his options, took a breath, and plunged ahead. "I didn't have lunch. I was just going to grab something quick. I didn't realize the blender was on when I plugged it in." He felt Jeffrey's gaze on him, but he kept going. "We were hoping to have it cleaned up before you got here."

She didn't look at all pleased. "Well, that worked."

"Don't worry about it. We'll get it."

It was clear she wanted to yell at him, but the hierarchy of the situation dawned on her, and she backed off. "Fine. But this mess had better be clean before dinner."

"It will be. No problem."

Maggie was still rocking Peter in the chair an hour later. Her cheek rested on his head, and she knew he was asleep. Poor kid. She'd about scared him to death. The soft creak of the door brought her thoughts up from the sleeping child. Keith stuck his head in, and she gasped softly.

"Keith, how's…?"

He put his finger to his lips, glanced back out into the hallway, and then stepped in before closing the door quietly behind him. Making no noise at all, he tiptoed over to where she sat. She surveyed him seriously. "How's downstairs?"

"Clean. Finally. We've got the curtains in the wash right now. Everything else is done."

She sighed in relief, and the chair started rocking again. But he didn't leave. Instead, he sat on his heel next to the rocking chair and brushed his thumb under his nose. "Listen. Inez came home and about had a conniption."

Maggie's eyes widened in fear and then closed as she shook her head. "I'm dead."

"No. No. That's what I came up here to tell you. I took the rap for you."

Her gaze smashed into his as she tried to understand what he was telling her. "You what? Why?"

Gentle and compassionate, he gazed at her, his deep brown eyes setting her spirit on solid ground. "She can be a little harsh if things aren't just right, so I told her I did it. So as long as you don't say anything, she'll never know."

Gratefulness for his chivalry traced through her, but still he'd put himself out there to get yell at… or worse. "But why? Why would you do that? It was my fault."

"Hey, things happen." He shrugged, then reached over and ran his hand over Peter's head. "Besides these two need you more than I need my skin." With a tight smile, he stood, and her gaze followed him up.

"Will you be back for dinner tonight?"

He nodded ever-so-slightly. "I wouldn't miss it."

Five

"Is she asleep?" Keith stepped up behind Maggie as she closed Isabella's door.

In the first second Maggie jumped. In the second she nodded, feeling the security his presence brought her all the way to her core. "Too much excitement today."

"I hear you there." He followed her across the hall, and she felt his every move. "You going to tuck Peter in?"

"Yeah."

"Mind if I come along?" He was leaning against the wall, shoulder to wrist. The hat and bandana were gone again, which wasn't helping her breathing any.

"If you want." She pushed the door to Peter's room open and without waiting for him to follow, she walked over to the bed. However, when she got there, the first thing she noticed was the tears on the little face, and concern poured over her. "Peter-boy, what's wrong?"

Sad, heart-wrenching eyes gazed up at her. "You're not leaving are you?"

"Leaving?" She knelt down next to the bed and took his hand in hers, forgetting anyone else was in the room with them. "Why would I be leaving?"

"Because of what we did." His little lip quivered. "I'm sorry. I didn't know Isabella was going to touch that button."

"Oh, baby." Compassion for him slid through her. "Baby, baby. Come here."

He sat up and fell into her arms, hugging her like she'd never been hugged before. "I don't want you to go."

"Hey. Hey." She stroked his head as his desperation pulled her closer to him. "Shh. It's okay. It's not your fault, remember?"

"But I don't want you to leave."

"Hey, slugger." Keith knelt down on the other side of the bed, and Maggie looked at him through the darkness. He reached across the bed and ran his hand over Peter's back. "Maggie's not going anywhere. I'm going to make sure of that."

How he could sound so sure, she didn't know. But Peter sniffed and backed up from her. Still leaning on her, he looked at Keith. "Really?"

"Really. Now you get on to sleep. Tomorrow's another day, and maybe we'll go horseback riding again if you want."

A breath of excitement punched through the sadness. "Really?"

"Yeah, but only if you get some sleep now."

Peter scooted back down under the covers, and Maggie helped him pull them up around him. However, when he was settled, she wasn't sure what to do next.

"You want to say it?" Keith asked her when she didn't start immediately.

Although it was more than her brain could handle, she nodded. She reached down and took Peter's hand in hers and then from across the bed, Keith offered her his. Her heart slammed into her chest as she looked at it for one second and then forced herself to remember his generosity earlier in the afternoon. She laid her hand in his. Rough but strong just like him, it supported hers effortlessly. Trying not to think about it, she bent her head.

"Dear Lord, we thank You tonight for all the good things You did for us today. We ask You to send Your saints and angels to be with us tonight. Keep us safe, hold us in Your love, and be with us always. Amen."

"Amen." The deep voice and the soft one blended together, sending her heart into fits.

"Good night, sweet prince." She pulled her hand back, bent forward, and kissed Peter's forehead. "You get some sleep. Let Jesus take care of everything else."

On the other side of the bed, Keith stood. He reached one hand down to the little shoulder. "'Night, slugger."

Maggie pushed to her feet and turned for the door. Three steps and she felt his presence right behind her. It was comforting and anxiety-producing at the same time. At the door Keith opened it for her, and they stepped into the hallway. Once there, he slid the door into the jamb and turned to her.

"I think you've got a fan," he whispered.

"Yeah, well. Lotta good that's going to do me." If the day had convinced her of anything, it was that she could never be perfect enough for this place. Some day, some way, she would do something just wrong enough to be fired, and it wouldn't even have to be as major as yogurt on the ceiling. Her heart ripped in half at the thought of leaving these kids, of breaking their hearts by walking away. It would kill her as surely as it would kill them. "I gotta go. 'Night."

"Hey." His hand coming around her wrist stopped her from escaping into her room. "What's wrong?"

Sniffing the misery down, she turned to him, but her gaze was on the carpet. "Let's face it. I'm not cut out for this place. It's obvious. I'm not used to schedules and dressing fancy and soccer lessons and piano lessons. Mrs. Malowinski's was nothing like this. I don't know how to do any of this right."

Beaten down by the need to appear perfect in a too-perfect world, she looked ready to admit defeat. Keith knew exactly where she was coming from. He'd been there. "Well, it looks to me like you're doing something right. Those kids love you, Maggie, and you've only been here... what? A week."

"Yeah." She laughed sarcastically. "And I'll only be here what? Four more days." She wrapped her arms over her middle, and one hand drifted up to wipe the tears from under her glasses. "Face it. I'm not good enough to be here. I couldn't be if I tried."

"Okay. Now you stop right there." He picked his hand up and held up his index finger. "First of all, you have done more for those two kids than anyone has since they've been on the planet. Second of all, you are perfect just the way you are."

She actually laughed at him that time. "Yeah, right. Look at me. I've worn the same shirt for three days now because I don't have the guts to ask if I can use the washer nor do I even know where it is. I got reamed out the other day because we were only two minutes early to dinner, and with today's stunt, well, let's just say it's only a matter of time."

Keith shook his head at the list. "Wait a minute. Back up.

They didn't show you the house? You don't know where the washer is?"

Embarrassment tramped across her face. It took her more than a few seconds, but finally she sighed. "They warned me not to go snooping around, so I didn't want to go looking on my own."

"Oh, well, that one's easy enough." He reached over and took hold of her wrist. "Come with me." With her trailing him like a bike with the kickstand down, they took the kitchen stairs to the bottom level. In the kitchen he turned to the right instead of to the left and opened a small door. He flipped the light on, and there in gleaming white was the washer and dryer. "Ta-da! Now was that really so hard?"

She fought the smile as long as she could, but finally it broke through.

"Good. Problem number one, solved." He turned to her. "Now, my next question is, how you got to the end of your clothing supply in less than a week."

Leaning against the open door and making circles on the floor with her toe that he realized was sticking out the front of her white sock, she kept her gaze on the floor. "Because I brought everything I owned. It was all in that suitcase. The one we carried from the barn."

Incredulousness dropped over him. "Everything you owned was in there?" How that could possibly be, he didn't know because that suitcase weighed next to nothing.

"I was headed back to Mrs. Malowinski's when the dean called me about this job, and Mrs. Ayer didn't really give me the chance to get anything new once I got here. Not that I could have, I had two dollars to my name the day I showed up... still do."

Processing all that she was telling him was getting harder by the minute. "Okay. Wait a minute. Time out. One thing at a time. Who is Mrs. Malowinski?"

Maggie fought the humiliation rising in her chest. Sure, there was nothing to be embarrassed about, but still... People always reacted so strangely when they knew.

The forcefulness of his voice was gone, and he softened. "Maggie? Hey. It's okay. You can tell me."

She glanced up at him, and his face held nothing but compassion and concern. She took a breath, closed her eyes, and willed the wall to hold her up. "She's my foster mom, or she was until I turned 18."

"Foster mom?" He shook his head a half-shake. "I don't understand."

Willing the tears to stay in her heart, Maggie detached herself from the story as she had learned to do so long before. "My parents were killed in a car accident when I was eight." She set her jaw and lifted her chin to show him she was over that tragedy. "There weren't any relatives to take me, and they hadn't named any guardians in the will, so… I went into the foster care system."

"Oh, Maggie. I'm sorry."

She shrugged slightly. "It's not that big of a deal. It was okay. At least it was once I got to Mrs. Malowinski's house. She was really great. She had six of us… all foster kids. It was chaos, but it was okay because she loved us."

The worry in his eyes drilled through her when she glanced up at him. Her gaze fell again. She fought to pull it back up to his. She didn't want him to think she was damaged goods or anything.

"How long were you at Mrs. ….?" he asked softly.

"Malowinski. Four years. Fourteen to eighteen. Then the state kicked me out, and I was on my own for good."

"The state kicked you out?"

She shrugged with one shoulder. "It's the rules. When you get to be eighteen, good luck. See ya." She waved her hand as if making a joke. "I got lucky though. I got a scholarship at Kingsville, so it worked out."

She stifled the yawn that attacked her. Slowly she pulled her hand up to her hair and slid it sideways through it to the back. "I know what it's like to grow up thinking nobody cares." Her smile was sad. "That's why I wanted this to work out so bad."

He regarded her for a long minute. "Yeah. I can see that."

This time she really did yawn. "Man, I'm done for. I'd better get up there. We've got dance and art lessons in the morning."

"Oh, joy," he said, trying to laugh. "More lessons."

"Tell me about it. I've never seen two kids with such tight schedules. They make Donald Trump look like a bum." With a push to get her going, she started up the stairs as he snapped off the light behind them. He was climbing behind her, of that, she

51

was sure. She could feel him there. As she climbed, she knew she had to say what was in her heart, and here, in the dark, she had just enough distance from it to be able to say the word. "Thanks."

"Thanks? For what?" He sounded surprised.

"For what. Yeah right. Well, let's see for not letting me face plant that first day in the foyer, for carrying my suitcase for a mile so my arms wouldn't drop off, for taking us horseback riding—although I'm still trying to recover from that one." She pulled herself up the top stair. "Oh, yeah, and for putting your neck on the line for me today. You didn't have to do that, you know?"

At her door, she stopped and turned toward him.

His smile was more sad and concerned than she had ever seen it. "I'm glad I did."

For one single moment all seemed right with the world. Then tension and awkwardness descended between them.

"Well, I'd better get some shut-eye," he said, pointing past her to the darkened hallway beyond.

"Yeah. You and me both." Her hand rested on the knob as she leaned her head on the door and gazed up at him. "Thanks, Keith."

"No problem."

It was nearly five in the morning before Keith got to sleep. He had to do something, speak up, tell his father about her, but how? It was a question that would be with him the rest of the weekend.

Six

Horseback riding with the kids on Friday was great because this time Keith convinced Maggie to trot, which was more fun watching than it should've been. Friday night he made it a point to be upstairs in time for prayers. On Saturday morning, he hit the breakfast table with one goal in mind.

"I'm going to run into town today to pick up some stuff," he said as if he hadn't thought every word through a million times since they'd walked out of the laundry room.

"Oh?" she asked. Sitting at the table, she picked small pieces off of a blueberry muffin.

He hunched over his bowl to avoid looking at her so that maybe she would believe he really didn't care one way or the other. "Yeah. I was thinking. If y'all want to come with me, you can."

The picking stopped, and she stared at him. "Us? Why would we go into town?"

"Well, I needed to hit Wal-Mart to get supplies for my place when I get banished there again on Tuesday." He shrugged to take the edge off that statement. "I thought you might want to go get some things for you. You know, clothes and stuff."

She narrowed her eyes and then raised her eyebrows. "Yeah, like I have the money to do that."

How he ever thought he could do this and be nonchalant about it, he didn't know. He swallowed the nervousness along with the Cheerios. "Well, I could loan you some until you get paid. I'm sure you'll be getting something by next Friday."

"Yeah, like my pink slip."

He started to protest, but when he looked at her, she smiled softly. It was obvious she was teasing as well as considering his offer, so he ducked his head over the bowl and let her alone with her thoughts.

"Maybe I could get a few things," she said but quickly added. "Not much. Just a couple."

The smile from his heart couldn't be stopped. "Cool." He finished off the last of the Cheerios, stood, and grabbed his hat from the table. "I'll be up to pick you guys up about 12:30."

"That'll work." She was gazing up at him, which had a way of short circuiting his brain. "If you're sure you don't mind…"

"Hey, I don't ask if I mind."

The more she thought about it, the more Maggie knew he was too good to be true. Stable, kind, generous. How could you get all of those in one package? There were only a couple of problems. One, she had no way to know if he felt the same way. Two, maybe he was nice to everybody, and she was reading way too much into his kindness toward her. Three, and this was the biggest of all, by Tuesday morning he could be a memory in the rearview mirror. This job was an eggshell crack away from disintegrating around her.

She felt it every minute that he wasn't around, and so it was comforting to have the promise of a whole afternoon in his company. Car seats standing sentinel on either side of her on the top step, she stood with Isabella in her arms, and Peter peering out from behind her leg. For the 78th time she checked her watch. He should've been here by now. If Patty Ann caught them out here with no better explanation than she had prepared, Tuesday might come a lot sooner than Tuesday.

Relief poured through her when the shiny red Dodge Ram pickup pulled around the corner and up to the front. He hopped out and yanked the back door open. "Sorry I'm late. I had trouble with a water pump."

Maggie picked up a car seat and started to him. He took it from her, and she handed him the other as well. "Nothing serious I hope."

"Na. The motor went out. Just took a little gerrymandering." At the pickup, he worked to put Isabella's seat in first, then went around to put in Peter's. "So, you ready for a trip into big ol' Pine Hill?"

"I don't know. I haven't been outside these gates in what feels like forever."

Keith smiled as they each strapped in a child. "Well, then, by all means we don't want you to feel like a prisoner."

As she climbed into the pickup, Maggie had the feeling that she'd never felt so free in her entire life.

All the way into Pine Hill which was only a 20 minute drive, the conversation sailed smoothly. She was so easy to be with, so easy to talk to, so spirited but with a maturity and control Keith found fascinating. "So, you were from where originally?"

"Midland," she said, and she pulled one jean-clad leg up to her other. "My dad worked for the city. My mom taught. Then when I was eight, everything changed."

"You moved to Del Rio."

She shook her head on his glance over. "No, I went to Lubbock first. They had an opening. It was less than wonderful." Her soft laugh ripped his heart out. "I was there for almost a year. Then I moved to Carlton for awhile. That one wasn't much better, but I really liked the school there." The history stopped for a moment. "Mrs. Baker. Man, I haven't thought of her in a long time. She really started me into the reading thing. I could just lose myself and everything else in the pages. It was something sane to do when everything was going crazy around me."

Her voice slid into the memories, and Keith glanced at her again, sensing the things she wasn't saying. Finally she ducked her head and continued.

"That one last two years." She let out a breath. "Hard to believe I even made it through that one." There was no doubt the pain she was pushing down with each word. "There were two stops after that... San Antonio with... hmm, what was their name again? Abrigail... Abingail... Something like that. They were okay, but we were in a really bad neighborhood." She glanced back into the back and chose not to continue with that line of thought.

"Then there was Mineral Wells for six months, and then I landed at Mrs. Malowinski's."

"In Del Rio."

"Yeah. She was great. Real inspiration. Unbelievable lady." Maggie let out a long breath as her gaze drifted out the side window. "I think she saved my life to be honest with you."

Sadness, fear, and hard-fought acceptance laced every memory. After a moment, he felt her gaze slide to his, and he glanced at her. She smiled. "It's been a long ride."

"Well, maybe this is where all of that was leading." Why he said it, he had no idea, but he wanted with everything in him for it to be the truth.

"I hope so." She looked out the side window again. "I really hope so."

Keith had never met anyone as unassuming and unpretentious as Maggie. Up and down the aisles of Wal-Mart they walked. They'd already gotten two pairs of shoes—a pair of tennis shoes and a pair of white dress shoes—both of which were on yellow tag, please-take-them-we're-begging-you sale. Once they made it to the clothes, things didn't improve. He'd pick up a shirt or pants or a skirt for her to consider. She liked it until she saw the price tag, and then she'd shake her head and put it back. At the extreme-clearance sale rack she found a shirt for $5 that wasn't much better than what she had on.

It wasn't that he cared what she wore, but he knew there were people back at the mansion who cared very much. If he had any chance of getting them to consent to let her stay, he had to find a way to convince her to get something nicer without totally cutting her off at the knees over her wardrobe.

"Maggie!" he said in frustrated disbelief when she put a white scrunch skirt back on the rack. "Why did you put that back? $12 is not that much."

"Twelve dollars is twelve dollars. That could buy five bags of cereal if you get the right ones." She walked around the rack as he pushed the cart with Isabella in the front and Peter sitting amidst Keith's purchases in the back.

His brilliant idea wasn't going to work if she kept this up. "Tell you what. I'll pick something, and you have to at least try it on."

"But…"

"I didn't say you have to buy it. Just try it on."

She scrunched her face as he started sorting through the rack next to him.

"What size?" he asked.

"Keith."

"I said, 'What size?'"

She exhaled hard and crossed her arms in front of her. "Eight."

"This is nice, and it's an eight." He pulled a red tank top from the rack. From the other side of him, he fingered a blue blazer and sorted until he found the right size. Holding them up, he wished he'd paid more attention on his shopping trips with Dallas. "These are good." He put those two in the cart. "How about orange?"

That idea was rejected nearly the second after he'd made it, more by him than by her. On the next rack he stopped. Smoke colored with white flowers and vines, the dress looked just like something Dallas would wear; however, this one would never fit in Dallas' price range. "And this." He flipped it into the cart.

Maggie raised her eyebrows skeptically.

At the next rack, he examined the choices. "Nice. Yuck. Here." He flipped another skirt into the cart. Pushing forward, he was halfway to the next rack when his cell phone beeped. He pulled it out, hit on. "This is Keith."

"Keith! Man, dude, where have you been? I was about to call out the FBI."

"Hey, Greg." He pushed the cart a little farther on and started sliding the hangers in each direction. His brain put the conversation with Greg on autopilot. "What's up, man?"

"I've called your place and left like five messages. I called the stables and left a message there too. Where have you been?"

"You know if you want to catch me, my cell's the best way." He held up a dark turquoise and white striped top. Maggie didn't look convinced, but he put in the cart anyway. "Besides I've been staying up at the mansion this last week." He held up a white skirt and added it to the others. "So, what's up?"

"Well, I was wondering when the big engagement shindig is for one thing."

"Oh." That threw Keith off for a minute. "Week from today."

"At the mansion?"

"Yeah."

"Well, are you coming over some time so we can hang out before the old ball and chain gets back or what?"

Keith shifted the phone to the other ear, picked up one more shirt and then another skirt and put them in the cart. "How's Friday?" He felt guilty about leaving his best friend hanging—even if he did have a zillion other things to think about.

"I need to go potty," Peter said from the cart, and Maggie looked at Keith. The multitasking was beginning to fry his nerves.

"Friday works for me," Greg said. "You want to just meet at Tonie's for pizzas, and we'll go from there?"

Maggie waved Keith down even as she lifted Peter from the cart. "We'll be right back."

Gratefully, Keith nodded. "Yeah, okay." His attention swung back to the conversation. "Friday at Tonie's." He sorted through the next rack, found nothing, and pushed the cart forward. They were running out of options.

"And what time's the big party start Saturday?"

"Uh." It took some searching to locate the information in his brain. "6:30. Dallas is flying in that morning at ten. I'll go pick her up and then her folks get here at..." The correct times slip-slid through his mind, not stopping long enough to lodge there. He pulled another shirt out, examined it, and put it back. "Umm, one, one-fifteen, something like that I think. I'm sure we'll pick them up, and then head back up to the mansion."

"You talked to Dallas recently?"

"Uh, yeah." This conversation was raking horrible feelings through him. "Last night. Night before last. She's good. Studying her brains out. You know Dallas." He caught sight of Maggie on the other side of the store but coming toward him. "Listen, Greg, I've gotta get. I'll talk to you Friday."

"Don't be late."

"You know me."

"Yeah. I know you. Don't be late."

Keith laughed at that. "Later, man." He hung up just as she walked back up. She started to put Peter in the cart, but at hip level she realized how much stuff was in there.

"I'm not buying all of this."

"You're right. You're not. I am. You want to try it on or just take it?"

Her gaze came up to his, and shock laced the edges of it. "Keith…"

"No. This isn't a discussion. You're getting whatever fits, so do you want to try it on here or take it home and try it on there? Your choice."

She shook her head in frustration and checked her watch. "It's almost two. The kids are exhausted. We'd better get back, or Patty Ann is going to go ballistic… if she hasn't already."

In the front of the cart, Isabella did a forward bob as sleep dragged her down. Keith looked at her, and although he wanted some confirmation that the clothes would fit, he knew Maggie was right. "Okay, but don't weasel out on me. You will keep and wear anything that fits."

"Me? Weasel?" Maggie shot him an innocent look that stole his heart. "I never weasel."

The kids were down for a nap, which took next to no effort to pull off. Maggie went to her room where the Wal-Mart bags were stacked on her bed. She shook her head. Somehow in the time she'd been gone, he'd accumulated far more than she'd wanted to get. Worse, he had sent her to the pickup with the kids so she couldn't see how much it had all cost. With a sigh and knowing she couldn't keep it all, she pulled the turquoise and white striped shirt out. She held it up to her and turned to the mirror over the dresser.

A smile slid through her heart. He was crazy. She really loved that about him.

"Hey. Sorry I'm late," Keith said in one short string of words as he strode into the dining room at 6:05. He put his hat on the chair at the head of the table and was almost in his own chair when he took one look at her and stopped dead. "Wow." He tilted his head to the side and ran his gaze up and down her. "Nice."

Her smile was a mix of happiness and shyness. "Like it?" With her hair pulled up and back from her face, the white collar just over the first turquoise stripe set off her skin.

Slowly he lowered himself into the chair. "Are you kidding?

They won't know who you are when they come back."

"Eat. Eat. Eat." Isabella knocked her hand on the high chair tray. The food was already on the table.

"Did y'all already pray?" he asked, looking at Maggie, which wasn't exactly safe at this point.

"We were waiting for you."

His heart filled his chest. "Well, there's a good excuse." He held out his hand across the table to her, and she took it.

Taking Isabella's hand in hers, Maggie bent her head. "Dear Father, we thank You for this food and this time together again. Watch over us, and be with us tonight and always. Amen."

He loved hearing her pray, and it was getting harder and harder to not let his brain catalog everything else he was starting to love about her.

"You don't go to church?" Keith asked later as he followed Maggie to her door after their few minutes on either side of Peter's bed. She pulled on his heart like a magnet, dragging him with her, making him want to stay with her as crazy as that sounded.

"Church?" The question turned her around.

"Yeah, you know. Big building with the steeple on it."

Annoyance drifted over her. "I know what church is. Why are you asking?"

He shrugged. "Just a question. You pray like you were born in church. I just thought... Well, I wondered... Tomorrow is..."

She lifted her chin in understanding. "You're wondering why I don't go on Sundays."

"No." Sheepishly, he glanced at her. "I was wondering if you were planning to go tomorrow."

That thought wound through her eyes. "Well, I don't know. I don't really have a way to go unless I take my car, and I don't know how far I'd trust it. Besides, I can't just take the kids, and I can't leave the kids either. Something tells me Patty Ann would take a very dim view of that."

He laughed. "Not to mention Inez."

"Yeah. There's a comforting thought." She sighed. "I don't even know where the churches are around here, or what time they start." With one hand she lifted the waves of hair out of her face.

"But you'd go if that stuff wasn't a problem?"

She anchored her arms over her middle. "Well, yeah, probably. But they are... a problem."

Keith's gaze took all of her in. The A-shirt, the tan pants, the gentle undulating waves over her soft, innocent face. He shouldn't make the offer, and yet not making it would kill him. They would only get this one chance, and as stupid as that was, he would never forgive himself if he didn't take it. "Tell you what. You get the kids ready and meet me out front at 9:30."

Her eyebrows lowered.

"The car seats are still in my truck."

She shook her head. "But..."

He hated pleading on most occasions, but this time it felt more like the only way to keep her from saying no. "Please, Maggie. Let me do this for you."

She gazed at him. "Why?"

His smile was barely there. "Because I want to. That's why."

Seven

Isabella was perched on Maggie's hip, Peter on Keith's as the four of them walked into the little church on the other side of Pine Hill. Keith hadn't been in this church in a long time. When he sat down in the bench and put Peter on his lap, Keith's gaze went to the front. In his mind the casket still sat right there. With barely a sigh, he was right back there—the incomprehension, the sadness, the fear wrapping around him.

Stoicism dropped into his heart. He wouldn't cry. He hadn't then, and he wouldn't now. At that moment Maggie looked over at him and smiled. If he'd had only a small amount of sanity less, he would've reached over and taken her hand. He knew what that hand felt like in his. It was wrong, but he wanted to feel it again and again forever.

Hardly smiling at her, he turned his gaze up front. He could do this. For her, he could do this. He needed to if only to pay her back for giving him a piece of himself he had lost so long ago. Bowing his head, he let his mind go back to the memories waiting there.

Her perfume, her gentleness, her tenderness. His heart filled with the memories of the woman who had shaped him into the man he was today.

"I'll be back, Keith. I promise," she said again in his memory, and he had no trouble at all recalling that voice. "You be good while I'm gone."

Emotion surged to the surface, but he beat it back. He hadn't done the best of jobs of keeping that last promise. He'd tried, but it wasn't exactly the easiest assignment in the world.

The service started, and Keith stood Peter next to him. Once on his feet, Keith glanced over at her. With Isabella on her hip and God in her eyes, Keith wondered how much she looked like his mother surely had, standing in this church with a little tow-headed boy standing right next to her.

He put his hands on the bench ahead of him and arched his shoulders forward. She had been gone for seventeen years, but to him, she had never really left.

"You want to stop somewhere and eat?" Keith asked when they were back in the pickup.

Maggie turned to him pensively. "We'd probably better get back. I'm sure lunch will be waiting."

"Yeah. Right." It took him more than a minute of driving before he got the emotions firmly put back in their place. Then he glanced over at her. "So, what do you say, horseback riding tomorrow? We could go out to the waterfall."

"Waterfall?"

"It's not bad. Real easy ride. The kids will love it." His heart was now talking for him. "We could take a picnic, spend a few hours, let them play in the water. It's supposed to be nice tomorrow."

"I don't know. Inez might..."

"Let me worry about Inez."

Maggie looked over at him, obviously still not convinced. "You don't think they will be mad?"

He didn't really care what they would think. "Na. It's one day, one afternoon. How could they get mad about that?"

Maggie did her best to have everything ready Monday morning, but life wasn't cooperating. Peter seemed to have grown two inches overnight, and suddenly nothing fit. She would have to mention that to someone, the prospect of which did not sound inviting. Isabella was not in the best of moods, and Maggie wondered if she might be getting sick.

There were no real, solid signs, but a general lethargy that seemed to drag on the little girl's spirit.

"Are you not feeling good?" Maggie asked, and Isabella looked at her from the changing table with wide eyes that told her no more than she already knew. "Well, I think swimming is out for you today, little one." With the child's clothes changed, Maggie picked her up and turned Peter for the kitchen. "Let's get some breakfast. We've got lessons to get done before Keith gets back to take us riding."

Her heart bounced on the mention of his name. Church the day before had been so wonderful. It was strange because she wouldn't have pegged him for a church-goer, and in truth he had looked rather out of place. Yet he took her because he knew she wanted to go. Something about that made her heart dance.

At breakfast, he was normal Keith again—down-to-earth, nice, and work-focused. Ike called again, apparently they had made it back from the race. Q-Main had gotten third. She couldn't tell how he felt about that. In fact, information about reality was having a hard time crowding out information about how her heart felt every time he was around.

He stood from the table and grabbed his hat. "I'll be back about eleven. I talked to Inez. She'll have lunch ready to take."

Maggie nodded, watching him, and wishing she could stop time. Here, in the breakfast area, him standing there, hat in hand, life felt so right, so perfect, and she never wanted that to end. "We'll be ready."

Ready they were. Standing on the top step as if they belonged nowhere else. Keith had to pull in a breath before he could hit the door with his shoulder to get out of the pickup. Ike would never understand, but that was okay. They had today. And right now, to Keith, that's all that mattered.

"Who's ready to go riding?" he asked as his heart soared ahead of him up the stairs.

"Me!" Peter jumped from the step into Keith's arms. He was happier than Keith had ever seen him.

"Well, what're we waiting for?"

They got the kids into the pickup. Maggie crawled in the front and locked her seat belt. "I don't think we're going to get to do the water thing."

"Oh? Why not?"

"I don't think Izzy's feeling all that great."

Keith looked back into the seat behind Maggie. "Why not?"

"I don't know. She's just not herself this morning." The concern was evident in Maggie's demeanor.

"You think she needs a doctor?"

"No. Not yet anyway, but I also don't think she needs to be inviting a cold either."

He had yet to put the pickup in drive. "You still want to go?"

She smiled at him. "I think the sunshine will do her some good." Her gaze fell to her jeans. "Besides, who knows when we'll get to do this again."

The melancholy of what happened tomorrow hung over her, and with everything in him, Keith wanted to make it evaporate. "Then we'll have a great day today and let Jesus take care of everything else."

Surprise jumped to her face, but when she looked at him, he smiled. After a couple seconds she nodded.

"Oh, it's beautiful." They were the only words Maggie could think to say when the horses approached the waterfall. The shelf of rock high above dropped the water over its edge like a hand dropping pearls. In the bright sunlight the water glinted and glimmered like a thousand tiny diamonds.

Her gaze stayed on the falls as she got off and pulled Isabella down too. "Oh, baby girl. Look at that. Look how pretty."

"P'itty," Isabella said, and happiness burst through Maggie. She nosed her face into the soft blonde curls.

"You are the cutest thing ever. You know that?"

"Come on, you two," Keith said, tilting his head and smiling at them as he stood there, the picnic basket in one hand and Peter's hand in the other. "You're wasting daylight."

Through the calf-high flowers, Maggie stepped over to him and followed him right up to the second shelf of rock which stood between the fall above and the pool of water below. Carefully she sat down. "This is incredible. I've never seen anything like it."

"One of the hidden treasures of the place," Keith said. "The drive up is murder on vehicles, so most people don't bother to come out here."

"But the horses didn't have much trouble," she said with concern.

"No. Luckily they're open access to out here." Kneeling, he started laying out the picnic—sandwiches, potato chips, and little silver bags of juice.

Maggie wondered if he would die of starvation before they got back. She'd seen him eat, and this didn't look like nearly enough. "You come out here a lot?"

"Not much anymore. I used come out here a lot."

She helped him and then set Isabella on her lap and tore her a piece of sandwich off. "What happened to that?"

He shrugged. "I got busy. Things to do. People to see. Places to go. You know how it is."

"So, they keep you pretty busy, huh?" She took a half sandwich for herself.

"Always something. They'll be taking Q-Main to Del Mar in a couple of weeks, and we're trying to get Transistor and Dragnet ready too."

Maggie laughed. "Where do you come up with these names? They sound like some kind of sci-fi aliens or something."

Keith smiled. "Some come with their own names if we buy them somewhere else. Some we come up with on our own if we've bred them in-house."

"In-house?"

"From our own stock. You breed them so the mare's qualities compliment the stud's and hopefully you get a racehorse that's fast as lightning and strong as an oak."

He was feeding Peter. She was feeding Isabella.

"That's not always easy I take it?" she asked, fascinated by the topic and by his apparent knowledge on the subject.

"No. It's not that easy. Sometimes instead of the best of both worlds, you get the worse of both worlds. Then you've got a nag that has the manners of a spoiled brat."

She laughed. "You've had a few of those I take it."

He scratched the bottom of his chin. "More than our share, but we're learning."

"We're?"

"Me and Ike, the trainer."

She lifted her chin in recognition of the name. Ike, the fifty-something guy who although way out of her age-bracket was still the gentleman every girl dreams about snagging. "You guys get a long pretty well, huh?"

"He's like a second father to me." Keith's gaze faded from her out onto the falling water as he chewed his sandwich. "I loved horses, couldn't get enough of them, and Ike took me under his wing and showed me the ropes. He still does."

"You've been here awhile then—at the Ayer's estate?"

He smiled. "Yeah, awhile." His face slid through the memories. "I graduated from A&M when I was 24. I've been here ever since."

"And how long is 'ever since'?"

His gaze came back to her. "Five years."

She nodded, doing the math in her head. "And you like it here?"

This smile was more wistful than the others. "Yeah. I love it here."

The day passed like none had ever past before for Keith. When the sun got hot, they found a cool shade near the falls and let the kids take a nap. Lying on the ground, Isabella next to her and Peter's hand in hers, Maggie looked like she belonged nowhere else. She never complained even when he knew she must be uncomfortable having been in the same position too long. Every move she made, every effort, every word came with the question of what was best for the kids clearly in mind.

"You're good with them," Keith said when they were both asleep, and he had ambled back over to the little group from his trip to check the horses.

"Yeah, well. They're easy to be good with." She twirled one finger through Isabella's curl.

Keith sat down and wound his arms around the backs of his knees which were Indian-style under him. "You wouldn't believe the nightmare those two have been through. Those other nannies were…" He exhaled his disgust.

"Yeah, I figured as much." Her gaze fell to Peter.

"What does that mean?"

Maggie's gaze came up to his, and Keith didn't like what he was reading there at all. "The other day... yogurt day. Peter kept cringing away from me like I was going to hit him." Her gaze fell. "I've seen that look before with kids that have grown up being beaten."

Real, honest concern swept through him. "You don't think they've ever..."

She shrugged slightly. "I wouldn't be surprised the way he was acting, and he's so quiet. He's terrified to get dirty. Any little wiggle throws him into terror." She exhaled. "Lots of signs. Lots of pieces, and when you put them all together..."

Somehow Keith had never realized this could be a possibility. Yes, the kids weren't treated like kids but beaten? That wasn't something he'd ever thought was happening to them.

"You should've seen him petting the cat the other day," she continued. "It was like he was petting it with one hand, and watching out of his eye for the reprimand he knew was coming. They have them on such a tight schedule. You get chewed out for being two minutes early. I don't know. They've got everything, you know. The playhouse, the toys, the nice house, but they aren't allowed to be kids."

Deep in the middle of his heart, at that moment, Keith made the solemn promise to himself that whatever he had to do to keep her here, he would do it. For their sakes. They deserved that much.

"Having everything isn't what makes you feel loved," she continued although his heart already felt like it was overflowing like the falls. "It's knowing that you're loved just because you're you." She slid her fingers over Peter's hair. "Every kid deserves that." The words stopped so she could take a breath. "I wish I could give that to every kid alive. Just the solid, unshakable knowledge that they are good enough just the way they are, that they are loved for who they are. Just that much... it could change the world."

Had the world quaked out of existence at that very moment, Keith couldn't have moved. Finally he understood the attraction of her. She cared—not about the money and the cars and the status. She cared about the person.

"Well, I for one, hope you get that chance," he said softly.

Her gaze slid up to his, and she smiled gratefully. It was the most perfect moment of his life.

"It's about time you get back," Ike said, stepping up as Keith put Buck into his stall.

Instinctively Maggie backed away without really moving. She cradled Isabella a bit closer and reached down to shield Peter as well.

"I took the day off. I told you that," Keith said, and there was a bite to his words.

"Well, the operation didn't. Hodges' truck showed up, and they only have half the load."

Not really understanding but wanting to not get in the way just the same, Maggie shrank back. If she could've thought of a way to get the kids back to the mansion without riding in the pickup, she would have done it.

Keith exhaled. "Fine." He turned to her slightly. "This'll just take a minute."

"No problem," she said so softly, she wasn't sure he'd heard. Keith and Ike started to the office, and Maggie followed with the kids, very cautiously and hanging back as much as possible. She considered telling him they would wait in the pickup, but he and Ike were in a heated discussion, and she didn't want to break in and add more stress to the already tense situation.

At the office, Keith yanked the door open and stomped inside. Ike followed him but stood at the door with it open. Maggie, careful to shield the children, stood ten steps back and faded against the shadows next to the hard, gray wood of the barn.

She could hear the angry voices rising as the tension stretched over them.

"Maggie, why is Keith so mad?" Peter asked at her knee.

"Shh," she said, pulling him closer. "Don't worry. They're just trying to get some things settled." How do you explain something you don't even understand?

"I'm sorry, Mr. Ayer," the young driver said, backing past Ike out the office door. "It won't happen again."

"You darn right it won't happen again. Tell Hodges we get jerked around one more time like this, and we'll find a different supplier permanently." Keith whacked the clipboard into the young man's chest. "You understand that?"

"Oh, yes, sir. Yes, sir, Mr. Ayer. I'll tell him."

"Good. Now get off my property."

The words spun through Maggie's brain in a whirlwind of concern and incomprehension. Mr. Ayer? Why did he keep calling Keith that? And why had Ike let Keith handle that when he was obviously the most senior of the two? Mr. Ayer. Mr. Ayer. The name twisted through her, and she pulled Peter closer to her, trying to make time run backward even as she swayed under the reordering of the world around her.

"They'll do it again," Ike said when the young man was gone. He put one hand on his hip where his brown belt went through the loops just so.

"I know they will." Keith looked so mad, Maggie wasn't sure what he would do next. "Get Mac on the line and tell him we'll start buying from them on Friday. Then call Hodges and tell him they're out."

The glance that Ike sent in her direction did nothing to settle Maggie's nerves, which were in knots inside her. "What about your dad?"

"Let me worry about Dad. He doesn't have to put up with this junk every day like we do. Friends don't jerk friends around like that. Hodges just barked up the wrong tree." Keith stomped back into the office, and Ike followed. Once inside, the voices were too indistinct to make out, and with her head pressed against the barn wall, Maggie fought to block them out altogether.

Keith was Mr. Ayer's son. Mr. Ayer, Conrad Ayer was Keith's father. Her breathing became shallow to the point of being non-existent as her heart broke through that understanding. Slowly her mind traced through the last week. Over and over again, she had humiliated herself in front of the boss's son. She had leaned on him when her own stupidity caught up with her. Worse, she had told him things, things you didn't tell people who could get you fired.

She felt like the biggest idiot on the planet. Her eyes fell closed against the thoughts. Stupid. Stupid. Stupid. Tears came to her eyes, stinging and harsh, but she beat them back. Sniffing, she squared her shoulders. He must think she was the most gullible imbecile to grace the planet. Yeah, right, he worked so hard out here. What a joke. He was the crown prince of a billion dollar estate!

70

At that moment the voices approached the door, and Maggie sucked in the emotions swirling around her. She wouldn't let him win. He would never know that she hadn't known. More than that, she would never let him so close again.

He was Keith Ayer. She was the hired hand, and for her heart and her sanity—not to mention her job, she'd better remember that.

"I'll be up at the mansion 'til morning," Keith said to Ike who followed him out. At the office door, Ike stopped, holding the door open with his back. "Dad and Vivian will be back bright and early tomorrow."

His voice had a hard edge to it that pulled up fear in Maggie's chest, and it wasn't only her. Peter's fingers dug into her jeans in a crunch. Isabella whimpered at her chest, and Maggie pulled her closer. "Shh. Little one. Shh."

"Maggie, you ready?" Keith asked, looking past Ike.

"Oh, y-yeah." Her voice cracked, and she shook her head in aggravation at herself.

He turned in the direction of the pickup, and Maggie stepped that direction as well. When she passed Ike, he looked at her with a mix of disgust and revulsion she couldn't miss. She ducked her head, lest he see the tears in her eyes. Hurt piled over hurt the farther she walked. When they walked out of the barn and she saw Keith standing at the truck, her heart cracked in two.

She closed her eyes and then pulled them back open, fighting the hurt with everything in her. "We'd better get back. I've got to give the kids a bath before dinner. They smell like horse." At her side Maggie opened her door and then Isabella's, but Peter never moved from her knee. "Patty Ann will toss me out on my ear if she gets wind of them."

"Pete, come over here," Keith said, his anger dissipated.

But Peter was going nowhere. Quickly Maggie latched Isabella in and then took hold of Peter's hand. Around the back of the pickup she strode, purposefully raking the hair out of her face. On his side, Keith stood solidly by his door, waiting for Peter; however, Maggie never gave him the chance to so much as touch the child. "I'll get it."

He backed into the space of his door, but only that. She didn't care. Anger snapped through the hurt, and at the moment that was a far better choice. At least that way she didn't have to worry about crying in front of him and completely humiliating herself.

When Peter was latched, she reached up and ruffled his hair. "Good boy." Then she stepped back and slammed the door. "What're you standing around for? You want Patty Ann to fire me?"

Keith seemed not to have a good answer for that as he stared at her in concerned incredulousness. "No. Why would I want that?"

Maggie swallowed every word she wanted to yell at him. Instead she stomped around the front of the truck and got in on her side. On his, Keith got in too. He started the pickup and backed out.

All the way home, she felt his gaze chance on her every so often, but she kept hers planted outside the side window. If she just kept her distance, tomorrow would be here in no time, and by tomorrow, she was sure she would never have to worry about getting too close to him again. Once he told them everything he knew, she would never again be welcome at the Ayer mansion. Of that much, she was one-hundred percent positive.

She was mad. Furious. Livid. That much Keith was absolutely sure. Why, he was having trouble getting his brain to figure out. Okay, so he'd lost his temper at the stables, surely she wasn't so naïve as to think you could never get angry. After all, he did run a multimillion dollar operation. That meant he had to make some decisions and that sometimes things needed a serious adjusting. Like Hodges and his manipulations. That was one that needed rectified in a flat hurry.

When they pulled up to the house, Keith barely had a chance to get Peter out of the back before she was around the pickup to get him. Whatever had happened to their nice day together had been soul-splittingly triumphant in ruining everything. Maggie wouldn't even look at him.

Everything in him wanted to make her look at him like she didn't want to jump off the side of the earth to get away from him. "I'll be back for dinner."

"Whatever."

It was all he would get as she turned and stomped up the

steps. Consternation such that he had never felt crashed around him. She acted like she hated him, but only an hour before, they were under the tree watching the kids sleep. The aggravating issue stayed with him the rest of the afternoon and through dinner, during which she hardly said two words and never so much as looked at him, and right through her taking the kids upstairs.

He had never felt so panicked in his life. Whatever it was, it was major, and the question of why she had done such a drastic 180 kept drifting through him. At first he wrote it off to mood swings, but when he was in his room later, his thoughts fought to put the whole puzzle together, and no matter how hard he tried, it just didn't fit. Finally, although it was taking his life in his hands, he knew he had to go ask. His heart slammed into his chest, warning him that this might make it worse, but in truth, he couldn't see how it could get any worse. Quietly he left his side of the mansion and made his way to hers.

The soft light of the hallway nightlight guided his steps until he was standing at Peter's door. Keith pushed it in slightly, not wanting to disturb their already-in-progress ritual.

"And please help us have a good day tomorrow," Maggie prayed, her head down, bending over Peter's bed. Keith heard the struggle in her voice, and he knew without a doubt that she was worried about the coming morning. He wasn't looking forward to it either. If things could just stay like this, he would be perfectly content to live here forever.

"Guide us, protect us, keep us, help us, and love us. Amen."

There was a soft rustle of blankets.

"I love you, Maggie." The words drifted to Keith, and he peered in. Peter was in her arms, hugging her like he never wanted to let her go.

"I love you, too, little one." The hug lasted a few more moments, and then she pulled him away. "Now you get some sleep." She pushed to her feet and stopped. Softly she kissed her two fingers and then pressed them to his forehead. "Good night, little prince. Sleep well." Even after she was finished, she didn't move for a long moment, and out of respect for her privacy, Keith backed out into the hallway to wait for her.

When she came out, he heard the sniffle and felt the anguish pouring from her even though he couldn't clearly see her face. In the soft light she shut the door before wiping her eyes and letting out a long, slow breath.

"Maggie," he said softly, and she jumped a foot and spun to face him.

Her face fell into a glowering distrust even though he was leaning against the wall, not exactly poised to pounce on her. Bitterness scrawled across her face as she turned slightly away from him. "What do you want?"

"Can we talk?"

Head down, she headed across the hall to her door. "We don't have anything to talk about."

He pushed away from the wall and stepped over to her door. There, he again leaned against the wall and lowered his head so he could look at her. "I think we do."

She shook her head and reached for her doorknob. "It's late. I need to get to bed."

Gently he reached out and touched her wrist, praying she wouldn't leave. "Maggie, please. I know you're mad. I want to know why."

"I'm not mad." She shook her hair back defiantly and looked at him. Chin up, that unmistakable air of determination flowing through every fiber of her. "Why would I be mad?"

The middle of him ached with the hate in her eyes. "I don't know. Why are you?"

Her gaze broke from his and darted across the hall. "Look, I get it. Okay? I know the score. It took me awhile, but you don't have to worry. I get it now."

Concerned incomprehension traced through him. "Maggie, you're not making any sense. What are you talking about?"

When she smiled at him, there was nothing in him that liked it. She looked cold and hateful and detached. "You're the prince of Conrad Ayer Industries. My bad. I thought you were just a nice guy who cared."

The words hit him like punches, and he dropped his hand from her wrist. "You... you didn't know."

With her jaw set, she shook her head. "No, and you didn't bother to tell me that little detail either."

His head dropped as understanding poured through him. No wonder she'd seemed so unnaturally normal around him. That explained a lot. Too much really. He sighed that understanding into his heart. "I'm sorry. Really I am. I just... I assumed you knew."

"No. I didn't know." Abhorrence and hurt dripped from the statement. Her gaze dropped from him to the carpet. "Well, you got what you wanted. Congratulations. Mission accomplished."

Panic plowed into him. "What does that mean?"

"Oh, come on, Keith. I'm not stupid. I know a spy when I see one."

That punch just about leveled him. "What...? A spy? I wasn't spying on you."

She laced her arms over themselves. "Oh, yeah? Then why've you been hanging around all week? Why've you been asking me about my past? Why've you watched my every move with the kids—even coming up here at night to check on us?" She put air quote marks around the last three words with her fingers. "I'm not completely stupid, you know."

Hurt and hate bled through her gaze. "I just hope you can explain it to Pete and Izzy when I'm gone tomorrow because they're going to be crushed thanks to you—not that you ever really cared anyway."

That one brought his defenses up. "Okay, now that's not fair. You know I love those two."

"Yeah. So you say. But how do I know that's the truth? How do I know anything you say is the truth?"

With determination he turned full on her. "Okay. That's it. Look at me." When she didn't, he put his hands on her shoulders and turned her to face him. "I said, look at me, Maggie." Her gaze met his, but there wasn't an ounce of trust anywhere in them. "I love those two kids like they were my own. I don't like what's been happening to them any more than you do, and despite what you think about me, I do not want you to leave. I have not been spying. Watching, yes. Spying, no. Now, you can hate me forever, that's fine, but don't you dare use that as an excuse to leave them because they need you... more than you can know."

"Oh, yeah? Well, what about your dad and Mrs. Ayer? They'll be back tomorrow, and I'm pretty sure Patty Ann and Inez will have plenty of stories to relate when they get back." She set her mouth. "Let's face it. Like it or not, I'll be out tomorrow."

His hands dropped from her shoulders, and he leaned back against the wall. "You don't know that."

"Yes, I do, and so do you." Her head fell to the side. "I may be what the kids need, but I'm sure not what the parents want. I knew that the first day. It's only a matter of time now… even if they don't fire me outright tomorrow."

The thought of her leaving, driving away, never coming back stabbed through him like a twin-edged sword. "I'm sorry. I really am."

"Yeah, well. It was an impressive show while it lasted. That whole working out at the stables thing. You sure had me fooled."

He felt like he'd gone sixteen rounds with the heavy weight champion of the world. Even his breath was gone. "That wasn't a show. I really do work out there."

"Yeah. I'm sure. And it's such hard work, too."

Her sarcasm bit through him, taking his knees out from under him. He slid down the wall, hearing in her voice exactly what every other person he'd ever met believed about him.

She stood there, over him, arms intertwined, ready to kick him once more with her words if she hadn't finished him off already. He could feel her gaze, but the numbness of hurt gripping him wouldn't let him look at her. She hated him, and he didn't blame her.

"I really do work," he said softly to the air in front of him. "I know. That's hard to believe." He shook his head and let it fall back onto the wall so he was looking at the top corner of the opposite side of the hall. "I don't know. Maybe that's not even really true. You're probably right. I'm just a spoiled little rich kid who wouldn't know what hard work was if it bit him in the butt." The inescapable truth of his lousy excuse for an existence cracked over him, and his spirit plummeted.

He'd tried so hard to prove to everyone that he wasn't just Daddy's little puppet, that he was his own man, that he could make it on his own. What a joke. She saw through that sham as surely as everyone else did. The feelings of worthlessness clogged the top of his chest, and for the first time in his life, he let them come. She hated him almost as much as he hated himself, and that was saying something.

Then, slowly, gently, he felt her not leave but bend down next to him, and this time her gaze was soft. "I'm sorry. That really was uncalled for. I shouldn't have said that."

A smile of sad acceptance slipped through him. "No, you just said what everyone else is thinking… except they don't have the guts to say it to my face."

Her gaze surveyed him as she searched for some way to take back her words and ease the hurt she'd caused.

He let his head fall to the side so he could look at her. It was over. He might as well finish it off. "I'm engaged."

"En…?" The word snaked through her face slowly, and her hand dropped from his shoulder. "What?"

Their friendship was completely trashed now. There was no reason not to burn it all the way to the ground. Besides, Keith knew it would be better to kill whatever was left of them now, get it over with in one, gut-crashing whack than to drag it out. That was cruel and would hurt her more in the end anyway. This way she didn't have the stupid idea that he was worth getting to know. She would see what a jerk he was and get out while the getting was good.

He twisted his lips into a half-smile, half-frown, fighting not to let the words dig into him. His gaze fell to his knuckles, which were sliding back and forth through his palm. "Yeah. June third." He nodded without feeling it. "Dallas Henderson, Lowell Henderson's daughter."

Her eyes widened. "Lowell Henderson—the senator?"

"That's the one." Keith exhaled hard. "She'll be here Saturday. Big, huge bash to celebrate the engagement. All the most powerful people in Texas, that kind of thing. It's the wedding of the decade or so I'm told."

Carefully Maggie let herself down onto the carpet next to him and leaned her back on her bedroom door. It took more than a minute for her to respond. "And this is a good thing, right?" As strange as that sounded, she actually sounded concerned, as if she cared one way or the other.

"Of course it's a good thing." The words came with firmness, and he was glad for that. "It's just… I should've told you… sooner."

Her gaze did a little circle dance until she let her head crack back on the door. "Well, I wish you would have, but I understand why you didn't." She didn't say anything for a long moment, and then she let her gaze fall over to his. "Is she nice?"

He nodded slowly but never looked at her.

"Good," she said, and he heard the feelings lacing the sides of that single word. "You deserve nice."

Eight

Maggie had the distinct feeling that the sunrise would find her heart no longer beating. It had withstood so many blows the day before, there was no way it would make it to morning. They had talked a bit longer, but Keith looked beat with a whip, and she didn't feel much better. So with a simple good night, they had left whatever they were, whatever they might have been at the threshold of her door.

It was hard to get herself going, but she knew there really wasn't a choice. Yes, Keith had been a nice addition to life at the mansion, but that was a dream. Today was back to reality. Quickly she pulled the red top and blue blazer on. She might not fit here, but at least she could pretend to look like she did.

When the limousine pulled up at the front of the mansion, Keith pulled up right behind it in the red Dodge. He wanted the first shot at his dad if at all possible.

"Here, let me get that," he said, taking three bags from the driver who was piling them on the driveway. "How was your trip?"

"Wonderful," Vivian said.

"Great until the flight home," his father said with characteristic blustering.

"Oh, now, Conrad. It was not that bad. Besides, we got it ironed out."

"Hrmpt." It was his father's standard comeback in any disagreement with Vivian.

"Well, we're glad you're back. We're all still in one piece." Keith opened the front door and stepped back for them to enter. However, even he wasn't prepared for the welcome on the other side. There standing on the bottom step stood Maggie, looking like a CEO, a look of sheer determination etched on her face and both children firmly in hand.

"Good morning, Mr. Ayer, Mrs. Ayer. It's great to have you back." With a slight push, she nudged Peter forward to greet them.

"Well, aren't you precious this morning," Vivian said, and she actually bent down to Peter's level.

Keith's gaze went from them to Maggie as she descended the last step and leaned toward Vivian so Isabella could go to her mother. Never before had Keith been so awestruck. Her hair was pulled back so that it was a slim cascade down her back rather than in unruly waves around her head.

"Oh, and little Isabella. Look at you. You grew so much while we were gone." Vivian's arms were around the child, and Isabella squealed in delight.

Both Vivian and his father laughed.

"Good morning," Patty Ann said staidly as she descended the stairs behind them.

All gazes snapped up to her, and the levity evaporated in one whoosh. Vivian gave Isabella back to Maggie and straightened, pulling on her suit jacket. "Hello, Patty Ann. I'm glad to see everything's still in place."

"Yes, Ma'am, it is." The look of disapproval she shot Maggie hit Keith on the ricochet.

Maggie was right. Patty Ann was out for her, and unless he did something quick, She-Wolf #1 would rip apart all of Maggie's hard work and leave it in shambles.

"Dad, I hate to take you away like this, but we had an issue with the feed again. Do you mind…?"

His father let out a long exhale. "Five minutes back and already there are problems."

"Hey, they didn't take a vacation like you did," Keith said, trying to lighten the mood.

"Ma'am," Patty Ann said, "we need to go over this week's schedule."

"Of course, Patty Ann," Vivian said, "but let me get settled in first. I smell like airplane."

With one more haughty glance at those assembled in the foyer, Patty Ann turned on her heel and marched up the steps. Keith noticed the visible although only barely sigh that went through Maggie. She looked over at him, and there was only the slightest of smiles. Then she took Peter's hand. "Come on, Peter, Heshiki will be here for your karate lesson in fifteen minutes."

The child followed Maggie up the stairs, and Keith felt the weight of his current undertaking fall on his shoulders.

"Are we going to do this or not?" his father asked harshly.

Pulling every bit of divine guidance to him, Keith turned to follow his father. "Guide me and protect me, Father," he prayed softly. "And Mom, if you're listening up there, I could use all the help I can get here."

As he stepped into his father's office, courage came into Keith. He shut the door behind him. "We need to talk, Dad."

"That's what you said. What's up with the feed situation?"

Keith shook his head, sat down, and pulled his hat then his bandana off his head. "That can wait. This is more important."

"Oh?"

"It's about Maggie. Uh, Ms. Montgomery."

His dad sat down with a thump. "Uh-oh."

It took everything he had not to drop his gaze, but he stayed steady. "You need to know that while you were gone she and I got to talking, and well, there are some things you need to know about her."

His father waved him off. "We already know about her background. Vivian and I have talked about it, and we know that her kind are not suitable for employment here…"

That comment slammed into Keith like a wrecking ball. "Her *kind?* What *kind* is she, Dad?"

The scowl of disapproval dropped through his father's features. "Oh, you know."

"You mean that she was a foster kid? That she was bounced around all over the state because every place she went sucked? Is that what you mean by her *kind?*"

"Look, Keith, I'm sure…"

"No." He held up his index finger. "Dad. For once you're going to listen to me." Hard determination solidified in his chest. "Now, she's been through hell and back through no fault of her own. Do you know why she was in the foster care system? Do you?"

There was a grunt but no real reply.

"I'll tell you why because her parents were killed in a car accident. That's why. A car accident, Dad. She was eight years old, and she was thrown out of the only world she'd ever known and sent first to one house and then to another. Then to another… not because she was a bad kid but because they were temporary solutions to a permanent problem."

"Look, that's really tragic, Keith…"

"Tragic?" Sanity began to tilt sideways. "Dad, she didn't lose one parent. She lost both of them. Zap they were gone. Just like that."

"Like I said, it's tragic…"

Frustration catapulted him from the chair. "Cripes, Dad! You don't get it, do you?" He paced over to the wall, and his hand raked across his head. "You don't get what something like that does to a kid. And you never have." He spun on the emotions. "It changes you. Way down inside. It changes you in ways you can't even explain, but it's deep, and it's forever."

"Keith…"

"And it doesn't go away even if you want it to, even if you wish it to, even if you pray to God to take it away. It doesn't go away. Even if you work hard, if you go to college and get a degree, it's still there. It's there even if you get successful and make a b-zillion dollars… It still doesn't go away. It's right here." He put his hand, little finger edged in to the center of his chest. The breaths were coming in hard fast gulps of air. "Every time you dare to look. It's right there. I know because I've lived with that pain for the last 17 years. Not that you've noticed."

His father's gaze dropped to the desk.

"And now, you're going to fire her and tell her she's no good, that she's not worthy of this job—just like she hasn't been worth keeping at any place she's been 'til now? Is that what you would want someone to do to me, Dad? Huh? Is it? Well, let me tell you something, you do that to her, and you are doing it to me."

He let his eyes fall closed to corral the emotions because they were starting to jab into him with such force he couldn't control them. When he opened his eyes, it was not her pain but her caring that he saw. "Besides Dad, you should see her with Pete and Izzy. They love her. They really do. I've seen it. They trust her, and even you have to admit there hasn't been a single other one they've trusted so far... not to even mention loved."

He took a long, calming breath. "So if you have the nerve to fire her, the minute she walks out that door, you've just trashed whatever family you have left. Those two kids will never be the same, and I'll never be able to have any respect for you again."

The words hung in the air, and finally, Keith knew he could do no more. "Well, I've said what I came to say." He swiped his hat and bandana off the little table and turned to walk out. The door was open before his father said anything.

"Keith, wait."

He stopped, but he didn't turn.

"Look, I know I made some mistakes with you. I know that. I admit that. I should've been there when... Your mom... Well, she was a wonderful woman. When I lost her..." The words stopped. "I'll talk to Vivian. We should at least give Ms. Montgomery a chance."

He wanted more, so, so much more, but at this point skirting an outright firing was a step in the right direction. Slowly he turned, and the thought went through him that he had never seen that look on his father's face. "She deserves that much."

All day Maggie expected that at any moment someone would walk in the room and expel her permanently. However, karate came and went, lunch came and went, naps, playtime. Each slid by as if the guillotine wasn't hanging over her neck.

By dinner, she was careful to have both children in their best clothes standing in the anteroom to the dining room at ten until six. It would've been far less intimidating if she had thought that maybe Keith would be by to eat with them. Of course, that was completely impossible. For reasons she couldn't adequately explain, he did his best to remain as scarce as possible when the others were around. It was only at that moment that she wondered about that.

She hadn't seen him all day, save for the few minutes welcoming the Ayers back. Of course, it was for the best. He was engaged, not to mention everything else. It was better if he went on with his life, and she went on with hers. All she had to do now was convince her heart of that.

"Well, well, this is a surprise," Patty Ann said as she strode over to them to inspect the children. "Did you reset your watch to on time?"

Maggie absorbed the barb. "No, Ma'am. We just had a little practice at getting it right while you were gone. Trust me, it's well in hand now."

"Well." The word was more a grunt of disapproval.

The inspection grated across Maggie's nerves. They didn't deserve to be treated like show animals. "May we go in now before you make us late?"

Patty Ann's eyes narrowed dangerously. "Don't patronize me, Ms. Montgomery. I could have you fired like that if I so choose."

"Really? It must be nice to have so much power. Too bad you don't know how to use it to make life better for anyone."

"Patty Ann, are the children here yet?" Mrs. Ayer called from inside the dining room.

Without waiting for the secretary to make her customary premier entrance, Maggie pushed the door open and guided the children in. "I'm sorry, Mrs. Ayer. Patty Ann was a little late getting down to make her inspections. I'm sure it won't happen again. Right Patty Ann?"

The two gazes at the table went to the secretary.

"No, Ma'am," Patty Ann said, with hate dripping from the statement. "It won't happen again."

"Here Peter. Give your mommy a kiss," Maggie said, tramping through all the other emotions to get to genuine love for the children. Peter gave Vivian a kiss and then reached his little hands out to the sides for a hug. Taken aback, Vivian glanced up at Maggie. Then she bent and gave him a hug. It wasn't much, but it was a start.

"You been back up to the mansion?" Ike asked Friday afternoon when Keith was in the stable office filling out the feeding schedules.

"No. Why?" It killed him to say it. In fact, there wasn't a single moment since he'd walked away that he hadn't thought about her, wondered about her, wanted to talk to her to see how things were going. He had stopped Jeffrey for the 411 the day before when the gardener was working on the guesthouse lawn, Keith's lawn from now until June third.

From Jeffrey's account nothing had changed, no major firings or personnel confrontations, and Keith was pretty sure Jeffrey was tapped into the Inez connection, so he would've known if something major had gone down.

Head down Keith wrote as if nothing in life was more important.

"I guess you'll be off this weekend?" Ike asked although there was more to the question than he let on.

"Yeah. I told you that six weeks ago, remember? Tanner's coming up early. He'll fill in. If you need more help, you could always call John."

"So everything's cool in paradise then?" Ike asked, digging still.

"Of course. Why wouldn't it be?"

Ike's gaze borrowed into Keith, trying to discern if there was more he wasn't saying.

"Oh," Keith said as if he'd just remembered something, "and I won't be here at all tomorrow. I'm picking Dallas and her folks up at the airport." How he could get all the way to nonchalance, Keith couldn't tell, but he was doing a pretty good job of sounding nearly together about the whole situation.

"Well, I'm glad." Ike crossed his arms and leaned on the filing cabinet. "Dallas is a wonderful girl."

"Hey." Keith looked up with a smile. "You don't have to sell me on Dallas. I'm marrying her, remember?"

Ike looked pleased with that answer. "I'm glad. I was a little worried there for awhile."

"Worried?" Keith smiled. "No worries, man. This is the happiest time of my life." He grabbed his keys from the shelf. "Gotta go. I'm meeting Greg for drinks."

"Greg? Uh-oh. Not too heavy on the uptake there."

"Me?" Keith flashed him a grin. "I'm a good boy."

"Yeah. Yeah. That's what they all say." Ike became very serious. "Take it easy, okay? You've got a lot to get done tomorrow."

Keith held up his hands. "I'll be good. I promise."

"Everything's ready for tomorrow," Vivian said as they sat at dinner Friday night. "The governor's office called. He and his wife will be here."

Maggie's fork slowed in her hand. The governor? They didn't mess around.

"We may have an issue with the press. Patty Ann has security lined up to keep them outside the gates, but you know they always come up with some sneaky plan to get in where they aren't wanted." She glanced at Maggie but quickly returned her gaze to her husband. "We've got florists, caterers, the photographer. I think everyone's lined up."

"Good," Mr. Ayer said. "Lowell is expecting this to be a great photo op. It may even have national legs, so they are pumping it that way. The wedding definitely will be, and he may even get a little mileage out of the engagement."

The roast stuck in Maggie's throat. Very softly she cleared her throat and turned to fuss with Isabella who had been eating mashed potatoes with her fists. "Oh, baby girl. No. Don't do that."

"The children will need to make an appearance," Vivian said, and Maggie froze.

"The children, Ma'am?"

"Yes. We'd like to have them in the garden for pictures and such, but please keep them from making any scene. We can't have that with the governor here."

"Oh, of course not, Ma'am." The responsibility wrapped around her, squeezing the breath from her lungs.

"Patty Ann has the next 24 hours planned down to the minute, and I expect that everything should go off perfectly."

Maggie didn't answer as the statement wasn't meant for her, but her heart hurt. It all sounded so scripted. She wondered if Patty Ann had scheduled each kiss too. Then she snapped that thought in half. How she would ever make it through watching Keith kiss someone else was completely beyond her.

Isabella picked that moment to overturn her milk. In the next instant Maggie was on her feet, mopping up the white substance.

"I'm sorry, Ma'am. We'll just go and let you all finish." She pulled Peter up. "Give your mom a kiss."

He did as instructed, and then with his hand firmly in hers and Isabella planted on her hip, they escaped the suffocating atmosphere of the dining room. If they never had to go back, it would be too soon.

"Well, it's about time," Greg said when Keith made it to the table at Tonie's 30 minutes late and not happy about anything in life.

He wasn't in the best of moods, and it was getting worse by the second. "Sorry. I lost track of time."

"That's a bad habit, you know." Greg eyed him. "Dallas is going to have to put a leash on you to get you where she wants you on time."

Keith didn't want to talk about Dallas. He didn't want to talk about the party or the mansion or the next two months. Tonight he had one goal in mind. Forgetting everything.

"Man, dude. Go easy on that stuff," Greg said when they had been firmly ensconced at Billy Joe's Dancehall and Bar for five hours. His wire-framed glasses set off his preppy look like a picture frame. "You got a big day tomorrow. Passing out tonight ain't the best idea in the world."

Keith turned alcohol-laden eyes on his friend. "What are you, my babysitter?"

Greg's face fell into concern. "What is up with you tonight? I haven't seen you like this since the night your dad got married."

"Yeah, well. I guess the joy of being married runs in the family."

The worry on Greg's face deepened. "Did you have a fight with Dallas?"

"No." He took another drink.

"Well, you're gonna have a fight if she finds out about this."

"Are you gonna sit there all night and ruin my good time, or are you gonna try to find you a hot babe to help you drive home?"

The displeasure on Greg's face didn't leave. "The way you look, I'm going to have to drive you home."

"Oh, yeah. Dad would love that." His body swayed under the

weight of the alcohol, which he was adding to by the second. "Hey, remember that time in college when you dropped me off, and I passed out on the front lawn. Boy, that was a howl, wasn't it?"

"Yeah, a howl." Nothing in Greg's voice said he'd enjoyed that episode.

"Or, hey, how about... how about the prom? Remember... when I was with what's her name?"

"Kaci."

"Yeah. Yeah. Kaci." He looked at Greg. "Boy, you're good..." His train of thought slid away from him. "What was I saying? Oh, yeah. Kaci. Dang. Now she was fine." He took another drink. "I wonder whatever happened to her."

"She's married. Three kids. Upstate."

That surprised Keith. "Really?"

"Yes, really. Her mom's a friend of my mom."

Keith nodded although he didn't really care.

Greg bent his head to catch a glimpse at his watch. "Well, it's about that time, brother. How're we going to get you home and tucked in safe and sound?"

Ache ripped through him, and Keith bowed forward, trying to withstand the thoughts that were flowing through him in disparate directions. He couldn't catch them, not even one. All he knew was that he hurt so bad he just wanted it to stop. "Do you think I'm making a mistake?"

"Considering what you have planned for tomorrow, I think this whole idea was a mistake."

"No, man. Do you think I'm making a mistake... with Dallas?"

Serious concern crowded over Greg's face. "Come on, Keith. Listen to yourself. That's crazy. Dallas is the best catch in the state, and you're going to throw her overboard? Dang, man. What has gotten into you?"

"Nothing."

"Well, I hope nothing disappears by tomorrow because Dallas will hang you out to dry if you ditch her now. She's not one to toy with. Not to mention her dad." Greg shook his head and mock shivered. "He'll filet you and serve you with dinner if you hurt Dallas." He set his face. "No, you've just got a bad case of cold feet, my friend. It will pass. Trust me. Once Dallas gets off that plane and she's in your arms again, you'll forget all about second thoughts. Now, we'd better get you home before it's time to get you to the airport."

There were so many other things Keith wanted to talk about, so many other things that were twisting through his brain and his spirit. However, Greg didn't stick around to hear them. Instead, he walked off to find something, or someone or… Keith lost the thought in the sip he took. He'd gotten on this train the minute he'd taken his dad's advice to "make it official" with Dallas, and there was no getting off now. Unless he found a way to forget or to escape.

"We're here, Sir. Sir?"

The words wound through Keith's brain, fuzzy and incomprehensible.

"You have to get out of the car, Sir."

Car. It was something about a car. Keith pulled himself to upright and dragged himself out of the backseat of the car. Swaying dangerously when he was on his feet, he reached for his wallet. "What do I owe you?"

"Your friend already took care of it." The driver looked at him skeptically. "You be okay getting in?"

Keith looked up at the stairs that looked a million miles high. "Yeah. No problem." And then he was standing by himself, not sure of anything other than he was home. Holding the railing to keep himself moving, he climbed the steps. At the top he pitched forward to the door. Key. He pulled his keys from his pocket and tried them, one after another. The second time around the key ring, he realized he must have forgotten to bring the right key.

Standing there as the world spun in front of his eyes, he reached over and punched the doorbell. There was no sanity left to tell him not to. Over and over he hit it, hoping someone would rescue him before he really did pass out. The door opened, and oblivious to who was standing there, Keith stumbled forward.

"Mr. Ayer!" Inez said in horror. "What in the world…?"

"Sorry. I dropped my key."

"Key? But…?"

"Who is it, Inez?" his father called from the top of the stairs.

"Umm, it's… Keith, Sir."

"It's me, Dad." His voice was coated with a slap-happy grin. "Aren't you glad to see me?"

By the time his dad made it down the last step, happy was the last word that would've described him. "What the…? Where have you been?"

"Sleeping." He grinned. "Where you think I've been?"

Pure, unadulterated anger poured through his father's face until it was red and puffy with it. "Get out." He pointed back for the door as Inez gasped.

"Out?"

"Now." His father turned him around to the door. "You are not welcome here."

"But…"

"Go home. Clean yourself up, and by tomorrow morning you'd better look like tonight never happened." At the door, he gave Keith a push which really wasn't necessary.

Somehow his hands caught the railing as he stumbled down the stairs. "But, Dad…"

"Good night, Keith." And his dad shut the door.

On the first sound of the doorbell, Maggie had come full awake. There was always uneasiness about sleeping in the mansion. The kids could wake up, and she wouldn't hear them before someone else did. Someone could come in. She was never really sure why, but she had slept lighter here than at any place she'd ever laid her head.

With one swipe she had her button down shirt from the day before over her, and at the door she quietly let herself out. There were voices down the hall, and when she heard Mr. Ayer's, she pressed herself into the space next to the wall cabinet.

"What is it, Conrad? Who was there?" Vivian asked from next to the staircase.

"My idiotic son."

"Keith? What's wrong with him?"

"He's drunk. Imagine that." He let a string of cuss words follow that statement as Maggie closed her eyes and willed this night to go away. Tears stained her heart and spirit as her thoughts went to him.

Vivian sounded almost as panicked as Maggie felt. "Did he leave?"

"Leave? I threw his butt out." Mr. Ayer muttered a few more choice words. "He's enough of a headache when he's stone-cold sober."

No, this night hadn't been good from minute one, and it was getting worse.

"What about tomorrow?" Vivian asked with fear.

"Well, I would tell you to ask him, but I don't think he could tell you his birth date much less anything really important right now."

"But the Hendersons? He's supposed to pick them up at one. And what about Dallas? She can't see him like that. It will ruin everything."

"You don't think I know that?" The low rumble of a guttural growl filled the expanse of space. "I knew it. I knew he would find a way to mess this up. Pulling something like this tonight of all nights. The only way this could be worse is if he had done it tomorrow night."

"Oh, don't even say that."

"As important as this is, there was no way he was going to not screw it up."

Vivian sighed. "Maybe he'll be better by morning."

"Yeah, and maybe the sun will rise in the West."

Their voices trailed off down the hallway, and Maggie stood, fixed in place. He was out there, by himself, hurting, and it was knifing into her spirit that his father didn't care more than how that affected his political connections. It was the craziest thing she had ever even considered in her life, but her heart wouldn't let her go back to bed. If they caught her, she would be out. But if she didn't go, she would never be able to live with herself.

Quietly she eased to Isabella's door and peered inside. Sleeping as usual. Then she opened Peter's. How they could sleep through the racket of the doorbell, she had no idea, but she was grateful they had. When Peter's door was closed, Maggie took a moment to close her eyes. "God, help. This is crazy, but I can't leave him out there. Not like that."

On cat feet she went down the kitchen stairs. The door just off the side of the kitchen was her best bet. It would let her right out near the trail. Then she could go up front and see if he was still there. There wasn't even a squeak as she let herself out. It took more than a moment for her eyes to adjust to the darkness. It was, after all, nearly three in the morning. Praying with each footfall, she pushed through the trees to the trail and met Keith's stumbling descent full on.

"Keith!"

"What…? Huh…?" He barely got stopped, and even when he did, he was still swaying.

"It's me. Maggie." She took one look at him and knew it was bad. He was wasted, but more than that, his eyes were stained with tears and falling closed with each word he managed to slur out.

"Maggie? What're you doing out here?"

"Well, I would ask you the same question except I think I know. You need help getting home?"

He laughed. "Oh, you know me. I don't have a home. I'm just traveling through."

"Through, huh? Well, you want some company while you travel?"

He looked at her with sad, sullen eyes. "Why're you being nice to me? You should be back in there with the rest of them."

"We're friends. Remember?" She wished with everything in her that she knew Ike's number. He would know what to do. He would know how to get Keith somewhere safe. But she didn't know Ike's number, so she said a prayer that her best would be good enough. "So which way is your place?"

"That way." He pointed an unsteady finger down the trail. "The guesthouse. Isn't that what they call it? Yeah, the guesthouse." He laughed. "Funny, how long have I been a guest here? You'd think they'd have started calling it Keith's place by now. But then that would mean they wanted me to stay, which of course they don't."

Maggie sucked in a long breath. So he wasn't doing work at the guesthouse that first day. Well, that was about par for how smart she had been about everything else. "Come on. Let's get you home."

It had been the longest walk of her life. All the way Keith kept asking why she was being so nice and telling her how he didn't have a home and how he should've known his father would yell. He was one of the most pathetic individuals she'd ever seen, and the others in the running, she really didn't want to think about. The only good thing was he'd actually managed to stay on his feet the whole way, which was a blessing considering she couldn't have dragged him two inches if she had to.

At the guesthouse he reached under the front flowerpot and produced the key. By now her body temperature had dropped to below freezing, and she stood on his front porch hopping from foot to foot to stay warm. The door finally gave, and mercifully he stepped in. She followed him right to the living room where he fell onto the couch, landing with one leg still trailing behind him.

He was home. He was safe. This was none of her business. She tried to tell herself just to leave. She had done more than she should have. Still, if she just left, tomorrow could ruin his life for good. Not that he didn't deserve it after this little stunt, but still, she didn't want to see his life ruined as hers had been by a night out partying. That was too much responsibility to put on any night.

She went into the kitchen, found the phone and the little list of numbers taped to the cabinet. There was only one she recognized. It took a long breath to get herself calm enough to dial the number, and it took another one not to hang up. Finally, thankfully, someone picked up.

"Hello?" He was asleep, and Maggie's courage nearly failed her again.

"Ike?"

"Yeah?"

"This is Maggie. Listen, Keith's in trouble."

Nine

"Okay, that's it, Keith. Get up. You had your fun. It's time to get going." Ike didn't sound happy. In fact, Ike didn't sound like Ike, he sounded more like Keith's father than he ever had.

"Wha...?" With a yank Ike spun him off the couch, and Keith landed on the floor with a gut-wrenching thump. "Ohhh." Pain punctuated by nausea swirled around his head. "What happened?"

"You had a fight with a bottle, and by the looks of it, the bottle won. Now you've got two hours to get yourself together enough to look presentable, and by the looks of things that ain't gonna be easy to pull off. You want eggs or just coffee?"

Keith was struggling to piece the night together. He leaned his head forward and scratched the side of it. "How'd I get home?"

"Well, apparently after an unscheduled stop at the mansion, your little friend stupidly brought you here. If it'd have been me, I'd have left your butt wherever you fell."

"The mansion?" He searched his memory, but it wasn't there. Then his mind stumbled on the next part of the story. "Maggie?"

"Yes, Maggie. She's way too nice for her own good. Let's just hope it wasn't for nothing, and she still has a job this morning." Ike came out of the kitchen. "Now, are you just going to sit there, or am I gonna have to get out my hot shot?"

Activity. It was the only accurate word to describe the chaos Maggie woke up to the next morning. Two trucks of flowers had pulled up just as she was coming down the stairs with the kids.

Four workers and their supervisor descended on the place, Patty Ann directing them all. "That goes out back. That one stays here on this table."

"Patty Ann, what time is the caterer supposed to be here?" Vivian called from the top step.

"One, Ma'am."

"And what time are the Hendersons scheduled?"

"6:15, Ma'am." Patty Ann didn't even have to glance at the checklist to answer the questions, even as she pointed out where each arrangement went. "Outside. Ms. Montgomery, may I have a word?"

Great. This couldn't be good. "Sure, what's up?"

"This probably goes without saying, but I'm going to say it anyway in case you are not attuned to such matters. These two are not to be in the yard today for any reason. We have a lot of very important preparations for tonight's party, and the last thing we need is two little sets of paw prints on everything. And that goes double for tonight. They are to come, be present for the first hour and pictures, and then I want them inside, out of sight, and definitely out of Mrs. Ayer's hair. Any slip…"

Maggie didn't like the reference or the tone, but she was already living dangerously on the edge, so she simply smiled. "Don't worry, Patty Ann. They shall be seen at the appropriate times but never a peep shall they utter—just like children should be."

It was clear Patty Ann surmised she was being made fun of; however, it wasn't clear enough that she could protest. "Good. Remember that. Your job's riding on it."

The water from the shower felt good. If Keith could stay here forever, he would. With a sigh, he let his thoughts drift through the coming day. In two short hours Dallas would be here, and as Ike was wont to yell at him, he'd better be cleaned and pressed when she stepped off that plane. Worse, it would only be a couple more hours before her parents would be here.

Keith leaned his head as far back as it would go under the torrent of water at that thought. The one and only reason Lowell Henderson had consented to this marriage was because there was a large bank account backing it. Big donors had a way of holding sway over candidates' decisions, and Keith's father was a big donor.

"Keith!" Ike called from the other side of the door, banging it in case Keith hadn't heard the summons.

"What?" It was more of an angry scream than a question.

"We got ten minutes to be gone if we're going to get your truck. Get a move on."

Nothing in Keith liked this new side of Ike. Nothing.

As soon as breakfast was over, Maggie and the kids disappeared up to the playroom. All lessons for the day had been unceremoniously cancelled. That was okay. At least she didn't have to worry about a minute-by-minute schedule. Instead, she went into Peter's closet and laid out one of the new outfits that had shown up when she mentioned to Patty Ann he was growing out of his former wardrobe.

Wednesday they had gone down to violin lessons, and when they returned, there was a whole new wardrobe as if the other had never existed. Maggie hadn't meant a complete overhaul. One or two new items would've been enough. However, that wasn't how the mansion ran. It was a way of living she was slowly learning she would never understand.

When she'd assembled Peter's attire for the evening, she went into Isabella's room and searched through the mountains of pink ruffles. It seemed they were on every piece of clothing the child had. Appropriate outfit in hand, Maggie walked to the window to lay it out on the dressing table. However, her gaze betrayed her, and she looked down into the hubbub below. In a few hours the party would be going. In a few hours there would be guests galore. She wondered as she put her head on the window if the guest of honor would in fact show up.

She'd left just after Ike got there the night before, and she hadn't heard a single thing from that side of the estate all morning. Although she wasn't sure how, she knew last night did not happen because of fun. He was too downtrodden when she'd caught up with him. She wondered what had made him sad enough to go jumping off the deep end like that. She also wondered who was with him and why on earth they had left him off at the mansion. What friend dropped someone off into that no-win trap?

Below the trees, she could make out the people working. Each preparation made was one less thing between her and tonight. If she could've gotten out of it, she would have. But short of quitting, there didn't seem a good way to do that. No. She would be there, with a smile on her face—for him and for her job, and which was the bigger motivation, she wasn't sure.

His head still hurt, and it probably wasn't going to quit any time soon. Four Advil and enough coffee to drown a horse hadn't really helped except to convince Ike that he was serious about the repentance. With everything he had, Keith wanted to jump off the planet for this one day. Be somebody else. Take a train ride to nowhere. Hijack the Space Shuttle and fly it to Mars. Nonetheless, here he was standing, solid and smiling, as Dallas walked off the plane. In one second she was walking toward him, in the next, she was in his arms.

"Oh, baby! Aren't you a sight for sore eyes," Dallas said, throwing her arms around his neck. The impact nearly sent him tumbling backward, but he caught himself at the last possible second.

"Hey, babe. It's great to see you too." When he pulled back, she smiled for a half-second, closed her eyes and pressed her lips to his. It had been so long since he'd kissed her, Keith was taken off-guard as much by the suddenness as by the ardor. It seemed not to matter to her at all that they were in public with half a thousand people milling about around them. For the first instant he stiffened and then rational kicked in, and he pulled her into his arms. The kiss was passionate as so many of their kisses had been. Truth was, Dallas had never lacked in that area.

When the kiss broke, her gaze found his. "Man, it's good to be home."

In her white silk shirt with the black stripe hugging her chest, Dallas resembled every other co-ed home for the early April break. Her white-blond hair was swept back, and only a few bangs were released to slide down across her forehead. Creamy-white skin, perfect complexion, crystal-clear blue eyes—she was picture perfect from head to toe. Even her jeans were graciously ripped in all the right places. "So, are you happy to see me?"

"Of course. How was the trip?" He took her hand in his between them, but she hung onto his arm as well.

"Oh, horrific as usual. Bad food. Long lines. Smelly seats. I'm just glad to be down on the ground, with you." She tightened her grip on him which would've been more of a hug except they were walking side-by-side through the airport. No matter, she laid her head on his shoulder. "I am so excited about tonight. I can't stand it."

Keith said nothing, knowing it wasn't necessary.

"We're supposed to drop Mom and Dad off at the Crowne Plaza on the way in. They decided to get the limo to take them to the mansion."

"Oh. Okay." He was walking, talking as if his head and heart weren't killing him.

"Dad said they may even stay for brunch tomorrow if your mom and dad can swing it. In the city of course. Dad has to get back to Washington early tomorrow. They're voting on the Taylor-Radkin bill Monday. He can't miss that."

"No. Of course not." Keith fought to find something else to talk about. Something normal people would talk about. "I guess you checked your stuff?"

"Yeah. If you're going to check one thing, you might as well check them all these days. It's such a hassle. Just getting through security is like... ugh."

His smile was almost real. "Well, you're here. That's all that matters."

She pulled him to her again and kissed him sideways. "Have I told you lately how much I love you?"

Something resembling happiness drifted over him. "I don't think so. Why don't you remind me?"

On the down escalator, she stood one step above him. Gently she ran her hand under his chin, tilting it up so she could bring her lips to his. When the kiss broke, she smiled at him devilishly. "Mmmm. It's too bad we have to get Mom and Dad. I'd love to go back to your place and get re-acquainted."

Keith nearly tripped getting off the escalator. She certainly didn't waste any time. He scratched the back of his neck as he caught the knowing smile of the woman descending behind them.

"Well, that's going to have to wait. We have a party to host tonight if you didn't remember."

"I remember just fine." She held out her hand that sported the iridescent rock Keith had given her on the all-night private cruise they had taken when he'd popped the question. The cruise was a little over-the-top for Keith, but his dad had said with a proposal like that, she couldn't say no. And as always, his dad was right.

Dallas liked to be wined-and-dined. The best restaurants. The finest of everything. It had been abundantly clear from the start that she was enamored with his place in the world, and what that place could offer her.

"Oh, I was looking on the Internet the other day, and I found a great place over in the Woodlands we've got to check out while I'm here. It's not too big. Four bedrooms, three baths. It's got a swimming pool, and a garden…"

His life began to coil around his chest, squeezing so tightly, Keith thought he might either pass out or be sick right there. He forced a smile to stave off running. "Really? It sounds… nice."

"And, I heard from Hayden & Elliott Thursday. I can start July 1 even if I don't have my official license yet. They'll just put me under one of their junior partners until my results come in."

"Great." By now they were standing at the carousel, her still draped on him from shoulder to foot.

"Have you thought more about what we talked about? You know applying at Devonshire? Daddy said it would be a great first step for you, what with the horse thing and all."

"The horse thing," he said under his breath. Then he brought himself to a stop. "I haven't really had time." He scratched the back of his head, which felt very different without his usual headgear. "We've been really busy getting the horses ready for Grand Prairie."

"Oh." That stopped her for about two seconds. Then she shook her head back. "Well, have they won anything this year?"

"We got third in Grand Prairie. Ike's going to Del Mar…"

The carousel picked that moment to turn on.

Her attention snapped to it. "Oh, good. Maybe we can grab my stuff and go somewhere decent to eat before Mom and Dad get in." Dallas checked her watch. "What's close out here?"

The turn in the conversation, coupled with his unbelievable headache, spun the question around in Keith's head. "Uh, I don't know really."

Suitcases started ca-thunking down the silver spiral.

"Mine are black. Salvatore Ferragamo."

Like he could tell the difference. It took fifteen bags before she noticed one of hers. He pulled that one off.

"There are five," she said, but she was so intent on the others coming off, she didn't see the skepticism in his face nor the shake of his head. From his vantage point, high maintenance should have been stamped on her business card.

"Dad. Mom." Dallas leaned in to give her mom a side-cheek kiss. "How was your flight?"

"Ugh. Stressful," her mother, Beatrice, said in frustration. "Next time we are definitely taking the Speaker up on his offer."

"What offer is that?" Dallas asked.

"He's Texan. We're Texan. His private jet knows the way with no reprogramming," Beatrice said, reveling in the attention of the horribleness of having to fly with regular people.

"It's nice to see you, Mrs. Henderson," Keith said, extending his hand. "And you Mr. Henderson. I'm glad you made it safely."

"Have we heard anything official from the governor yet?" Mr. Henderson, a white-haired, distinguished but pompous man, asked as he pulled himself up to his full six feet.

"Uh. Not yet, Sir." Keith stumbled through the minefield in the man's eyes. "At least we hadn't when I left, but that was a couple of hours ago." He checked his watch for emphasis, but the thought of what happened in four and a half hours made him pull in the stale air around him. Exhaling slowly, he forced those thoughts from his mind. "We'd better get going. Midday traffic can get a little nuts on the weekends."

"Patty Ann! Are they here yet?" Vivian yelled from the top of the stairs.

In the hallway leading to the kids' wing, Maggie's attention snapped that direction. Isabella was down for a nap. Peter was trying to take one too; however, with all the commotion, him actually sleeping was a long shot.

"No, Ma'am. I haven't seen them."

"Well, call Keith's cell phone. Find out where they are."

"Yes, Ma'am."

As stupid as it was, Maggie wondered if something major was keeping them. She had clearly noted on the schedule Patty Ann had issued at noon that Keith and Dallas were due back on the estate by 3:30. It was now sliding toward four.

Maybe they'd had a wreck, or maybe someone's plane had been delayed or irrevocably detained. Maybe there was emergency legislation pending in the Senate, or maybe Dallas forgot all about the weekend and took off for Barbados.

"Not to worry," Patty Ann said as she came up the stairs. "They are at the guesthouse. Ms. Dallas is getting settled in. They will be here at 5:30."

"Oh, that's a relief," Vivian said with a sigh.

Maybe to her…

"I always forget how provincially bachelors live," Dallas said, lounging on the beige-toned sofa. "Just wait. A woman's touch will make all the difference."

Keith brought in two glasses of tea from the kitchen. "Lightly sweetened," he said, handing her the glass.

She took a sip, her gaze staying on him as he sat on the couch next to her. "You know," she said as she set the glass on the glass-topped coffee table, "I was hoping I'd get more than a little tea once we got here." With a motion he knew he should remember, she swung herself over closer to him. "We've got an hour before we have to be anywhere. You have any idea how we can fill that much time?"

Her kiss, once his most prized goal, was demanding and insistent. She pressed herself into him even as he fought the instinct to back away. With both hands he took her shoulders and pulled her from him. "Hey, tiger. Whoa there. Patty Ann is going to come down here and skin us both alive if we're late."

"Let her. It's our party. We can be late if we want." She came at him again, but Keith managed to stop her progress.

"And your parents won't be happy if we aren't there to meet

them. Not to mention my parents." The thought of which stabbed a knife of guilt and fear right into him. However, at the moment he was facing down one situation, and at this point one at a time was all he could manage. "Besides, that will make tonight so much better."

He smiled slyly at her. "Surely you can wait a few more hours."

She spun petulantly and crossed her arms. "Well, yeah, but you'd better make this worth it."

It hurt to smile. "You know it."

Ten

"Don't even think about it," Patty Ann said from behind Maggie as she retied Peter's shoe in the upstairs hallway. That shoe was forever coming untied, what she would've given for his old ones. At least they stayed tied.

"About what?" Maggie asked, turning and tying simultaneously. She was bent down on the ground, and with Patty Ann behind her there was a distinct possibility of being kicked the rest of the way to the carpet.

"You. You look like a high school math teacher on her first day of school."

Maggie's eyes widened in incomprehension. "I... why?" She looked down at herself as she stood. The turquoise and white striped shirt wasn't exactly horrible.

Patty Ann walked around her slowly. "No. No. No. This will never do. Do you not know the governor is going to be here along with some other very important people? We can't have you walking around as if you just stepped out of the Wal-Mart parking lot."

The jab hurt—even from Patty Ann.

Maggie looked down at her attire once more. "It's not like I'm the guest of honor. No one's even going to see me."

"You represent this family." Each word exploded like a bomb. "Never, ever take that for granted. The way you look reflects on their standing in society. It is not acceptable for you to go around looking like the help."

"Hello. I am the help."

"Pft." Patty Ann held up her hand. She scrutinized Maggie carefully. "I hate to even ask this, but don't you have anything better? Anything?"

The small list of clothing slid through her mind. "I have a pink top that's kind of silk-looking, but except this skirt, I don't really have anything to go with it."

Patty Ann considered that. "What size do you wear?"

"Eight." The word was at least six syllables long. "Why?"

A moment of consideration and the decision was made. "I'll be right back."

The entrances were scripted to perfection. The Ayers first as hosts. The governor and his wife as honored guests. The Hendersons as parents of the bride-to-be. And then, last but not least the happy couple. His father had even sent the limo down the driveway to the guesthouse to get them. It seemed this side of ridiculous for them to actually travel outside the gate to a discreet turnaround and then come back, but when it was in the schedule, questions just got in the way.

"Oh, look, here they are," Vivian called to the assembled guests when Keith and Dallas walked arm-in-arm into the lavishly decorated backyard. Applause broke out around them. The backyard looked like a garden had exploded. White and pink flowers were everywhere. Soft candles burned in various places although the hot Texas sun was doing no bowing to its puny counterparts.

As he stepped with Dallas into the sea of faces he hardly recognized, Keith smiled as if this was the only place in the world he'd ever wanted to be. Somehow, he hadn't seen this part when he'd asked her to marry him. Somehow the thought of flashbulbs and formal greetings hadn't entered his mind.

"Son, Keith," his father said, puffing himself out with pride. "May I introduce you to Governor Keyes."

"Governor." Keith shook the man's hand like an expert. "Mrs. Keyes. This is Dallas Henderson. My fiancée." The last word lodged in his throat, but with a push he got it out. "It's so nice of you to come. We so appreciate it."

From her post in the corner next to the outside wall, Maggie watched him. He was hard not to watch. Smoke-colored tailored pants. White shirt casually buttoned. He looked the part of the handsome billionaire heir. The problem was he didn't look at all like Keith.

Dallas on the other hand looked like she belonged nowhere else. Something in Maggie had hoped that Dallas wasn't all that pretty because at least then, Keith's assessment that she was nice would've been balanced by the fact that she wasn't also beautiful. Well, that worked. No, Dallas wasn't pretty. She was gorgeous.

Her dress, a white number that plunged deep and rose high, accentuated a figure that said it was made for that kind of dress. The light golden hair was pulled to the side in a loose ponytail that hung over her left shoulder, wisps of hair sliding off both sides. Worse, her necklace and earrings alone had to cost more than Maggie would make in her lifetime. Yes, Dallas Henderson was beautiful, and the fact that she was nice too completely torpedoed any outlandish hopes Maggie had managed to put together about her chances with Keith. Even though her stomach twisted in knots at the sight, she watched them, mingling and sipping champagne, his arm around Dallas as if it belonged nowhere else.

Her attention returned to Peter and his sister, making sure they didn't go far. That wasn't too much of a problem because Peter seemed to be permanently attached to the silk pants Patty Ann had loaned her. They felt great, but they probably cost more than all her other purchases put altogether. Worse, it wasn't totally clear where they had come from. "Guard them with your life" was not what you wanted to hear when you'd be on the front lines with two children.

So, with no better options, Maggie resorted to sitting on the little bench that had been added along with who-knew-how-many-other things to the backyard. It was like a completely different place. They'd even moved the playhouse, which must have taken more than a little effort. She sighed as she looked around. Here she was, in the midst of the Texas elite, and even though she was physically here, she was for all intents and purposes completely invisible.

It hadn't taken Keith more than five minutes to locate Maggie. From the first second he caught sight of her over in the corner by the miniature yellow rose covered trellis, he'd wanted nothing more than to find a way to break away from the stuffed-shirts and thank her for her kindness the night before. However, he knew that wouldn't be possible tonight as much as he wanted it to be. Too many people were watching his every move. Besides, tonight was about showing off—for his father and Dallas, and Dallas's family. He felt like a trophy on a shelf, having been taken down for others to ooh and aah over. Still, his gaze betrayed him every so often and drifted where the rest of him wanted so badly to go.

"Well, Dallas, I'm glad to see Keith found you back," Ike said with a big Texas grin as he ambled up to the happy couple.

"Ike, I'm so glad you could come." She put her arms around him and leaned forward. Keith wondered how her dress stayed on. The top of it was held together with a couple of gold chains which plunged down the backless part of the dress to the waistline. When she pulled back, Keith held out his hand.

"Ike."

"Keith." Warnings and an ultra-critical evaluation of the situation flowed through Ike's eyes and smile right into Keith, pulling guilt out in fistfuls. Then with a real smile at Dallas, Ike raised his glass. "Congratulations, you two. I hope you will be very happy together."

As Ike stepped away, Keith closed his eyes for the barest of moments. When he opened them again, his gaze snagged on the young lady with the white pants and modest pink blouse sitting in the corner of the yard with two little children. Her hair was pulled up in that way that let it cascade down her back, conservative and yet not stuffy. Next to her sat Peter, and on her lap sat Isabella. She was playing with them, talking to them, just like she always did. If he could just go over…

"I'd like a picture with the happy couple," the governor said to those standing around. "Phillip."

The governor's photographer stepped up. The two couples smiled, and the picture was recorded for all of posterity.

"Well, well, it's good to see you standing on your own power," Greg said an hour later as Keith stood at the tree, taking a breather from the socializing. He was about full-up and overflowing on his small talk quotient for the year.

Keith held out his hand to his friend. "You made it."

"Yes, I did. Even more remarkably you did." Greg shook Keith's hand. Then sipping the champagne he leaned on the tree next to Keith. "So, you made it to the airport looking all happy and chipper I guess?"

"No thanks to you."

"Me?" Greg sounded genuinely surprised. "What'd I do?"

"Next time you call a cab, tell them which house is mine if you don't mind."

"I did."

"No, you didn't. You sent them to the mansion. Big difference." Anger snapped into Keith. "Thanks to you my dad hasn't spoken to me all day."

Greg shrugged that off. "Hey, now. That's not my fault. It was all I could do to convince you not to be a total idiot and try to drive home. Because of me, you're standing there in one piece. You should be thanking me."

They stood in the silence of a skirmish neither wanted to continue at the moment.

"So, what's the story on Peter's new friend?" Greg asked, lifting his chin toward Maggie and the children who were still in the corner, at the party and yet not really visible.

"The new nanny." Keith took a sip of champagne to keep his heart from cracking in two.

"Does the new nanny have a name?"

"Maggie. Maggie Montgomery." The name slid through him, knifing into his heart with the complete understanding that whatever he wanted with her would never become his reality. He looked around at the party. No, his reality was about his father's money and his position in this life. Anything more substantial was a dream that would never be any more than that.

"Hello there," the tall, dark-haired, good-looking guy with the little wire-framed glasses said as he stood next to the bench where

Maggie sat.

"Hi."

"Cute kids."

"Thanks." Somehow she had thought spending the whole night in the corner alone could get no worse. She was wrong.

"They're the Ayer kids, right?"

That pulled Maggie's uneasiness to the surface. "I'm sorry. Who are you again?"

"Oh, sorry." He sat down and pulled his dark blue jacket with him, which to Maggie was not an improvement. "Greg Parker. I'm Keith's friend." He held out his hand to her.

The name pulled up a thousand emotions she was trying desperately to bury. "Oh, it's nice to meet you Greg, Keith's friend." Isabella was toddling around the bench, and just as she got to Maggie's leg, she reached out but missed, landing on her bottom. "Oops, baby girl. Try it again." Maggie lifted her to her feet as Greg's hand fell back to his jacket.

"Gie. Gie," Isabella said, her eyes shining.

Maggie's attention dropped to the little face she had grown to so love. "Gie. Gie? Is that Mag-gie?"

"Gie. Gie." Isabella pounded Maggie's knee with her hand.

Greg smiled. "You're good with her."

"It's my job."

"Yeah, Keith told me you're the new babysitter."

"Nanny."

"What's the difference?"

"A babysitter goes home when the parents get back from wherever they were. A nanny... well..." She snagged Isabella from escaping too far and swung her onto her lap. "Come here, you."

"So you don't get like time off or anything?" He took a sip of champagne although he never really took his gaze off of her.

"Nope. Not so far."

His face fell. "Isn't that like slave labor? Don't they have to give you some time off?"

Maggie shrugged. "I don't mind. What else do I have to do, right?"

"Ms. Montgomery," Patty Ann said, stepping up beside them. From her outfit any normal person would've assumed she was the bride's mother at a wedding. Ivory Chanel suit, upswept hair. It was a little much for a garden party.

"Yes, Ma'am." Maggie stood, picking Isabella up with her. She felt Greg rise at her side, and she wondered about that.

"Mrs. Ayer is ready for the formal pictures to be taken, so the children are needed."

"Oh, of course." Maggie glanced back at Greg. "Excuse me."

She was there for the pictures of that much Keith was one-hundred percent sure. What he was less sure of was where she had gone after the pictures. As the sun relinquished its hold on the party and the soft lights came up, Keith couldn't help but glance back at the empty corner. Frustration poured through him when even after minutes and minutes she didn't reappear there.

He checked his watch and realized she must be putting Pete and Izzy down for the night. His gaze traveled up to Isabella's window, and sure enough the soft light in her window was on. At that moment he would've given everything he would ever own to ditch all of this and go up there to help her tuck the kids in. The light in the window faded to black, and he didn't even have to try to remember the soft prayers she would say as she bent over Peter's bed.

"You're not getting tired already now, are you?" Dallas waltzed up and draped her arms over his shoulders.

"Just taking a breather."

She leaned over to him and nuzzled his ear. Self-consciousness dropped over him. "Hey. You're pressing your luck there." He ran his hand over her back.

"I haven't forgotten what you like," she said, pulling her bottom lip under her teeth. She glanced back at the party. "Do you think anyone would miss us?"

At that moment Keith caught sight of his father across the grass, standing and talking to both the governor and to Mr. Henderson. His father's glance in Keith's direction froze his blood. There was resolve in his gaze and a smile of self-satisfaction underneath. His stance on the situation was clear. Marry her or else.

"Hey, you two. Get a room," Greg said good-naturedly as he walked up to where they were huddled.

"Jealous?" Dallas asked, smiling up at Greg.

"Well, I wouldn't be if Keith here would hook me up with the nanny."

Dallas tilted her head in curiosity. "The nanny? What nanny?"

Greg lifted his chin to indicate the back corner, and Keith's heart did a nosedive. Somehow that wasn't what he expected. "Maggie. I'd love to ask her out, but you know the Ayers, they are taskmasters."

"They're not so bad once you get to know them," Dallas said, turning on her full-wattage charm in Keith's direction.

"Yeah, well, tell that to whoever hasn't let Maggie off yet. How long's she been here anyway?"

Keith had to swallow to get the answer out. "Couple of weeks."

That got Dallas's attention. "A couple of weeks, and she hasn't had any time off?"

Keith's shrug hurt for more reasons than he could name.

"Well, Greg, you leave it to me." Dallas laced her arm through Greg's and bent her head furtively. "I'm sure they will take the advice of their future daughter-in-law. Besides we owe you one for hooking us up. The least we could do is return the favor."

Ugh. She had to go and remind Keith. The night he never wanted to remember. The one she would never let him forget. It was a dance at A&M which were always rowdy and way-fun. Keith and Greg had gone to scope out the prospects for a night of fun, and Keith spotted Dallas almost instantly. She was a sophomore at the time, and he didn't know her from Eve. During a slow song he'd finally gotten up the courage to ask her to dance; however, when he approached her to ask, she surveyed him like he was dirt personified.

Stupidly he had asked her anyway, and it was with no small amount of insinuated insult that she had turned him down, making a point to do it loudly in front of her friends. He hated remembering that moment. It always made his heart stop his breathing.

But Greg, being the friend he always had been, assured Keith it was only because she didn't know who he was. So Greg took it upon himself to fix the situation, and fix it he did. By the time they left Dallas was hanging on Keith's every word, and before the next three sunsets, they were a couple.

"Do you think she'll come back down tonight?" Dallas asked a little too into this whole set-up thing than Keith would've liked. "What, does she like have to put the kids in bed and stuff?"

"That's generally in the job description," Keith said, hating how mean he sounded.

"Well, maybe we can't do anything tonight," Dallas said as she patted Greg's arm. "But I'm here the whole week. I'm sure we can get something to work out."

When the kids were in bed, prayers said, and tucked in, Maggie went to her own room. She didn't turn the light on. They might see it from the party. Instead she knelt down next to her bed as tears of letting go streamed down her face onto the little white flowers. "Dear Lord, I know I never had a chance with Keith. I know that as well as You do. But please, I ask You, keep him safe. Help him to be happy with Dallas. Help them to have a long and happy life together because he deserves that much."

The night wound down eventually. The governor and his wife left. The guests left. Even the Hendersons had to call it a night. Keith was running on empty. After the night before, the draining afternoon, and the overtaxing evening, he was about ten seconds from curling up on one of the little benches and calling a stop-time forever.

"Well, we really should be going too," Dallas said as she laced her arm through his.

"Are you staying at the guesthouse?" Vivian asked, and Keith wanted to throw up at the obviousness of the question.

"Where else?" Dallas asked as if she was thrilled with the house and everything about it. She shrugged to get closer to him. "Oh, and Mrs. Ayer… Keith and I were thinking about having a little party Monday evening. Nothing big, just a few close friends."

This was news to Keith, so he perked up his ears lest he miss something important.

"We invited Greg, and he wanted to bring a guest."

Vivian's face asked the question as much as she did. "And the problem is?"

"Well, it's who he wants to ask," Dallas said, and then she leaned in, lest anyone happen to hear. "Maggie Montgomery."

Vivian's eyebrows shot up. "The nanny?"

Dallas smiled. "You know Greg. Never one to shoot very high."

The comment raked right over Keith's nerves.

"But we were kind of hoping we could help him out. Do you think Maggie could have Monday night off?"

Vivian smiled serenely. "I'm sure we could arrange that."

Eleven

All day Sunday Keith thought of little other than Maggie. Of course he had plenty of other things to occupy his mind and his time like Dallas and her incessant come-ons. He'd ducked the issue the night before by practically falling asleep in their limo ride from the mansion to the guesthouse. It wasn't an act. He was done for. Nonetheless, the barrage of innuendos had started the moment he woke up.

Had he not had the brilliant idea of breakfast in bed, talking her out of anything else would've been next to impossible. More to the point they were to meet his parents at eight o'clock to ride with them into Houston to meet her parents at nine o'clock, and the prospect of all the parents on top of everything else was making him seriously queasy.

"I wonder if Greg called Maggie yet," Dallas said when she helped Keith take the breakfast dishes back to the kitchen.

The statement twisted through his gut.

"I really hope she says yes. It would be nice for Greg to have someone."

Keith turned to her questioningly. "Why is this so important to you?"

"Because." She stepped up to him and laid her arms over his shoulders. "I want everyone to be as deliriously happy as we are."

"Ms. Montogmery," Patty Ann said with her usual amount of iciness. "May I have a word with you?"

Maggie had chosen to keep the kids upstairs rather than running the gauntlet of tempers and exhausted nerves the next morning. She had asked Inez if she could take breakfast up for the kids for a Sunday treat, and despite her assumptions of what the maid would say, permission was granted. Now, it seemed she had been caught.

She unfolded herself from the floor and walked to the door, pulling her shirt down behind her. "Yes, Ma'am."

Patty Ann stepped into the hallway, and Maggie's uh-oh meter went off the charts. Still she followed her out with only a quick "You two be good."

"Ms. Montgomery. Three things. First, Mrs. Ayer wanted to extend her appreciation for your job performance last night. The children were there for the appropriate impact at just the right moments and not seen other than that. Very well done."

That surprised Maggie. "Thank you."

"Second of all, here is your paycheck for the first two weeks of your service. You will be receiving payment from here on out on the fifteenth and the first. There are no advances, so budget accordingly."

Maggie accepted the little envelope. "Yes, Ma'am."

"And finally, you are being given tomorrow off."

"Off?" The word smashed into Maggie. "Why?"

"So you can go into town and deposit that or do errands or whatever it is you do on a day off."

Maggie's thoughts went into the room behind her. "What about the kids?"

"Not to worry, they shall be taken care of."

"Keith, I talked with Lee Ferrell of Devonshire, Inc. last week," Mr. Henderson said as they sat around the table eating brunch. "He is really interested in talking with you about your future in Houston."

Dallas elbowed him and smiled.

"Oh, really?" Keith asked. He cleared his throat because the roll went down the wrong pipe.

"With your background in your father's company and your degree, Lee thinks you would be a natural to run their Midland assets."

Midland? He cleared his throat again. He glanced at Dallas. "Umm, we had planned to live in Houston."

"Oh, of course. Running things in Midland doesn't mean you have to live there." He laughed as if it was the most absurd thing he'd ever heard. "You'd just have to go out there once or twice a week. Day trips for the most part."

How much had Mr. Henderson talked with Mr. Ferrell? It sounded like suicide to accept the offer. His father-in-law knowing the everyday details of his job and presumably his home life as well? He already had one watchdog. He didn't need two. "Sounds interesting."

"I was telling Keith yesterday there is a nice little starter place in the Woodlands," Dallas said. "It's perfect distance from Hayden & Elliott. We're going to go look at it this week. Right, honey?" She snaked her arm through his, and Keith had to fight not to remove his arm from the encroachment.

"Well, I can't say how pleased I am with the foundation the two of you are building," his father said, and he really did look proud. "Years ago when I started out, it was with a five dollar bill and a dream. I can't imagine where I would be now if I had the start you two are getting."

Dallas beamed her appreciation. "We're so lucky."

"There's a phone call for you in the kitchen," Inez said, standing at the door to the playroom. For as many hours as they had spent with no one seeming to notice they were still on the planet, Maggie wondered why suddenly today everyone seemed to be showing up.

"K. I'll be right there." She stood, pulled her top down, and leveled her gaze at Peter. "You be good and take care of your sister. Got it?"

Peter's eyes widened in fear.

"Don't worry." She winked at him. "I trust you."

After a moment he smiled and nodded. With that she went down, wondering who in the world would be calling her. Mrs. Malowinski was the only one she could think of, and that made no sense because she didn't have the number, which Maggie assumed was unlisted, and unless it was a tragedy, her foster parent would never call anyway.

She picked the phone off the cabinet like it was a bomb that might explode. "Hello?" It was laced with uncertainty.

"Maggie. Oh, good. I'm glad I caught you."

How a telemarketer had tracked her down here, she would never know. "I'm not interested in whatever you're selling."

He laughed. "No. No, Maggie. This is Greg... Parker. Remember? From the party last night?"

Maggie glanced over at Inez who she was sure was listening. "Oh, hi, Greg. Umm... if you're looking for Keith..."

"No. I'm not looking for Keith. I'm looking for you."

Awkwardness twined through her as she pulled her arm up over her middle. "Me? What...? Why?"

"Listen, Keith and Dallas are having a little get together tomorrow night. Nothing fancy. Just some old friends. I was wondering if you might want to go with me."

The question knocked her backward. "With... I... Umm... Well..."

"Please say yes. I know. I shouldn't beg, but please say yes. Everybody else is going to be coupled off, and I don't want to go alone. I just broke up with my girlfriend last month, and well, I haven't had much of a chance to meet anyone new... But I don't want to pressure you. If you don't want to go with me, I'll understand."

Ugh. Why did he have to sound so nice? Why couldn't she just be a little more cruel? A little more selfish? It would've solved a lot of problems.

"Please, Maggie. We can go late, leave early. You'll never even have to know I'm in the room."

She laughed a little laugh at that. "Well, maybe I want to know you're in the room."

He seemed to breathe in that statement. "Cool. So you'll go with me?"

"Yes, Greg. I'll go with you."

"Tomorrow I'm going to need to run into Houston for awhile," Dallas said as Keith's dad and Vivian monitored the conversation from the other side of the limo on their way back to the estate. "I need to get a few things for the party, and several things for your place." She angled her attention to his parents. "Bachelors. They live on such a bare minimum."

His father laughed. "Keith never was one to need much."

"Tell me about it. His place is positively minimalist."

Keith wanted to tell her that he hadn't touched a single decoration nor furnishing in five years. Each and every piece was handpicked and put there by Vivian before she knew he would be using the place. However, even at this moment he couldn't be that cruel. So he accepted the jab and lowered his head to the proper level of embarrassment.

"So, you're having a party tomorrow night," his father asked, smiling at Dallas while he simultaneously glared at Keith. How he could pull that off with them sitting right next to each other, Keith wasn't sure, but he felt it just the same.

Dallas shrugged. "Just a few friends. Nothing big. We'll start with hors d'oeuvres on the patio. I'm thinking paté with a nice red wine, and then for the meal something light. Lamb or duck."

"I didn't know you were such a chef," Vivian said, clearly impressed with the menu. The limousine rolled into the turn and then through the gate.

"Oh, no. I'm not. I thought either we could have it catered or we could just use your staff."

Keith noticed Vivian nearly swallow her teeth, and it was all he could do to keep from laughing. Instead, he simply leaned over to Dallas and kissed her cheek. "Whatever you want, baby. I'll be there by 6:30."

Instantly the color drained from Dallas's face. "6:30? Where are you going to be?"

"Working of course. We've got to get Dragnet ready for Oak Tree. Isn't that right, Dad?"

"Hrumph." It wasn't really an answer at all, but Keith liked the sound of his father's awkwardness just the same.

Dallas was having trouble putting two words together. Vivian was clearly holding back a fit of anxiety, and his father was puffed and as red as a lobster.

"Well," his father finally managed. "I will be going into Houston tomorrow and then up to Amarillo Tuesday for meetings."

"Amarillo?" Vivian asked, her world spinning around her.

"You didn't tell me that."

"I've been busy with other things."

The car pulled up to the mansion and stopped. If he hadn't known better, Keith would've sworn his father and Vivian were racing to get out. However, Dallas never so much as moved. He looked at her. "Ladies first."

Her eyes widened. "We're getting out here? Why can't they take us to the guesthouse?"

"It's only a half mile walk," Keith said, teasing her. "What? Are you afraid you're going to melt?"

She didn't look happy. In fact, she looked downright mad. "No." But she got out anyway.

On the trail, Keith tried to take her hand, but she anchored her arms over her middle. He didn't fight it. After all that's what he'd wanted for 24-hours, for her to stop hanging all over him. He put his hand in his pocket and absorbed the beauty of the day. The trees rustled above them, bringing him back to center. "So, what do you think about riding out to the falls on Wednesday? I think I should be able to get the afternoon off."

"The falls?" she asked, and there was a note of panic. "On horses?"

"Well, yeah. I mean we could take the Dodge, but the horses let us take the slow way."

For as much as Dallas had hinted around the subject of being with him in the last day, she suddenly looked pale at the prospect. "Isn't it kind of hot to be riding?"

"You think it's hot now, wait until July." But his own comment knocked the words away from him. July. Everything would be different come July.

"Maybe we can go see the house in the Woodlands on Wednesday, put down an offer. I'd like to get that checked off the list as soon as possible. And Tracy and I are going to go in and finalize everything with the florist on Thursday. I wanted to do a final fitting on my dress before I leave. That would have to be Friday. I don't want to wait until the last minute on that. Mom and Vivian have the guest lists all ready on-line so I'll be putting the invitations together at school. I'd wanted to do it this weekend, but Mom was waiting on a few from her side. It's such a nightmare to get 600 guests in-sync for something like this."

The thought of 600 guests almost overwhelmed every other

thing she'd just said. Keith inhaled to stop his thoughts from swimming through all the details. Finally it struck upon something that had to be taken care of immediately.

He rubbed his thumb across the bottom of his nose as the nerves tingled there. "Listen, about tomorrow night. I know the staff at the mansion would be glad to do the party, but I think it would be better if we hired someone on our own."

Her face fell. "Why?"

He shrugged. "Well, it's our party, and they're not our staff."

It took a long minute for that information to wind through her. At the turn for the front door she shook her head. "It sure is hot out here."

"Yeah, it is."

Dallas spent most of the evening on the phone with Tracy making plans for the next day, and Keith spent it getting the place ready for a party. It wasn't that bad, but still. He wanted it nice for Dallas not to mention the other guests he wasn't even sure were coming. Some deep, demented part of him wanted to call Greg to find out if he'd asked Maggie, but that was playing with fire. He was sure to find out soon enough, and to him, seeing her again couldn't come soon enough.

"I think I'm going to turn in," Dallas said when the phone call ended. "I'm supposed to meet Tracy at her place in Houston at eight, which means leaving here at what?"

"Six-thirty," Keith said. "If you want to miss at least some of the traffic."

"Huh." That deflated her even further.

"And you need to call a caterer first thing," he said, infinitely more into the actual details of having a party than she was.

"Okay. Fine." She slumped onto a chair and watched him pull out the vacuum. "Are you going to do that now?"

"Unless you want to do it tomorrow. I've got to be at the stables at eight, and I won't be back until at least six or six-thirty."

"But I told everyone to be here at six-thirty."

"Thus I'm vacuuming now." He was getting tired of this conversation.

"But I wanted to spend some time with you."

"What do you call this?"

She pursed her lips. "Vacuuming? Come on, Keith. This was supposed to be fun."

"Yes, but it can't always be fun. There's work involved too." With that he started the vacuum and pushed it over the carpet. Dallas watched him for only a couple of seconds, then with a huff, she launched out of the chair and stalked down the hallway. Keith exhaled and rolled his eyes. If he was lucky, she would be asleep before he got the rest cleaned because one thing was for sure, she wasn't coming back to help.

Maggie had meant to be gone before nine. She had to get to the bank and cash her more-money-than-she'd-ever-seen-in-her-life check. Then she had a little shopping to do. With the white silk pants back to their original owner and everything from Wal-Mart on its second go-round, she decided to get something nice for tonight. Something that didn't scream poverty.

Where she would get this outfit, she had no clue, but that was part of the excitement. The two biggest problems were the kids and her car. When she went to leave, you would've thought someone had died. Both kids looked completely abandoned and then started wailing. She tried to calm them down, but when that didn't work, Inez shooed her away. Reluctantly she left, not seeing that she had much other choice.

Walking down through the trees, Maggie thought about her shoes that first day, and she smiled. Two sizes too big. Just like this job. Still, somehow, it had come to fit her like the new white tennis shoes on her feet. Her thoughts stumbled back to a Wal-Mart, and a shopping cart, and him. Sad acceptance slid through her. They were good together—Keith and Dallas—that much was obvious.

As much as that hurt, she had to let him go because he'd chosen his life, and his life wasn't her. Still a quarter mile from the guesthouse, she heard the familiar drone of the Dodge coming up behind her, and she couldn't stop the smile.

"Hey, stranger," Keith said through the open passenger window. "What're you doing out in these parts?"

She turned to him, and when she found the other side of the pickup empty, her heart nearly wouldn't let the words out.

"Rescuing my car from your barn."

That brought a slice of worry across his face. "What? Are you escaping?"

"Enjoying my day off." Maggie was still walking, and he was driving very slowly next to her.

"Day off? Wow. They actually let you out of prison?"

She laughed. "It's not that bad."

He drove a little farther. "You know, we are going the same direction if you hadn't noticed. Why don't you get in, and then you wouldn't have to walk?"

"I like walking. I'm showing off my new tennis shoes, remember?" She lifted her foot high, so he could see them.

"Nice." His face said he clearly did remember. "Well, before you wear them out..." He stopped and reached across the seat to pop the door open for her.

Maggie beat back every feeling of the wonderful familiarity of getting in his pickup. Once inside familiar had never felt so safe.

"So, you're going into town then?" he asked as the pickup made its way the last 300 yards to the turn beyond the guesthouse.

"Yeah. I've gotta cash my paycheck so I can pay you back."

Confusion dropped on his face. "Pay me back? For what?"

"Gee, you have a long memory. Clothes. Wal-Mart. Shopping. Does any of this ring a bell?" It was so weird to be talking to him like this. With his beat up cowboy hat over the light blue bandana, she would never have guessed how he looked at the party on Saturday. It was like he wasn't even the same person, or maybe that person wasn't the same as this one. She couldn't really tell how he could be both.

"You don't owe me anything."

"Hey now. That was the deal, remember? You buy them. I pay you back."

The pickup bounced past the last knot of trees into the clearing where the barn stood.

"Yeah, but..."

"Besides," she said, and she couldn't stop the smile. "I got paid." She held up the envelope with her check, so I don't have to be a mooch anymore."

When he looked at her and smiled, there was no condescension anywhere in it. "Good for you." The pickup rolled to the barn, and he parked so her car would be able to get out. At the barn door she watched as he unlatched the bolt and pulled it down. He made it look so easy. The door swung open. "There you go. Safe and sound."

"Well, thank you very much." She turned to him, and her heart did a flip-flop. "I guess I'll see you tonight."

The word slammed into Keith like a brick. "Tonight?"

"Oh, yeah." She hesitated for a second. "Dallas's party? That is tonight, right?"

His thoughts swirled as if in a blender. "Oh. Y…yeah. That's tonight. She asked you?"

"No, Greg Parker called me. It's the funniest thing. We just met the other night at the party, but he seems like such a nice guy. Besides, I figured he's your friend, so how bad can he be, right?"

There was teasing in her tone and her eyes, but Keith's brain was having a hard time getting past her being with Greg. "Oh, yeah. Right."

For a full ten seconds no one moved. Then Maggie smiled. "Well, miles to go and not much time to get there. Be good. I'll see you tonight." And with that she got in her car, got it started, and backed out past him standing at the barn doors. With a wave she started off. Just as she got to the trees, he remembered.

"Maggie!"

But she was gone.

When she came back, he would have to open the door for her. He wished he had thought to ask her when that would be. He wished he could just think logically about anything when she was around. Then the thought of her with Greg twisted through him. Greg was a nice guy. He would surely treat her right. That wasn't the problem. It was worse than that. It was that he never wanted to see her with anyone else. Ever.

Maggie was so bad at this. Shopping was not her specialty. She didn't know the first thing about what looked right together and what didn't. Growing up she was just happy if it didn't fall off and only had a couple of holes. Now, inexplicably, here she was trying to find something that would conceivably compete with all the other girls who were sure to be at this party.

She couldn't out-do them. That was a given. All she hoped for was to not look like someone's poor step-niece that nobody wants around. Rack after rack, she looked. She even tried a few things on, but the fits weren't right and the prices were worse.

"God, what am I going to do?" she asked the One who had become her best friend when there were no others around. She looked in the mirror at the off-shoulder lime green thing she was wearing. It was awful. Nothing about it looked right.

Quickly she checked the watch she had bought at the last store she couldn't find anything at. "Great." Now on top of not having anything to wear, she was going to be late. "Look, God, I know I have no right to ask for a miracle at this point, but I'm asking anyway. Please. What am I going to wear?"

It wasn't until she was in her own clothes and pulling her white sneaker on that the thought occurred to her. The dress. The one from Wal-Mart. She'd hung it in her closet in the very back, thinking it was too nice to wear at work. Presumably it was still there. Her memory slid down it, and she decided that yes, it would work, provided it actually fit. Of course, there was no way to know that considering she'd never actually tried it on. It was the one she had figured on taking back the minute he put it in the cart.

"Ugh." Why? Why did every single train of thought always lead her right back to him? "Maggie, girl. You've got to put him out of your head. He's taken. Dallas-taken. They are together. You are not. Stop thinking about him!" But that was easier said than done.

How many times Keith had been up and down the road leading to the guesthouse that day, he had no idea. The excuses were endless, and by four o'clock, he was beginning to hope Ike wouldn't catch on.

"Man, I forgot to grab the extra ropes from my garage at lunch," Keith said. "Tanner said he needed them for tomorrow."

"You know, I think Dallas must've fried your brain," Ike said with a laugh. "You're a mess."

"That's one way to put it."

"Gee, I'd hate to see you after the honeymoon. You ain't going to get any meaningful work done for a year."

Keith shook his head at the implication. "I'm going to run over and get them."

Ike waved him off, and Keith escaped from the office with a sigh of relief. Now if she would just show up so he could help her, he wouldn't have to come up with some other lame excuse. Eventually Ike was going to get suspicious.

How he made that bolt look like it would slide through butter, Maggie had no clue. Sweat popped out on her forehead as she took hold of it with both hands and pulled. She had the feeling that even if she hung on the thing, she wouldn't be able to get it to unlatch. "Grrr."

Taking hold of it again, she yanked. Once. Twice. Just before she actually tried the hanging on it thing, she heard the drone of the Dodge, and her gaze snapped up the trail. Self-consciously she let go and backed up as she watched him drive toward her. When he stopped, his grin could've been no bigger.

"You need some help?" He slid out of the pickup, looking every bit the rugged, hardworking ranch hand cowboy. Those arms, sleek and tan, bulged from beneath the dirt-stained denim shirt, and Maggie had to force herself to breathe.

"That would be nice." She shaded her eyes with her hand as she backed farther from the barn door.

He stepped in front of her.

"Ike going easy on you these days?"

He twisted slightly. "What's that mean?"

"You've spent more time here today than working." Then the thought of why scratched across her brain. "Oh, yeah. I bet Dallas has got you going crazy over the party. Huh?"

"Oh. No. Not really." He slid the bolt out of the holder with ease.

She put her hands on her hips. "Now how do you do that? I've been out here for ten minutes trying to do that."

"It's not hard. You just have to know the secret." He smiled at her wickedly.

"Uh-huh. And you're going to keep my car hostage by not

telling me this secret?"

He leaned on the barn door and folded his arms across his chest as he sized her up. "Well, if you're really nice..."

"Hey, now. When have I not been nice to you?" She was teasing, but his face fell just the same.

He turned back for the door. "It's easy. You just have to push the door in a little bit." With one hand he pushed the door, with the other he slid the bolt up and down into the latch with no problem.

Maggie still wasn't convinced. She stepped up into the space between him and the door. "Let me try that." Reaching up with one hand, she took hold of the bolt. Then with the other and her hip, she pushed on the door. Sure enough the bolt slid free with nearly no effort. "Wow. That's some secret."

Keith felt like all the air in the meadow had evaporated. Three inches from him, she stood in her yellow top and three-quarter length pants, looking all smart and sassy. With everything he had, he wanted to reach out to her, put his arms around her and forget about everything else in his life.

She worked the bolt a few more times to make sure there wasn't some catch. Then she let the bolt down and pulled the door open. "Ha. Now my car isn't a hostage."

Deflecting the feelings of wanting her, he crossed his arms again. "What makes you think it was a hostage to begin with? All you had to do was knock on my door, and say, 'Keith, could you come help me?'"

She tossed her hair over her shoulder. "What like some little damsel in distress? I can handle things on my own just fine, I'll have you know."

"Uh-huh. Like smoothie-on-the-ceiling fine?"

At first she looked hurt, but then her eyes glinted when she realized he was teasing. "That was a fluke."

"And falling down the stairs?"

Annoyance crossed her face. "Nerves."

"And being caught out in the rain with no umbrella?"

Her face scrunched. "I never did that."

He grinned. "Give it time."

"Grr." She reached out and whacked the side of his arm with her hand; however, in the next second she was yelping in pain. "Oww. What are you made of steel?"

At first he laughed, then the thought of how many problems that would solve crossed through him. "No. Unfortunately flesh and bones."

"Yeah," she said, still shaking her hand. "Hard ones."

"Come on. Let's get this car taken care of. I'll run you back up to the mansion."

"Yeah. I'd hate to be late when Greg gets here."

It was like a punch to the gut. "Yeah, we'd hate for that to happen."

Maggie drove the car in and made a point of working the bolt herself when she came back out. It was not fair for a guy to stand around looking that good. It just wasn't. She was having enough trouble getting her brain to think clearly as it was. Those muscles. That tan. That smile. They all called to her senses, threatening to take her places that she knew she could never go.

She jumped into the pickup, glad for the cool air of the air conditioner. When he slid in behind the wheel, she knew she had to say something, something casual and friendly—lest her mouth take her where her heart wanted to go. "You been out working today?"

He glanced over at her. That hat. The bandana. Her brain kept cataloging every single thing she liked about him.

"Trying to get Dragnet ready for Oak Tree." In his voice there was darkness lurking in the corners.

"And that's not going well?"

"Oh, Dad just has no patience with the really important things. He gave us 'til May to have him ready, and there's just no way that's going to happen." After a moment he sighed and slid down in the seat as they crossed back onto the road. "Not that it matters to me much anymore."

"Why's that?"

He glanced at her. "May. By June. I'll be out of here, and it'll be his problem."

That whacked her backward in the seat. "You're leaving

then?"

It seemed he couldn't get comfortable as he shifted side-to-side. "Dallas has this place picked out in the Woodlands. That's a little too far to commute every day."

"Oh." Somehow she hadn't realized he'd be leaving.

The pickup rolled to the front of the mansion and stopped.

"Well, this is it," he said, looking over at her.

She fought to smile. "Yeah. I guess I'll see you tonight."

"Sounds like a plan."

Twelve

Maggie heard the doorbell. It raked across her nerves, pulling them right to the surface. She closed her eyes as she prayed for courage and sanity and anything else she might need to get through this night. The dress was far better than anything else she'd tried on that day; however, it was much shorter than what she was used to wearing.

On her way out the door she tugged the skirt down, trying to get it below her knees. "Stop fidgeting, Maggie," she berated herself. "Stop it." But still she fidgeted. She couldn't help it.

Carefully she descended the stairs, feeling like it was the night of a prom she'd never gone to. She certainly couldn't have gotten any more nervous had she been in a formal gown with a corsage on her wrist. At the bottom of the steps by the door stood Greg with Inez. When he looked up, he smiled.

"Well, hello there." His gaze stayed on her all the way to the bottom. In all of her memory, she couldn't remember anybody ever looking at her like that.

"I'd better get back to the kitchen," Inez said, and she removed herself from the situation.

Greg surveyed her. "You look beautiful."

Once more she smoothed the skirt down. "Thanks."

He offered her his arm. "Shall we?"

Keith was midway through pouring Tracy wine when movement at the patio door caught his attention. He looked up and everything else dropped away. There, on the arm of his best friend, was every dream he'd ever had. The smoky-gray dress hugged her curves and set off the mass of waves undulating around her face.

"Oh, Greg! You made it." Dallas greeted them like a four-star hostess. "And you must be Maggie. Hi, I'm Dallas."

"It's nice to meet you." Maggie put out her hand, and Keith had to force the air into his lungs.

"Hey, Keith, man." Greg put his hand in the air, and Keith caught it as he had countless times. But never before had his gaze stayed on the beauty standing behind his best friend. "Thanks for asking us. This is Maggie."

"Maggie," Keith said, holding out his hand to her like he'd been caught in a trance.

"Hi. Uh, thanks for asking us."

"Our pleasure." Man, she was going to be hard not to watch all night.

"Pâté?" Dallas asked, stepping up with a silver serving tray.

"Oh, thanks." Maggie took a small piece of bread with the meat spread on it. She took a bite, and Keith had to keep from laughing at the look on her face. "Mmm."

"Hi, Greg," Tracy, Dallas's best friend and maid of honor, said as she stepped up. From Keith's recollection Tracy and Greg had been out about three times when they were all in college. If his memory served correctly, Greg's exact assessment was "too much drama for me."

"Tracy." Greg put his arm around Maggie apparently to emphasize he had a date, and Keith's fist balled automatically. "This is Maggie Montgomery."

"Oh." Tracy spun her wine glass toward her face. "Do you work with Greg at Corporate Accounting?"

"Uh, no." Maggie hesitated.

"She works at the Ayer mansion," Greg said, pulling her closer to his side. "She's the new nanny."

"Oh," Tracy dragged the single syllable to six. "Well, I guess that's about par for the course." She surveyed Greg with smiling condescension. "We all know how you like slumming with the middle class."

Had she not been a friend of Dallas, Keith would've shown her the door and thrown her out himself.

"Yeah, well," Dallas sighed dramatically, trying to salvage the wreck. "I wonder what's keeping Allison and Jared. They should've been here by now."

"Oh," Keith said, wanting only to put his arms around Maggie and get her out of here and away from the snobs he called friends. He hated the defenseless vulnerability on her face. "Jared called and said they were going to be a little late. He got stuck at the office."

Dallas sighed again and looked at her watch. "Well, should we wait on dinner then? I told the caterers seven."

Keith's concern meter was hitting overload. He wanted to protect Maggie and help Dallas, but he wasn't doing much good at either one. "We can be a little late. It won't kill anyone." Although as he glanced at Tracy standing smugly to the side, he thought if she popped her mouth off at Maggie again, she might very well not be around to enjoy the Duck a L'Orange.

For her part Maggie had effectively shrunk to invisible next to Greg.

"Oh, where are my manners?" Keith asked, snapping back into host mode. "Would you two like some wine?" He grabbed the bottle and two glasses from the serving table.

"Sure," Greg said right next to Maggie, and the only thing she could think was that she never should have come. These people were way out of her league. They talked in languages she didn't understand. They ate food that tasted like it had been recycled from the trashcan. And most of all, they drank.

She wondered at that moment about Keith's night on the town Friday night. Was this just normal protocol with them? Drinks and more drinks. Her gut twisted around that thought. And then he was standing there in front of her with the bottle and the glass, smiling at her with that smile that reminded her so much of a guy she knew. Only that guy wore a beat up cowboy hat and didn't go around sipping Chardonnay.

"Um…" Her gaze swept past him to the others. Saying it might well banish her from them forever, but the truth was she would never be invited again anyway. That much was obvious. "I don't drink."

Keith's face fell in confusion with the statement, and he

looked at her like she had just dropped there from Mars. Greg looked down at her, and his smile fell away as well too.

"What?" Greg asked.

Maggie dragged in a breath as her gaze fought to find somewhere to look that wouldn't knife her to death. "I don't drink." She tried to smile to soften the blow as she scratched the side of her head. "Umm, I hope that's not a problem."

Utter silence fell over the whole place. Even the trees stopped rustling.

Keith was the first to break the silence. "Of course not. I've got lots of other stuff in the kitchen. Coke. Sprite. Water. Whatever you want."

She had never felt more rescued in her life. "Sprite. If you don't mind."

Finally his smile was back in full. "Of course. I'll be right back."

He stepped past her, smelling better than any human had a right to. The whiff of soft, musk cologne sent her head swimming, and her gaze followed him all the way to and through the back patio door.

Tracy and Dallas were already talking about wedding plans as they took seats on the perfectly positioned outdoor furniture. Greg guided Maggie to the little swing with the metal frame that rounded up and over the top. It was on the same patio but far enough away they could have a modicum of privacy.

On the swing he leaned toward her. "I'm really sorry about that. Tracy and I… Well, we were together for awhile. She can be like that sometimes."

"Don't worry about it," Maggie said, trying to take her own advice. She reached over and put her hand on his knee for emphasis. "It comes with the territory."

Keith stepped back into the yard and walked right over to her. "Here you are." He produced a wine glass with clear, bubbly liquid. "Enjoy."

Her heart skipped through her chest. Somehow she had expected a green plastic bottle to announce to everyone how different she was. Instead the wine glass said she fit with no question. "Thanks."

The wink was almost non-existent, but she saw it just the same. "No problem."

Throughout drinks and dinner Keith watched her. There was no doubt that this was not her element, and yet... yet, she held her own. Allison, thankfully, was much less of a snob than Tracy, and between her and Dallas, they made sure Maggie was included as much as possible.

"Nice party," Greg said, sliding up by Keith who stood at the entertainment center talking with Jared.

"Thanks."

Jared excused himself and walked off.

"She's something, huh?" Greg asked, indicating Maggie who sat across the room with the women. She wasn't in the conversation, but the light that permeated her every move was right there with her.

"Yeah, something."

"I wonder if she's like seeing anyone."

The thought had never occurred to Keith. "I don't know. She came with you, didn't she?"

"Yeah." Greg took a drink. "But you know my track record with women. They're always attached to someone else."

The knife went right through Keith's heart. "Yeah, well maybe this time you'll get lucky."

Greg tipped the glass up. "Here's hoping."

"Thanks for coming. It was fun." Dallas stood at the top step of the guesthouse, Keith at her side as Greg and Maggie stood on the porch saying their good-byes.

"Thanks for asking us. We had a good time," Greg said.

"Yeah. It was wonderful," Maggie said, fighting with everything in her not to look at Keith. It was nearly impossible, but looking at him standing there with his arm around Dallas was going to kill her.

"Good night," Greg said and turned her toward the cars.

"Night," Dallas called happily.

Maggie would be happy too if she was going back in with Keith. The guests were gone. The party over. Now they could be alone. That thought hit her hard. It was clear Dallas was staying there. Of course Maggie wasn't naïve enough to think that nothing was happening when they were alone. She closed her eyes to block out that thought.

Then just at the end of the steps, Greg swayed into her. She looked at him with concern. "Are you okay to drive?"

"Yeah. I didn't have that much."

Maggie glanced back at the guesthouse, but Dallas and Keith had already gone in. She looked back at Greg, and her mind went through the evening. Two wines on the patio. A couple during dinner. One or two more after. With a breath she watched him walking to the car. It was barely there, but still it was.

"Maybe I should drive."

Greg laughed. "We're just going to the mansion."

"No. I mean maybe I should drive you home."

"Home?" He jerked backward to look at her. "I'm fine. I barely had anything."

She put her arms around herself and glanced back at the house. "Yeah, well... I'd feel better if we all got home in one piece."

He snorted. "If you drive me home, how are you going to get home?"

There was money in her purse now. Sure there were other things she could get, but none were more important than this. "I'll take a cab. It's no big deal."

Greg looked at his watch. "But it's after 10. You won't get back here until like midnight."

"Yeah, thus, we'd better get going." She walked around the car to him. "Keys."

He was obviously not ready for this confrontation, and he hesitated. However, Maggie wasn't taking no for an answer. Finally he relinquished the keys. As he walked to the other side, she laughed. "But don't go to sleep on me. I'm going to need some directions."

"That was great," Dallas said as they picked up the debris from the party.

"Yeah, except Tracy's stupid comment to Maggie."

Dallas waved that off. "Oh, you know how Tracy is. She talks before she thinks."

Something inside of Keith lodged at the comment. He wanted to say more, but what more was there to say? *I think your friends are inconsiderate snobs?* That was honest, but not very prudent.

"Oh, but didn't Greg and Maggie make the cutest couple?" Dallas cooed. "I told you. He's got a thing for her. I could tell by how he looked at her. You mark my words. Those two are going to get together."

Worse words had never been spoken. At the front window, Keith pulled the curtain back and peered out into the darkness. They were gone. Presumably to the mansion, or would Greg take her back to his place first? That was not an encouraging thought. Keith shook his head. Surely not. That was all the way back into Houston. The timing alone precluded that. Still, he couldn't help but think even if they didn't tonight, if Greg pursued this, it wouldn't be long. That's just the way things worked in their crowd.

"So, Mr. Ayer," Dallas said, wrapping her arms around him from behind before he knew she was there. "What do you say I give you a little preview of June third?" She sidled her way around him and leaned on the windowsill. Softly she reached up and kissed him. There was no doubt she was beautiful. There was no doubt any other man alive would have wanted her. But the sad fact was there was also no doubt that the one woman he really wanted had just left with his best friend. That was the way things were, and although it might kill him, it was time he accepted it.

"Here?" Maggie asked, turning cautiously into the driveway.

"Yeah. Apartment 215 at the end there."

She nodded.

"Just park under the awning."

Again she nodded, guiding the little sports car into a space and with a sigh of relief turning it off. The light from the headlights slashed through the night and died. They were left under the amber nightlight above.

"Thanks for bringing me home," Greg said, putting his gaze the floorboard. "You really didn't have to do that."

"Yeah, well. I'd rather know you're home safe and sound than to worry about if you'd become highway pizza on the way home."

She fought to make her voice light and cheerful. The night had been nice. Greg was a nice date, and overall, she knew it was a night she would remember.

"You can come up," he said, glancing past her to the apartments beyond.

She glanced the direction he'd indicated. "Oh, no. I'd better get home."

"Well, you can at least come up and call the cab."

That hurdle hadn't crossed her mind, but he had a point. "Okay." Nerves like she'd never had before snaked through her as they got out of the car. He started up the stairs first, and she followed.

At the top he opened the door and flipped on the light. She followed him in, her gaze taking in every detail of the room. Clean and neat. Just like him. At the kitchen counter, he grabbed a phonebook and paged through it.

"You got any one you like in particular?"

She shrugged. "It doesn't matter."

After a minute more of searching, Greg reached for the phone, dialed the number, and placed the call. When the cab was on its way, he turned to her. "Would you like something to drink? I don't have much. Water. Milk. Beer."

She scrunched her nose and shook her head. "No thanks."

Greg nodded, and Maggie was pretty sure he already knew what her answer would be when he asked. He walked over to where she was standing, looking like each step might be his last.

"I had fun tonight just so you know."

Her smile was genuine. "So did I."

His gaze dropped between them. "Really? I mean I really felt bad about Tracy and her being so rude to you."

"No, hey. Don't worry about it. I lived. It's okay."

When he looked at her, Maggie's gaze was swept up in his. Between them his fingers brushed hers, and before she knew it, he leaned toward her. It wasn't what she'd expected. Why she didn't know, but somehow him being a nice guy who would call a cab with no pressure and then kiss her before she left wasn't where she thought this night would go. His lips brushed hers but only that. It was nicer than she thought it would be.

Her eyes came open, and she looked up to find him gazing right through her.

"Can I call you sometime?"

Her heart had no other answer. "I'd like that."

The cab ride back was eternal, and Maggie had to fight not to fall asleep the whole way. Once at the estate she paid the driver more than she had thought it would be and then slipped from the cab and around to the back. Quietly she let herself in the kitchen door. Inez had carefully gotten her the message that she would leave it open.

Up the stairs and to her bedroom door she went, but when she was there, she couldn't just go in without checking. Softly she slipped to Izzy's door and opened it. The child in the baby bed was barely visible, yet she looked older than Maggie remembered. "Good night, little one."

Then across the hall to Peter's room. He was curled in a ball, his thumb in his mouth. A question went through Maggie's mind at his posture, but then she thought rationally, she'd never actually seen him in the middle of the night before. Softly she kissed her fingers. "Good night, sweet prince. I love you."

And she tiptoed out.

Five and a half hours later, Maggie was up again. Over and over she stifled the yawns, but she was determined not to let her one day off hurt her job performance. It was back to lessons and lunches, and although the night before had been a nice distraction, this was life.

The day slipped by almost without notice. She was so in-tune with the schedule, it was like it had never been a problem. Even Patty Ann almost smiled when they were down at the dining room door at 5:45, cleaned, pressed, and ready. Dinner went well although Mr. Ayer was not present. Maggie considered asking about that, but she didn't have the courage.

Mrs. Ayer mostly ate in silence, and although Maggie wanted to say something to her, she couldn't think what that something should be. When dinner was finished, Maggie had Peter kiss his mother, and they went upstairs to take baths.

Isabella went through first, and her new favorite word seemed to be "Gie. Gie." It was cute to hear her say it over and over, but Maggie was afraid the others would throw a fit if they heard. So in her best interest, she knelt by the tub, washing off the slick little body. "Say, 'Mommy.' Yeah. 'Mommy.'" She held her lips just right on the Mmm part of Mommy to demonstrate the letter. "Mommy."

"Gie. Gie!" Isabella squealed excitedly.

"No." Maggie laughed. "Mommy. Mmmommmy."

"Gie. Gie!"

"Well, I guess Mommy is going to have to wait 'til tomorrow." She grabbed a towel and dried the first little one off. "Okay, Mister. Mister. Your turn."

Like the trooper he was, Peter stepped forward. Maggie took hold of his shirt and pulled it up. His pants were halfway down when she noticed the dark brown circles on the back of his arm. "Peter, what happened?" Concern drained through her as she gazed at him. "Did you fall?"

Slowly side-to-side his head moved, but his gaze was on the tile.

"What...?" Maggie turned him to the other side, and there were identical marks on his other arm. Gently she turned him to face her. "Peter, who did this to you?"

He wouldn't look at her.

"You can tell me. I won't be mad." Maggie's mind was flying through every bit of training she'd ever had on how to get a child to tell you something they didn't want to tell you.

"Izzy cried," Peter said softly. "I tried to tell her to stop."

"Izzy?" Maggie's gaze went to the baby playing with the towel on the floor. She surveyed the child in one glance. "Was she hurt?"

"No. She got in trouble. I tried to tell her to stop."

"What did she get into trouble for?" Every point in Maggie's body was in full defense and concern mode.

Peter didn't say anything, and Maggie realized the intensity of her voice was scaring him. She forced herself to calm down and breathe.

"It's okay, Peter. Really. You can tell me."

"She was trying to climb the ladder on the playhouse." The words came slow and deliberately. "Ms. Haga got mad."

It was all she could do to keep her emotions from reaching the surface. "Did she hit Izzy?"

Peter's head moved back and forth.

"Did she hit you?"

Again his head moved back and forth.

"Peter, this is important. Did Ms. Haga hurt you?"

His head stopped, and he stood there, staring at the tiles.

Maggie's heart had ceased beating. "It's okay, Peter. I won't get mad. I promise."

"She wanted me to be quiet because I was telling Izzy to stop crying."

Maggie's intensity felt like it might overwhelm her. Still she forced herself to calm down so she could put her hand gently on his back without scaring him. "Peter, did she hurt you?"

When he looked at her, there were tears welling in his brown eyes. "She shook me real hard. I told her I was sorry, but she was really mad. I tried to tell her…"

"Oh, baby boy." And Maggie pulled him into her arms, wishing she had never heard of such a thing as a day off.

Thirteen

Keith had tried every excuse he could think of to get out of going to the Woodlands, but neither Dallas nor Ike would hear any of it. His future was calling, and there didn't seem like much he could do to get out of it.

"This house is so perfect," Dallas cooed from her side of the pickup. She looked so strange sitting there, so out-of-place.

Keith tried not to think about who looked better sitting there. It wasn't easy.

"Do you think we should just put an offer in now, or should we try to haggle with them?" Dallas asked.

"Why don't we just see the house first, and then we'll decide." Put it off. That was his motto. Put it off until the very last possible moment. It was the best he could think to do.

"We're going to go over to the stables," Maggie said to Inez Wednesday afternoon. "I talked to Jeffrey. He said he would come get us and take us over there."

"You're going riding?" Inez asked with concern.

"Ho'sies!" Isabella said.

"I don't know. We'll see. The kids need some fresh air."

"There's fresh air in the backyard."

"Yeah, but there's not ho'sies!" Maggie shot the maid a grin. "Ho'sies!"

With Peter's hand in hers and Isabella planted on her hip, Maggie stepped from the gardener's truck, scanning the area for the Dodge.

"You want me to wait for you?" Jeffrey asked.

"No. That's okay. If they're not here, we'll wait."

He didn't look particularly pleased about that, but he nodded and drove off. In the dust cloud that followed, Maggie stepped, hoping this was the right thing to do. Maybe together they could figure out what to do about Ms. Haga and the little marks. Holding onto both children, she walked into the breezeway of the stables where she listened with every step for voices but heard nothing. At the door to the office, she knocked. A minute she waited. Then she knocked again. "Hello. Anyone here?"

She ducked into the office, which felt good compared with the stifling humidity of outside. "Hello. Keith? Ike?" Still nothing. She glanced back through the breezeway outside. No movement anywhere. Finally she made the decision. "Come on. Looks like we're going to have to wait."

An hour slid by as Maggie held Isabella who played for a little while then fell asleep. There didn't seem to be a good place to lay her down, so Maggie willed her arm not to drop off as she held the sleeping child who got heavier by the minute.

"When is Keith going to get here?" Peter asked clearly losing his patience as well.

"Soon I hope." At that moment her ears picked up the voices in the breezeway, and she froze. Too late to make a new decision, she sat unmoving as the two figures walked into the office.

Ike was all the way in the room before he realized she was there and stopped. His smile at her wasn't altogether happy. "Ms. Montgomery. This is a surprise."

She stood, praying she could get all the way up without falling. "I'm sorry. We were waiting for Keith."

Puzzlement ripped through Ike's gaze. "Keith? Keith went to the Woodlands with Dallas." Ike walked through the office to his desk as a young man, several years younger than Maggie followed him in. At the desk the two talked in quiet tones as Ike handed out the rest of the day's work schedule.

The young man turned to go and at the door tipped his hat to her. "Ma'am."

Maggie stood there, not sure if she should sit or run. She nodded to the young man who ducked out.

"Ms. Montgomery, why are you here?" Ike leaned back in his office chair and surveyed her from head to foot.

She pulled herself up to her full height. "I'm... I need to talk with Keith."

"Keith. Hmm... well, let me give you a little piece of advice about Keith Ayer. Mr. Ayer is not available for your entertainment or your amusement, no matter what you may have been led to believe." His disdain for her dripped from the statement. "Now I don't know what fancy ideas he might have put in your head about things, but let's get one thing perfectly straight, shall we? He's engaged, and chasing after engaged men just doesn't make it very far on the sniff factor around here. Now, I advise you to go back up to the mansion and stay there. I don't want to see you hanging around the stables again because you're just not welcome down here. Got it?"

How she kept from crying, Maggie would never know. Her pride hurt. Her arm hurt. Her heart hurt. Everything about her hurt including her overwhelming desire to help the children. She wanted to tell him that, to tell him this was only about them. Instead she resettled Isabella on her shoulder and squared her jaw. He was just like all the rest of them—condescending and spiteful. "Yeah, I got it. I'm sorry for taking up your time." She grabbed Peter's hand and stumbled from the office, not knowing where she was going or how she was going to get there. Tears blurred her vision so that she wasn't sure she was even going in the right direction, but stopping wasn't an option.

Out into the sun they went, through the dust, and out to the road. Her tears, hot and salty, slid down her cheeks.

"Ma'am!"

The word barely slowed her down.

"Ma'am! If you want a ride, I could take you," the young man from the office said.

Maggie yanked the tears back into her eyes and turned to him as he ran up to her. "Oh, okay. Thank you. That would be great."

It was Friday before Keith managed to make it to the stables again. There was just something about Dallas that made him feel guilty if he wasn't entertaining her at every moment. He walked into the office at eight o'clock and grabbed the feed schedule from the wall. No doubt he was going to get ribbed for missing two days in a row.

"Well, the dead has arisen," Ike said as he and Tanner came into the office. "Nice of you to join us again."

"Yeah. Yeah. Yeah," Keith said, shrugging off the teasing. "I'm going to go check the hay out in the stables."

"Good plan," Ike said and waved him out. "It would be good for you to get something accomplished this week."

With a push out of the office, Keith strode through the stables, looking in to check each horse individually as he did every morning. He was really going to miss this morning ritual when he was chained to some desk in a few months. "Good morning, Dragnet. You're up mighty early." He rubbed a hand over the chestnut's head.

The office door banged, and he looked up. "Y'all all ready to head out for tomorrow?" Keith asked the retreating back of the young cowboy who would presumably take his place once he was gone.

"Oh." Tanner spun on the heel of his boot. "Mr. Ayer. I didn't see you there."

"Sorry." Keith came abreast of him, and they started out. "Anything exciting happen while I was gone?"

Tanner, never one to be quick on the draw with words, hesitated. He glanced back to the office door and then swung his gaze forward again. Even as he walked, it took another long moment for him to say anything. "Well, there was one thing."

Nothing in Keith liked the hesitation or the glance. "Why? What happened?"

"Well…" Tanner glanced back again. "Mr. Jones would kill me if he knew I told you this."

"Well, Mr. Jones doesn't own this place. What do you say, you tell me and let me decide?"

"Well…" It seemed to take a tug of his courage to get the

words out. "The other day, when you were gone, the lady who works at the mansion came by."

"The lady?" Keith was having trouble picturing Patty Ann anywhere near the stables.

"Yeah. The young one with the nice hair. She had the two kids with her."

Instantly Keith was worried. "Maggie? Maggie was here?"

Tanner nodded.

"Why? What did she want? What did she say?"

"I don't know." Tanner shrugged, shrinking back from the weight of responsibility. "Mr. Jones talked to her, and when she left, she was real upset. I think she was going to walk all the way back with them kids, but I took her back so she wouldn't have to walk."

The story twisted and twined through Keith as his brain fought to decide what to do with it. "You don't know what she and Mr. Jones talked about?"

"No, Sir. I just know she was real upset when I took her home."

Keith nodded. "Well, thanks for telling me, Tanner. You did good."

"I hope she's not in trouble. She really seems like a nice lady."

"That she is, Tanner. That she is."

The Dodge pulled to the front of the mansion in a small cloud of dust. Keith hopped out and slammed the door. He stalked to the front door. He needed to know what was going on. Had he been thinking, he would've come up with a less intrusive way to find out. However, he wasn't thinking—not about shoulds and protocol anyway. His only concern was about her, and that thought overtook every other one.

At the door he didn't ring the doorbell, but he was met by Inez just the same. "Where's Maggie?"

Inez looked positively terrified. "Ms. Montgomery? I think she's upstairs. Why?"

"Keith." His father's voice rumbled through the entire mansion. "I need to see you."

"I'm not here on business, Dad."

"Keith!" The name was harsh and sharp. "I need to see you. Now."

Loathing for his whole insufferable life crawled through Keith. "Fine, but this better be quick." He stalked to his father's office, entered, and shut the door. Something told him he didn't want the entire mansion privy to this little discussion.

His father walked around the desk but didn't sit down. "I got a call this morning."

Keith wasn't interested in playing cat and mouse. "And…"

"It was from Bill Hodges." He let the name hang in the air for a moment. "He said somebody had cancelled his contract without notice, and he said we owe him for the remainder of the contract as scheduled whether we accept the deliveries or not."

Anger boiled in Keith's gut. "First of all, you told me to make a decision. I made it. Second of all, we don't owe him a dime. In fact, we paid for three loads that were either late or partial shipments. In my books that means if anything, he owes us. Tell Bill Hodges he's off his rocker if he thinks I'm going to deal with someone who jerks me around and then says it's my fault."

"I'll have you know that Bill is a friend of mine."

Keith was in no mood to coddle. "Then I'd suggest you pick your friends a little better." He turned for the door.

His father sounded like he was about to explode as he cleared his throat. "Have you told Dallas about the other night?"

"The other night?" It took him a moment to frame the reference even as he stopped. Slowly he turned. "You mean Friday? No, why would I tell her about that?"

"Because Keith, you're not in college any more. And you're not in high school. You can't go around cavorting with drunkards and expect your wife-to-be to never find out about it."

"Dad, I'm almost 30 years old. I'm not 16. I can drink if I want to."

"You're not hearing me, Keith. Responsible adults do not stay out all night and come home plastered. You have to get your priorities in order here. Dallas and her family can't have bad publicity over some stupid thing you did."

"I had a few to drink. That's not a crime."

"Make no mistake about this, you get stopped in the shape you were in the other night, and jail is going to look good compared to the hell you will reap from that family, and let me tell you, Lowell Henderson is not one to forgive easily when his name's at stake."

Keith's patience with his father was about to run out, but he held it in two fists just the same. "You don't have to tell me about Lowell Henderson. I've seen him work up close and personal. Now if you'll excuse me."

"Don't you dare make a mistake with this one." His father's menacing tone snaked through Keith. "Dallas deserves better."

That did it. He turned in one swing. "For the love of Mike, Dad! What do you want from me? Huh? What? I've done every single thing you've ever asked! Private school. College. Master's degree. And now I'm marrying Dallas Henderson. I'm moving away, to a house that's six times too big and ten times too expensive. I'm getting a job at a desk that I'm going to hate just so maybe, maybe you'll finally get off my back about not being good enough. And now you're going to stand there, and tell me even this much isn't enough? What am I supposed to do, cut my wrist and bleed so you'll see I'm trying to make this work?"

Hurt laced through him, and he hated that. "I don't know why you don't just say what you're really thinking and get it over with. I'm a disappointment. I have been from day one, and if you could ship me back to the factory and order a new son, you would do it in a heartbeat."

"Keith, you're blowing this out of proportion."

"Out of proportion?" Hurt snapped into raging anger. "This is my life we're talking about here, Dad. I'm sorry I'm not more rational, but I'm kind of dealing with a mountain of junk at the moment." He shook his head. "I don't have to stand here and listen to this."

"I've decided to put Ike in charge at the stables," his father said as Keith stepped out of the door.

Keith turned, very, very slowly. Hurt, anger, resentment, and complete exasperation rained through him. He wanted to scream and yell, but he knew how little that would accomplish. Finally he shrugged. "Well, it's your operation. It always has been. In two months I'm out of here for good anyway. Do whatever you want with it." And without waiting for his father's reply, he stomped out.

At the front door he came a breath away from going out. Then he remembered his original mission, and he turned back for the stairs. Two at a time he climbed them, not caring if it was proper or not. He didn't really care about anything at the moment. They didn't care about him, why should he care about them? At the top, he didn't so much as pause as he headed to the playroom. When he got to the door, he stopped for one second and listened.

Instantly peace and serenity drifted through everything else. He smiled at the lilt in her voice and the happy sounds of the kids. He would have given the world to have what they had now. Quietly he pushed open the door and peered inside. She sat in the chair with Izzy on her lap, reading. It was a scene he wished he could get very used to.

"Maggie," he whispered, and her head jerked up.

Her eyes went wide. "Keith. What…?"

He put his finger to his lips and ducked into the room. The closer to her he got, the more his lungs screamed for air. It was like being sucked into a black hole of exhilarated anticipation. "How's it going?" He sat down on his heel next to the rocking chair. Unconsciously, he ran his thumb under his nose. "I heard you came by the stables the other day."

The depth of Maggie's agony had never reached so low. He was here, and yet he wasn't. Tears jumped into her skull, stinging everything in their path. Ike's words rang in her head, and as much as she wanted it not to be true, he was right. This was Keith Ayer, and she needed to remember that.

"I'm sorry," she said softly. "I just thought maybe we could go riding, that's all."

Keith's face fell into concern. "Tanner said he thought you were upset."

It took everything she had to shake her head and smile. "I just thought… You know. I wasn't thinking. You have enough to do without us coming around to bother you."

"Bother me? What does that mean? You haven't been bothering me. I love having y'all out there."

That makes one of you, she thought, but she was smart enough to know voicing it would be disastrous. "I know, but you have work to do."

He shook his head at that, and his jaw went hard. "Yeah.

Work."

Concern plowed through her on his tone. Her gaze surveyed him. "What does that mean?"

"Nothing." He looked at her and smiled. "Listen. Okay? You three are welcome at the stables any time you want to come." He reached over and ran his hand down Isabella's curls. "I love seeing you."

Maggie nodded, but she knew better. She'd seen reality in bright, living, unforgettable color.

"Are you sure that's all?" He looked like he wanted her to say everything that was in her heart. He was so close, so unbearably close, she was afraid she just might.

"Yeah. What else would there be?"

"What did you say to Maggie?" Keith asked, slamming the office door behind him. He was itching for a fight, and Ike was as good a place to start as any.

"Maggie?" Ike stood and went to the filing cabinet. "I'd say you have more to worry about than some little gold digger like her."

Fury overtook him in a breath, and Keith grabbed Ike by the perfectly pressed shirt and slammed him up against the wall. "What did you say to her?"

Ike's eyes went ice cold. "You're something else, you know that? You've got Dallas Henderson staying in your house, presumably in your bed, and you're all hot and bothered about some little kids' babysitter."

"You say one more thing like that about her, and I swear…"

"Look, Keith." Ike pulled calm to him as he put up his hands to show he wasn't about to take the first swing. "I know, you're freaked out about the wedding. I get that. I can't say I wouldn't be either, but get serious here. You just got demoted from owner to employee, and now you're worried about this?"

"He called already, huh?" Keith backed up. The world seemed to be crashing around him.

"Yes, he did. I've told you he doesn't take kindly to anyone undermining him."

"Undermining…? Whoa. Now just hold it right there. You

agreed with me about the Hodges thing."

"Yes, I did. I still do, but your dad doesn't know that, and so he will take out his displeasure on whoever's name is stamped at the bottom of the order. Besides, this way he can tell Hodges he's taken care of the problem."

The word snarled around Keith's gut.

Ike put his hand on Keith's back, which to Keith wasn't the smartest move anyone had ever made. "Listen to me, Keith. You've got like two months left here, tops. Just lay low and keep yourself out of trouble. The less he hears from you the better. Trust me, in two months you'll be married and far, far away from this place and from him. None of this will even be on the table anymore."

Keith turned, and the ice from Ike's eyes had descended into Keith's heart. "What makes you think then will be any better than now?" As far into the future as he could see, life had no prospect of getting any better than it was at this very moment. "I've got hay to check."

"We're leaving at noon. I expect you to take care of everything while we're gone," Ike called.

"Yeah." Keith walked out. "What else is new?"

Sitting at the counter over a ham sandwich and chips, Keith re-ran the morning through his mind. Ike had said something to her. Of that, Keith had no doubt. But what had he said? How low had he sunk to convince her to stay away? His thoughts traveled back to the party on Monday. Tracy cut Maggie to ribbons, and Maggie never so much as swung back.

He wondered if that's what she was doing now, ducking back and hoping to become invisible so no one would see how hurt she really was. The thought sent an ache through his heart that he wondered if he'd ever before felt. She was hurting, and there wasn't one, single solitary thing he could see to do about it.

"Hey, babe," Dallas said, coming in from the garage with a fistful of packages. "I didn't expect you to be here."

"Lunch time."

She ca-thunked the packages onto the counter. "Oh, hey, Dad called today. He got an interview set up for you in two weeks with

Mr. Ferrell at Devonshire. He said, to emphasize your education and to go easy on the last five years." Dallas walked up and ate a chip from Keith's plate.

"What else did he say?"

"Just that he and Mom will be coming up to Vermont again for graduation. You are remembering graduation, aren't you? May 13. You've got your flight booked and everything?" She ate another chip.

He hadn't even thought about it. "Oh, I was going to do that this week."

She didn't look pleased with the answer. "You need to get that booked. You're going to have to pay triple if you wait too long."

Like she'd ever thought money was a problem for him before.

"Or I guess you could take your dad's private plane up there." That thought seemed to appeal to her as she crunched another chip. "That way we could just fly back together. Yeah, why don't you just do that?"

Yeah. Why didn't he?

Fourteen

"Please make note of the party next Saturday," Patty Ann said, pointing it out on Maggie's schedule. The personal secretary's office in the East wing was so dark and gloomy Maggie had to make herself not shiver at the looming doom that seemed to glare at her from the corners. Worse, it was cold. Ice block cold.

"Okay."

"Mrs. Ayer does not want the children around that night. Nowhere. No how."

That stopped Maggie's nodding. "Where are we supposed to go?"

"The playroom is acceptable, but stay out of sight and absolutely no noise. This is a very important affair. Many of Mr. Ayer's biggest business associates will be in attendance."

Maggie scratched the side of her head. "Okay."

"Mr. and Mrs. Ayer are due to fly out this evening to attend her nephew's wedding on Tuesday."

"Tuesday? Who gets married on a Tuesday?"

"Those," Patty Ann said with exasperation in her voice, "who can afford to be married in a private ceremony in Buenos Aires."

"Ah." Maggie lifted her chin in understanding.

"That's all that you need to be aware of. Everything else is self-explanatory."

Meeting over, Maggie stood.

"Oh, and Ms. Montgomery. Your paycheck."

At least that was getting to be a nice habit.

"May 13," Dallas said, pulling Keith to her as they stood in the terminal. Her eyes danced with the date. "Get that jet fired up. I'll be waiting to see you."

"I wouldn't miss it." His hand felt big on her waist. Where had the I-can't-wait-to-be-with-you feelings he'd had when they first got together gone? Now it was like going through the motions with someone he didn't even know, and as he stood there with her, he wondered if he had ever really known her or if he had been in love with the idea of being in love with her.

She kissed him once more. It was more of a peck really. "And don't forget to call the bank on that house loan like we talked about."

"Got it."

"Oh, and I'll email you the details on the Ferrell thing once Dad sends them to me."

Keith nodded. "I'll be watching for it." He couldn't figure out why she didn't just get on the plane already.

She stopped and gazed right into his eyes. "I love you."

He tried to smile. "Love you."

"Final boarding call Flight 85 to New Haven."

Dallas looked up at the speakers. "That's me." She sighed. "I hate leaving you. You take care of yourself." She readjusted his collar.

"You too."

"I love you, babe."

"Love you, too." With one more kiss, he glanced beyond her to the boarding ramp. "You'd better get, or you're going to miss your plane."

"Okay." She pulled herself away from him and turned. "Bye."

He waved.

"Take care."

He smiled.

"I love you."

And then, finally, mercifully, she was gone. Keith let his eyes go closed as he breathed in what it was like not to have to be somebody else to impress her. Sooner or later she was going to see the truth, and sooner or later she was not going to be happy about that truth. The only question was just how long sooner or later would take to get here.

"Ms. Montgomery, phone call," Inez said that evening when the kids were down for the count.

Maggie swung her legs off her bed and followed the maid down the stairs and into the kitchen. "Thanks."

Inez nodded, snapped off the light, and left.

Dallas was gone. Maggie knew this because she'd heard Inez and Jeffrey talking about it. All day long, she had hoped Keith might make an unscheduled appearance, yet he never had. "Hello?"

"Maggie. Oh, good, I'm glad I caught you."

"Greg?" Her heart fell through the name.

"You remembered."

"Of course I remembered. You have such little faith in my memory. What's up?"

"I was thinking we should get together again. Maybe tomorrow night. What do you say?"

"Oh, Greg." She sat down on the chair in the breakfast nook. "I don't know. The Ayers are gone, and I have no idea when I'll get another day off, but it definitely won't be tomorrow."

"Nights? You don't even have nights off?"

"Not really." Her mind tripped back over the little bruises that had faded from everything but her memory. If it was up to her, she would never have so much as another minute off.

"That sounds like slave labor."

She sighed. "It's not so bad."

"Hmm." He seemed to think through their options, which from Maggie's point of view didn't seem exactly abundant. "Well, you're free now... to talk I mean?"

"Yeah." Softness for him drifted through her. "I'm free to talk now."

"I'll take it."

His parents were gone. Keith knew that. Dallas was also safely back in Vermont. He knew that because she had called when she got there. Sunday morning was his first chance, and he wasn't going to blow this one. He stood on the front steps, pressed and ready for church. All he wanted was to spend a couple of hours with the only person who still represented sanity in his world. He rang the doorbell, and nerves crashed through him. What if she told him no? What if she laughed in his face? He reached to ring it again when Inez opened the door.

"Mr. Ayer?"

"Inez." He ducked, knowing she could as easily as not close the door in his face. His hand found his pants pocket. "Is Mag… Ms. Montgomery here?"

Confusion slid over her face. "Umm, yes. I think she's upstairs."

With his head tilted he looked at her. "Do you mind?"

It took a breath but she opened the door wider. "Go on."

"You're an angel, Inez."

"Yeah, well, they'll strip my wings if they find you here, so be careful."

The thought of church always brought with it a pang of guilt and a pang of regret. Maggie wished she could load the kids into the little Chevette and no one would know. But there was fat chance of that happening. "God, I hope You know I would be there if I could."

A soft knock sounded on the door, and she looked up. Joy jumped through her followed immediately by painful indifference. "Keith."

"Hey. You guys busy?"

He was in his un-Keith outfit again. Nice pants, a button down white cotton shirt that revealed a solid gold chain at his neck. It made her think of Dallas, which made her heart fall even further.

"No, come on in."

"What's up?" He sat down Indian-style on the carpet in front of her.

"We're learning our letters." She pointed to another one.

"P," Peter said with no trouble.

"And what starts with P?" she asked.

"Peter!" he said jubilantly, and she held up her hand for him to slap.

"Very nice." Keith beamed his approval, which Peter obviously soaked up.

For her part, Maggie couldn't look at Keith. It just hurt too much.

"Listen," Keith said, and his gaze drifted over her. She hated the way he looked at her because it always made her think she was doing something wrong by being with him. "I was going to go into church. I wondered if y'all wanted to come with me."

Her gaze jumped to his, and he smiled softly.

"I… I don't know." She looked at her watch. "We don't have much time. I can't get the kids and me ready that fast."

"Then you get you ready, and I'll get them ready." He stood from the floor and reached down for her hand.

Maggie put her hand in his, and gently he pulled her up. When she was standing only a foot from him, the scent of his cologne invaded her senses, and she fought not to get lost in it. "You sure?"

"Positive."

There was no other place Keith was meant to be other than right there, in that little church, holding Isabella with Peter between them. His heart filled his chest as he watched Maggie show Peter how to fold his hands and how to bow his head. He wanted only for her arms to be wrapped around him as easily as she wrapped Peter under her wing and guided him through his prayers.

So many things would've been so very different about Keith's life had that one night not happened. He could see in Maggie all the things he had missed when his mother had died–a calm hand to guide him, a compassionate heart to shield him from the cold, harsh world, a way of peace in an unstable, volatile existence. That's all he now prayed for, some way to find what Maggie so effortlessly gave to Peter.

Keith let his gaze trail to the front. "God, I'm asking here. I don't know how to do this. I see how she is, and I know I want that. But everything is so messed up. Dad's furious. My job's in the gutter. I don't even know if I want to be with Dallas anymore. Nothing is making sense anymore. Nothing."

The congregation sat, and Keith sat with them, resting Isabella on his knee. The little girl snuggled in to his chest and stuck her thumb in her mouth. Just to stay here. He would've settled for that.

"People talk about discerning God's will in their lives," the preacher said. "They talk about not being sure what will find them favor in God's eyes. In Psalms 37:4 and 5 it says, 'Delight yourself also in the Lord, and He shall give you the desires of your heart. Commit your way to the Lord, trust also in Him and He shall bring it to pass.'

"'Delight yourself in the Lord, and He shall give you the *desires* of your heart.' To understand this verse, you must first get hold of what the word 'desire' means. Desire is made up of two parts. 'De' meaning 'of' and 'sire' meaning 'the Father.' So desire literally means 'of the Father.'

"Contrast this with what we often think desire means—our wants, our needs, our plans. That's not what it means at all."

The sermon had Keith's attention, and he shifted slightly in concentration.

"When the Scripture says, 'He will provide you with the desires of your heart,' that means that He will provide you with what He knows you really need—those things that He has put in your heart. Now, what happens a lot of times is we have what seem to be competing desires—two things that are tugging us in different directions. This is where the question of discernment comes in.

"My best advice on this subject is to walk through the doors that He opens for you and stop pounding on the doors that are locked. You may think that door number 2 will lead you to everything you've ever wanted. So you try it, and when you find it locked—it doesn't work out or roadblocks seem to drop from the sky, so you start pounding on the door. Many people pray, asking for what they want to have happen.

"But God..." He pointed upward. "God in His infinite wisdom *knows* that door will ultimately lead you to heartache and pain, so He chooses to keep it locked for your sake. But if you're like me, you just know that whatever's on the other side of that door will lead you to what you want, and so you will pound and kick and bang on that door, sure that it will lead you to what you want.

"And if you're like me, you might even get mad at God for not opening that door. 'God, please, if You'll just let it work out this way...' No." He stopped, his face intense. "No. That's not going for the desires of our hearts, that's not walking in His ways. That's walking in our own ways and asking God to bless it. He won't.

"No. God will never bless what He doesn't instigate. Why? Because He will not bless what is not from Himself. So what's the answer to this dilemma? How do we know what God wants us to do? Simple. You walk through the doors that are open. Quit banging on the ones He has closed. Ask Him to lead you and to guide you and to open up those doors you are supposed to walk through. Then, as the doors open before you, you will know that you are in God's will for your life. And when you get to a door that is locked, know deep down that He locked it for a reason. You may not be able to see that reason right at this moment, but He has your ultimate best in mind, and if you let Him, He will guide you to your ultimate best."

The preacher stepped away from the pulpit. "Let us stand."

Keith stood, but the sermon was on-loop in his brain. *Walk through the doors that are open. Stop banging on those that are closed.* He felt like he'd been banging his whole life. Banging to get his father's approval. Banging to feel whole again. Banging to get someone to notice him just for him. "God, he makes it sound so easy, but it feels so hard. Please help me to know which doors it makes sense for me to go through. I've never needed anything more in my life."

When they got back to the mansion after church, Maggie couldn't get out of the pickup fast enough. His presence was threatening to overload every 'No' circuit she had. Gentle and kind, he was right there the second she needed anything—carrying kids, helping them in, smiling at her in that way that curled her toes. It was starting to frazzle her nerves.

"Hey, why don't you leave the car seats in, go change, and we'll go riding?" Keith asked when Maggie started to remove the car seat from the Dodge.

That slammed her to a stop. "Today?"

He tilted his head to the side. "I'm off. Y'all don't have lessons. Come on. What do you say? It'll be fun."

No! Her head screamed so loud she thought it would explode. The only problem was, it wasn't her head that had the controls anymore. "Okay."

"Y'all good?" Keith asked Maggie as she sat on Nell with Izzy in front of her.

"Great."

How one simple word could make his heart pound, he had no idea. He swung Peter up and then got on Buck. Reins in hand, he turned them and headed out to the waterfall. He hadn't exactly told her where they would be going, but he didn't think she would mind. Just a couple hours to be sane, and then he would find a way to deal with the headache of his life.

To say the falls were breathtaking would've been an understatement. Maggie had the distinct impression that Heaven couldn't be as gorgeous. However, what really stole her breath away was the once again scruffy cowboy riding in front of her. He had traded in his pressed white cotton button down for a green and gray plaid shirt with the sleeves ripped off. Coupled with the bandana and the cowboy hat, Maggie knew she was in for a full day of trying not to stare.

"How'd you do?" Keith asked as he stood at her feet, waiting to help her off the horse.

"Great." Maggie handed Isabella down and then swung her own leg over and off. She felt him standing behind her, his hand out lest she stumble. "I can take her." She reached for Isabella. "Come here, you."

"Gie. Gie!" Isabella squealed happily, and Maggie didn't miss Keith's heart stopping smile.

"I think you've found another fan."

Maggie smiled, took Peter's hand, and they walked over to the shade of the tree near the second shelf of rock. It was so unbelievably peaceful out here, like the rest of the world didn't exist. She sat down and set Isabella on the soft, cool grass beside her. Instantly Isabella rolled, crawled, and then stood. She toddled off just as Keith walked up and swept her up in his arms.

"Where do you think you're going, missy?" He blew on her belly, and then lowered himself to the ground as she giggled appreciatively.

Maggie fell back onto the grass herself. "Oh, I could live out here."

Keith stood Isabella on the grass as Peter sat down next to Maggie.

"You and me both." Keith breathed in the day. "Just that sound."

"It's enough to put you to sleep." She let herself drift away on the lilting splashes of the falls. A yawn danced through her. She hadn't been this truly relaxed in longer than she could remember. Every muscle, every thought. The soft breeze blew a curl across her face, and she brushed it aside. "I think I could go to sleep right here."

"So go to sleep."

Her eyes came open, and she laughed at him. "I'm on duty, remember?"

"Well, I for one think you could stand to take an hour off." He picked up Isabella who was climbing all over him. "Go to sleep. I'll take care of them."

The offer was too good to be true, she thought as another yawn attacked her. If Greg hadn't kept her up so late talking, it might not be such a struggle to stay awake now. "Are you sure?"

"I'm sure. Relax. I've got this."

It was as if two seconds after he'd suggested it, Maggie was asleep. She had rolled to the side, taken her glasses off, and curled up with her face lying on her hand. As he played quietly with the kids, Keith watched her. She was beautiful—especially minus the glasses. They threw harsh lines over a face that was anything but harsh. He wondered about them, and about the car, and about the clothes. It was as if more than the bare minimum meant she had asked for too much.

His thoughts traced to Dallas and over how different they were. It wasn't that Dallas was a bad person exactly, more that she was shallow in ways he couldn't even adequately explain. Even the college education was about how much money she could make with it rather than about following her heart's desire.

Isabella had long since settled into the crook of his arm, and she too was dozing. He looked down at her, and the thought came to him that this was it. His heart's desire. To have a family, raise them, be there for them, hold them at night, tuck them in. It was as simple and as complicated as that. He glanced over at Maggie, and his thoughts traced to Dallas.

Sure, he knew about her dreams of the house and the cars and the jobs, but what about her deeper dreams? What about what she really wanted? Gazing at Maggie, he knew that complicating her life by pursuing her wasn't fair. She was happy where she was, and it was clear from the party that she would never be happy where he had to be.

Still, when he looked down into the now-sleeping eyes of the child in his arms, he couldn't help but wish that things could be so, so different. A life with Maggie. Simple and honest. Family and a few friends. He shook his head at those thoughts. It would never happen, and he was setting himself up for more heartache by thinking that it could.

When she woke up, Keith was sitting with his back to the tree, holding Isabella and taking a nap of his own. She reached over and pulled her glasses on making as little noise as possible. It was nice to have this chance just to watch him. He looked so peaceful and content. Next to his thigh laid Peter. The three of them made a picture she knew she would remember forever.

It occurred to her then what a good older brother he was and in almost the same thought what a good dad he would make some day. Strong and sure. Gentle and loving. Dallas was one lucky woman. Maggie's heart panged at the thought.

At that moment he stirred and opened his eyes. His smile was slow but obvious. "How long have you been awake?"

"Few minutes. You have a good nap?"

He took a long breath. "Yeah." He leaned his head first one way then the other to get the kinks out. "Whew. I haven't done that in awhile." His gaze found hers, and there was no awkwardness anywhere to be seen. "I take it things are going good at the mansion."

She shrugged. The thought of telling him about Peter crossed her mind, but she crossed it off again instantly. There was nothing he could do, and getting him in the middle of it was pointless.

"Okay." She rolled onto her back so she was looking up at the sky. "Keep the kids occupied and out of sight. That's about the extent of it."

There was no response, and she let her head fall to the side so she could look at him. She brushed an errant strand from her face. "So did you get put in the closet for parties when you were little too?"

Confusion traced across his face. "In the closet?"

"Yeah, like 'we don't want to hear from them or see them no matter what.'" She deepened her voice in emphasis.

His face fell in concern. "Did they tell you that?"

She rolled to her stomach. "Basically. Apparently they are having some ultra-important party next Saturday. I think Patty Ann may lock us in the playroom to keep us from ruining it. I just hope she doesn't throw away the key." Maggie laughed at her own joke.

However, Keith wasn't laughing. "They're banishing you?"

"Banishing. Yep. I'd say that's a pretty good word for it." She picked up a blade of grass and twisted it through her fingers. Then she rolled back onto her back. "It could be worse. We could be invited like last time."

There was a long pause during which the only sound was the waterfall.

"Or you could escape altogether," he said softly.

That brought her around to look at him. "Escape? Yeah, right. They'd have my head."

"Not if they knew where you were escaping to." He smiled.

She was intrigued and just a little more than concerned. "Such as...?"

"My place?"

The suggestion smashed through her, and Maggie shook her head, sending the strands of hair spiraling through the breeze. "No. You don't want us. Besides how would I put the kids to bed?"

He shrugged, and it brought her attention to his sleek, tanned arms. "I have two extra rooms that nobody uses. We could put Izzy on the floor. Peter in the bed. You could take the room right next to them."

The words were like a torrent, one coming as fast as his light southern drawl would let them.

"Y'all could come over early. We could make supper. Watch a movie..."

"Hold…. Hold on." She waved her hands to get him to stop. Then she pulled up to her knees. "You're not serious?"

But he never wavered. "Yes, I am. Please, Maggie. Please. Let me do this for you."

It was the epitome of stupid. "You sure you won't mind?"

"No way. I think it will be fun."

Fifteen

Keith grabbed the phone on the third ring. "This is Keith."

"Hey, dude, are you not picking up your messages again? What is up with you and not returning my calls? You're going to give me a complex if you don't watch it," Greg said with a laugh.

"Not my fault. Some of us have to work," Keith said, shifting the cell phone to his other ear as he hauled a slab of hay through the stables to Dragnet's stall. "What're you up to?"

"Numbers. Clients. Problems. Same as always. You?"

"Horses. Hay. Problems. Same as always." He threw the hay over the gate and stopped only a second to pat the horse. "Haven't heard from you in awhile."

"Aren't you lucky?"

"Hey, you said it, not me."

"I guess you got Dallas to the airport and back home in one piece."

"You know me. Mr. Responsibility," Keith said, dragging two more slabs off the bale of hay.

"Seems that part comes and goes as I remember."

"Oh. Uh-huh. Hello, pot, this is the kettle calling." He slung those slabs over the gate to Buck.

"Well, you may have a point there," Greg said. "Considering I got driven home the other night, that might not be too far from the truth."

"Driven home? When?"

"The other night," Greg said as if Keith already knew. "After your party."

Keith stopped and leaned against the graying wood of the

stables. He took his hat off and wiped his forehead. "After the party? What're you talking about? Who drove you home?"

There was a pause.

"Well, if you must know. Maggie took me home."

Even the hat stopped. "Maggie?" A picture of her lying in the afternoon sun traced through him. "Why did Maggie take you home?"

"I don't know. She didn't trust me to drive, I guess."

"She took you all the way into Houston?" Panic rose in him with each question.

"That's where my home is."

"I know that. Why did you make her drive you back? If you didn't think you could drive, you should've asked me."

"Hey, dude, I didn't make the decision. She did, and believe me, I wasn't going to go back up to your door and ask you to take me at that point."

Keith thought back to that night, trying to remember if Greg had been that bad off. Surely he would've noticed if he was. Then the thought occurred to him that Greg was taking Maggie home at the time. If he was that bad and Keith let her get in that car…

Then another thought occurred to him. "Wait a minute. How'd she get home?"

"We called her a cab. She wouldn't take no for an answer."

"But it had to have been… what? Midnight or better when she got home."

"That's what I kept trying to tell her, but I'm telling you that lady's got a will of steel."

That much Keith knew.

"I think I'm going to ask her to our company picnic," Greg said.

"Oh, when's that?" Keith asked as if he was still breathing.

"Saturday after next. The fifteenth. I hope she'll come. We really had a good time together the other night."

Keith thought asking the next question just might kill him. "So you haven't asked her yet?"

"No, we talked the other night until like midnight, but it was just general stuff. My work. Her work. College."

This conversation was making Keith nauseous. "Listen, man. I've got to get back to work or Ike's going to skin me alive when he gets back tomorrow."

"K, but don't be a stranger."

"I couldn't get any stranger, could I?"

"Hey," Greg laughed. "You said it not me."

They signed off, but it took Keith a full minute to get his body to move again. Greg was going to ask her out again. That was bad news. They had talked until midnight. That was very bad news. Well, it was good news, but as good as it should have been, it hurt like everything. And then there was the whole issue of her taking Greg home. What did they do when they got to his place?

Keith knocked that thought away with a solid thwack. He didn't want to hate Greg. Greg had been there through some of the toughest times of Keith's life, but how do you watch the woman you are falling in love with walk off into the sunset with the man who has been your best friend for 15 years? They were questions with no answers. Finally, with no better option Keith pried himself from the wall. There was work to be done. That was the only thing that didn't seem to be complicated any more.

Keith was sprawled out next to the jack on the spare trailer Tuesday afternoon, fixing another flat with a patched tire. At the rate they were going, they could outfit NASCAR with all the tires he'd changed in the last month. He needed to go in and get some new ones. He needed to get the track watered down. He needed to feed the horses. Truth was, he needed help because he was about to crack trying to do it on his own.

"Well, it looks like the operation hasn't completely fallen apart," Ike said, putting his cowboy boot on the trailer's running board as Keith fitted the repaired tire on and spun the lug nuts.

"Not on my watch." Keith yanked himself to his feet, rubbing the dirt from his hands with the rag. The dirt didn't move much, and he replaced the rag in his back pocket. He grabbed the wrench. "We've got to budget for some new tires. These are about to kill me."

"Put in a request," Ike said. "I'll take it up with the manager."

Keith stalked by him back to the tire. "I just did."

"Aren't you going to ask how we did?"

"Fifth," Keith said. "I can read you know."

"Gee, you're in a good mood."

"Huh. I wouldn't know why. You leave me here with six thousand things to do and no help."

"Hey, Mr. Ayer, how's it going?" Tanner asked, stepping up.

"It would be better if I had some help with this tire."

"Oh. Sorry. I didn't realize. Here. I'll get these." Tanner bent down and started twisting on the lug nuts.

"See, that's what I mean," Keith said, indicating Tanner. "You should hire four more of him."

"Put in a request."

Keith glared at him. "I just did."

Maggie hadn't heard a word from Keith since he'd dropped them off on Sunday. She knew that was for the best, but it didn't feel like it was. Thursday night Inez knocked at her door after the kids were asleep. "Phone."

Maggie knew who it was, but who it was wasn't who she wanted it to be. She tramped down stairs to the phone. "Hello?"

"Hey, Maggie. How's it going?" Just as she thought. Greg.

She dropped onto the chair. "Good. How about you?"

"Well, I'll be even better when you say, 'Yes.'"

Her head came up from her hand. "Yes about what?"

"About going with me next Saturday."

She bit her bottom lip. "Where?"

"To my company picnic. They have it every year. We go to the park and eat cold chicken. It's very romantic."

"Be still my beating heart."

"So you'll go?"

Trepidation trounced through her. "I don't know. I'll have to find somebody to baby sit."

"How about their parents?"

She laughed. "Like I said, I'll have to see."

They were going to have to quit talking until all hours, Maggie decided Friday morning as she yawned at herself in the mirror. Six hours of sleep was doing nothing for her sanity. Still, it was nice to have a friend. It was nice of him to listen. The picnic sounded fun except for the part about leaving the kids and the part about what he might expect from her afterward.

This would be their second official date, and at some point the laws of dating had to kick in. She thought about asking Keith for his assessment of Greg's intentions. It sounded like it should sound like a good idea. The problem was, it didn't. She didn't want to talk about Greg with Keith. Just like she didn't want to talk about Keith with Greg. It was very complicated and getting more so by the second.

"The cavalry has arrived," Keith said, ducking into the playroom at four o'clock on Saturday. He'd had to tell Ike he was going into town for supplies. Town and supplies would have to wait. Right now, he had more important things to do.

"Oh, hallelujah. I thought you forgot," Maggie said, launching off the carpet.

"Me? Forget? Never." He arched his chin. "Come on. Let's get out of here while the gettin's good."

Quickly Maggie gathered up the pillows and blankets, and the two little suitcases. Inez knew where she was going. She hadn't really had the guts to tell anyone else.

Keith swung Isabella to his hip and took Peter's hand. "Ready?"

"Let's do it."

Out the door, down the back stairs, through the kitchen that was filled with catering staff, Keith led the way looking like a Mission Impossible operative. Maggie wasn't arguing. If they got caught, there was no telling what might happen.

His pickup was parked just outside the tree line on the road. She carried the contraband and threw it into the pickup. Keith wasted no time getting the two kids in, and within two minutes they were gone.

"Whew," Maggie said, sighing in real relief. "That's a little too much intrigue for my taste."

He grinned. "What? You're not planning to join the CIA?"

"Unless that stands for the Children In America fund, no." Before she was even settled, they pulled up at the guesthouse.

He guided the pickup around to the back and parked it in the garage. Then he looked at her. "And now the fun begins." It was a good thing it was a two-car garage because the pickup wouldn't have fit in a single car garage. The garage though functional was spotless—auto equipment on one side; lawn care on the other.

Maggie got out of the pickup and pulled Isabella out as well. She stood the little girl on the concrete. Then she collected the overnight things from the front. Keith was already standing at the door to the house.

He scooped Isabella up. "Come here, you."

She squealed as he put two well-placed fingers into her side and tickled her. Then he flipped her over his shoulder, catching her feet.

"I brought the potatoes," he said over his shoulder at Maggie. "I hope you brought everything else."

Happiness danced through Maggie. He looked so carefree and peaceful, just as he had leaning against the tree at the waterfall. In the kitchen he swung Isabella to the floor and flipped his hat to the counter. Underneath was the familiar navy bandana.

"There's some blocks in the living room I got out, and for our viewing pleasure." He held up a *Nemo* DVD. "Oh, here." He reached for the stuff Maggie still had in her arms. "I'll put this down here."

She followed him down the hall, admiring how well kept the house was. She hadn't really had much chance to look around on either of her first two trips here. Now she took her time, glancing into rooms as they walked.

"My office," he said as he passed the first room. "The bathroom. Your room." He smiled at her. "For tonight." At the end of the hall, he turned into the last room. "And the kids' room."

It wasn't huge, but it was a nice size. Bigger certainly than anything she'd ever slept in until she'd made it to the mansion. "Nice." She walked to the large window overlooking the trees in the direction of the mansion.

"It's not the mansion," he said as if he was apologizing for that.

She turned to him. "It doesn't have to be."

His gaze fell from her to the things in his hands. "What do we do with these?"

"Here." She took them from him and laid them out across the floor next to the window. Peter's stuff and then Isabella's stuff. She'd packed clothes for church too in case he happened to suggest it. "Here's Peter's blanket. Put that on the bed." She handed over the blue and yellow flannel blanket. "And here's Izzy's." The pink blanket was twined through Isabella's suitcase handle, and it took Maggie an extra tug to get it free. Without really looking at him, she handed it over too. Then she planted her hands on her hips to survey the layout. "I think that's it."

He laid the pink blanket out on the carpet. "Cool. What time do you want dinner?"

Maggie almost started laughing. "You mean we don't have to be washed and ready fifteen minutes early? We won't be inspected? Oh, my. I don't know whatever we shall do. We might not know how to act."

"They keep you on a pretty tight leash up there, huh?"

"That's one way to say it." She stepped past him out the door. "Those two will never know how to make a decision for themselves. Everything is planned down to the second. It's crazy."

At the living room end of the hallway, she stepped to the side to let him lead. Although she'd expected him to go to the kitchen, he walked to the living room where Peter and Isabella were playing quietly.

"Let's see who can build the biggest tower!" Keith said excitedly joining in the fun on the floor. "Pete, you and me against Maggie and Izzy. Ready?"

Maggie barely made it onto the carpet without crashing. "Hey, now. You've got to give us a chance."

"Oh, yeah?" Keith's gaze danced at her. "Go."

Maggie laughed as she grabbed blocks from the center of the floor. He was the most alive person she'd ever been around, and life with him present was filled with it.

Two hours later they stood in the kitchen together. Taco meat sizzled in the skillet as he moved around the kitchen that couldn't be called small except his presence made it feel that way. It was strange because he wasn't tall, and he wasn't even all that big, but he was solid. Solid shoulders. Solid thighs. Solid arms. Solid in body and heart. And his presence had a way of filling every room he entered.

"Tacos and carrots," Maggie said as she stood at the stove, stirring the food in the pans. "What a combination."

"I didn't think Iz could eat the shells," he said as if once again he was apologizing.

"Hey," Maggie said over her shoulder. "I was teasing. You did good."

He seemed to soak the compliment in. "I got some extra spicy and some mild for the tacos. I didn't know what you liked."

"Mild. You put extra spicy in that stuff, and I'll have smoke coming out of my ears."

His smile lit his face. "That could be interesting."

"Says you." She pulled her wrist up. It was almost six-thirty. "We're going to have to hurry. Those two are going to really get thrown off-schedule."

He split the meat into two pans and put the contents of the two packages in, stirring each as he did so. "Oh, that would be such a tragedy."

She laughed. "It's okay. I'll just blame you."

Stirring slowly, he shrugged. "Wouldn't be the first time."

At first she thought he was slamming himself, but when she looked at him, his wink made her remember when he really had been blamed for something she did. The timer on the stove went off.

"Here. Back up. The shells are ready." He put an oven mitt on his hand to get the cookie sheet out.

She shook her head, fighting not to laugh. When the cookie sheet was on the potholder on the cabinet, he turned and caught her expression.

"What?"

"You. Is there anything you can't do? You cook. You throw parties. You clean yogurt off of curtains."

"I'm a man of many talents."

"I can see that."

"Is that ready?"

"As it'll ever be."

"Dinner time!"

When the food and plates had been transferred to the table, and Peter and Izzy were settled in their seats, Keith sat down and watched Maggie sit across from him. There was no describing that feeling. It filled him all the way to the top with a happiness and a peace he couldn't remember ever feeling. It was so different than sitting here with Dallas. That felt empty and awkward. This felt real. More real than anything he'd ever experienced. "Maggie," he said, watching her.

She smiled at him and held her hands out to the children on either side of her. Two little hands in hers, two in his, and she bent her head. "Dear Father in Heaven, we praise You for all the wonderful things You have graciously put into our lives. Help us never to take them for granted. We love You and we praise You. Amen."

His amen was husky. It was just so hard to get enough air in for the words to sound normal. Reaching across the table, he picked up Peter's plate and started filling it as she filled Izzy's. "So." He had to clear his throat to get more out. "Are we going to church tomorrow?"

She was intently filling the plate and didn't so much as glance at him. "I brought their clothes, and I told Inez we might."

So she'd thought they might as well. Something about that sent his spirit soaring. If this could just all be for real. That was the one and only thing that could make this feeling any better.

A movie. Popcorn in the living room. It was like the life Maggie had always dreamed of having but never thought would come. The kids sat on the floor in front of the television. Maggie sat on one side of the couch, and Keith sat on the other.

"I didn't know you were a Nemo fan," she said teasingly.

"I told you, I'm a man of many talents."

"Cool. I think I'll bring Barney over on Monday."

He smiled as he put a now-shower cleaned arm over the couch back. She did the dishes. He took a shower. It all felt so normal. The only thing she would've asked now was that he could be sitting beside her, with that arm around her. Something told her that would feel even better than this did.

"I don't know. I might draw the line at Barney."

"I don't blame you. He even gets on my nerves."

"Shhh." Peter said. "The movie's starting."

Keith laughed softly. "Shh," he mouthed to her. "Behave."

"Me?" she mouthed back. "You behave."

"I didn't start it."

"Oh, yeah? Well, I'm going to finish it if you don't watch it."

He raised his eyebrows. "You're getting very brave."

Heat flamed to her face. Why did he have to look so handsome? It was getting harder and harder to keep her heart from going on little trips with her in his arms as the world slipped by. She grabbed a pillow, anchored it to her chest, and pointed at the television. "Watch the movie, and behave yourself."

The only good thing that could be said about the bathroom by the time bath time was almost over was that water could be cleaned. The floor was covered in it. Maggie, too, was covered in suds and water from Izzy splashing bubbles and rubbing them all over the white and gray marble tub sides. By the time Keith brought Peter in, the bathroom was awash in water and suds.

"You look like a scrubbing bubble," Keith told her, scraping a small handful of suds from her hair.

"It's not my fault," she said as Izzy started pounding on the water again, sending suds in 70 directions at once. Maggie tried to wipe them off her face with her sleeve, but it was unclear how successful she was. "Iz. Ugh. Come on. Stop that."

"I take it the bubble bath was a hit," he said from his position on the floor where he was removing Peter's clothing.

"You could say that."

Once again Izzy started squealing and whacking the water. Suds flew in all directions.

"Grr. Okay, you. That's enough fun for one night." Maggie stood and grabbed a towel; however, still sitting in the tub, the child was covered with suds from every angle. "Oh, great. Now how are we going to get you cleaned off?"

"Here." Keith stood and reached up to release the removable

showerhead. "You pick her up. I'll hose her off."

Seeing no better way to do it, Maggie did as instructed. "Okay, but you be careful with that."

He grinned. "Me? I'm always careful."

"Uh-huh. Yeah, right. Well, you remember that." She lifted Isabella who was even more slippery from the suds than she normally was. Holding the child up, Maggie shrank back so he wouldn't get her completely soaked as he angled the water at the child. Isabella squealed and kicked. "Hey, now. You're hard enough to hold onto when you're not doing that."

The spray from the hose drizzled up onto Maggie's glasses. "Hello. Now I can't see."

"Oh, here, let me fix that." Keith angled the hose around Isabella so that it sprayed Maggie's arm higher, drizzling water all over her.

"Hey! Are you kidding me? I'm not the one taking a bath here!"

"Isabella," Keith said as if he was mad. "You shouldn't get Maggie all wet like that."

Isabella squealed and kicked, and on the floor Petter giggled. Maggie's heart lifted at the sound even as she fought to be mad at him.

"Finished." Keith shut the water off. He stepped back, but Maggie was still covered with water droplets and holding a dripping wet, kicking baby.

"Hello. Some help here. Towel please."

He laughed as he pulled the soft taupe towel up from her knees. However, when it was in his hand, he stopped as he looked at them. "Who should I dry off—you or her?"

"Let's start with her." Maggie turned, and Keith covered Isabella in the towel.

"How you ever manage to do this without me every night is beyond me," he said with a wink.

"Yeah, it's completely unbelievable." But she wasn't mad. She was having the time of her life. She took Isabella, wrapped in the towel, in her arms.

"Oh, here. You're wet." He put his fingers on either side of her glasses and removed them.

"I wouldn't know why." She rubbed her face in Izzy's towel. Then she lifted her face for him to replace the glasses.

When they were on, he gazed at her. "Perfect."

The moment froze, and it was as if suddenly she couldn't move. Her breath filled her throat as she gazed into his soft hazel eyes. *Move!* her brain screamed, but she couldn't. It was as if her body had short-circuited. "I'll… I'll just go get her ready."

"Yeah. I'll give Pete a bath."

However, neither one of them moved. His eyes held so much that she couldn't get enough of them. Hope, happiness, an offering of a life different than any she had ever lived. Then Isabella kicked in Maggie's arms, and Maggie's attention dropped to her. "Okay. Okay. Let's go."

As Maggie walked out, Keith watched her. That was it. Her. That's all he ever wanted. Every second he was with her confirmed that fact, and every second he was without her was spent wondering how long it would be before they could be together again.

Shaking off the thoughts, he bent down and swept Peter from the carpet. "Come here, you. It's your turn."

Sixteen

Isabella was asleep on her little pallet on the floor. Peter was tucked into the big bed. Maggie stepped over to the bed, and Peter's gaze drifted to her.

"Where's Keith?"

"Oh." The question took her off-guard, and she glanced back at the door. "I don't..."

"I'm here," Keith said, pushing the door to gently. "You didn't think I'd miss prayers, did you?"

Maggie couldn't get all the emotions lined up in logical order in her heart. It would've all been so easy if he had just not been Keith Ayer, and minus the hat and the bandana, it was hard not to notice that he was. Pushing those thoughts away, at the bed she knelt on one side, and her heart flipped over when Keith knelt on the other. He reached across the mattress for her hand, and with her heart doing somersaults through her, she laid her hand in his. Strength and safety flooded through her spirit as he held her hand, his thumb gently stroking her knuckle.

Praying under these conditions was more than she could do. Just to get a word out was impossible. Closing her eyes, she willed her mind to stay with her. "Dear Lord, please be with us tonight. Keep us safe, and help us all have a good night sleep. Please keep all the boys and girls in the world safe, and help them all to have a good night. Amen."

The two amens blended together, and they yanked tears to her eyes. She sniffed them back and pushed up to her feet. Anchoring her gaze on Peter, she smiled lest it betray her by following Keith up and around the bed. "Get some sleep."

Peter nodded and snuggled down into the covers. She put her fingers to her lips, kissed them, and put them on his forehead. "Good night, sweet prince." She was careful not to trip on Isabella on her way to the door where Keith was already waiting. Ducking, she stepped past him and out into the hall.

Her steps took her to the door of her room. Spending more time with him than she had to was dangerous to her heart and to her sanity.

"You going to bed?" he asked, sounding strangely disappointed.

She had her arm anchored to her middle. "I'd better if we're going to get to church tomorrow."

He looked as if he was going to protest, but he just nodded. "Okay. See you in the morning."

As absurd as it sounded, Maggie was a little disappointed he didn't stop her. But then, that was nuts. She went into her room and pulled her little duffle bag from the floor. The only piece of clothing she had bought on her disaster of a shopping trip was a decent pair of pajamas. She pulled them and the matching robe out of the bag and put them on. The soft blue satin slid across her skin. How life had changed in the last month.

Ready for bed, she climbed into the low-rise sleigh bed. Her prayers slid through her with no effort. Her parents, Mrs. Malowinski, the kids, the Ayers, and then his name as it always did, found its way into her mind. "God, please help me find a guy as nice as Keith. That's all I ask." She laid there, replaying the evening in her mind. Start to finish it had been perfect.

Her mind traced over Peter and Izzy sleeping in a strange house, and concern drifted through her. Peter wasn't the most tranquil child on the planet. He probably hadn't slept outside his own room ten nights since he'd been alive. She had this horrible vision of him lying there all night, listening to the scary sounds of a strange house as she had in each new house she slept in when she was a child. And he would do that, too, lie there all night, scared out of his mind and never come get her. That was the kind of kid he was.

She listened to the sounds in the house to see if Keith was awake. However, the hum of the dishwasher was the only one. Slowly, quietly, she swung her legs out of the bed and grabbed her robe. It wouldn't hurt to check on Peter once more. She went to the door and slid it open. She looked up and down the hall. Nothing. A step and she was in the hallway. Two more and she was at the children's door, her hand securing her robe at her stomach. Softly she twisted the knob and pushed it open.

So she wouldn't have to risk making noise to get it open again, she left it ajar an inch and stepped into the room. Isabella, thumb in mouth, lay on the floor. Her little eyes were closed with the dreams behind them. Maggie smiled at the sight. Then she stepped twice more and found Peter, too, already asleep. To her, that could only mean one thing—that he felt as safe here as she did. That thought slid through her.

Grateful tears swept over her heart. Peter deserved to feel safe. They all did. She let her hand brush the comforter as she turned, intending to head back to the door, but the glow at the window stopped her. Intrigued, she stepped over to it, trying to determine the origin of the soft glow in the nighttime sky.

The thought hit her. The party. Yes, it would be going on up on the hill beyond. The break in the yard trees allowed the glow to be visible only in pieces but it was there just the same. Thoughts and memories swarmed through Maggie, and she pulled her arms to her chest to deflect them. One hand rubbed slowly up the other arm as she stood there, lost in yesterday, gazing into it as if it was right there in front of her.

Keith was on his way back to his room from getting a drink when he noticed that the kids' door wasn't shut. That was odd. His first thought was Peter. Maybe he had already gotten scared and had gone to find someone to make it better. However, with a glance, he realized that Maggie's door was shut tight. Something wasn't right, but he decided to check it out before he bothered her.

With the lightest touch on the kids' door, it opened, and there in the pale light of the window stood Maggie. The waves of hair, the curves—there was no one else it could be. His heart snagged on the sight. There was something so intimate about it, as if she knew no one knew she was there. For a moment he thought about leaving before she knew he was there, but then he heard the soft sniff of overwhelming ache, and concern traced through him. Wanting not to scare her but to help just the same, he stepped into the room and over to where she stood. "Maggie?"

She turned to him, and the anguish in her eyes overtook his heart with the hard whack of a two-by-four across the chest. Her face contorted, and she closed her eyes, squeezing them to stop the pain, but it squeezed out tears instead. They rolled down her cheeks on the paths others had already made.

"Maggie, what's wrong?"

She didn't answer. The words seemed to jam without ever making it to the air.

It was all he could think to do. "Hey. Shh. Come here." He pulled her into his arms and vowed to hold her there until all the tears were vanquished.

Maggie knew she should pull away. It wasn't right for her to be here in his arms, soaking in his strength as her grief poured out of her heart. But the truth was she needed him right now, more than she had ever needed anyone. The memories were too much for her to bear alone. They were too heavy, and too overwhelming.

So many nights spent thinking about the one that had changed hers forever. So many days spent trying not to think about it. With her head on his chest, she let her tear-blurred gaze drift out to that glow in the night sky beyond the trees, and the grief hit again. She pulled her hand to her mouth, trying to get her brain to stop thinking. The tears were going to drag her down until she might never get to the top of them again.

Still, gently, solidly he stood, just holding her and letting her grief run its course. Her thoughts bounced back and forth from present to past as waves of anguish gushed over her. It was a night, just like this one. Early spring. It was a party, just like that one. The social event of the season. The man. She'd never had a name for him—just the man. He'd partied, and then he left and changed her life forever.

Sorrow reached up and yanked a sob from her, and suddenly she couldn't breathe. Thinking ceased, and feeling took over. And oh, the feelings she'd thought were buried so deep—anger, hurt, fear, grief, sorrow. The sorrow was the worst of them because it was the one that couldn't be controlled. She had known that almost from the very beginning.

It was the one that would never let her go if she ever let it to the surface, and now it was here, dragging her down into its undercurrent, yanking at her with a grip that said it would never let her go. Another sob wrenched free, and Maggie had the horrible sensation that she was drowning in the grief. Her knees went weak beneath her, and the only reason she was still standing was because he was holding her up.

"Shhh," he said, and she realized he was stroking her hair. "Shhh." His hand on her hair felt so good, so soothing. His arm around her felt like strength itself.

Every rational part of her said she should pull away that he was going to think she was a complete idiot, but her legs wouldn't move and her body felt shaky and weak. Tired washed through her spirit, taking rational thought with it. She let her will melt into the fatigue. Life itself slipped away from her grasp, and she let go and watched it leave. They were gone. They were really gone, and they were never, ever coming back.

Her grief gave way to a blank numbness as she sniffed and wiped at the tears. She pulled in air in short little gasps and sniffs. Still, he didn't let her go.

"Come on," he said softly, and she nodded, why she didn't know. All she knew was that, here, with him, she was safe. He would take care of life while she was unable to. That was comforting although she couldn't really put it all into words as to just why.

His arm never left her as he guided her out the door and down the hallway to the living room. Once there, he sat down with her on the couch. She leaned into him, her grief over-spilling its banks again. He didn't question it, he just held her until this spasm too had past.

"Do you know what I remember?" she asked, and it was as if she didn't feel any need to start at the beginning.

"What's that?"

"I remember waking up the next morning and wondering why they hadn't come." She shook her head. "I don't even remember the night before. I've tried, but I really don't remember them leaving. I was going to stay at a friend's house, so it really wasn't a big deal. But I remember waking up on that couch the next morning and wondering why I was still there and not in my bed."

She let out a soft laugh. "It's weird. I can still picture that room. Man, it's like it was yesterday. It was yellow. Not like a bright yellow but a really pale, mustard yellow, and the curtains were white so there was this really intense kind of light everywhere. It's weird because I thought for a moment I must be in Heaven, and then I realized I wasn't."

Her mind let the memories come freely. She felt no need to edit them. "I laid there for like the longest time trying to figure out why I wasn't in my bed. I don't know that I had ever not waked up in my bed, so it was weird, you know? And then I remembered they were supposed to come get me. They'd told me eleven or something like that. But here it was morning, and they still weren't there to get me."

She squinted into the memories, trying to pull them up, but they'd been buried so long, it was difficult. "I don't know if I even knew something was wrong at that point or not. I just thought there must've been a mix up." Her heart snagged on the next memory. "But when I walked into that kitchen, and Mrs. Davidson was sitting at that table." She let out the memory in a slow exhale. "When she looked at me…" Maggie had to take a breath on the memory of the woman, her eyes red and tear-stained. That look. That one look had changed her life.

"Everything happened so fast after that. There were all these people around, and everyone was talking all quiet. I really didn't understand what was going on. Just that I was alone, and Mom and Dad weren't there. And then even the other people left. They all left." She stopped. Thoughts that had been there her whole life although she had never said them out loud came through her. "You know, I've always wondered what would've happened if he'd have left two minutes later. Just two minutes. Everything would've been so different."

"Your dad?" Keith asked, and the sound of his voice surprised her. She jerked her head up and then lowered it because she was having too much trouble dealing with the past to deal with the present too.

"No." In a strange way, she'd never thought about the fact that her parents could have left later. Somehow that had never occurred to her. They were right where they should've been. It was the other guy who shouldn't have been there. "The guy that hit them."

Keith absorbed that blow. For no real reason, he had never realized there was another driver involved. "It was his fault?"

On his chest, she nodded. "He was drunk."

The breath he had been taking vanished. In its absence a hundred thousand pieces of things she had told him and things she hadn't fell into place. He wanted to say something, but nothing would come. Her world had been ripped apart by someone else's thoughtlessness, and in the next second the understanding of how many times that could have been him smashed into him. How many times had he told his friends he was perfectly fine to drive when the reality was he really wasn't? How many bars had he left, never thinking of whose life was between him and home? Too many. That was for sure. "So do you know what happened?"

She was shaking a little, cold he suspected, so he reached over and pulled the little throw blanket from the couch edge. Gently he put it around her, the blanket sliding easily over the soft blue material of her robe. Once it was there, he slid his hand up and down her arm for reassurance that he was still there.

"He ran a stop sign," she said softly. "There were no skid marks at all. They were both killed instantly. It was just a mess of smashed metal when it was over—nothing recognizable at all."

"So you saw the car?"

Inexplicably she shook her head. "That's what everybody said, but they never took me to see it." Her voice sounded hollow as if there was no feeling beneath the memories. "It's so weird. I've gone through that night a million times in my head. Sometimes I'd wake up in the middle of the night, and I'd try to picture the accident. Who was where. How dark it was. The lights. The sounds. I don't know. It's like if I could find something that could've been changed, something that didn't add up, it would bring them back like it never happened. Like if I could somehow find some evidence that God had overlooked that He would have to reverse His decision and let them come back."

She exhaled at that thought. "Pretty stupid, huh?"

"No. You're just trying to make some sense out of something that doesn't make any sense."

The hollowness returned to her voice and her breathing. "He was supposed to get time." She squinted into the memories.

"Manslaughter something, but he paid his way out of it."

Once again, Keith's breathing snagged on the statement. "He walked away?"

She nodded. "Just like I did. Only I never got over it." Her hand pulled the robe's belt out slowly and then let it drop. "I wonder if he ever did."

The story wound through Keith, pulling up memories as it went. "That's why you drove Greg home."

"Huh?" Her head moved, and this time she sat up although she swayed with the movement.

Now, looking at her, sitting there, there was so much he wanted to say but no real way to say it all. "He told me about the other night. How you took him home."

Her gaze dropped to the carpet. She tried to crush the feelings flooding through her face back down. "I didn't want..." She put her hand to her nose to stop the tears.

Soft gentleness for the courage she showed in the face of such a struggle drifted through him. He reached over and laid his hand on her back. "I know."

She looked back at him, and the tears overtook her again. "It's just so unfair. I wish no other kid ever had to go through this. I wish I could make it so that every kid had a home and parents who cared. I hate it that any kid ever has to be afraid and alone. None of them deserve that."

Keith watched her. "And neither did you."

Her tongue drifted under her top lip as she fought the tears, but they were too strong. Her face crumpled into the pain again, and she gasped the breath in. Gently he reached over and pulled her back to his chest. She didn't fight it, and for that he was glad. He wanted her to know he was here for her, that she could share her grief, and he would help her through it the best he could. Her cheek and hand rested on his chest, and he could feel her soft sobs.

He wanted with everything in him to say something that would make it better, but what could he say? What could anyone say? It had all been said in one, thoughtless, reckless act by someone he would never know.

"Thank you," she said softly.

He tilted his head to be able to see her. "For what?"

"For listening. I've never told anyone that before."

Gratefulness for her trust in him drifted through him. He

hugged her tighter and kissed the top of her hair. "Hey, I'll always be here for you no matter what."

When Maggie woke up the next morning, her heart still hurt, but in a different way now. Now it was with the undeniable understanding that she wasn't carrying this pain alone. And somehow, in some strange way, that helped. In the kitchen she found him making eggs and sausage with Peter perched on the cabinet.

"Good morning," she said, her happiness not a total façade although she did have a headache.

"Morning." Keith smiled at her and then grew serious. "How are you?"

"Good." She nodded. "I could use some aspirin though."

"Two aspirin coming up." He reached into the cabinet above Peter. "'Scuse me, Mr. Ayer."

Peter giggled as Keith leaned him to the side and grabbed the bottle. He produced the aspirin and handed them to her.

"There's orange juice in the refrigerator and milk on the table."

She took the aspirins and grabbed a glass from the table to pour some milk. "How long have you been up?"

"Since Peter knocked on my door at 6:15." Keith reached over and tickled his fellow chef. "We got up and played Mario."

"Mario?" Maggie's displeasure slid through her. "Before breakfast?"

"Not our fault some people sleep all day. Huh, Peter?"

"All day?" Maggie checked the clock. "It's 7:30!"

"Like I said." Keith grinned at her wickedly. "If you're not up at the crack of dawn, we're wasting daylight as Ike would say."

Maggie knew he hadn't meant them to sting, but the words did anyway. She pulled her robe around her a little tighter. "Well, I'm going to go get ready and get Izzy up. Unless you need a woman's help to finish this."

"A woman?" Keith asked Peter. "We don't need no stinkin' woman. Do we?"

Although she was sure Peter didn't fully understand the comment, he grinned and shook his head anyway.

"Fine," she said, flouncing on the word, "but if you burn down the house, don't come whining to me."

"How many times have we cooked eggs and never needed her help?" Keith asked Peter as Maggie walked to the hallway. "Now she thinks we're going to burn the place down without her. Huh. Like we would do that."

Maggie laughed. He was crazy.

It seemed Keith could spend hours with her, and no matter how many there had been, he always wanted just a few more. "Want to go eat?" he asked after church.

"No. We're probably pushing our luck. We'd better get home."

He nodded. He knew that as well as she did, but still, he wanted to find some way to stave off her leaving, some excuse for her to stay. "You want to go riding today?"

Her gaze was softly apologetic. "We better put in some face time at the mansion or someone's going to get suspicious."

Suspicious of what he didn't really know or care. All he cared about was that she was leaving, and there was nothing he could do about it.

"I'll get Pete," Keith said, sliding out.

"I can get it," Maggie said quickly. She grabbed the suitcases and blankets. If she could just get away from him without letting him know she didn't want to leave, somehow she could go on with life as if the last night had never happened.

"You can get it?" He laughed at her. "Yeah, and I'm Houdini." He slid Peter to the ground. "Down you go, Buddy. Go help Maggie with the pillows."

Maggie gave him one, but it dragged the ground. She had to check her heart rate as Keith came to her side carrying Peter's car seat to get Isabella out. Amazingly he managed to snap the second car seat out with Isabella planted on his hip. They started up the walk, laden with kids and equipment.

"You know, for two little kids, you guys sure don't travel

light."

"You think this is bad, you should see their rooms." Maggie's gaze slid back to him as she opened the kitchen door and they walked in. He laughed. Then his gaze traced past her, and the smile fell.

"Oh, good morning," he said, visibly straightening, and Maggie knew it was bad even before she turned around.

Gathering her courage she turned slowly. It was worse than she ever could have imagined. She fought to find her own smile which had evaporated as thoroughly as his had. "Mr. Ayer. Mrs. Ayer. Good morning."

Mr. Ayer was the first to get anything out. "Would someone like to explain this?"

"I'm sorry, sir," Maggie started. "Patty Ann said that you all were not to be disturbed last night, so we…"

"We?" he asked, looking at Keith.

"I… Well…" She glanced back at Keith who stood staring at his father. "I mentioned to Keith that we weren't really invited, and…"

"That did not give you the right to take our children out of the house without our permission," Mrs. Ayer said.

Maggie deflated. "I know. I'm sorry. I just… I didn't think it would be a problem if we just went to Keith's. I told Inez."

"And thus we haven't called out the National Guard," Mr. Ayer said. "But we are still not pleased that you didn't tell us where you were going. We do not appreciate our children being taken just anywhere. Who knows what could've happened to them?"

"But we weren't just anywhere. We were at Keith's." She looked back at him, but his face was rock-hard.

"I should go," he said. He smiled at her, kind of, handed Isabella to her, and then he dropped the other stuff to the floor and shoved through the kitchen door with a bang. The last she saw of him was that familiar stride, stomping down the walk.

To say she didn't understand anything at all about the situation would've been an understatement. However, understanding wasn't going to help her much anyway. She turned back to face the wrath of people she had no real way of placating. "I'm really sorry. We would've been back earlier, but we went to church…"

That seemed to stop Mr. Ayer. His face dropped into

incomprehension. "Church? You went to church?"

"Yeah." She felt Peter at her knee, and she reached down to shield him from any ugliness. Her heart was pounding in fear, and she was sure his was too. "Keith's been taking me some times. Not all the time. Just a few times. I know… We should've told you that too. I'm sorry."

Mr. Ayer's gaze surveyed her in a way she couldn't quite read. "Keith went to church?"

She wasn't sure what the right answer to that question was, so she tried the honest one. "Yes."

"And you've taken the children?" Mrs. Ayer asked, clearly furious.

"Yes, Ma'am." That was it. She was fired. She was sure of it.

"I do not believe this," Mrs. Ayer said, standing. "Ms. Montgomery…"

"Vivian." Mr. Ayer's hand on her wrist stopped her, and she looked down in consternation. With a gaze heavy with haze, he looked up at his wife. "May I speak with you?" He glanced at Maggie and the kids. "Privately."

Mrs. Ayer didn't look at all happy, and it took her a long time to answer. "Fine."

They walked out. It would have been nice to be relieved, but Maggie couldn't get all the way there. True, she hadn't been fired outright, but it was less than clear that she wouldn't be when they came back.

Seconds turned to minutes. Then she heard the whimper. Peter. Carefully she spun right where she had been standing. She sat on her heel and hugged him to her. "Hey, baby. Shh. It's okay."

"Where did Keith go?" Peter rubbed his eyes, and she knew it was getting time for lunch and a nap.

"Keith had to go home, sweetheart." At least she hoped that was where he had gone. She pulled Peter to her again, and as she kissed his hair, her gaze went through the window in the kitchen door to the outside. The pickup was long gone. He was upset, the bang of the door had told her that, and it was bad, the look on his face told her that. She wished she could somehow turn back time and start over. She shouldn't have asked him to help her. She should've made the best of it at the mansion.

"Ms. Montgomery," Mr. Ayer said, striding in the room. Mrs. Ayer followed him, her arms folded at her chest.

Maggie stood and waited for the death sentence to be pronounced.

"We are not happy that you did not inform us you had taken the children, but..." He paused as his gaze went to his children. "We believe you had their best interests at heart." His gaze leveled back on her. "In the future we expect you to inform us where the children will be at all times."

"O...kay." She shouldn't have had any courage left, but to her heart, this was important. "We have gone riding a couple times at the stables and to church. Will those be acceptable if I tell Patty Ann where we're going?"

Mr. Ayer looked like she had punched him. "So long as you tell Patty Ann."

Mrs. Ayer didn't look at all pleased, but he turned and ushered her out before she could take a whack at Maggie. When they were gone, Maggie finally took a breath.

"Come on, you two, we'd better get you ready for lunch."

She was gone, of that much Keith was certain. He should've been smart enough to nix the idea of them coming to his place when it first came up. Of course his father would never approve of them going to his place. That thought knifed through his heart. He loved those kids, and to be treated as if he wasn't good enough to be around them hurt.

He tried to find something to do at his place, but after an hour of frustration, he decided it would be best to go get some work done. He pulled on his faded blue jeans and grabbed a sleeveless shirt. If she was gone, what was the point of wanting to be here? He might as well move to the Woodlands now and get it over with. That thought brought him up short. He'd never called the realtor as Dallas had told him to.

Frustration at being treated like a three-year-old no matter where he went crawled through him. It was like none of them cared what he thought. They knew what was best. He was supposed to follow along.

At the stables, he noticed Tanner's beat up pickup, but Ike's was nowhere to be seen. That was a relief. At least he wouldn't have to go more rounds with the newest manager. Keith stalked into the stables and met Tanner who was tossing hay to the horses.

"Oh, good afternoon, Mr. Ayer, I didn't know you were scheduled today."

"The house was getting to me."

"Tell me about it," Tanner said. "My roommates were getting on my nerves."

"The silence was getting on mine."

At that moment a blonde-headed young lady stepped out of the office. "Oh! I'm sorry. I didn't know there was anybody else here."

Keith stopped and looked at her, trying to fit her into a logical place. It wasn't until Tanner walked over to her and laid his arm around her that Keith figured it out.

"Mr. Ayer, this is my girlfriend Jamie. Jamie, this is Mr. Ayer."

Keith held out his hand. "Keith, please."

She smiled and shook his hand. "I'm sorry. I was just helping Tanner so we could go out tonight."

When Keith stepped back and surveyed her, it was clear that she was indeed in work clothes.

"I didn't think you would mind," Tanner said, and the strain of apprehension was evident.

Happiness for them drifted through him. They were lucky to be together without a million things standing in their way. "I don't mind. Glad to have you aboard, Jamie."

"Thank you, Mr. Ayer." She caught his look. "Keith."

"The interview is Thursday," Dallas said that evening as Keith's real life crashed in around him. "10 a.m. You should email me your resume, so I can go over it."

"I know how to do a resume." He sat at the table over his dinner that was already cold. Eating didn't sound appealing. Living didn't even sound appealing. Finally he stood and took his dish and the phone to the sink.

"Still, you haven't had much practice with things like this," Dallas said. "I'd hate for you to mess up this chance. It's such an incredible opportunity."

"I won't mess it up, Dallas."

"I didn't mean 'mess it up'—like be an idiot, but you have to understand these companies are not your father. They aren't going to overlook the details."

"What details about me do they need to overlook?" Frustration seeped through him.

"You know what I mean, Keith. You don't exactly have an extensive history outside your father's influence."

That would've been a challenge. "I worked all while I was in college, and I was the manager for the racing operation here from the time I graduated. We've turned a profit on the racing every single year, and this year our revenues are on-pace to double."

Dallas sounded less than impressed. "That's good for a hobby, but a real company…"

"Listen, Dallas, I've got things to get done."

"But we haven't even talked about the house. Did you call Jane at the realtor office? She needed to know what our offer would be."

"What is our offer going to be?"

"Well, that depends if we go through the bank or if your dad will underwrite us."

Keith scratched his head. "We'd better go with the bank. I don't really want to be tied to family if at all possible."

Her side went quiet. "It's going to be hard for us to do it on our own. With neither of us having a real job yet…"

"I have a real job."

"You know what I mean. The bank needs something more solid than what we plan to do. Are you sure you can't ask your dad? That would really help."

"I'll see what I can do."

"Have you talked to him about the jet?" Dallas asked. "I talked to Rachel, and she might catch a ride with us."

"Who's Rachel?"

"Oh, a friend from Advanced Legal Theory. She lives in Tennessee."

"But we'd be coming to Texas."

"Well, yeah, but Tennessee's right on the way."

"Right…?" Keith was having trouble breathing. Dallas seemed to take it for granted that not only was whatever his, hers, but that apparently included whatever was his father's as well. "We're going to have to talk about this whole plane thing."

"Oh, Keith. I'm sorry. Heather just showed up. We're going to dinner. Ristorante Reppucci."

He had no idea what Ristorante Reppucci was, but the fact that she pointed it out must mean it was expensive and meant to impress him. "Oh. Okay."

"I'll talk to you tomorrow night."

Oh, good. Something to look forward to. "See ya."

And they signed off. When Keith hung up, it was like dropping a fifty-pound pack. He sat down on the couch with a thump. He wiped his hand over his face, trying to block out the last 24-hours, but that wasn't easy. Her on the couch, in his arms, reliving a nightmare he wished she had never been through. Then this morning in the mansion's kitchen. Why was it, even when he helped, they found a way to throw him to the ground and then kick him in the gut?

Dallas was right. He needed to call the realtor. He needed to get out of here before they permanently killed his spirit and everything he'd ever managed to put together underneath him. As he stood and headed for the back, he wondered if she was gone. Probably, and with everything in him, he tried to convince himself that was for the best.

Seventeen

The interview was all but a disaster. Keith knew it the minute he sat down in the chair, and it only went downhill from there. Lee Ferrell was the kind of guy who made you feel an inch high and about as worthless as a maggot-infested donkey. Oh, he talked a good game, but Keith knew without a shadow of a doubt that Mr. Ferrell would never so much have said, "Hello" had Keith not had the connections he did. Never in his life had he been so glad to leave a place.

When the phone rang Thursday night, Keith had the feeling of falling into a black hole of self-flagellation. This would be a lesson in humility he could do without. "Hello?"

"Hey, how'd the interview go?" Dallas asked, sounding far too enthusiastic about it for Keith's taste.

"Fine."

"You got it, right? I mean he offered you the job, right?"

"I don't know. He said he'd get back to me."

That stopped her. "Oh. Well, it's just a matter of time. Have you called on the house yet?"

The house. Why was that so hard to remember? "I was going to, but I couldn't find the number."

"I left it on your desk with all the other information." She didn't sound pleased. "Come on, Keith. You've got to get on this. That house is going to sell, and then we'll have to start all over."

"Look, I've been a little busy here. We're trying to get Dragnet ready. Ike and Tanner are heading out again with Transistor."

"Oh, good grief. Enough about the stupid horses already. This is our future we're talking about here. Can't you get anything right?"

The shot found its mark. He shifted on the couch to keep from screaming. "Listen, Dallas. I'm not yelling at you about whether or not you've got every little picky detail done. I do have a life, you know?"

"Playing horses is not a life. It's a hobby, if that. You need a real job, Keith. Now don't screw this up for me. I do not want to come home to an unemployed husband who doesn't have a house for me to live in."

The conflagration was flaring into dangerous territory. "Fine. I'll get it done. Is there anything else you need?" He stopped only one syllable short from calling her "Your Highness."

"Yes, you need to stop by the caterers and give them the final menu and head count. I'll email that to you. The invitations are all out, so that's taken care of..."

Down the list they went, and for everything in him Keith wanted nothing more than to hang up on her. After five minutes of lists and tasks, she finally took a breath.

"It would really be nice if we could get into the house by the end of May. That way we could get it set up with our gifts, and when we get home from Hawaii, it'll all be ready for us."

"Yeah, okay." Keith just wanted to get off the phone. Hawaii had never sounded so much like hell. "Listen, I've got to go, and I'm sure you've got studying to do."

"Yeah, some." She sighed. "Man, I wish I was there with you."

He couldn't even say it. "Yeah. Well, good luck with everything. I'll talk to you soon."

In all their talks, Maggie had never thought to ask Greg for his number. The number of Parkers in the Houston phone book was staggering, and she wasn't about to call every Greg, Gregory, and G plus varied initials listed. So, Thursday night with a sigh, she resorted to corralling Inez long enough to plead for Keith's number. She wouldn't have done it, but she saw no good way around it. Worse, she felt like a heel for not having called him sooner. It was just that her previous attempts hadn't panned out.

Even though the Ayers had left that morning for several large

Washington fundraisers over the weekend, Maggie knew that taking a day off at this point could be a deal breaker. Besides there was no way she was going to put the children in jeopardy over a company picnic. So, Thursday night she waited until the mansion was quiet and the kitchen quieter. Then she snuck downstairs to the phone. Even two long exhales weren't enough to settle her nerves. Her heart pounded in her ears as she dialed the number. "Please be home. Please be home."

"Hello?" Man, she loved that voice.

Her smile came without her willing it to. "Hey. How's it going?"

There was the longest pause of her life on the other end. "Maggie?"

"Yeah, it's me." She sat down in a heap on the chair. She raked her fingers through her hair, jerking once to get her fingers all the way through it. "Listen, I won't keep you, but I wanted to say I'm sorry about the other day. I should've told them where I was going."

He sighed. "Yeah, well. They probably wouldn't have let you come if they had known."

There were so many questions surrounding that answer that Maggie could scarcely count them all. "Well, for the record, I am glad we went even if I got into trouble over it."

"So, they didn't fire you then?"

"No." She sighed. "Not this time anyway." The words were there, but she had to force herself to say them. "Listen, the real reason I was calling was to find out if you know Greg's number."

"Greg's...? Why?"

"Oh. Brilliant me. I kind of said I'd go with him to his company picnic, and now, it looks like it's just not going to work."

"Oh? Why not?"

She sighed again, her spirit dragging down with the weight. "Well, the Ayers left this morning for Washington, and I never got the guts to ask for Saturday off. Now that they're gone, I really can't just ask off."

"Have you had a day off since you started?"

"One. The night of your party. But I just can't take off this weekend. It's just not going to work."

As thrilled as Keith should have been about that, nothing in him was. She deserved to be happy, and if Greg made her happy, then Keith would do everything he could to see that she got that chance. "Why don't you just ask Patty Ann to get a babysitter?"

Maggie hesitated.

He waited, but she said nothing. "Would that really be so bad?"

"I just... I just wouldn't feel right leaving them here with someone they don't know. Especially when their parents are gone."

"You could leave them with Patty Ann." He laughed at his own joke.

"Yeah, and Attila the Hun might be available too." She didn't sound like she was laughing. In fact, she sounded downright despondent. "Besides, Patty Ann went with them, so..."

He hated himself for what he was about to say. If there was a way around it, he would've pounced on it, but there wasn't. "So, do you want to go to this deal with Greg?"

"Well... yeah. I mean he's a nice guy. We have fun together and everything. Plus, I'd hate to back out now."

Keith exhaled. How he would ever get the words out of his mouth, he had no idea. They stung just thinking them. "Maybe I could babysit."

Maggie didn't say anything.

"Maggie? Where'd you go?"

"I... I'm here."

"Well, what do you think? I could come to the mansion whatever time you need me on Saturday. I'd love to spend some time with Pete and Izzy. Only Inez would know, and if I know Inez, she wouldn't say anything to Patty Ann."

"But... I'd hate to ask you to do that. You've got work, and..."

"Not on a Saturday night I don't." Keith laughed. "It would beat cleaning my house."

Again her side went silent.

"What?" he finally asked.

"Do you think they would mind? I mean if they found out?"

He didn't know how much she knew, but she obviously knew enough. "It's one afternoon and evening. Inez will be there. We'll tell them it was a last minute thing."

Still, she didn't say anything.

"Maggie?"

"Why would you do that? You could get in trouble covering for me... again."

"Maybe I like to walk on the wild side."

As planned, Keith showed up right at two o'clock on Saturday. He went in the backdoor, having left his pickup at the guesthouse. This way if something bad went down, Inez could take over, and he could slip out the back.

"Good afternoon," he said to Inez who stood at the sink peeling carrots.

She shook her head, and when she smiled, the dimples on her cheeks stood out. "You are a piece of work, you know that?"

He walked over to the carrots and popped one in his mouth. "How's that?"

"You just keep showing up like they actually want you here."

He put a hurt look on his face. "You don't want me here?"

She put a hand on her hip and shook her head. "I shouldn't. If they find out about this, you're toast."

"That's why they are not going to find out about this." He lowered his gaze at her. "Right? This is between us."

Inez glanced back at the stairs. "Babysitting? You've never offered to baby sit before."

"Not true. I did a lot when Pete was first born. They just wouldn't let me."

She still didn't look convinced. "You seem to be sticking your neck out a lot recently. Do you have a death wish or what?"

Keith grabbed another carrot and popped it in his mouth. "I'm getting married, aren't I?"

The doorbell rang, and Inez reached down to wipe her hands. However, Keith held up his. "Don't move. I'll get that." He strode through the mansion to the front door. One peek through the sidelight told him this was in fact happening. Wrenching the doorknob, he swung the door open. "Well. Well. Look who found their way back."

"Keith." Greg looked positively stunned. "I didn't know they would let you within 30 yards of this place."

"Ha. Ha." Keith stepped back, and Greg walked in. Careful not to let his emotions slam the door, Keith closed it. "You here for Maggie?"

Greg readjusted the light green cotton shirt. "Umm, yeah. Is she ready?"

"I don't know. Just a second. I'll go check." Keith was determined to remain light and cheerful as if this wasn't killing him. That worked all the way up until he met her coming quietly out of her room. The turquoise and white striped shirt always did funny things to his stomach. "Greg's here."

Maggie spun like she'd been caught stealing the Hope Diamond. "Oh, man. Do you have to sneak up on people like that?"

He smiled. "Only the ones I like."

She looked at him then with a face full of hope and fear. "Are you sure this is okay? I don't want you to miss work for me."

"It's fine. I'm fine. The kids will be fine." At least he could say the words like he meant them. "Go. Have fun. Don't worry about us."

Still, she didn't look convinced. Her gaze traveled down to her shirt and white skirt. "Is this okay?" She smoothed down the shirt. "I don't want to look overdressed."

The words drifted through him, touching with an ache every soft spot. "You look amazing."

With Keith right behind her, Maggie made her way down the stairs, hoping she wouldn't fall and wondering how she was ever going to make it out that door with both Greg and Keith in the room. Midway down, she caught Greg gazing up at her, and she smiled and pushed a stray strand of hair over her ear.

"Wow. You're going to put all the other ladies there to shame," Greg said. When she stepped off the bottom stair, he stepped over to her and put his arm around her. "You look beautiful."

Nerves overtook her then. It was bad enough for him to say it. It was worse for Keith to be standing right there to hear it.

"Well, Keith, we'll see you." Greg extended his other hand to his friend although he never removed his other arm from her. Somehow it was weird to watch Keith shake Greg's hand from this vantage point.

"Have fun," Keith said, looking at her in the way that made her knees feel like jelly.

"We will," Greg said, and he turned them both and started out.

Keith had never been in such a battle in his life. Not one part of him wanted to let them walk out that door and down that walk. But he knew it could be no different, and thinking that it could would only cause everyone heartache that they didn't deserve. Softly he closed the door, but he couldn't just leave. So he stepped to the sidelight and pulled the little sheer curtain there back ever-so-slightly.

They looked good together in a way that ripped his heart out. They would be good together—good for each other. Greg needed someone patient and kind and strong. And Maggie deserved to be treated well by a genuinely nice guy. It was just that watching it happen knifed through him with an intensity he hadn't counted on.

The little sports car drove away smoothly, and somehow every moment of watching her slip farther away made it hurt all the more.

"Are they gone?" Inez asked from her leaning post on the breezeway to the kitchen.

Keith glanced at her, knowing he was busted. "Yeah."

She gazed at him for a long moment. "Do you want to talk about it?"

There were certain people in the world that Keith knew, or thought he knew, he could trust. Ike had been on that list until recently. Inez had been on it until he left for college. "You still make those chocolate shakes like you used to?"

She smiled. "I think I might remember."

The drive to the park had to be one for the memory books. Spring had definitely arrived. Bluebonnets and orange paintbrushes washed everything that wasn't green in breathtaking color. The day would have been absolutely perfect, save for the fact of who she was here with.

"So, are you planning on working for the Ayers forever?" Greg asked, glancing over at her. His strong hands with long fingers rested easily on the steering wheel.

"I'm surprised I'm still there." Her fingers played with her skirt.

"Oh? Why's that?"

Maggie shrugged although her gaze was down. "I'm not exactly cut out for living like the rich and famous. Give me a little house in a little town with a little grass and a few kids, and I'll be more than happy."

He glanced at her. "No big, fancy parties?"

She shook her head. "Just someone who loves me and enough money to live." She hadn't seen it coming, and if she had, she didn't know if she would've had time to react. But suddenly his hand was over hers. His fingers fell in the space between her thumb and her palm. Her heart leaped into gear as her gaze jumped to his.

His look was laced with a smile. "Maybe that dream isn't as far away as you think."

"Okay, Keith, what gives? You haven't been around this place this much in five years, and now every time I turn around, there you are again." Inez set the frothy drink in front of him, seemingly as a bribe to get him to open up.

However, he didn't want to go there. "Do you remember when we used to drink these when I was little?"

"Do I? What I remember is you coming home from football practice wanting a bag of French fries and three of these."

Inez laughed. "I thought I would never get you full."

Keith took a sip. "Those were good times."

"Yes and no," she said, tilting her head to look at him.

His heart clogged his chest. "I really made a mess of things, huh?"

"How so?"

"High school. College. He hates me now, even more than before."

Inez shook her head slowly. "He doesn't hate you. He loves

you. He just can't figure out how to show that."

"Yeah, and that's why I've been banished. He treats me like I'm somebody he could fire tomorrow if I take a step out of square."

"So you dance outside the square to prove to him that he can't."

He couldn't argue with that, so he didn't. "It would've all been so different if she had lived."

There was a long, slow exhale from the housekeeper. "He's hurting too. You've got to know that."

Keith shook his head. "What does he have to be hurting about? He's the king of this place. To him, we're all expendable." He stirred the drink very slowly. "It must be nice to know you're not."

"Well, in a month you'll be in your own house with your own wife leading your own life."

That didn't help although he knew she meant it to. "The Hendersons are just like him. I won't be their son-in-law. I'll be their slave."

"Is that how you feel here? Like a slave?"

He couldn't say it, so he just nodded.

"Have you told your dad that's how you feel?"

"Yeah, right. There's a plan that would get me shipped off to Siberia."

Inez continued to look at him. "You know, your mom would never have wanted this. She loved you so much. She would've never wanted you to have gotten run over like you have."

Keith snorted. "I think God took the wrong one."

"As bad as that sounds, I've thought that too on occasion. But what is it they say, 'Only the good die young.'"

"Boy, truer words were never spoken." He spun the glass slowly. "We've been going to the church again. The one she used to take me to."

That stopped Inez. "We?"

He glanced up. "Me and Maggie."

She lifted her chin, but said nothing.

"It's nice. You know? I didn't realize how much I missed it." Tears sprang to his heart. "It's hard because I remember so much sometimes—the way she was always at my games, the way she would hold those signs up that said, 'Yeah, Keith!' At the time I

197

thought I was embarrassed by them. Now I wish I could go back just for a day and feel her arms around me, telling me it will be okay."

"You know, she may not be right here telling you that, but I'll bet she is up there in Heaven, holding those signs up and cheering you on."

The tears made it all the way to his eyes. "You think?"

Inez smiled. "I know so."

"How about here?" Greg asked, indicating a semi-vacant table under a tree.

"Looks good." Maggie followed him and set her plate and cup down on the picnic table. The happy sounds in the park enveloped them. On one side company team members played tag football. On the other a myriad of people filled their plates.

"Must be some company," Maggie said, picking up her fork.

"Yeah. There's something like a thousand employees at all the regional firms. A lot of them show up for this." He stabbed into the potato salad. "It's good to get in some face time, network. That kind of thing."

"So what do you do exactly?"

He swallowed that bite and took a drink. "I work in accounting. I like it pretty well. Better than being in the computer wing."

"You don't like computers?"

"When they work, yes. Hit the button, down comes your answer. I like that, but to try to fix one or program one? No way. Not my forte."

"So you like living in Houston then?"

"Greg," a middle aged lady said, walking up with a man behind her. They both sat down. "This is my husband, John."

Greg wiped his hands on the napkin and then extended it to the older man. He sat for only a second longer. "Oh, and this is Maggie Montgomery. Maggie, this is Virginia. She works with me."

"We're cubicle buddies."

"Oh," Maggie said.

"So you're Maggie," Virginia said, gazing at her with a smile Maggie wasn't wholly sure she liked. "Greg's been telling me about you. You're the one who works for the Ayers."

She ducked her head. "Yeah."

"Must be quite the ticket up there. Do you get your own butler and maid?"

The pleasant day evaporated from sight. "Oh, no. Not really."

"Maggie baby sits the kids," Greg offered.

Virginia lifted her chin in understanding and then nodded. "I bet they're a couple of little brats."

This was a true and genuine ambush, and if Maggie'd had a little better handle on what she could say and what she couldn't say as a representative of the Ayers, she would've told this woman off. However, the fact that Greg had to work with her, coupled with the fact that she didn't want to embarrass the Ayers made her hold that thought from finding the air. "They're really good kids."

"Yeah. I bet. Do they pay you to say that?" And Virginia let out a whoop the size of the rest of her.

"And the I-Express flies through the air to the landing pad. Ka-boom!" Keith let Isabella dropped about four inches onto the changing table after the flight up the kitchen stairs. "Okay, you. Let's see how much damage you did."

He pulled the pink bloomers down and detached the Velcro. "Ugh! What have they been feeding you?"

Isbella laughed.

"Yeah, you think it's funny, huh?" His hands worked as he continued to talk to her. "Keith's gotta change this nuclear waste diaper. Real funny."

"Keef!" she squealed, throwing her arms out to the sides.

He leaned down and kissed her. How could you not just fall in love with that face? "You are too cute."

"Do you dance?" Greg asked as the band started off to the side. Thankfully Virginia had gone home, and the evening had cooled off. Both welcome turn of events.

"A little." Maggie was doing her best to keep tired from her, but it wasn't easy. She wondered about the kids and about Keith.

They were probably in bed by now, and she wished with everything in her that she was there with them.

"That makes two of us. Maybe your little and my little will keep us from being helplessly bad." Greg held his hand out to her, and she put hers in his and stood. He led her to the dance floor, and after only a few sways, she gave up and let the gentle pressure of his hand pull her to him.

He was quite a bit taller than her, and only a step up from being truly awkward about holding her. It seemed disingenuous to let him hold her so close, but she was tired and his presence was the only thing keeping her from falling to the ground and sleeping there until morning.

"Thanks for coming with me," he whispered into her hair.

She pulled back to look at him. "You're welcome."

And then, even as they swayed, he lowered his lips to hers. It was a brush and barely that, but it set Maggie's alerts on full-force. Before she had the chance to react, he pulled her back to him, and she was caught there with no way of extricating herself without breaking his heart.

"Now I'm not very good at this," Keith told Peter as he knelt by the bed. "I don't know all the words like Maggie does."

"That's okay," Peter said, rubbing his eyes. "She taught me how to say it."

Keith's smile danced across his heart. "Okay. Then let's hear it."

"Dear Jesus, we love you." The little voice yanked tears to Keith's eyes. "Please be with us tonight. Watch over us and help us have a good sleep. Please keep all the boys and girls in the world safe tonight, and let them know that You love them as much as You love us. Amen."

He could barely get the word out. "Amen."

Peter was looking at him when he stood.

"You get some sleep so we can go to church tomorrow."

And with that, Peter closed his little eyes. Keith let himself out of the room and checked his watch. Somehow he'd thought they would be back by now. How long could a picnic last? Unless they had decided to do dinner afterward or worse, back to Greg's apartment. It was amazing how bad one thought could hurt.

Eighteen

"Thanks for coming with me," Greg said, and he slid his hand through her hair at her neck.

"You're welcome." Maggie's gaze wouldn't fall from his. She knew he was going to kiss her, and for the first time, she wasn't running.

When his lips found hers, it wasn't melting she felt so much as just gratefulness for him being there. After a lingering moment, he pulled back and looked at her. "Can I call you?"

She smiled. "You better."

Keith had told himself over and over again that he should go. Sitting here, by her door was beyond pathetic. However, when he heard the noise first at the front door and then at the stairs, his head came up and he watched for her to appear. It was nearly midnight, and it didn't take a doctorate to know what that meant.

"Keith," she said in surprise when she noticed him as she traced down the hallway. "What're you doing here?"

He looked up at her as his heart broke for how beautiful she was. "Waiting for you."

She glanced worriedly at the doors. "Are they asleep?"

He nodded.

"You didn't have to wait. Inez could've kept an eye on them."

"It's okay." He didn't get up. In fact, he didn't move. "Did you have fun?"

She stopped, and after a moment she let herself to the floor against the opposite wall. "Yeah. Did you?"

He tried to smile. "Izzy's sweet. Peter said his prayers."

She nodded, but her gaze didn't leave his face.

Finally he looked at her. "So are you going to see Greg again?" He tried not to let her hear the shattering of his heart.

Her gaze fell from him to her skirt. "He said he'd call me, but you never know what that means. You know how guys are."

Yes, he did. He knew exactly how guys were. Keith looked at her, and for all the screaming in his head, he couldn't foist his disaster of a life onto her. "He'll call. Greg's a smart guy." He sighed. "So are we going to church tomorrow?"

She smiled slightly. "If you're up for it."

It sounded like Heaven. "I wouldn't miss it."

Keith was back at the mansion the next morning before they had even finished breakfast. "Good morning." Bright and cheery, he sounded so different than the night before.

"Good morning to you," Maggie said. "You get any sleep?"

"Keef!" Isabella squealed, throwing her hands out to the sides.

"Izzy!" Keith said, mimicking her. He walked over and gave her a big hug.

Maggie eyed him, worried for reasons she knew and some she couldn't quite figure out. "You're early."

"I couldn't stay away."

Church was wonderful as usual. To Keith the only bad thing was when the service was over. His talk with Inez had brought more memories of his mother back. In a strange way he had purposely forgotten even those things that he loved about her. He wondered about that as they drove home.

"What do you remember about your parents?" he asked, not to make her feel uncomfortable but because he needed to talk to someone who understood.

Maggie narrowed her eyes as if she was watching the memories on a fuzzy screen. "Weird things mostly. Like how my dad liked to smoke a pipe, but my mom wouldn't let him. How my mom put her hair up in a ponytail when she cooked. And my dad always slammed the backdoor so we knew he was home. It's strange what you remember."

"Yeah." He let himself get lost in memories of his own, most so obscure he could hardly catch hold of them.

She looked at him across the Dodge seat. "Why do you ask?"

His gaze stayed on the road because he couldn't bear to look at her just at that moment.

"Keith?" She sounded so worried, all he wanted to do was to put her at ease; however, he couldn't get any words out to do that.

He ran his knuckle under his nose to keep the emotions from coming to the surface. He shook his head one way and leaned his head to the side. "Does it ever go away?"

Maggie's heart was ripping in two from the anguish on his face. He was trying so hard to hide it, and yet it was right there. "What?"

"Missing them." He let his wrist down onto the steering wheel hard. "Crud. I'm sorry. I wasn't going to drag you into this."

Her gaze never left him. "Well, I'm in this, so you might as well tell me."

The fact that he never looked at her told her more than she could ever have seen in his eyes. He shook his head again but only barely.

"My mom died when I was 12."

"Twe...?" Her breath slid away from her. "Oh, Keith. I'm so sorry."

The smile wasn't really a smile, and his gaze never left the road. "It's not your fault."

Maggie was so focused on him, it was like the rest of the world had dropped away. "What happened?"

It took him more than a second to get the words out. "Car wreck."

She moaned as her ache mixed with his.

"They went on a trip one weekend, and she never came back. It was like the only thing I had left was the memories."

"The funeral?"

"I don't remember much about any of it. I think I only went to the funeral. Besides that I stayed with Inez."

That surprised her. "Inez? Our Inez?"

"Yeah. That was back before Dad knew about the wonderful world of nannies. In fact, I don't know that he really cared too much what happened to me or who was taking care of me." He sniffed, and Maggie could tell he was embarrassed by it. "They're what got me through it. The staff. But mostly Inez and Ike."

It was like taking a whack with a hard tree branch, but Maggie absorbed the pain and kept her focus on Keith. There was so much pain there. So much he wasn't saying, so much she wondered if he had ever said. It occurred to her that the roles from the week before had been reversed—except for the part about holding him while he let it out. Knowing she wanted him to feel as safe as she had felt, she reached across the seat and ran her hand down his soft gray cotton shirt. His arm solid underneath. He always looked so stylish when he wasn't work-dirty. It was a dichotomy she was only now beginning to understand.

"I don't know how much choice they really had in the matter," Keith said, continuing as though if he stopped, he might break down. "I was a pretty attention-hungry kid. Inez would get me ready for school, and the second I got off the bus and changed, I was down at the stables with Ike."

For all the animosity Maggie had toward Ike to that moment, she knew then that she would never be able to hate him in the same way again. "What about your dad?"

Keith snorted. "What about him? He was never here, and when he was, all he did was tell me everything I was doing wrong, and believe me, that list got longer every time he got the chance to use it." Vehemence seeped into his tone. "I hated him. He hated me. So we just stayed out of one another's way as much as possible."

With apprehension telling her she must be out of her mind, Maggie's gaze fell and then slipped back up to him. "Is that why he was so mad last week?"

For the first time, Keith's gaze came over to her. "Oh, you noticed that too, huh?"

"It was kind of hard not to."

For a single second his face let that go through it. Then he tossed it off as if it meant nothing to him. "I'm just sorry you got in the middle of it."

Maggie smiled. "It was worth it."

Surprise jumped to his face.

Her glance slipped into the backseat. "The kids had a great time at your place." She considered the foolishness of telling him, but she'd come this far, and she wasn't about to step on him like his father had. She let her gaze trail to his face. "And I did too."

That brought an actual smile to his face, but it was melancholy and poignant. As they turned into the gate, he nodded. "I'm glad."

Although Keith wanted to stay with her all day, he knew that wasn't possible. The jockey was coming at 2 to take Dragnet through a simulated 2 o'clock start. They didn't have much time to get him ready. One month. So Keith left Maggie with the kids and the car seats in the front door of the mansion. He heard Inez come in from the kitchen just as he escaped out the front door, and he was glad for the timing.

It wasn't a stretch to think the maid had her theories about him and Maggie, and he didn't want to hear the innuendos and implied understanding. Inez didn't understand, and the less chance he gave her to act like she did, the better it would be for his heart. Nonetheless, a piece of him stayed right there at that door, with the kids and with her. And something told him, it always would.

"I called the realtor," Dallas said on Monday night, and Keith braced for the coming storm. Her voice was cutting and sarcastic. "Thanks to you, that house sold. I cannot believe you let that perfect house slip through our fingers because you're *busy*."

Anger bit into him. "I am busy, Dallas. I know that surprises you, but it's the truth."

"Well, I'm not swimming in extra time here either, Keith, but I've gotten everything I'm supposed to do done. Why do I feel like you don't even care about us anymore?"

He was spinning through the accusations. "There are other houses. Maybe there's something better."

"Better? That's not the point! The point is this one was *perfect* and because you were too lazy to make a phone call, now it's gone."

"You know, you could have made that phone call as easily as I could have."

"Do you know how much I have to do? I've got graduation in three weeks. Finals. I'm studying for the boards. I'm trying to plan a wedding from 3,000 miles away, and you're not helping my stress level."

The anger dissipated, mostly because he knew she was right. "Look, I'm sorry, Dallas. Really I am." He hadn't been concentrating on the wedding or Dallas or anything else in the real world. True, thinking of the wedding brought a tightness to his chest that he couldn't adequately explain, but still, he was the groom-to-be, he'd better start acting like it. "Listen, I'll make up for it. I'll find another house. Even better than that one."

"And where are you going to find this better-than-perfect house?"

"I'll make some calls. Surely that wasn't the only wonderful house in Houston."

"Well, don't make it too close to Houston. I don't want to live in the city-city."

"Not too close."

"And I want a pool, and at least three bedrooms and an office."

The list was pushing him deeper into the cushions.

"And the kitchen needs to be state-of-the-art. I'd like two sinks if possible, and granite cabinets. Oh, and state-of-the-art appliances. And no fake wood floors either, if you get wood floors, I want them real wood."

At least she wasn't picky.

"I'll make some calls tomorrow."

Keith wasn't sure where his week had gone by the next Sunday. Basically, it had disappeared into a dark well of looking at houses and trying to get some work done. The work wasn't so bad. The houses were another story. Bedrooms, bathrooms, backyards, floor plans, financing. It was enough to give a monk a migraine. During the day he burned up the phone lines. At night he burned up the modem. He had looked through so many virtual tours, his head felt like it was still spinning. On Sunday he'd had enough looking. He needed some peace.

Showing up on a cold call to the mansion wasn't the best idea in the world, but he didn't have much of a choice. Besides even if his parents nixed the idea, at least they would know the church thing was his idea and not Maggie's. He rang the doorbell, knowing that just walking in would be a mistake.

Inez opened the door.

Keith's nerves jumped to the surface. "Hi. Is Maggie here?"

Slowly Inez surveyed him head-to-toe, and her getting Maggie was less than certain.

"Who is it, Inez?" his father's voice boomed through the entryway.

The maid turned. "It's Keith, Sir."

Uh-oh. Not good. Not good. Not good. Keith wanted to disappear. If the earth opened up and swallowed him, that would've been kind.

His father appeared at the door, and his eyes hardened as he gazed at his son. "I didn't know we had a meeting today."

The breath Keith tried to take in didn't get his lungs. Instead it lodged at the top of them, making it impossible to talk. "I... Umm... I was wondering if Maggie and the kids wanted to go with me to church."

The middle of his father's eyebrows narrowed. "Church? Why?"

"Be...Because I was going anyway, and..." He glanced out to his pickup and wished he had never thought of something so absurd as to come get her. "But that's okay. I can go alone. I'm sorry. It was just a thought." He started to turn, hoping he could get out of here without a yelling match.

"Were you planning to take them in that thing?" his father asked, indicating Keith's pickup with a nod.

Keith turned back. "Well, yeah. It'd kind of be a long walk otherwise." The joke fell like a pancake under an army boot.

However, his father examined him without rebuke. "Inez, page Ramon. Have him bring the car around front."

The middle of Keith pitched forward. "The car?"

"If you're going to go, you might as well go with a real driver."

How his father could give such backhanded assistance, Keith wasn't at all sure.

Inez came back. "He's on his way, Sir."

"Good." His father nodded. "Go tell Ms. Montgomery it's time for church."

"Yes, Sir."

Maggie hadn't seen Keith for a whole week, and it was starting to grate her nerves not knowing where he was or if he was all right. She and Greg had talked twice during the week, and although he hadn't asked her out again, that was just a matter of time. Had she met and fallen for Greg first, this would all be perfect. As it was, perfect felt a million miles away.

She sat on Isabella's window seat and gazed out at the backyard. She wondered about Keith if his week had gone well, if the horses were coming along, if things were going well with Dallas. Yes, she would've even taken talking about Dallas to have the opportunity to talk with him about something.

"Ms. Montgomery?" Inez asked as she knocked on the door.

Instantly Maggie was on her feet. "Yes, Ma'am?"

The look on Inez's face went from happy and hopeful to condescending and cold. "Mr. Keith is here to see you."

A joy she had never before felt flooded through her.

"Keef!" Isabella said from the floor where she and Peter were playing.

Maggie knew she would need all the reinforcements she could get. She swung Isabella to her hip. "Come on, Peter. Let's go see why Keith is here." She followed Inez out the door.

"He's at the front," Inez said but turned for the kitchen.

"Okay." Maggie walked to the main staircase and started down it. On the curve halfway down, she caught his gaze, and the smile couldn't be stopped. However, she had to keep it as professional as possible because Mr. Ayer was standing there watching. "Hi. Inez said you wanted to see me?"

"Hey," Keith said. "I wondered if you wanted to go with me to church." He seemed subdued and hesitant. His hands were behind his back, and his head was down more than it was up.

"Oh... I don't." She glanced at Mr. Ayer. "I don't know if the children..."

"I've called the car, Ms. Montgomery," Mr. Ayer said. "If you would like to take the children to church, I think that would be acceptable."

She looked from his father to Keith and back again. "Are you sure you don't mind?"

The saddest but almost not there smile she had ever seen met her. "I think it would be good for them."

The Dodge was one thing. The limo was quite another. Maggie helped Peter strap in while Keith got Isabella settled. When both children were ready, Maggie sat down on the plush seat that faced backward, and Keith sat next to her although at the far other end of the seat. He buckled in and then tapped the dividing door. The car rolled out.

This was beyond anything Maggie had ever expected. She wasn't made to ride in limos. She wasn't even made to stand on the street corner and watch a limo drive by. Limos weren't a part of her world. However, the thought slid through her that they were how Keith had grown up. That thought stabbed into her as it illuminated in brilliant colors why they could never be together. Nonetheless, she was sure he was enjoying this chance to exhibit his status in the world. After all, wouldn't everyone?

Keith hated this. With everything in him he hated this. In fact, if he would have thought of it, he would've told her he would meet her there. This was like wearing a big sign across your forehead—*Hello, hate me because I'm rich!* He tried to quell the crawling shame, mostly because he didn't want to spoil this ride for Maggie. She was staring out her window, surely thinking how far she had come in the world.

His gaze drifted over to her silhouette. She wasn't looking his direction so he let his gaze linger there, watching her. She could even make a limo ride bearable, and for him, that was a stretch. He wanted to ask about her week and the kids, but it was clear she was lost in her own thoughts, so he kept his own to himself.

Maggie followed Keith who held Isabella up the steps and into the church, wishing it didn't feel like everyone was staring. Their arrival out front had been less than ordinary, and now it was as if everyone in the church was glancing at them, whispering, wondering who they were. Maggie hated the attention, but they were here, so she had to make the best of it. With Peter's hand in hers, she stepped into the bench, and Keith followed her in. Her heart stifled the breath from her when he was once again by her side.

There was something about standing next to him, something so familiar and yet exciting just the same. He didn't look at her even when the service started, and that worried her. They stood there together, yet separate. Joined by the children, and yet not. It was a strange space in life to occupy.

By the time the sermon started, Keith knew with everything in him this was a total mistake. He felt the gazes on them even if he didn't look around to actually see them. Worse, his mind kept going to how right this would feel if he could let himself think that. Her by his side, saying the words and seeming to guide their little group through the prayers without effort. He couldn't explain it, and after a while he stopped trying if for no other reason than every time he tried, he kept coming to the same conclusion, and it was a conclusion he liked but could never make happen anyway.

In complete frustration with himself and everything about his miserable life, he anchored his attention to the preacher. Somehow, Keith knew he had to find something else to think about or his mind was going to get so tangled it would never work right again.

"The pots," the preacher began. "Six pots, set off to the side. I wonder if we have ever really thought about those pots. Here's Jesus at a wedding. His disciples are there. His mother is there, and as the wedding progresses, they've run out of wine."

Oh, terrific, Keith thought, shifting in his seat. *We come to church, and they're going to talk about getting drunk. This is exactly what Maggie needs. Not to even mention me. We shouldn't have come. I knew we shouldn't have come.*

"Now one thing you have to know is that in this time period, to run out of wine during a wedding celebration was a major insult to all the guests. It would heap dishonor on the host, and presumably the host was a friend of Jesus because... well, Jesus was invited, and you don't invite just anybody to a wedding. So here's Jesus and his friends, and it becomes clear to Mary that they have run out of wine.

"Mary on faith goes to Jesus. 'They've run out of wine.' Jesus puts her off. 'It's not my time.' But Mary, her faith in what Jesus can do never wavering, looks to the servants and says, 'Do whatever He tells you.' And what does Jesus say? 'Take those pots, and fill them with water.'

"Take those pots? But what were those pots? If you're like me, you think they were pitchers just like you would normally think you would put wine into. Ahh, but that's not what it says. It says, 'Now there were six stone waterpots set there for the Jewish custom of purification...' The Jewish custom of purification. That means those pots are there for the Jews to *wash themselves,* to purify themselves in order to be clean enough to share a meal.

"Notice. Jesus doesn't say, 'Take them and wash them with Dawn detergent and then go out fill them with water.' In fact, He doesn't even mention washing them out first. He just says, 'Take them, and fill them with water.'"

The preacher paused and looked out at the crowd. "What does this mean to us? It's very simple. We are not required to get our act together and then go to God. We *are* those dirty pots—full of the filth of our lives, even the filth of our own attempts to wash our sinfulness away with our religions and our rules. Those rituals can never save you. Even if you live by the rules, you are still unclean. You still need to wash and to be washed. And then Jesus comes along and without requiring you to get clean first, He points to you and says, 'Fill that one with My water.' The living water that He refers to later on. 'Fill her with My water. Fill him with My water.'

"And then, as if that's not enough, He tells the servants to take some of what has come out of these pots to the headwaiter who will judge the wine, the fruit that comes from these dirty, filthy, stinking pots. Think about that. All these people have washed themselves in these pots, and now these servants are going to take what they know was water only minutes before to the ultimate judge to seek his approval to share it with others. Isn't this just like you and me?

"We are these pots, once filthy and dirty, but now not only filled with the living water, but filled with the wine of a new life. And the fruit that has come out of us is now taken to the ultimate judge. Does the judge take one sip and spit it out in horror at our filth? No. You know the end of the story. He praises the bridegroom for saving the best wine for last.

"Understand this," the preacher said slowly, "Jesus is the new wine. He is the best, and He wants to fill you right now. Not when you get your act cleaned up, not when you've gotten yourself presentable. Right now. He is standing here calling you to be filled with His new wine. The question is: Will you let Him do it, will you do whatever He says, or are you still going to try to do it on your own? It's your choice.

"Let us stand."

Keith could hardly move, and even when he did, it felt like someone else moving him. How many years had he known he was not good enough? How many hours had he spent beating himself to a pulp because he couldn't be what his father wanted? How many hours had he spent first trying to escape through a bottle and then hating himself for being so weak?

The guilt was crushing. The deep understanding that he could never, ever measure up was like a million pound weight that he labored to carry every day. Even when they had first started coming to church, he knew it held a peace he hadn't known in years, but he felt so unworthy of the peace it seemed to offer.

Now as he stood fighting to breathe, he realized he was one of those waterpots. He was filthy and dirty and vile. He had sin upon sin, worldly answer after worldly answer, and as much as he had wanted to gain the peace he could feel being offered here, he had convinced himself he wasn't worthy of it. He was too bad to ever fix, and he knew it to the bottom of his soul.

Guilt and shame for all the things he had done swiped through him, raking gashes in the façade of I'm-all-right as it went. Sins he remembered and many he didn't gushed to the surface, reminding him how far he had fallen since he had stood in this space with his mother all those years before. It couldn't be true. It couldn't be as easy as the preacher made it sound, and yet.... Yet, he could see those pots, sitting in the corner, dirt-stained and contemptible at the very least. That's how he felt—dirt stained and contemptible.

Fear and shame gripped the grain of hope the preacher's words held, and Keith crushed his eyes closed as the battle rose inside him. "You don't understand, Lord," he prayed in the depths of his heart. "You don't understand all the bad things I've done."

"And you, Keith don't understand what I can do if you will let Me."

The voice was so real, Keith didn't even question its existence.

"But I've done so many horrible things. Things I can't even forgive myself for. How could you ever forgive me?"

"I can do all things. In fact, I have already forgiven you. All that remains now is for you to accept that forgiveness."

He thought the guilt might squeeze his breath right out of him. It was like he was suffocating. His head swam for want of oxygen. "How, Lord? How?"

"Trust. Walk through the door I open, and trust that the next step will appear."

"Keith," Maggie said, and when he came back to the church, she was looking at him with worry. "It's over. Are you ready?"

He looked at her with uncomprehending eyes. His insides were exhausted from the battle. "Is it real?"

Her gaze fell increasing with concern. "What?"

"What you have. Is it real?" He really needed to know.

"What I have?" she asked, clearly not understanding.

Keith glanced to the front. "The praying. The believing." He looked back at her. "Is it real?"

She smiled but barely. "It's the most real thing I've ever found in my life."

For the first time he took a real breath, and slowly he nodded. "Then I want that. I want what you have. But I don't know how. I don't know how to be there—where you are. Can you show me?"

His gaze seemed to sink into hers.

"I'd love to."

Nineteen

Maggie knew she was pushing her luck, but she also knew Who she had on her side, and so she put the day in His hands and let go. When they got back to the mansion, Patty Ann met them at the front door. It was enough to make Maggie question God's sanity.

"Where did you take the car?" Patty Ann asked in angry exasperation. "The Ayers will be late."

Pulling Isabella closer to her side, Maggie lifted her chin. "We went to church, and we took the car because Mr. Ayer said we should."

Patty Ann surveyed Keith, clearing knowing he was to blame for this, but Maggie held her ground.

"Mr. Ayer didn't say anything about him needing the car."

"That's because Mr. Ayer didn't know about the Coopers' brunch in…" Patty Ann looked at her watch and went ashen. "Oh, my. I've got to get them in that car, or they are going to be far more than fashionably late." She practically ran up the stairs.

Keith was all-but doubled over as his gaze stayed on the floor. Hesitantly he glanced up at her. "Well, I'd better get…"

The thought seized her with a vehemence that took her breath. Quickly she darted a glance up the stairs before she bent closer to him. "Come back and get us in thirty minutes."

Confusion slid over his face.

But she was perfectly calm. "Trust me."

Keith waited until the limo had been gone for ten minutes before he had the guts to go back to the mansion. Even then, he parked on the trail close to the kitchen. His heart was jumping through his chest and at the door he had to exhale hard to get his emotions to calm down. He opened the door and found Maggie, a whirlwind of activity in the kitchen.

He let the door bang softly behind him, and when she looked up and smiled, life stopped.

"Oh, good." She licked her finger and slapped the two pieces of bread together. "Inez is off, so don't laugh at my cooking."

"O… kay."

"The car seats are right there. If you'll get them ready."

Keith picked them up, questioning his sanity. He must be crazy. That was the only logical explanation for any of this.

"So, I'm driving," Keith said when they were all in the pickup and strapped in. "Mind telling me where we're going?"

Only then did Maggie hesitate. It was nearing 100 degrees outside, and keeping the children out in that for hours didn't sound like a great idea. "Well, you said you could drive out to the waterfall if you had to."

"There's a couple places that are a little scary."

"Depends who's driving."

Keith was amazed. Maggie had weathered the bumpy, uncomfortable trip out to the falls with grace and humor. She was simply amazing. There was no other word for her. At the falls, she unpacked lunch. She fed Isabella. He helped Peter. When lunch was over, Maggie told the kids to play under the tree, and both seemed so happy to be there again, they obeyed.

"Now," Maggie said, sitting on her knees and pulling one last thing from the lunch basket as the peaceful sound of the falls enveloped the afternoon, "were you serious about what you said at church—about being where I am?"

Reaching up to scratch his collarbone, Keith nodded.

"Well, then I brought you something. It's not new or anything. If I'd have had the chance to get a new one, I would have, but you didn't give me a lot of notice." With a short breath she handed it across to him, never really meeting his gaze. It was a black leather book with a worn zipper around the outside. The lettering across the front, faded to a nearly unreadable gold held five simple letters: Bible.

"It was my parents' Bible," Maggie said softly, looking more at it than at him. "It's what I have left of them."

Gratitude and guilt smashed together in the middle of him. "Oh, Maggie, I can't…"

She smiled serenely. "Just until you can get one for you."

Gently, reverently, Keith held the Bible, fighting not to let his hands shake for the trust it represented. He slid the zipper around it and let it fall open. For all the wear on its outside, its inside was remarkably intact.

Maggie watched him as he flipped it first from one page to another. "One thing that really stuck with me was that I remember Mrs. Malowinski telling me that faith isn't just believing He's there. Real faith is trusting Him to guide your every step to your greater good. He wants that for you, you know? Your greater good."

The protests crowded through him about his own life, but he chose to use hers as an argument. "But how can you believe that? How can you trust a God Who took away your parents?"

Her gaze fell. "This life isn't perfect, and there are things that happen, bad things, set into motion by people who make really bad choices. God does not alter the physical laws of this world. If velocity says a car traveling at this speed hits another at that speed, there are consequences to that impact. God allows the laws here to work so that we can live our lives. Otherwise, if the law of gravity worked sometimes and not others, we couldn't even walk out of our house because we might float off the planet."

She paused and then shook her head. "But there's more to it than that. God can take anything, *anything* and use it to teach us, to strengthen us, to guide us—if we let Him." Her gaze found Keith's. "Sometimes it's the things that are the hardest that teach us the most."

"But if He loved us…"

"He wouldn't let bad things happen."

There was nothing to do but nod.

Maggie's gaze went over to the children. "What if Peter needed an appendectomy. Emergency situation. You have to make the decision. Do you sign the paper to allow them to operate on him?"

Confusion slid through Keith. "Well, yeah."

"But it's major surgery. It's going to be painful for him."

"But he'll die if I don't."

Slowly Maggie let that sink in. "That's what God knows. That without our learning to trust His love in the good times and in the bad, to trust that He knows best what will ultimately give us life, we will die because we'll never have His life in us, and His life is what will live forever. If we don't have that, we die."

Keith wanted to argue, but he didn't have the words.

"I know, it's a lot to absorb in one day," Maggie said with compassion, "but the good news is, He doesn't require you to know it all. Just take this step. This one right here. That's all. He knows where you're going, and if you trust that, He will show you the next step and the next and the next."

"Like the doors," he said as his mind processed what she was telling him.

"Huh?"

"You know, the doors the preacher was talking about the other day. How God opens one door, and when you walk through that door, He will open the next."

"Yeah, like that."

Still, he clung to the arguments. "But how do you do that? How do you remember?"

"Well, how do you remember to feed each horse every day. You've got to have like what? Ten of them?"

"Twelve."

"But that's got to be hard to remember to feed them every, single day."

Keith shrugged. "No, not really, you just get used to doing it. Once you do, it's not hard to remember."

Maggie nodded, and although it took a moment for the depth of that to sink in, Keith finally caught what she was saying.

"It's not one big declaration, and it's done," Maggie said. "It's remembering in the little moments in your life—to trust Him, to trust what He's guiding you to do, to listen, and to know with everything in you that He will lead you exactly where He meant for you to go. Like praying and living with Him, that's not me trying to prove I deserve for Him to live in my life, it's a sign that He is. Simple as that."

"But it sounds so hard. So... I don't know. Big."

"It is big, but He doesn't require big. He asks you to take one step."

"Walk through one door."

Maggie nodded. "Trust me, He's more than capable of opening those doors in front of you."

"Are they all easy?"

Her eyebrows shot for the sky. "Walking through those doors?"

He nodded.

"On your own they are some of the hardest things in the world to do. In fact, the world will most likely think you are crazy for doing them. Look at Mother Teresa of Calcutta. Any normal person would've balked at going into the places where she went— the home of the destitute and dying doesn't sound like a fun place to spend your life. Yet she did it because that's where God put her."

Concern seeped into him. "I couldn't do that."

"You don't have to. All you have to do is what He gives you to do. That's what's so cool about God—He doesn't think you have to be someone else before He'll love you. It's not a contest. He loves you right now. Right here. Just like you are, like the waterpots today."

"But don't people go off into missions and stuff?"

"They can, but they don't have to. Mrs. Malowinski lived in Del Rio her whole life, but she was right where God put her, doing His work. Sometimes it's the little things, those things that the world doesn't see and will probably never know about that mean the most to those whose lives they touch." She shook her hair out of her face. "I, for one, am grateful she answered His call. Her taking just that step probably saved my life. I sure wouldn't be who I am today if it wasn't for her."

Keith gazed at Maggie, his heart falling through the peace and serenity there. "Thank God for Mrs. Malowinski."

Monday night Keith was sitting on the couch with the Bible open in his hands when the phone rang. He reached for it without really paying attention. "Hello?" His gaze continued to absorb the words on the page.

"Well, it's about time. Where have you been?"

Instantly Keith sat up and closed the Bible. "Dallas."

"Yes, Dallas. Did you forget about me?"

"I… no. Why?"

"It's Monday night. You always call me on Monday night. It's like these days we don't talk unless I call you."

Guilt crawled over the peace he'd had for 24 hours. "Sorry, Dallas. I've been…"

"Busy. I know. Did Ferrell call you yet?"

"Uh, no." He hated that admission.

"Well, Dad talked to him today, and he's decided to give you another chance." She didn't sound particularly happy about that. "They'll call you to confirm, of course, but he's got you scheduled for Thursday at 3:00. I'm telling you, Keith, guys like Ferrell don't ever give guys like you a second chance. Trust me, Dad had to pull all the strings there were, so do not mess this one up."

Nothing in Keith liked any of this. "Fine. I'll do my best."

"No, Keith. Not your best. You get that job… whatever it takes."

Anger stamped through him with Army boots. "Anything else?"

"Yeah. Have you found a house yet?"

"I… Well, no. Well, kind of." He felt like he was on the inspection line, and he was failing miserably. "I mean I found a couple you might want to check out on line." His thoughts spun away from him even as he tried to catch them. "Here. Let me get to my computer."

And for the next hour they played house shopping via phone lines and modems. By the time they were going through their fifth virtual tour, Keith was exhausted. He didn't care about tile and granite and landscaping. He just wanted to get back to the black book lying on the coffee table in the living room. It represented the only sanity left in his life.

"Oh, I forgot to tell you," Dallas cooed when she was sufficiently convinced he had actually been looking for a house. "I found an Aston Martin Concept car I'm going to do some checking into. It is the coolest thing you've ever seen."

Confusion went through him. "Don't you still have your Jag?"

"Well, yeah, but I can't show up at Hayden & Elliott in a

Jag—everyone will think I'm poor." She laughed as if the thought was ridiculous. "I mean come on, by that point I'll be Mrs. Keith Ayer. I have to make a statement, you know?" She sounded so excited about being Mrs. Keith Ayer, unfortunately she didn't sound nearly as excited about being married to Keith. "I'm going to make an offer of a million. We'll see where we go from there."

"A… million?" Keith choked on the word.

"It will probably have to be custom made. They aren't mass-producing them yet, so that's even sweeter."

"Dal…"

"Oh, hang on." She left as Keith's mind spun through the car and the house and the move and the wedding. "Keith? Listen, Chris Ann just showed up. We're going shopping for my trousseau. Let me know when you've seen the houses we looked at in person. Maybe we can go together when I get home."

The calendar on the pegboard stared back at him. May 13. Dallas's graduation. Less than three weeks away. He was no longer breathing.

"Gotta go. I love you," she said.

He mumbled something incoherent, said good-bye, and hung up. It was only 9:30, but overwhelm tramped through him and without going back to the living room, he turned for his bedroom. Maybe if he was really lucky, he would go to sleep, and this whole nightmare would be just that when he woke up again.

Maggie wondered how he was doing with the Bible. She hadn't seen him since Sunday, and although her sensible side said she was crazy, a little voice in the recesses of her heart kept saying, "Call him."

On Tuesday night, she waited until the kids were down and the house was quiet before she snuck down to the kitchen. Quietly, carefully she grabbed the phone and slid into a chair. Wishing the buttons wouldn't beep so loudly, she dialed the number. As it rang, her glance chanced across the clock. It was eleven-fifteen. He was in bed. She shouldn't be calling him.

"Hello?" He didn't sound asleep exactly, more distracted.

"Hey, there," she said softly. "Did I wake you?"

"Maggie?" There was a hint of hope in that name.

220

"Yeah, it's me. You can't get rid of me, huh?"

"That's a problem?"

"I don't know. Is it?"

He inhaled and then exhaled as if he was pulling life in and releasing every bad thing trapped in him. "It isn't to me."

They had talked for over an hour about him being up well past dark sitting here in his living room with the little lamp over the recliner on as he read the Bible. He had so many questions, so many things he'd read that he wanted some guidance on. She answered the ones she could. The ones she couldn't, they talked over until he was satisfied in what they had come up with to explain it.

It was so easy to talk with her. So natural and relaxed. He had the feeling that he could ask her anything, and she wouldn't jump all over him for being an idiot. As the clock started back up toward one o'clock, he knew he had to let her go, but he had one more question that was dogging his every step.

"Okay, one more question and then I'd better let you get some sleep," he said.

"Okay."

He took a breath because the question seemed so pivotal to everything. "If someone gave you a million dollars, what would you do with it?"

She didn't say anything for a long, long moment. "Well, I'd take some of it and put it toward scholarships for foster kids. That's the only way I got to go because someone else had thought to make a scholarship available. And then..."

Keith waited as his heart filled with her first answer. It wasn't a car. It wasn't a fancy house with granite countertops. It was helping someone else out. He liked that.

"Well..." She didn't continue right away. "I've never really told anybody this..."

Something told him they were now swimming in the depths of her being, just like the night they had spent on his couch. He waited, wondering what came next.

"I want to be a foster mom someday. I want to give back what I was given—a chance, a life, a shot at normal. I want to give that to as many other kids as I can." Her voice faded out on the soft dreams. "So I'd use whatever was left to do that."

Nothing in him had a hard time picturing her—a gaggle of kids in a rainbow of colors around her. There was no doubt in him that her presence with them would be a turning point in their lives. It sure had been in his. "Well, I hope someday you get that chance," he said, wishing only that he could join her dream instead of being stuck in his own.

"Mr. Ayer," Tanner said on Wednesday as Keith worked to fix the gate leading to the track. Ike was busy with Dragnet, and the gate was all-but nonfunctional. Just to open it you had to drag the whole thing, and it was getting so bad that dragging it didn't even work anymore.

"Yeah." Keith lifted the gate from its hinges, swung it to the side and leaned it against the opposite fence. The support pole it had been attached to leaned awkwardly to the side, pulling the rest of the fence with it. He went back and examined it, pulling it one way and then the other. Whoever had poured the foundational concrete obviously didn't know what they were doing. It was cracked and chipping and so unstable that the pole had no choice but to fall. "What's up?"

Keith grabbed the shovel from the fence. "Would you bring me that wheelbarrow?"

"Oh, sure." Tanner did as instructed. "Listen, I hate to ask this, but Jamie's been all over Pine Hill, and everybody she's interviewed with wants a full-time employee if she's going to work for the summer. She's going to school the second summer session starting in July, and full-time's just not going to work. I know there's probably nothing, but she wanted me to ask if there was something she might do out here. Just to earn a little gas money."

With a whack of the shovel, Keith knocked a whole chunk of the concrete loose. He scooped it up and dumped it in the wheelbarrow. "I don't know, Tanner. The only thing I really know much about is the horses, and except when you and Ike are gone, we've pretty much got that covered."

"Well, what about when we're gone? I mean, surely there's something…"

Keith gave another good whack and the pole wobbled. "Here.

Hold this, or the whole fence is going to come down."

Tanner went to the other side of the pole and put his hand on it. In one motion it was stabilized. Keith continued to whack the concrete and dig it out from around the pole.

"We're going this weekend with Q-Main," Tanner said. "Maybe she could come and feed the horses to give you a break. She's really good with them, and if anything was major wrong, she could always call you."

The concrete was now coming out in large chunks. Deeper and deeper into the hole Keith dug. "Well, I'm going to be out of pocket tomorrow. I've got another interview with Ferrell in Houston." At that he cracked the shovel against the last few base chunks. He'd been trying to forget that interview. "So I guess you can bring her over and show her the ropes."

"Really?"

Keith liked the hopeful sound in Tanner's voice. He wished there was a millionth of that hope in his own. "Sure. Why not?"

"Ms. Montgomery, telephone," Inez said, knocking on her door after the kids were in bed.

"Okay, thanks." In one motion she was out of bed and had her robe on. Racing down the stairs, she willed herself not to trip. Through the kitchen, to the phone, she nearly slid right into the window before she got stopped. "Hello?"

"Maggie!"

Her heart slid through her. "Oh. Hi, Greg."

"Hey. Listen I don't have much time, but a bunch of us are going out tomorrow night, I was wondering if you wanted to go."

NO! screamed through her. She sat down on the chair in a heap. "I have to work."

"Maggie, for Pete sakes. You're their employee not their slave. Ask off. They can't make you work 24/7."

Some part of her said he was right, but the rest of her was saying she would rather be here, doing her job, than out with him and his friends. But she could hole up here and pass up every opportunity and then what? Get fired and have nothing? That didn't sound like a great plan either. Besides Greg was a pretty respectable Plan B. "Okay. I'll ask."

Twenty

Ten a.m. Houston, Texas. Noise. People. Cars. Chaos. Keith hated every second of it. He strode into Devonshire, Inc. knowing somehow he had to make this work—for Dallas, for his father, and for Mr. Henderson. Anything less than wowing Mr. Ferrell would be another giant nail in his coffin. He rolled his shoulders around, trying to get them to be comfortable in the dark business suit as he walked from the elevator to Mr. Lee Ferrell's secretary.

"May I help you?" She didn't sound happy nor even really alive, more like a machine.

"Umm, yes. I have a ten o'clock appointment with Mr. Ferrell."

"One moment please." She punched two buttons on the phone in front of her. "Your ten o'clock's here, Mr. Ferrell. Yes, sir." She punched the button again. "He'll be right with you."

"Umm, Patty Ann." Maggie knocked softly on the secretary's door. "May I speak with you?"

"Come on in, Ms. Montgomery." At her desk, Patty Ann sat ramrod straight, her red suit jacket looking like it was still on a hanger across her shoulders. "Is there a problem?"

"Umm, no, Ma'am." Maggie slid into the black upholstered chair and fought the shiver that always attacked her in this room. "I know it's really short notice, and I'll understand if you say no." Actually, she was hoping Patty Ann would say no. That would solve a lot of problems. "But I got invited out for tonight, and well, I was wondering…"

Patty Ann sighed.

"Like I said, I know it's short notice."

Patty Ann narrowed her gaze on Maggie causing another shiver. "Only tonight?"

"Oh, yes, Ma'am, and I wouldn't have to actually leave until seven or so, and I will be here tomorrow morning as usual."

There was a long pause as Patty Ann surveyed her. "Very well. I'll make arrangements."

"Mr. Ayer," Lee Ferrell, a short, little weasel of a man said from behind his enormous desk, "I do not have to tell you that I'm a very busy man, but in deference to your father-in-law, I have made an exception. So tell me what assets can you bring to Devonshire, Inc. that I'm not aware of?"

Keith had never felt so small. "I'm... hmm." He cleared his throat. "As we talked about before I've got managerial experience."

"Yes, with horses." Mr. Ferrell's sarcasm dripped from the words. "That's impressive."

"And I've got an MBA from A&M."

"Yes, as every other applicant does. Mr. Henderson, however, hinted at a more... shall we say a more enticing incentive."

Very slowly Keith shifted in his chair. "What incentive was that?"

Mr. Ferrell's gaze fell to the desk. "Well, Devonshire and Ayer Industries have several intertwining interests as well as several competing interests. The power grid that a dovetailing of their mutual assets, a thinning of the competition between us, coupled with your future wife's connections could be very shall we say convincing."

It was literally as if the devil was sitting across that desk saying, "You can have all of this..." The problem was, this devil had leverage like none other.

The legalities alone were enough to crumple Keith's knees, and he fought not to squirm under them. "Well, sir. I don't know if..."

Ferrell lifted his chin, his eyes flashing with malevolence. "Don't forget, your father-in-law has a lot riding on your answer. I am personally a large contributor to his bid for re-election. So please consider carefully."

"I..." Keith's gaze fell to his hands.

"We can negotiate your salary. I'm quite sure your contributions will be worth whatever you ask."

A million dollar car and a house the size of Vermont flashed through his mind. This could be well be the answer to the question of how he would ever pay for Dallas' dreams. However, his spirit was screaming that this was wrong, horribly, horribly wrong. To accept a job that he would hate forever, a job that would put his character, honor, and integrity in jeopardy, a job that would erase who he was from the planet forever? How much money was worth that?

His father would be furious, not to mention Dallas and Mr. Henderson. Then, like a sojourn in an oasis amidst the chaos, Keith's mind traced its way to a little church, in a little pew, standing next to the only one in the world who made him never apologize for who he was. What she would say was a question that didn't even need to be asked. His heart told him the answer. This wasn't right, and it never would be—no matter how much they wanted to convince him that it was.

He stood slowly, knowing this decision would cause a chain reaction he couldn't clearly see the end of. However, he knew this was a door he couldn't afford to open. "I'm sorry for taking up your time, Mr. Ferrell, but I'm going to have to decline the offer."

The little man's eyes narrowed to the point that he was glaring at Keith. "Son, declining this position is not in your best interest. Your father-in-law…"

"Well, sir, I think accepting this position is not in my best interest, and if my father-in-law has any integrity at all, he will understand why I cannot accept your offer." Keith held his hand across the desk, but Mr. Ferrell never moved. Finally he let his hand drop, and he walked to the door.

"You are making a grave mistake, Mr. Ayer."

At the door, he stopped, breathed through the thoughts of each fork in this particular road. The thought of taking the job coiled around him, sucking the air from his lungs so that suffocation seemed likely. Then he pulled in a full breath as the thought of opening this door that led to a thousand unknowns went through him. There was no challenge, no barrier to that breath. It was the only confirmation that he needed. With that, he opened the door, stepped out, and never looked back.

Maggie knew as well as anybody what today was. She and Keith had talked about it, under the tree on Sunday. Today he took another step away from her into his new life with Dallas. It hurt, but all day long, Maggie had prayed for Keith, that the right doors would be open to him so that he and Dallas could have the best start in life possible.

Just before dinner, Patty Ann showed up at the door to the playroom with a woman whose eyes were so dark, they were almost black. The rest of her was small—small shoulders, thin arms, hands with long, spindly fingers. Across the room, Peter took one look up and shrank back against the cabinets.

"Ms. Montgomery, Mrs. Haga is here to relieve you for the evening."

Maggie stood there, stunned into speechlessness. Mrs. Haga? Why had she not remembered this was a possibility? "Oh, I..."

Mrs. Haga stepped into the room. "Come, children. It's time for dinner. We must get washed up."

"Oh, they've already been..."

There was no hesitation as Mrs. Haga glared at Maggie. "They are children. No amount of washing will make them perfectly presentable, but we shall try. Come, children. Now!" She clapped her hands with the words, and Peter scrambled to his feet.

The look on his face ripped through Maggie with such force she could hardly breathe. "Mrs..." But they were already being marched across the hall.

"You are officially off-duty, Ms. Montgomery," Patty Ann said, and with that, she closed the door.

Slowly Maggie sank to the window seat. How could she go back now? How could she tell them what that monster had done to Peter? The thought of leaving them here like this threatened to annihilate every sane thought she could manage to think. And yet, what was the alternative? Marching downstairs to take them back? Telling Patty Ann? Calling Greg to tell him no when he was probably already on his way?

"Oh, God," she prayed softly. "They are just babies. Please protect them."

Dallas made the connection on Keith's cell phone ten minutes before he got back home. He had stopped at Wal-Mart for supplies, and something about just walking and thinking had kept him there far longer than he should have stayed. It was almost seven when he got to the last turn before the gate. He'd even decided against going to the stables. Surely Tanner and Ike and Jamie had been able to handle everything.

"So, how did it go?" Dallas asked in anxious excitement.

The first hurdle. "Well, he made me an offer I couldn't refuse."

"Fabulous!" Dallas squealed. "Tell me all about it. I want the details."

He was far more casual than he ever thought he could be. "Well, there's only one that really matters."

"What's that?" She had never sounded more excited.

"I refused it."

That stopped her. "Refused it? Refused what?"

"The job. The offer. All of it."

"Wh...?" She laughed, kind of. "Keith, that's not funny."

"I'm not laughing."

"You... You told them no?"

He let out a solid breath. "Yes, Dallas. I told them no."

"Are you out of your mind?" She was shrieking now, and Keith had to hold the cell phone away from his ear lest he go deaf. "Dad put his reputation on the line to get you another interview, and you turned them down!"

Well, her father had put someone's reputation on the line, but it wasn't his. Keith turned into the gate, and his heart slammed into his ribcage. There, sitting at the base of the mansion's steps sat Greg's little silver sports car. For one reckless moment, Keith thought about stopping, but instead he gunned it to get behind the trees before they came out. Seeing them, together, would've been more than he could take.

"I cannot believe this! How stupid can you possibly be? That was the job of a lifetime! What were you thinking? You couldn't have been thinking. You couldn't have! You turned down an offer that would have set us for life!" She was still shrieking when he turned the pickup into his own driveway and punched the garage door. She was shrieking, but he was no longer listening.

Keith's mind went to where they were going on a Thursday

night—the movies, a play, dinner, dancing? There wasn't an option he liked. Just the thought of them together was enough to toss his sanity overboard into waves of helplessness and hurt.

"Keith!" The incessant diatribe stopped. "Keith!"

His name brought him back as he put the pickup in park and got out. "What?"

"Are you listening to me?"

The correct answer was no. The prudent answer was... "Sorry. What did you say?"

"I *said* we could still get you another interview with Ferrell. Maybe he would believe there was just a misunderstanding, and you were playing hardball."

"Dallas." He stopped her. This discussion was becoming annoying. "I'm not going back. I don't want to work for Lee Ferrell. I don't want to work at some firm that sucks your life out to inflate their bottom line."

"Keith, wake up. This is the real world we're talking about here—not some dinky, little pet farm. Now, we are a month from walking down that aisle, so you'd better get your head pulled out and start thinking like a man instead of like a little kid, or we're going to have a serious problem on our hands."

"Look. I'm not cut out for office life. I never have been."

"You have an MBA! What were you going to do with that? Feed horses your whole life?"

He didn't have the sanity to explain that the MBA was his father's idea nor that feeding horses all day was what had kept him from throwing himself off a cliff for all those years. Instead, he shook his head. "I've got to go."

"Go? We're not finished yet."

"Yeah? Well, I am." And he clicked the phone off, threw it to the counter and went to take a shower. Trapped in this monkey suit, he felt dirtier than he had his whole life.

"Give me a good scotch any day. It's the best way to unwind," Greg said as they sat at the bar, waiting for their table. "Are you sure you don't want anything?" He tipped the glass up until the ice cubes clinked against the side when he put it down.

"No, no thanks." Maggie's gaze wandered through the

darkened bar area of the restaurant. She'd never been in a place so fancy. She knew she should be adequately impressed; however, the only thing she could concentrate on was how badly she wanted to go home to check on how Peter and Isabella were doing. *Dear Lord, please keep them safe.*

The shower hadn't helped much. Keith knew he should be worried about Dallas and what happened next, but that paled in comparison with the fact that Maggie was out with Greg... again. The sun had dipped below the horizon, and Keith stepped out onto the porch, a beer in one hand, grief filling his heart. He leaned there on the doorpost and gazed across the patio to the swing she had sat on so many nights before with Greg. He couldn't get a clear picture of Greg, but he could see her as if she still sat there.

He took a drink, pushed away from the doorpost, and ambled over to the swing. All he wanted was to get closer to her even as it felt as if she was moving away. He sat down hard on the swing and let his mind wind through the memories. That first day—her coming down the stairs and falling into him, her walking with him after they got her car put away. Sitting at the waterfall, riding horses, showing up with the kids at the stables. Praying at Peter's bedside, sitting amidst a kitchen splattered with pink yogurt.

Fighting to push the memories from him, Keith took another drink, and then one memory seeped through all the others. It was her, standing at the window looking out into the dark night as the kids slept behind her. That memory tore through him, and ache for her pain clutched him. He remembered her crying in his arms, telling him about her parents and how life would have been so different if only someone she would never know hadn't made such a horrible choice.

A horrible choice. Keith's gaze fell to the can in his hand. How many horrible choices had he made? How many times had he just wanted the hurt to stop so badly that drowning it seemed the only option? As he gazed at that can, he saw with perfect clarity the life it had doomed her to live.

It wasn't a hard choice, more one that came of its own volition. Slowly he reached his hand out past the swing to the lawn beyond, and like the water trickling over the sides of the falls, he poured the rest of the liquid out. He closed his eyes, feeling the desire for it go. Then he sat back and let him feel what life was like on the other side of that door.

A scotch before dinner, two glasses of wine with dinner, and now they were at the bar with Greg's friends. Thankfully Virginia wasn't invited to this little soirée. At least that was one thing to be grateful for.

"Dance?" Greg asked, standing from his chair and offering Maggie his hand.

She put hers in his and let him lead her to the floor. Once there, he took her in his arms, and she put her head on his chest more so she didn't have to look at him than because she wanted to get closer.

He bent his head so his mouth was close to her ear. "You've been awful quiet tonight. Everything all right?"

Her thoughts flashed to Peter and Isabella. They were in bed by now, and her heart panged at the thought of not being with them. "Just a little worried about the kids," she said softly.

Greg backed up a little. "The kids?"

"Peter and Izzy." She shook her head to keep herself from crying.

That brought a look of true incredulousness to his face. "Why would you be worried about them? You're not their mother or anything."

Maggie ducked her head and forced herself to breathe. She huddled closer to him because running wasn't an option. The feel of his arms around her was so different than Keith's. She fought not to notice that, but she did anyway. Her heart filled her chest at that thought, and the tears came again. Greg was nice, but he would never be what she really wanted. What she really wanted was Keith, but he was so far out of her reach, all hoping would do was end up hurting her more.

No, she may not like it, but Greg was here, and she was going to have to be happy with that.

With everything in him, Keith wanted to call the mansion. Just talking to her might make the spinning of his life stop for a while. Still, without even being there, she had guided him through two decisions that he knew would change the course of everything for him. If only he could tell her that...

"This one, right?" Maggie asked as she pulled the little sports car up through the parking lot to Greg's space.

"Good memory," he said, the words slurring together.

When the car was parked, he looked over at her with a goofy grin. "Well, we're home."

"Yes, we are."

He continued to look at her in a way that was making her very nervous. "I guess you're coming up to call a cab?"

"I guess so." It was not what she wanted to do. Carefully she unwound herself from the car, and when she got around front, he was waiting for her. With his hand on her back, they walked up the stairs to his apartment.

Once inside, he went to the cabinet rather than to the phone. "Would you like something to drink?"

She couldn't believe he could even ask the question. "Uh, no thanks. I'd better get home." She walked over to his phone and pulled out the phonebook. Across the kitchen she heard the clink of ice cubes. Quickly she pulled the phone up, dialed the number, and asked for a ride.

However, midway through the phone call, she could feel him right behind her. Even after the cab company was gone, she held the phone, stalling a few more seconds. Finally she knew she couldn't stand there holding the phone until the cab came, so she hung it up. She turned and tried to smile at him. "Well, thanks for tonight." She pulled her purse strap up her shoulder and anchored it there with her opposite hand. "I had fun."

"You know." Greg set his drink on the countertop behind her. "You really don't have to leave. I'm free all night." He leaned in to her, and the smell of alcohol and smoke on him was overwhelming.

"That's nice." She pushed him away. "But really, I have to get home. It's after two."

"So?" He leaned in again, this time more forcefully.

"So. I have to be up in four and a half hours."

"All the more reason to stay." His breath, hot and sticky, grazed her neck as his hand brushed her hair back off her neck.

Maggie shrank back from his advance until she was pinned to the counter. "Hey. Greg. Listen. Not tonight, okay? I've really got to go." She was breathing heavily, but not for the reason he obviously thought.

Still he advanced. "The cab's not going to be right here. We could at least finish off the night right."

"Greg! Hello!" She used both hands and arms to get a wedge between them. "Stop it."

"Maggie." He pawed the back of her head. "Maggie, I want you so bad."

The sound of the horn out the front was the best thing she'd ever heard. "The car's here." She pushed to get free of him. "Greg. The car's here. I've got to go!" And with that, she broke free and fled.

The trip home was the longest ride of her life. It compared only to the moves she had made to different homes—only this ride was different than those. This time, she was trapped not by someone else's mistakes and decisions but by her own. How could she have been so blind as to trust Greg? Sure he was a nice guy, but nice guys tended to not be so nice when the alcohol took over. She'd learned that frightening fact more than once. It had happened often enough throughout her life to make her leery of the next time it did.

Lest she drown in the memories, she forced herself to think of something else. The kids were her first thought, and that too brought a slap of pain. She'd left them in the clutches of a monster, why? Because she didn't want to let Greg down? How stupid was that?

She leaned her head back on the seat and watched the lights of Houston stream by. So many, many things she would change if she could. So many heartaches she never wanted to feel again. As her mind wound to the one that could change everything, a single tear escaped her eye, and she didn't even reach up to brush it away. He had his life, and as scant as it was, she had hers. That was how it was, and she had to either accept it or let it kill her completely. The trouble was, she couldn't decide which would hurt the most.

Friday morning Maggie awoke with a start. Her first thought was how badly her head hurt. Her second was that the sun was up and brighter than normal. With a jerk she looked at the alarm clock. They had fifteen minutes to be downstairs for breakfast. In the next breath she was up and grabbing for her clothes. It took less than four minutes, and with no make-up coupled with a ponytail corralling the hair she hardly brushed, she raced first to Peter's room to wake him up.

"Pete. Peter. It's Friday morning. Time to get up, sweetheart."

The child rolled over and rubbed his eyes.

"Come on, sweetie. We're going to be late for breakfast." She went into his closet and grabbed an outfit. "I'll be right back to help you." With that she ran across the hallway to Isabella's room. The blinds were shut, causing the room to be a deep, shadowy gray. "Baby girl. Hey. Good morning." She went to the crib and laid her hand on the child's back. "Wake up, little one. It's breakfast time."

In Isabella's closet, she turned on the light and took out a pink outfit complete with baby capris. She snapped the light off and strode for the crib. Still asleep, Isabella barely moved as Maggie picked her up and took her to the changing table. It was like she was on autopilot, and in no time the little girl was changed and ready—except that she was still asleep. Maggie tucked her onto her shoulder and went to help Peter.

"Morning, little man. How are you?" She laid Isabella on Peter's bed and helped him with his shirt and then his pants. Frantically she raced to the closet for socks and shoes. Sitting on his bed, she swept him up to her lap and worked the socks and then the shoes on the little feet.

He rubbed his eyes. "Are you leaving today?"

"No. Sweetheart, but we're going to be fired if we don't get down to breakfast like super-fast." Maggie stood him off, leaped to her feet, and grabbed up Isabella. "Come on."

"What are you going to do then?" his father asked in dissatisfaction as Keith sat across from the desk, having been summoned for a meeting he would rather have skipped.

"I'm not sure, but Devonshire is not it." That much, and only that much he was sure of.

His father frowned. "You do realize that Dallas is accustomed to living at a certain level. Lewell is beside himself with worry for her."

"I'm sure." Not to mention himself, Keith thought. "But there are things in this life that are more important than having enough money to make everyone else respect you."

"Hhrump. Like what?"

"Like respecting yourself, and having values and principles you don't sell down the river for a few bucks." How he felt so calm, he had no idea. He slid his fingers together loosely. "We'll be okay."

Displeasure crossed his father's face. "How do you know that? You don't even have a job lined up nor according to Lewell a house."

"Because something's going to work. I just have to wait for the right doors to come open."

His father's face fell further. "You're talking in riddles, Keith. You have to make some solid plans here. You can't keep a wife happy on dreams and hopes and wishes. Dallas needs you to be a man and to start accepting your responsibilities."

"Even if that includes selling myself to the highest bidder?"

That stopped his father's rant.

Keith shrugged. "I'll find something, but it's not going to be at Devonshire."

Seeing no way to convince his son, his father stood. "Well, I hope you know what you're doing because Lewell is going to eat you alive if this doesn't work." He led the way to the door as Keith stood and followed him. "I'll tell you one thing's for sure, Lewell is not pleased, and that's a dangerous line to be crossing."

They walked into the hallway. Two steps and his father changed the subject.

"So is there a race this weekend? I was wanting to take Vivian if it's not too far away."

"Yeah. Q-Main is racing at Harrah's tomorrow." Keith stopped at the base of the stairs, and his attention snapped up as

Maggie and children came nearly flying down them.

"So Ike and Tanner are gone already?" his father asked.

"Uh, yeah. They left yesterday afternoon."

"Oh!" Maggie pulled up short midway down the bottom curve. "I'm sorry, Sir. Umm... we're a little late for breakfast."

Concern slid through Keith. She looked pale and harried and not at all like the Maggie he knew.

"Yes. I believe Mrs. Ayer is waiting for us all," his father said. He turned to Keith. "I guess that means you'll be taking care of things this weekend?"

"Here?"

His father glanced at his children and pursed his lips. "I think it might be wise if you check in on things, just to make sure."

On cat feet and without directly looking at Keith, Maggie slipped past them. Her heart was set on permanent spin. "I smell waffles." She shook her shoulder a bit. "Izzy, time to wake up, baby. Waffles."

They walked into the dining room, and a face that would've frozen Africa met them. "Well, it's about time," Vivian said. "Ms. Montgomery, if you are going to take time off to go on your little rendezvous, I expect you to not be late and keep the rest of us waiting."

Mr. Ayer stepped in behind her.

"I'm sorry, Ma'am. Really. My alarm clock didn't..."

"This is not a time for excuses." Vivian rapped on the table. "Inez."

Like she was a trained seal, Inez appeared with a stack of waffles and a plate of sausage. "It's turkey sausage, just as you requested, Ma'am. Would you like anything else?"

"A glass of orange juice please," Vivian said, and Inez walked out. "You would think after all these years, she would know not to set the milk in front of me. Ugh." Vivian picked up the crystal pitcher and handed it to Maggie to put down the table.

Maggie was still trying to wake Isabella up. She set the pitcher next to Peter. "Izzy. Sweetheart." Only then did the child move just a little.

"Vivian," Mr. Ayer said as he forked into the waffles, "Keith just informed me that one of the horses will be racing in Louisiana this weekend. I thought it might be a good time to get away—what with the wedding coming up and all. It might be our only chance before the middle of June. I thought we could leave this evening if you want to go."

"Do you have the box secured and the hotel booked?"

He waved the question off. "I'll get Cherise to do it when I go into the office today."

Mrs. Ayer glanced at Maggie. "Who will be watching the house?"

"I asked Keith to keep an eye on things, and Patty Ann will be here too."

She looked all-but horrified. "Keith? Are you sure that's a good idea?"

He stopped eating for a moment. "He needs some responsibility on his shoulders. Maybe that will help him get his head on straight."

She sighed dramatically. "Well, I guess it would do me some good to get away for a weekend. I certainly won't have a chance after this."

"Iz," Maggie said, pulling the child off her shoulder and sitting her on her lap as she tried not to listen to the conversation. "Let's eat some waffles, little one."

The little girl shook her head slowly, her curls sliding across Maggie's ribcage.

Worry snapped into Maggie. "You don't want waffles? But they're your favorite."

Again Isabella shook her head. Maggie corkscrewed her mouth as she looked down at the child. "I don't think you feel very good. We're going to have to let you lay down a little." She stood from the table. "I think I'll just take her upstairs."

Instantly Peter was on his feet. "I'll go too."

Maggie looked down at his plate with a full sausage and nearly as much waffle left. "Why don't you stay down here and eat?"

He wound his hand through hers. "I want to go with you."

Seeing no other option, Maggie nodded. "If you'll excuse us."

By lunchtime Isabella was decidedly sick. Even the pediatric hydration liquid hadn't stayed down. The night before was looking less and less worth it all the time. For the third time that day, Maggie put Isabella in her crib with the child already asleep. She laid her hand on her back and said a soft prayer. Then she turned and took Peter's hand as they tiptoed out.

"Ms. Montgomery," Patty Ann said, striding down the hall and meeting them at Isabella's door.

Instantly Maggie held her finger to her lips. "Shh. Izzy isn't feeling good."

"Yes. Well." Patty Ann waited until the door was closed but didn't lower her voice. "I wanted to inform you that the Ayers are going out of town this evening, so they will not be at dinner."

There were moments to thank God for small favors. This was one of them. "Okay."

"They will be back Sunday afternoon at four, so I hope you are not planning any last minute absences."

"Uh, no, Ma'am." Maggie felt Peter huddling behind her knee. "I'm here for the duration."

Patty Ann scowled. "Good." With that she turned on her heel and stalked off.

Maggie looked down at Peter. "Ugh. She's fun. Let's go see what we can do while we wait for your sister to get better."

It was stupid to even think it, but he knew they wouldn't get many more chances like this. At 5:30, Keith left the stables and drove to the mansion. His parents were gone. He'd seen them leave. Dinner was at six, and he didn't want to miss it.

"Oh, baby girl. Your little eyes look awful." Maggie sighed and looked at her watch. Across the room, Peter played with his blocks. "I guess I'll have to see if Inez will let us eat up here. You don't look like dinner material."

Knowing she was going to get reamed for it, Maggie went down to the kitchen. "Izzy's still sick. Is there any way we can take some plates upstairs and eat up there?"

Inez looked horrified. "Eating upstairs? Patty Ann would fire me on the spot."

"Well, Patty Ann is gone for the day." Maggie put her hands on her hips, not willing to roll over and play dead. "Peter is hungry, and so am I. Izzy can't come down here, and I'm not leaving her up there in the shape she's in. So that doesn't leave us many options, does it?"

Keith heard the voices in the kitchen and followed them that direction.

"But Ms. Montgomery, one spot on the carpet, and you know…" Her words trailed off as Keith walked in.

He looked at Maggie and overwhelming worry snapped into him. "What's wrong?"

Maggie crossed her arms. "Izzy's sick, and I can't just leave her up there to bring Peter down here to eat. And unfortunately I can't split myself in half to be in both places at once." She glared at Inez. The oppressiveness of the house was obviously beginning to grate her nerves.

"Oh." Keith didn't want to make the suggestion because he had really hoped they could eat together, but it was the best option. "Well, I could eat with Pete, and then I could watch them while you eat."

Her gaze was less than certain. "You're eating here tonight?"

"Looks like it."

Maggie was in the rocking chair with Isabella again, holding her, stroking her hair when suddenly she felt something strange at the back of the child's head. Worry collapsed over her. "What's this?" Rounded out, it felt like the outside of a golf ball. Isabella let out a whimper of pain as Maggie lightly rubbed across it.

"Knock. Knock," Keith said softly knocking on the door as he and Peter appeared there.

Maggie barely looked up.

"We brought you some dinner. Smuggled it up ourselves. Right, Pete?" Proudly Keith produced the plate, but Maggie hardly noticed. The plate in his hand lowered along with his eyebrows. "What's wrong?"

"Come here, and feel this."

Keith set the plate on the dresser and strode to where she sat. He sat down on his heel and gently ran his fingers over the place Maggie was feeling. The second he touched the spot, Isabella whimpered past the thumb in her mouth and huddled closer to Maggie. Concern dragged Keith's eyebrows together. "What happened?"

"I don't know. I was just holding her and rubbing her hair, and I felt that."

His scowl deepened. "Did she fall today?"

"She's been sick all day. Even this morning, I couldn't get her to wake up."

"Did she fall last night?"

"I don't... I don't know. She was with..." Maggie's mind snapped into gear, and she looked over to where Peter stood pressed against the door. "Peter, did Isabella fall last night?"

Keith spun slowly to look at the child who looked like he was facing a firing squad. "Pete?"

Maggie reached her hand out to stop Keith. "Don't scare him."

Keith nodded but stood and went to the little boy. He sat down on his heels to be eye level with Peter. "Pete, what happened to Izzy?"

Peter looked over Keith's shoulder to Maggie for help. "I didn't do it."

Anger and guilt slid through her. She should never have left. "It's okay, Peter. We know you didn't do it. Come here."

It was clear he didn't want to, so Keith picked him up and carried him to Maggie. "It's all right, slugger. You can tell us." At Maggie's chair he stood the child on the floor but kept his hand on Peter's back as he sat back down on his heels. "It's all right. We won't be mad. We just need to know what happened."

Tears the size of grapefruits welled in the little brown eyes. "She slipped."

"On what?" Maggie asked, her heart turning over.

"On the floor." His gaze fell to his shoes. "Mrs. Haga was mad."

Maggie's gaze went to Keith who looked at her with horror. "Can you start at the beginning, Pete? Tell us everything that happened."

He didn't start immediately, but Keith rubbed his back slowly to assure him it would be all right.

"We were taking a bath, and Izzy was playing like she always does when she hits the water. Mrs. Haga told her not to, but Izzy didn't listen. So Mrs. Haga said she had to get out." The story slowed to a crawl. "She took Izzy out of the bathtub and stood her next to it. I don't know why, but Izzy started to walk away, and…" He was obviously fighting not to cry. "Mrs. Haga grabbed Izzy's arm and pulled her backward. Izzy slipped."

"And hit her head on the tub," Maggie finished for him.

Miserably he nodded. "I didn't know she was going to do that, or I would've told her not to."

There were tears in Maggie's eyes too. How could she have been so selfish? She knew something like this was going to happen.

"Mrs. Haga didn't tell anyone?" Keith asked, his voice strangling through the question.

Peter shook his head slowly. "She told me not to."

"I should've known," Maggie said in horror. "I should've known."

Keith looked at her with patient, gentle eyes. "How could you have known?"

She gazed right at him. Lying wasn't even an option. "Because it's happened before."

The words hit Keith like shots from a double-barrel rifle. They knocked him backward on his heels. "What do you mean it's happened before? When?"

Maggie hesitated, but only for a second. "The last time I left. When I went to your party."

"My…?"

"With Greg."

The volleys to his heart were coming fast and hard, and Keith had to force the air in to keep himself calm.

"Peter had marks on his arm the next morning. Bruises."

Fury knocked through him as he stood and paced away from her. "And you didn't tell anybody?"

Her voice shook, and fear snaked through it. "I didn't know who to tell. They were as liable to blame me as anyone, and then where would the kids be?"

He spun. "Well, you could've told me."

She shook her head. "You were busy with Dallas, and besides…" Her gaze fell. "I tried."

That stopped him. "Tried…? But you never said anything."

Tears crowded her eyes, and anguish slashed across her face as she looked up at him. "I… We went… down to the stables, but…" Her gaze fell from his, heavy with words she wasn't saying.

"But…?"

Twisting as if in the breeze her gaze darted one way and then the other as she fought not to cry, but she sniffed anyway. "Ike saw me waiting for you, and… Well, he wasn't very happy I was there."

Slow understanding sunk into Keith. "That day Tanner found you walking."

She nodded as despair crumpled over her. "I didn't want to make things bad for you. I didn't want to get you into trouble." Her tears overflowed their banks as she ducked her head. "I'm so sorry. I should've told someone. I should've done something…"

"Oh, no. Maggie." He knelt down in front of her and reached his hand to just under her ear. "No. Listen, I'm the one that's sorry." He pulled her to him as the tears streamed down her cheeks. "I'm so sorry I wasn't there." His own grief pulled to the surface as he held her there sobbing. "Ike didn't know. He couldn't have."

She nodded but pulled back. There, she wiped the tears from her eyes even as new ones took their place. "I think he thought we were… That I was…" Maggie's gaze fell between them laden with embarrassment. She corralled the tears, but the effort was obvious. "I figured the less we bothered you the better."

Keith closed his eyes, willing himself to stay calm. When he opened them again, his determination to protect them all was steel hard. "Now you listen to me." He narrowed his gaze at her. "If you ever, ever need anything, all you have to do is call. I am right here." His gaze burrowed through hers. "Got it?"

Slowly she nodded, and the tentative trust was clear.

"Good." His gaze fell to Isabella. "Now, do you think we need to take her in or what?"

Twenty-One

It was midnight before they got back from the emergency room. Thankfully the bump was just that—a bump with a very slight concussion that would not be a problem. Because of lack of sleep and the emotional day, Maggie was completely exhausted by the time they laid the kids down and made it out into the hallway. She didn't even have the sanity to make a fast get-away.

"Maggie," Keith said softly when they were standing at her door, "I wanted to tell you thanks."

She turned to him incredulously. "Thanks? For what?"

"For trusting me enough to tell me. For coming to tell me the first time it happened. I just wish I had been there." Gently he pulled her to him, and his arms were the best place she'd ever been. He felt so safe and so indescribably stable. "I meant what I said about calling me if you ever need anything." His embrace fell away, but his hands found her arms. He lowered his gaze to hers. "Okay?"

She nodded but couldn't be fully certain this wasn't just some nice dream she had somehow fallen into.

"Now get some sleep. You look exhausted."

"Yeah." She tried to laugh it off. "After not getting back until like three in the morning last night, I feel like I've lived six days in one today."

Concern slashed through Keith. "Why didn't you get back until three?" In the next second he knew he shouldn't have asked as why smacked into him.

"Oh, you know. Those cab drivers have a racket going," she said, laughing again.

But Keith wasn't laughing. "Cab drivers? What happened to Greg?"

She shrugged and let her gaze find the darkness at her feet. "He was drinking."

If she was trying to make him crazy, it was definitely working. "Maggie, why didn't you call me?"

"Because it was three in the morning." She laughed softly even as her hand came up to her other arm. "Besides what was I going to say, 'Hi, Keith. It's me. My date is over. Come get me.'"

Irritation scratched through him. "Well, that would've been better than you riding alone in some cab all over the countryside in the middle of the night." The overpowering need to protect her jammed into his chest. "Now, you listen to me. I do not want you calling cabs to take you home in the middle of the night ever again."

Annoyance flashed through her eyes as her gaze jerked up to his. "You're not my father. Besides, how else was I supposed to get home? Walk?"

"No. You were supposed to call me."

She sighed, and it was obvious she was tired. "Look, Keith. I don't want to argue... especially about this."

He corralled his own emotions. "Yeah, okay. We can talk about this tomorrow. Go get some sleep, and don't set your alarm for in the morning. I'll cover for you."

Panic slid through her face. "For breakfast?"

He smiled. "And lunch and dinner the way you look." He lifted his chin. "Now go get some sleep."

Saturday Maggie slept in, and it was like the best vacation ever. They spent most of the rest of the day together except for the time Keith had to run to the stables to check on things. Isabella was feeling better. At least she was playing now. At dinner they talked about everything and nothing in particular. It was strange to

Maggie how easy Keith was to be with, so unlike Greg who seemed to be more show than substance.

By the time they tucked Peter in and said their prayers, Maggie found herself wishing this never had to end.

"So, are we going to church tomorrow?" Keith asked as she made it to her door.

"Bright and early." She opened her door.

"You know Dad and Vivian will be back tomorrow." Something in his voice stopped her. "We have to tell them. You know that, right?"

Dread slid through her. He was right, and she knew it. However, nothing in her wanted to face them with this information.

"I think we should do it together," he said slowly. "If you want me there."

Maggie turned. His presence filled the space between them. He was there, gazing into her eyes with concern and hope. "I don't want to get you into trouble."

"And you don't deserve to be in trouble. So if we both go…"

"Are you sure?"

"Very."

Church flew by, and in no time they were out at the stables so Keith could check on things. There was no reason for them to be there really, other than neither Maggie nor the kids wanted to see him go. At the stables they got out of the pickup and walked to the barn, Maggie holding Izzy in one arm and Peter's hand with her other hand.

"This won't take long," Keith said.

A young woman dressed in faded jeans and a T-shirt strode out of the barn. She had long blonde hair, and she was shorter even than Maggie by several inches.

"Oh, Mr. Ayer," she said, putting her hand up to block out the sun. "I didn't know you were coming. Tanner said I was supposed to feed them."

"I just wanted to make sure you remembered," Keith said with a smile. Then his glance chanced to Maggie. "Oh, Jamie. This is Maggie." He put his hand on Maggie's back, and her pulse jumped into a higher gear.

"Hi, Maggie." Jamie stuck out her hand, and Maggie shook it. "Hi."

"And this is Isabella and Peter," Keith said proudly.

"It's nice to meet you." Jamie stepped up and stuck her hand out to Peter. "You're a cutie."

He smiled slightly. Jamie ruffled his hair. Then she stood and looked at Isabella who was curled on Maggie's chest sucking her thumb.

"And you are adorable." Jamie ran her hand gently over Isabella's curls. "It looks like somebody could use a nap."

Keith nodded. "Maybe we should head on back to the house since Jamie's got this under control."

"No problem," Jamie said, stepping away from them. "Y'all take care."

"We will."

They walked to the pickup.

"She's nice," Maggie said.

"Tanner's girlfriend. She's helping out a little to make some gas money."

Maggie nodded. "Well, Tanner has good taste. I'm glad to see him with someone so nice. He deserves it."

The rest of the afternoon they stayed in the air conditioning of the mansion. Isabella didn't need to be out in the heat, and neither of them really wanted to be either. So they spent the afternoon in the kids' rooms, playing, wrestling, reading, and resting with the kids. It was nice to have a day to just do nothing.

However, the reprieve couldn't last. When the Ayers announced their return downstairs, Keith looked at Maggie, and she knew it was time for the inquisition.

"You ready?" he asked.

Had there been a way to say no, she would have. Instead she nodded, and with him holding Izzy and Maggie's hand in Peter's they walked out. Down the stairs they went, trooping one behind the other as if marching into enemy territory.

"Welcome home," Keith said, far too happy and normal sounding for Maggie to match.

"Well, it looks like it's still standing. That's something," Mr.

Ayer said, gazing at them as they made their descent. "We won. Q-Main ran a great race."

"That's great, Dad," Keith said. "Really great."

Mr. Ayer nodded and smiled happily. "I think I'll give Ike a raise. He deserves it after that one."

"Hello, Peter." Vivian reached down and gave her son the obligatory hug. "Did you have a good time?"

"Uh-huh. We went to see the horses today."

"Horsies," Isabella said, but there wasn't much of a squeal.

Maggie looked down at her. No, the bouncy child of a week ago still hadn't returned.

For an awkward moment no one said anything. Then Keith exhaled ever-so-slightly. "Dad, Vivian, we need to talk."

Mr. Ayer's face went ashen with the tone in Keith's voice, and suddenly Maggie knew why.

"Umm, it's about the children, Sir," she said before he could misconstrue Keith's intentions any further.

"Can't this wait?" Vivian whined. "We just got home."

"No, I'm afraid not," Keith said. "It's pretty serious, and we wanted you to know what's been going on as soon as you got home."

Mr. Ayer looked more confused than displeased.

"Could we go into your office?" Keith asked, and his father nodded.

"I'll let the kids with Inez for a minute," Maggie said, grateful that she didn't have to follow them all down the hallway. She took the kids to the kitchen and told Inez she would be back. It took everything she had to walk down that hall. When she slipped into the room, Keith was waiting for her at the door. He guided her to one of the mahogany-wood chairs covered in expensive black leather.

He sat next to her, his parents on the other side of the desk. Keith cleared his throat. "We wanted you all to know that we found a bump on Isabella's head on Friday night. It was pretty good sized, and we took her to the emergency room."

"A bump?" Vivian asked incredulously. "What from?"

Keith glanced at Maggie and then leveled his gaze on his father. "We managed to get the story out of Peter. It seems that the fill-in babysitter, yanked Isabella and made her slip. She fell and hit her head on the tub, causing the bump. We filled out a report on her at the hospital. It's standard."

"But she's been our fill-in for years," Vivian said. "She wouldn't…"

"It wasn't the first time." Maggie pulled in a breath and let out her fear. "She hurt Peter the last time she was here. I saw the bruises on his arms. He told me she shook him really hard. He's terrified of her."

"But…" Vivian started.

Mr. Ayer folded his hands on the desk. "Are you sure about this?"

Keith never flinched. "There's no doubt."

They walked out together so his parents could discuss the situation. With her arms wrapped at her chest, Maggie walked slightly in front of him, not saying a word.

"Are you okay?" he asked with concern.

"I just hope they don't think I did it."

Peace flowed through Keith. "Dad's smart enough to know we were telling the truth."

They got to the front door, and Keith stopped. "Well, I guess this is where I get off."

She spun toward him. "You're leaving?"

He grinned and winked at her. "What? Did you think I was going to stay forever?"

Sadness went through her. "A girl can hope, can't she?"

"Mrs. Haga has been notified that her services are no longer needed," Patty Ann said stridently. "So until further notice, you are on duty."

"I understand," Maggie said, nodding. The secretary's office seemed even colder today.

"That means you are not to even consider asking off until we have cleared someone new."

"Yes, Ma'am."

"And just so you know, that may not be any time soon."

Why did this feel like a sentencing session? "Don't worry about it. I don't plan on going anywhere any time soon anyway."

Monday night Keith drove into Houston. There were some things that needed to be said face-to-face. He climbed the steps to the second floor apartment and knocked. Putting his hand on his hip, he waited, rehearsing what he had come to say just as he had been for all of 24 hours.

"Keith!" Greg sounded happy to see him when he opened the door. "Come in, buddy. This is a surprise. I thought you must've forgotten where I live."

"No, just haven't had much time to make the trip recently."

Greg walked into the kitchen. "Can I get you something? Bud? Coors?"

The thought made Keith ill. "Uh, no thanks. I'm driving."

From the refrigerator Greg checked him with a disbelieving look. "Never bothered you before." Greg laughed as he brought one into the living room for himself.

Keith sat down on the couch. His gaze went to the coffee table as fuzzy memories of games of quarters drifted aimlessly through him. The parties were legend, and yet they didn't hold the amusement they once had. He retrained his gaze to his friend.

"So what brings you all the way down the mountain?"

"Well," Keith said, shifting slightly, "this is probably not my place, but I have to say something because it's going to drive me crazy if I don't."

Greg took a drink. "Sounds serious."

"It is." Keith paused to gather his courage. "It's about Maggie."

"Maggie?" Greg's head snapped up incredulously.

It took another breath to get the words out. "Do you know about her… well, her growing up?"

"She said she grew up in Del Rio."

Keith watched Greg take another drink. "Did she tell you why?"

Greg shrugged. "I don't know. Because she liked Del Rio?"

It was all Keith could do to keep himself from knocking Greg flat. "No. Because she was an orphan."

Across the room, Greg's face fell with the can.

"She grew up in the foster care system. Her parents died in a car accident when she was eight."

Concern slid over Greg's features. "I don't... Why didn't she tell me this?"

"It gets worse." Keith knew this was betraying every confidence she'd ever trusted him with, but he had to say it, had to get Greg to understand so he would stop being an idiot and hurting Maggie. "They were hit by a drunk driver."

"A drunk...?" Greg looked down at the can and thought for a long, long minute. "That's why..."

"Yeah." Keith's place in this situation had been left so far behind, it was no longer even in the rearview mirror. "Look, I don't want to step on any toes here, but her riding out into the boondocks in some cab for an hour by herself is not exactly safe. I told her she could call me, but I don't think she'll do that."

Greg shook his head. "Is she mad at me?"

"No." It killed him to say that. What he wanted to do was to lie and ruin every chance they had together, but he couldn't do that to Greg or to Maggie. "I just thought you should know that's all."

"Ye... yeah, man. Thanks for telling me."

His heart wouldn't let him go without saying it, but the words were pulling emotions from the center of him. "Treat her right, Greg. Okay? She's been through hell already, and she deserves better."

"Yeah." Greg nodded in understanding. "Okay. I will."

"Well, are you going to congratulate us or what?" Ike asked, walking into the office Tuesday morning.

Keith barely looked up from the paperwork. "Congratulations."

"Gee, you sound so happy. I would've thought you'd be bouncing off the walls for joy."

"I am. Inside." He sounded as surly as he felt. The talk with Greg hadn't made him feel any better. If anything, it had made him feel worse.

"We won, you know," Ike said, sitting on the other side of the desk.

"I heard."

"You behave yourself while we were gone?"

Keith stood, tired of this conversation. "I was an angel just like always." He grabbed his hat and stalked to the door. "Time to get some real work done. Don't burn the place down while I'm gone."

"Ms. Montgomery," Inez said long after the sun had gone down on Wednesday. "Phone call."

Already tucked in for the night, Maggie dragged herself out of bed. Isabella was recovering, and they were back to a modified lesson schedule. It was already getting old. She tramped down to the kitchen and picked up the phone. "Hello?"

"Maggie, it's Greg."

"Oh, hi." She sat down on the chair. Somehow she had hoped he wouldn't call back after the last episode. "What's up?"

"Listen, I think we need to talk. I'm really sorry about the other night. I was out of control, and I'm sorry."

She was tired of this conversation already. She was tired of trying to make herself like him in a way that she just didn't. "Hey, it happens."

"No, I was a total jerk, and you have every reason to hate me."

"I don't hate you, Greg. I just like to take things slower than that."

"But I shouldn't have made you ride home in the cab again. It won't happen again, I swear."

"Don't worry about it." Riding home wouldn't be a problem because she wasn't planning on going out with him again.

He hesitated. "Well, I was wondering if you wanted to go out tomorrow night."

Disbelief slammed into her. "Oh, Greg, I can't. We've had an impossible week around here. Isabella got hurt when I was gone last time."

"But couldn't they get someone else to watch them... just for awhile?"

"No, I don't think so."

"Dinner. Just dinner."

"No. Really."

"Pre-dinner for drinks, or coffee, or whatever."

Maggie laid her head on the table. "No, it's just not going to work, Greg."

"Maggie, please, don't give up on us because I was a jerk.

251

Please."

Us? It sounded like a death sentence. "It's not because of that. Really. It's just that they haven't hired a back-up babysitter yet."

"What happened to the one they had?"

"Long story. Listen, I've got to go."

But he didn't sign off. "Can I call you again sometime?"

She wanted to say no. With everything in her she wanted to say no, but he sounded so crushed, she just couldn't. "If you want."

Saturday night Keith got the call he had been dreading all week. After his talk with Greg, he had thrown himself into his coming life with Dallas like a good soon-to-be groom should; however, just because he was committed didn't mean he was happy.

"I wanted to make sure we're going to be able to take the jet," Dallas said, clearly stressed out. "I've got to be out of here by the 15th one way or the other."

"Oh," he said, hearing the yelling already, "Dad's going up to Amarillo that weekend. He's taking it. But I'm scheduled for the Friday night flight on American."

Dallas sighed. "Fine. I'll tell Rachel." She sounded tired. "Have you checked into any more houses?"

"I called the realtor yesterday. We're scheduled to go looking next Tuesday. She's got five houses to show us including two of the ones we looked at online."

"Well, there's something." She sounded only vaguely impressed. "How about the job search? Have you found anything yet?"

"I posted my resume on three sites on line, but I haven't heard back from anyone yet." This felt like work. Why did he have to have another job? "I checked with the caterer too. They are a go."

"Okay."

"You sound stressed."

"Huh. I wouldn't know why. I've got two more finals and packing and moving and the wedding…"

Keith's heart sank, knowing he was the cause of a good portion of her stress. "Tell you what. When you get here, you can take a mini-vacation. No finals, no stress."

"It sounds wonderful."

"It will be."

Sunday morning it was all Keith could do to keep himself from running up the front steps. He hadn't seen Maggie in what felt like forever, and as crazy as it was, the thought of being with her even for a few short hours was all that was keeping him going. He opened the front door and slipped inside. His heart was pounding so loudly, he was sure it was audible in the quiet of the house. He turned toward the kitchen where he found Inez washing breakfast dishes.

"Morning," he said.

"Oh, good morning. Ms. Montgomery said she'd be down shortly. She's getting the children ready."

"Dad and Vivian?"

"They had a luncheon in Galveston this morning. They'll be back later."

He nodded just as Maggie and the kids appeared at the bottom of the stairs. He had never seen a more breathtaking sight. "Morning," he said softly.

"Hi. Sorry we're late."

"No problem. You ready?"

"Guess so."

Keith couldn't get his mind to forget that this was probably their last Sunday together. Next week he would be in Vermont, and the week after that Dallas would be here with him permanently. The thought threatened to overload his brain circuits, so rather than fry anything, he simply shut them off. He wouldn't think about Dallas or anything else in his other life today. For these few hours he was Keith Ayer, the real Keith Ayer, and for the time he had left, he was determined to soak in as much life as possible because on the other side of this hour lay the death of him.

He stood next to her in the pew, wishing this was real, wishing it never had to end, wishing it could be a future with her he was looking into.

"Welcome, everyone to our service this May 7th..."

The rest of the greeting subsided into a swirl of confusion. The 7th? May 7th? Keith's mind wound through and around that date. It had been 17 years. Seventeen years today that his mother had died. How could he have forgotten? His heart slid through the thought. He hadn't even thought about it until now. Somehow that hurt as much as the date did.

The service started, but he didn't really hear it. It was as if in one breath, he was back with her, a young boy enthralled with the world. Her soft voice flowed through him like it hadn't in so many, many years. He closed his eyes and soaked in the feeling of her. He was a man now, but when he thought about her, he was once again 12 and 10 and 5, asking her questions, begging for her knowledge of the world and her understanding of his place in it.

She had always been able to make things right—with a kiss, a hug, a word of encouragement spoken at just the right moment. Peace, calm, joy. Those were the things he remembered about her. And now she was gone. Yes, she had been gone for many years, but in truth he had never let himself feel her absence until this very moment. Softly he let his heart whisper, "I miss you, Mom. I miss you so much. It's been so long."

Suddenly at his side, Peter reached up and slid his little hand into Keith's big one, and Keith opened his eyes and smiled down at the child. Love, so strong it ached, flowed through Keith. Yes, his mom had left, but if she hadn't, he wouldn't have Peter nor Isabella. He looked over to Maggie, holding his little sister, and the picture they made seared through him. If his mother had never left, he wouldn't have either of them. It wasn't that he would've chosen one over the other. It was more that only now could he see that even in the pain, there were some blessings.

"Mom, I never wanted you to leave. I've missed you so much, but these blessings. I was missing the blessings that are here that I wouldn't have had if the accident hadn't happened." He let his eyes fall closed. "God, I'm so lost here. I feel like I know what I want, and yet it's like I can never have that. Please help me to let them go, to let Maggie go. I made a commitment to Dallas, and I've got to keep it. Please help me."

In what seemed only moments, the service ended. He hadn't heard a word anyone had said. He followed Maggie out and to the pickup. However, when they were all strapped in, he glanced over at her. "Would you mind if we make a little stop?"

She shrugged. "No, that's fine."

He nodded. The last time he had been to the graveyard was when his grandmother had died five years before, but he'd never had the courage to visit his mother's grave. Never. It had always seemed so final. But today he would face it. Today he would face the tragedy that had defined his youth so he could move onto the tragedy that would define his future.

What Maggie had expected, she didn't know, but the graveyard was not it. "What's going on?" she asked in barely disguised panic as he turned into the parking lot gate.

"I just want to make a little visit while we're here."

Now? she wanted to scream. Today of all days? It was like fate was playing some kind of cruel trick. Gathering herself so that she wouldn't completely lose it in front of him and the kids, she got out of the pickup and unstrapped Isabella. However, it took everything she had to get her feet moving toward the walkway when Isabella was in her arms.

"What is this?" Peter asked, and Keith gave him some answer she didn't hear.

Walk. Keep walking. Don't think. Fighting not to let the memories overwhelm her, Maggie walked with him through the small wrought iron archway and past five rows of headstones. There Keith turned to the left, and Maggie followed, pleading with God to not drag this out any longer than it had to be. It brought back too many memories of another graveyard, half a state away.

Halfway to the far fence, Keith stopped, and even in her anguish, Maggie saw his. He seemed not able to face what lay in front of him as his head was back, and his eyes were closed. "I miss her so much."

Maggie stepped over to him and put her hand on his upper arm. "I know. Believe me, I know." At that moment she glanced down at the headstone, and reality scattered. "Oh, my…"

That brought Keith's senses back to him with a snap. He looked over at her, concern and grief whiplashing their way through him. "What, Maggie? What is it?"

She stood, staring at the headstone, her hand over her mouth. It was as if she had frozen in place right there.

Fear drove into him. "Maggie, what's wrong?"

"She… They…" Maggie was shaking her head as horrible thoughts went across her face. Then she looked at him in blank disbelief. "They died the same day."

He wasn't following. "What…? Who…?"

It was all she could do to get the words out. "My parents and your mom. They died the same day."

Twenty-Two

The trip home was spent in stunned silence. Neither of them knew what to say to the other, and so no one said anything. At the mansion Keith let Maggie out and made some lame excuse about needing to check on things at the stables. She, too, had things to do, and so they went their separate ways. The rest of the week was pretty much living that one hour over and over again. There was the shock of it, followed by the numbness.

Maggie did her best to be normal around the kids, but it wasn't easy. She wondered how he was doing, and she even thought about calling to check. But she always talked herself out of it. If he was doing half as bad as she was, talking to her would just confirm that it had actually happened. And somehow making believe it hadn't seemed easier.

"For someone leaving for a four-day party, you look like death warmed over," Ike said on Thursday evening. "You okay?"

Okay? It was such a strange word. How could you ever tell you were okay? Maybe others could, but your real thoughts and feelings were so unreliable, how could you ever be sure? Keith's thoughts swept him away from the conversation so fast, he didn't realize he hadn't answered.

With a concerned look, Ike swung onto the chair. "Is everything all right?"

Keith looked at him as the emotions threatened to break through the numbness. Vehemently he pushed them back. "What do you remember about the accident?"

"Accident?" Ike looked like he'd driven around a blind corner. "What accident?"

"Mom's. When she was killed. What do you know about it?"

The horrified look on Ike's face barely registered in Keith's fuzzy brain. "Why?"

"Because I want to know. That's why. I've never really known. One day she was here, and then she wasn't. Nobody ever told me what really happened."

Ike got up and went to the filing cabinet. "Well, it was a long time ago. I don't really remember all the details."

"Then give me the rough outline, Ike. Come on. I'm 29. I'm not a child anymore."

"I don't know that anyone really knows what happened. It was kind of... Well, it wasn't real clear. There was a crash, and she went through the windshield. That's all we were ever really told."

Keith's grief gripped him. "Yeah, but what did she hit—a tree, a sign, another car?"

"I don't think she hit anything. I think it just happened."

This was a one-way trip down a blind alley.

Ike came back to the desk. "Listen, Keith. It was a long time ago, and stuff like that is better just put to rest and left alone. There's nothing you can do about it now except accept it and move on."

Keith wanted to lash out, to take his anger and grief out on Ike, but that wasn't fair. Ike had pulled him through like no one else had. And there was no reason for Ike to lie. If he didn't know, he didn't know. Keith wrenched himself out of the chair and stalked to the office door. "I'm going to make rounds, and then I'm going to pack for Vermont. I'll be back Tuesday."

"Have a safe trip."

Greg called again on Friday, and again Maggie told him no. She knew Keith was already gone. The whole house was buzzing with the anticipation of Dallas's graduation and their imminent arrival on Monday. Monday. It seemed to occupy a space in a parallel universe—one in which he was again attached to Dallas's side, and Maggie was left to occupy the little, infinitesimal space she called life. "Dear God, please get me through Monday, and the Tuesday after that, and the Wednesday after that…"

"Dallas Celeste Henderson," the speaker at the podium read, and with that Keith watched her stride across the stage and accept first her diploma and then the hood of her new, vaunted position in life. He clapped politely, just like her parents did beside him.

They had all apparently decided to leave the unpleasantries until after Dallas's victorious walk. Tomorrow they would argue. Today they would celebrate.

"This is Keith Ayer, my fiancé," Dallas purred as they made their way around the well-appointed restaurant. "He's *Conrad Ayer's* son."

"Oh," several of their prey said. "Well, it's nice to meet you, Mr. Ayer."

Keith smiled, hoping he looked happy about the connection Dallas was so fond of making. They got to the refreshment table after a walk that would've left a camel dehydrated, and Dallas took a flute of champagne and handed him one. However, Keith held up his hand.

"No thanks."

"No thanks?" Dallas laughed. "What does that mean?"

"It means I don't really want to drink right now."

"Yeah, right." She pressed the glass into his hand. "For later."

He'd watered three flowering plants and two green ones, hoping it wouldn't kill them. If Dallas kept this up, he'd have the whole place watered by the time they left. They'd been at this party for three hours, and it was getting boring making small talk with people who cared nothing for him except because of his family's money. Nonetheless, he followed her around like a good little puppy dog until his feet ached from the monkey shoes he'd had to wear.

"You know, I'm really beat," he said as the clock slid toward eleven. "What do you say we go back to the hotel?"

"Ooo." Dallas slipped her arms around his neck. "Now there's an idea."

Being with Dallas was like taking a turn on a stuck CD. She had two modes sex and money. And then every so often he got really lucky, and she turned on the power mode. How she couldn't wait to be at Hayden & Elliott, how she planned to make junior partner before 28, how with his money and her family's connections, she was destined for full partnership before 32, it was only a question of if she would stay that long.

By the time they landed in Houston, Keith had never been so happy to get off a plane in his life. Although he had brought his pickup, Dallas insisted on the mansion sending the limo to get them. So Jeffrey had come for the pickup, and they rode in the limo. The rest of her stuff was being shipped to a storage building until they found a place of their own, which considering that house hunting started tomorrow, was only a matter of time.

"I'm so happy to be home." Dallas lifted Keith's hand which was intertwined with hers and arched it over her shoulder. "This is too good to be true."

"Yeah," he said, trying to be enthusiastic but not even getting close.

When they drove into the gates of the estate, Dallas just about squirmed out of her skin with excitement. However, the second the driver slid past the main circle, the squirming stopped. She sat up incredulously. "Why aren't we stopping? Where is he going?"

"To the guesthouse, Dallas. Where you're staying. Remember?"

"Well, yeah... but I thought we'd stop at the mansion first, to... you know. Say hello."

Keith laughed softly. "No one's home." His thoughts went to one who probably was, but he yanked that thought back.

"No one? Not even the staff?"

He lifted his eyebrows. "You want to say hello to the staff?"

She caught herself then and leaned back petulantly. "Fine. We'll go to the guesthouse."

"The square footage is 2,750," the agent said as she led them through the third house on Tuesday afternoon. They were all pretentious, all way over what they needed, and all meant only to impress anyone who happened to be impressible.

"That's a little small," Dallas said, folding her arms unconvinced.

"Yes, but it does have a pool and a library."

"Well…" Dallas said as Keith followed her around the vaulted entryway with the crystal chandelier hanging high above.

"It's okay, Ms. Henderson. I have lots more properties to see."

"Then let's keep looking."

If there was a house they missed, Keith's feet wouldn't have believed it. The next morning as he stuck them in his cowboy boots, they groaned. However, he had chores to do, work. Good, honest work, and he wasn't going to let some little triviality like his feet feeling like they were about to fall off keep him from it.

"Are you leaving already?" Dallas asked, coming from the hallway. Her silk robe tied just so around her body.

"Gotta get cracking." He stood and put on his hat over his bandana.

She wrapped her arms over themselves like an angry teacher. "Ugh. Do you have to wear that ugly thing? It's disgusting."

"I'm working in the stables. The horses wouldn't be impressed with a coat and tie anyway."

With a shake of her head, her scowl deepened. "We've got to find you something else. If I have to look at that thing every day of my life, just shoot me now."

It was a thought; however, he shoved that thought down. "I'll be back for dinner. We've got to get Dragnet ready to go for tomorrow."

"Dinner?" Dallas sat down at the table petulantly. "But I thought we were going to take a mini-vacation."

"No. I said you are going to take a mini-vacation. You've got all day to yourself." He kissed her on the forehead. "Help yourself to anything you need. I'll see you later."

"Yeah, later." And there wasn't an ounce of happiness anywhere in the words.

"I don't know," Ike said, striding into the office. "Paul's got Drag on the track, and he's about as jumpy as a June bug. I don't know how he'll fly at the race Saturday."

"Pulling him's not an option?" Tanner asked with concern.

Ike looked at Keith who sat at the desk, trying not to listen. "I talked to Mr. Ayer last week, and he's adamant that we're racing him." Ike put up his hands. "I've done all I can do."

Like clockwork, Greg called on Tuesday and Thursday nights. Maggie hadn't seen Keith in so long it was almost possible to make herself believe he really was just a nice dream. However, the pit of this-isn't-what-I-want stayed with her each time she talked to Greg.

"Friday night," Greg said. "Come on, Maggie. Why don't you just ask off? It can't be that hard."

She put her head in her hand and dragged her fingers through her hair. "Greg, we've been over this. They haven't hired anyone new, and I can't just leave."

"Even for one night?"

"Even for one minute."

Dallas was out shopping. Again. Keith wondered how there could be that many things to buy in all of Houston. She'd already bought new sheets for his bed, which she didn't even plan to take with them, new kitchen towels, new bathroom towels, and two new pillows that were on the couch but not to be touched nor sat on. He'd found that out the hard way.

Grateful for a small reprieve from her omnipresence, Keith turned on the satellite radio in the living room Saturday afternoon and sat down in the recliner. With the remote control he flipped through the channels until the race came in so clear it was like he was at the track.

"We're here at the third race at Fair Meadows." The announcer went through the lineup of horses, and when Dragnet's name was called second, Keith sat forward.

Elbows on his knees, he tapped his lips with his index fingers. "Come on, Paul. Just take it easy on him and get through this race. We can concentrate on winning the next one." Seconds slid by as the track personnel went through their race-start protocol.

Keith was glad he hadn't gone. Race day always razed his nerves. Traveling frayed them even further. Being around that many people and having to act like an owner rather than a trainer really was impossible. He hated the way people looked at him when they knew who he was. No, this was better, sitting here listening, alone and anonymous was much, much better.

"The horses are in the gate. Oh, number two seems a bit jumpy today."

"Settle down, Drag. Just settle down. Calm him down, Paul and get through this."

"Looks like they're working with him." A minute slid by. "Okay, I believe we are set. The horses are in their gates, and they're... off."

Keith sat forward, coaching Paul as if he could really see him. "Come on. Come on."

"To the first turn we go." The announcer slid through the horses' names. "Dragnet in fourth." The pounding of the hooves was so ingrained in Keith he heard them in his brain even if he couldn't really hear them on the radio. "Dragnet seems to be making an inside move. Yes, he has overtaken Melody's Dream on the inside corner. As they round the final turn... Oh! Oh no..."

Keith nearly fell off the chair. "What?"

"Oh, no. Two of the horses got tangled underneath. It looks like... Dragnet and Mostafar are down at the inside railing on the last turn. And Melody's Dream wins the third race at Fair Meadows. Troubadour second. And Walesland third."

Keith launched out of the chair and stalked over to the entertainment center where he put his hands on the wood on either side of the stereo. "What about Dragnet? What happened to Dragnet?"

"Oh, good. Good news. Mostafar has regained his footing and is being escorted from the track."

"What about Dragnet?" The frustration flowed through him

like lava from a volcano.

Another announcer took over. "This looks really serious for the Ayer Stables horse Dragnet. He's still down on the track. The trainer and medical team are on the track as well. Everyone in the stands is on their feet, and it's clear to everyone this does not look good."

Keith slammed his hand into the entertainment center. "I knew it."

The most gut-wrenching minutes of his life passed as Keith placed phone call after phone call to Ike with no luck. He knew the trainer was knee-deep in chaos so after ten tries, he resorted to sitting on the couch with his hands clasped on his knees praying. Finally nearly an hour after the race started, his phone rang. His gaze swept over the ID as he hit the on button. "Is he all right?"

Ike sighed so hard it yanked Keith's spirit all the way down. "It's bad, Keith. I've never seen one shattered like that."

"What...? What happened? Where are you? How is he?"

"The vet's here. They're fixing to put him down."

"Down?" Keith vaulted off the couch. "No, Ike! No! Don't do that."

Again Ike sighed. "Too late. I already talked to your dad."

The words took Keith's knees out from under him. "He... approved?"

"He suggested it." Ike sighed again. "The vet's said it would take a miracle for him to even live much less to ever really walk again."

For his own sake, Keith backed up from the story to keep from thinking about what was happening now. "What happened anyway? I couldn't really tell from the radio."

"I don't know. They were rounding the last turn, and they got tangled. Dragnet's front right leg shattered in the process. I'm telling you, man, it's bad."

Clinging to rational, Keith sorted through the accident. "How's Paul?"

"Emergency room too, but he's okay. A little banged up and shaken up, but he'll be all right."

"And Drag..."

Ike was talking to someone else, and Keith wanted to shake

him silly to get him to stop and fill him in on the details.

"It's a done deal," Ike said after a moment of pause. "He's gone." Even Ike had to corral the emotions to be able to continue. "Listen, I've got to get. I'll see you tomorrow, and we'll figure out what's next."

"I... Y...yeah. Okay. 'bye." Keith hung up the phone without really seeing it. Dragnet was gone. Just like that. And now he was never coming back. Grief jammed into Keith's throat followed in the next breath by anger. Surely there was something someone could have done.

Who makes a snap decision about a quarter-million dollar horse like that? His thoughts smashed through the image of his father, and he yanked himself off the couch, grabbed his hat from the table and stalked out.

"I'm hungry," Peter said after Isabella was asleep Saturday afternoon. Most days during this time they simply played in the next room until she woke up, but today even Maggie was getting claustrophobic. She wished they could go out to the stables and go riding, but with Dallas back, Maggie didn't have the guts to show her face anywhere she might be compared to the goddess.

"Well, let's go down and see what we can find." She took Peter's hand, and they trooped down to the kitchen. Inez was off shopping, and Patty Ann and Mrs. Ayer had gone to a luncheon for some organization Maggie couldn't even pronounce. "How about a ham sandwich?" Her gaze caught on the blender, and she smiled although the memory stabbed into her heart.

"Can I have peanut butter and jelly?" Peter climbed up the stool by the counter.

"Peanut butter and jelly?" Maggie was surprised he'd ever even heard the term. "Sure. If I can find some."

"We used to have those with Mrs. Ortega before she got in trouble and left."

Maggie opened the refrigerator. "Why'd she get into trouble?"

Peter shrugged. "For being in Mom's room. We used to go in there a lot."

The story was beginning to bring real curiosity to Maggie. "Oh? Why?"

"So she could play dress up with Mommy's earrings and stuff."

"Momm…" But she didn't get that question out as the front door slammed with an earth-shaking crash. Fear pummeled into her. No one just walked in unannounced like that, especially not with a foundation-cracking door slam for emphasis. "Peter, you stay right there." Wiping her hands on her pants, she went to the door and turned the corner to the foyer where she met Keith coming the other direction full-steam.

"Is my father here?" He looked like he might bulldoze anyone who stood in his way.

"Uh. No. I don't think so. He's gone until Monday, I think," Maggie said, shaken by the sight of Keith who looked more out-of-control than she had ever seen him.

"That figures." He glanced over his shoulder. "You're sure he's not here."

"You can go check if you want, but…"

A scowl marred his face. It was almost as if he wasn't even really seeing her when he looked at her. "I do not believe this."

"This… what? What happened?"

He glanced at her as anger flashed through his eyes. "My sorry excuse for a father told them to put Dragnet down without even consulting me."

It was serious. That much she understood, but not much more. "Hold on. Who's Dragnet?"

"The horse we had racing today at Fair Meadows." Keith seemed not to be able to contain the rage as his body rocked side to side with its power. "He went down around one of the turns, shattered his foreleg, and my brilliant father told them to just put him down." His fist came up and then dropped to his thigh. "They didn't even bother to call me before they made the decision."

It wasn't so much the news as how he was taking it that knocked into Maggie. She tilted her head to be able to see his face which was bowed. "I'm sorry. Is there anything I can do?"

He reached up and readjusted his hat, clearly fighting not to let any emotion other than rage find the surface. "Yeah. Can you get me a new father?"

She hated seeing him in such turmoil, and her voice became soft with compassion. "I wish I could." She shouldn't, she knew, but it was all she could think to do. With only a step toward him, she slid her arms through his. At first he seemed surprised, but then he bent his head onto her shoulder and clasped his arms around her so tightly she wondered if she would ever breathe again. Gently she rubbed his back with her hand. It was a funeral hug, just like the kind Mrs. Malowinski had taught her to give. The kind where you don't let go until the hurting person does. And so she stood there in the middle of the Ayer mansion foyer holding Keith for no other reason than he hadn't yet let go.

Finally his grip released, and he stepped back. There were no tears but anguish slashed across his face just the same. "Do you know when he'll be back?"

"I think Patty Ann said Monday." Maggie wished with everything in her that she could do something to ease the pain searing across his face.

"Then I guess I'll be back Monday."

She followed him to the door. "Are you going to be okay?"

Sad acceptance slid through the ache. "Do I have a choice?" And with that, he left.

Twenty-Three

"Hello. How was your day?" Dallas asked, walking up and kissing the side of Keith's cheek as he sat at the table, slowly spinning the Spaghetti O's on his plate.

They were cold by now. In fact they'd been cold for 30 minutes, but he hadn't had the energy to even get up.

"Ugh. The malls were swamped. End of school all those kids with nothing better to do. It was a madhouse." She walked into the hallway still talking all the way to the bedroom and back. "Tracy is going crazy. Her maid of honor dress came in like two sizes too big. They're having to do all these alterations. I'm glad mine is done, and the pictures are done, and the photographer's confirmed." She went into the kitchen and got some water.

"Have you heard from Jane yet? She said she'd call when that house she was working on listed." Dallas walked back into the dining room and stopped. "Keith, are you listening to me? Good grief, you look like the morning after the night before."

"Yeah," he said for no other reason than some of the times that was enough to satisfy her. It was as if his life had closed in around him in one swipe. He needed something, something to hold onto that felt solid and safe. "Umm, I'm thinking about going to church tomorrow. I was wondering if you wanted to go."

"Church?" She made the word sound more like prison. "What would you want to go to church for?"

"Well, we had some trouble with the stables today, and I thought…"

"Oh? What kind of trouble?"

He exhaled, feeling like he was giving her his heart. "They put one of our horses down at the track where it was racing. It shattered a leg."

Dallas paused for a long moment, and then it became clear she was waiting for more. "Is that all? You're moping around because of some dumb horse?"

Squish went his heart.

"Jeez, Keith. It's just a horse. What'd you think it was going to live forever?"

Why did he bother? He stood from the table, took his plate to the sink and dumped the Spaghetti O's down the disposal, liking the growling noise it made.

"Mom called today. They got five more gifts in for the wedding. Some of the crystal and the china. But now she's freaking out because we should've had them route all the presents to Texas." Dallas took a drink. "You know my mom. She'll find something to complain about, and if she can't find something, she'll make something up."

"So church is out then?" he asked, verifying in case he had misunderstood.

Dallas shook her head and laughed. "Sometimes you are so funny."

Maggie had known they wouldn't be going to church, but still, it hurt that they weren't. All day Sunday she went through their routine, and every time her mind traced to Keith, she said a prayer for him. She hoped he'd found some peace about the horse. She knew how attached he was to them, and any time you put that much effort and love into anything, losing it is like ripping the foundation out from under you. "Dear Lord, please be with Keith. Remind him that You are there and that You love him."

It was the second worst Sunday of Keith's life, and that was saying something. The night before he had wanted alcohol worse than he ever had in his entire life, and yet he had thrown all of it out the night after his decision on the matter. However, he hadn't counted on how badly un-dulled pain hurt. It felt like it would kill him outright, and long after midnight he had resorted to getting up and going to the living room to read Maggie's Bible that he had secreted in the hidden compartment in the entertainment center.

Dallas would never understand—not in a million years. So since her arrival, he had done his best not to think about the little book he had spent many nights reading before her arrival. It was so strange to be two different people. So strange. After most of the night spent reading, he found himself on Sunday half real Keith, half Keith Ayer as he stalked into the stables, trying to find something that would take his mind off of not being with Maggie at church.

Real Keith wanted answers as to what happened on that track and to lay down the law that this would never happen again. Keith Ayer, however, knew that wasn't his place. He wasn't the manager here. He was just putting in time. In two weeks he would ride off into the sunset with his new bride, and this place would be a distant memory.

As he fed the horses, he stopped at Dragnet's stall, the hay in his hands, the empty stall beyond the gate. With a shake of his head, his heart shattered, and he stepped past that stall to Nell's. "Good morning, girl. How's it going?" He threw the hay over and tried not to think about how empty the stables felt today. His thoughts went to when Ike and Tanner would return. Tomorrow at the earliest. Would it be better to ask for every detail like he wanted to or to just shrug it off as if it didn't make an ounce of difference to him? After all, that's how everyone else seemed to think he should act.

It was enough to make a stress headache feel like an aneurysm.

Just after lunch on Monday afternoon the pickup and trailer crept up the trail and stopped at the stables in a small cloud of dust. Keith, who'd just returned himself came out of the breezeway. Ike got out one side of the pickup, Tanner the other. Both heads were down, neither set of eyes came up to meet his. They stalked past him to the office. Frustrated, Keith turned and followed them.

"I think I'll go check the water," Tanner said at the office door. Ike nodded and went into the office. Keith caught the door with his fist and watched the younger cowboy stride out the other side of the breezeway. Then he turned his own steps into the office.

He ran his thumb under his nose as he watched Ike who sat at the desk, sorting papers. "So what happened anyway?"

Ike glanced up but continued with the paperwork.

Keith glowered at the snub. "You're not going to tell me? What's up with that?"

It was clear Ike was trying to figure out good words to explain it without angering Keith. "It's just... We... Well, you knew Dragnet wasn't ready." As if that was supposed to make everything comprehensible.

"Yeah, we both knew that. So what was Paul thinking pushing him then?" Keith put his foot on the hardwood chair and stared at Ike. "I thought we talked about that—hanging back these first few races so Dad would think we were following orders."

Ike glanced up, and nothing in Keith liked that look. "I was following orders."

"Orders? You're the boss, remember?" Keith laughed softly, but Ike didn't respond. The ignoring thing was beginning to irk Keith. "Ike, come on. Talk to me, man. We've been partners in this thing too long for you to shut me out now."

Ike stood and went to the file cabinet. "You're out of here in like a week. What does it matter to you?"

Livid was in spitting distance. "You're kidding, right?" Keith let his foot slide off the chair. "You know me better than that, Ike. I care about what happens to this place and to those horses. You of all people should know I haven't busted my butt here for five years to just leave. In fact, if it wasn't for Dallas, I wouldn't even move. I'd be here, taking care of things just like I always have."

Slowly Ike shook his head. He turned to face Keith. "Look, take some advice from an old cowboy who doesn't hit every trick. Be smart. Get out while the getting's good. Dallas is a great girl. Concentrate on getting married and making her happy. Get your house. Set up your life, and don't look back."

"Ike, for Pete's sake, what are you talking about? This place is my life. I can't just walk away even if everybody thinks I should."

The trainer's eyes fell closed, and his slow Southern drawl fell to a crawl. "We didn't have a choice about taking it easy on Drag. Your dad made it crystal clear that if we undermined his orders, we'd be gone."

Rage and confusion battled inside Keith. "He told you to race him like that?"

"I believe his exact words were, 'Win or you're fired.'"

"I need to talk to you," Keith said the second after he opened his father's office door less than ten minutes later. He'd already met Patty Ann in the foyer. She confirmed his father's presence in the mansion today although she had tried to explain that Mr. Ayer was very busy. However, Keith wasn't about to be put-off no matter who stood in his way. The rage boiling in him was going to explode somewhere and it might as well be in the presence of the one who really deserved it.

His father never looked up. "I'm busy."

"Yeah? Well, get unbusy. This is important." Keith stepped in and closed the door.

"If it's not about how you will be half a state away in two weeks, I don't want to hear it."

"You know, you could be just a little less happy about me leaving. If I didn't know better, I'd think you already have my stuff packed and sitting in my garage."

"I thought you said you were here to talk about something important."

Keith held his anger in both fists to keep it from spilling over. "You told Ike to push Dragnet, and then when he got hurt, you had him put down before anyone could even assess how bad he really was."

"Hrumph. It was a business decision, Keith. It's called cutting your losses. Besides we had insurance, so it's no big deal."

"No big deal? Insurance doesn't make putting that animal down right. This wasn't about five dollars on a spreadsheet, Dad. This was a racehorse. A quarter-million dollar, promising racehorse that had more potential than any one I've ever seen trained."

"Yeah. And he fell. Big surprise."

"Big surprise? Yeah, no kidding. We both know you set him up for that fall. You knew he wasn't ready and rather than having a little patience and putting in a little effort to get him ready, you pushed him into a race he wasn't ready to run. Then, as if that wasn't enough, you made sure he would fail by heaping your impossibly high expectations on top of an already impossible situation. What in the world did you expect to happen?"

His father stood. "I expected him to rise to the occasion." His gaze nailed Keith. "Unfortunately, there are so few on this planet who know the meaning of that phrase."

They were face-to-face, stare-to-stare, steel will-to-steel will.

"So everyone who can't stand up to what you think they should be able to do is expendable then?" Ache and anger met in Keith's gut. "Wow. There's a great life philosophy."

Impatience corkscrewed across his father's face. "Look, I can't be wasting money on some stupid horse that will never make it back to the track. I want a winner—not some crippled, money-sucking loser."

The understanding that his father wasn't only talking about the horse drifted through him. Keith backed up and folded his arms. "Wow. It must be nice to be so perfect you can sit up here in your mansion and make such sweeping judgments about the whole world. That one deserves to live, that one doesn't. You are the most arrogant, selfish, egotistical jerk I've ever had the misfortune of meeting."

"Keith Warren Ayer, I am your father, and I deserve some respect."

His hatred drained down the sinkhole of capitulation. It was pointless to fight. "Respect has to be earned, Dad, and from where I'm standing, you have never done a single thing to earn my respect."

Despite Keith's surrender, his father looked like a mad dog ready to attack. "Are you kidding me? You have had everything you've ever wanted. Nice cars, more than a roof over your head, servants at your beck and call..."

Keith laughed. "And I'm supposed to be impressed with that? Gee, Dad, you aim mighty low in the providing for arena." He had kept the feelings of never being good enough to warrant his father's attention from ever finding the air his whole life. For the first twelve years, his mother had filled in for the absence of his father; after she was gone, the staff had tried to fill in for both. But the reality was, there was a hole in him that had never been filled because his father was always too busy. Work and other things always came first.

He had thought it was just him. Now he saw with perfect clarity that nothing other than the image he portrayed to the world was at all important to his father. If it looked good on the outside, it was worth it. If it didn't, it was expendable.

"You're unbelievable, you know that, Dad? If someone's not

perfect enough for you, you think they are worthless. Well, you know what? I'm tired of trying to be perfect. I'm not perfect. I never have been. We both know that. So, I give up. I do. That's it. You can have your mansion and your horses. Run them all into the ground if you want. See what I care. I'm out of here."

He turned for the door with a shake of his head.

"Now you listen to me. I did my best," his father said. "I wanted to give you everything I could even though I knew it would never be enough to make up for her being gone."

The words ran over Keith's heart, and he stopped at the door.

"She always made up for how bad I was with you. But I did want what was best for you—even if I didn't know how to do that."

Keith turned slowly. He needed to know even though it would change nothing. "What happened, the night she died?"

"That was a long time ago." His father sat slowly. "It was an accident. A stupid thing that just happened. I wish I could go back and change so many things, but the past is the past. I can't do anything about it now."

"Why did she go on that trip?" Keith asked, not being able to stop the question. It had been running in the background of every moment of his life for 17 years.

His father shook his head slowly. "The same reason we do everything—because she was supposed to."

"But what was it? It couldn't have been a meeting. She didn't work. Did she go to see family… what?"

"No, your mother didn't have family in Midland." His father shook his head, first slowly, then more vehemently. "It was just some dumb thing that happened. Okay? It's over, Keith. She's gone. It's time to move on." His gaze fell to the papers as he started writing on the top one again.

Why was it so easy for everyone else to just go on with life and so impossible for him? He put his hand on the knob but stopped. He looked back over at his father, already buried in work again. "Do you miss her?"

With a look that yanked Keith's heart to the surface, his father looked up. "Every day of my life."

"So I guess you're going to the wedding," Greg said Monday night as Maggie sat in the night-darkened kitchen.

"I'm sure I'll have to take Pete and Izzy." Maggie held her head up from the table with only her fingers twined in her hair. It had been days since she'd seen Keith. Days, in fact, since she'd seen the outside of the house. They were already busy getting the backyard ready for the wedding, and that meant no one was allowed out there for any reason.

Two days before, workers had moved the back fence and more grass was planted and being watered even now. It was no place for little feet, so they had stayed inside and as much as possible out of view.

Mrs. Ayer was in a state, and save for dinner, Mr. Ayer made few appearances. When he was around, he didn't talk. When he wasn't around, there was a tension that permeated everything. Patty Ann had gone so far as to ask if it was necessary to have Peter's karate lesson in the courtyard outside the kitchen, and when it was determined there was simply no other place, karate lessons were cancelled until further notice.

Gardeners such that Maggie had never seen had also shown up shortly after the grass. They were planting more flowers than God had created and vast teams of workers were busy even now scrubbing the walls of the mansion until every crevice was clean.

"You don't get off even for the wedding?" Greg asked in horror. "Maggie, it's been weeks since you've had a day off. I don't know how you do it."

You remember what happens when you do take a day off, she thought but didn't say. "I guess you're going."

"Of course. I'm best man."

Lovely. "Oh? Who're you walking with?"

"Did you have to ask? Tracy, the Monster of honor."

More good news. "I wish I could get out of it, but Pete and Izzy are the ring bearer and flower girl. Which reminds me, we have a fitting for Izzy Thursday. Ugh. I wish this was over already."

"You and me both. I guess you've got your dress and everything already. The invites say black tie only. Thankfully Keith sprung for my tux, or that'd be another $500 bucks to spend on top of the gift."

Keith. The name knifed through her. "I hadn't really thought about a dress."

"Well, you'd better think about it, or they may send you to the dungeon." He laughed. "You know how they can be."

Yes, she did.

"Well, you know," Greg said slowly. "I've been thinking. If you're there and I'm there, maybe we could be there together."

Would this nightmare never end? "I don't know, Greg. I'll have to be taking care of the kids, and you'll be dealing with the best man stuff..."

He sighed. "Well, will you at least save me a dance?"

She smiled sadly. "You got it."

"If I wanted to look up an old accident report, how would I go about doing that?" Keith asked Dallas as they sat at breakfast Tuesday morning. All night he had replayed the fight with his dad and one word kept sticking. *Midland.*

Why hadn't he asked? Why hadn't that word jarred his memory into gear when he could have asked? But no. As usual he hadn't really thought about it until long after it was too late to ask.

"An accident report about what?" Dallas asked. Her cornsilk hair was pulled back from her face, revealing her perfectly chiseled nose and jawbone. She was beautiful even if not Keith's kind of beautiful.

He shrugged. "Greg and I were talking the other day, and he was asking about something. I was just going to look into it."

"Oh, well. If it was publicized at the time, you might be able to dig in a newspaper's archives, or do a search for the date and the location. It'd be like looking for a pin in a gutter, but you could try." She got up and took her plate to the kitchen. "Tracy and some of the girls are taking me out tomorrow night. Just so you know. I'll probably stay in Houston with her if that's all right."

"Oh, yeah." His mind was already back in Midland. "That's fine."

Tuesday Maggie went to Patty Ann's office while Inez watched the kids. She knocked. "Excuse me. I'm sorry to bother you, but I need to ask a question."

"Make it quick. The governor's office will be calling with the itinerary any minute now."

"Oh, okay." Maggie sat down in the chair. "Umm, I was wondering. How formal do you want me to be for the wedding? I imagine I'll just be working with the kids, so..."

Patty Ann exhaled harshly. "Let me guess. You don't have anything formal."

"Formal?" The word leveled her. "Uh, no. Not really." She pushed her glasses up nervously. "I just have my work clothes pretty much."

"Terrific." The secretary thought for a moment. "Well, if I advance your pay and give you tomorrow off..."

"Oh, I have money from before, but I don't... Umm, who will take care of the children?"

Patty Ann looked like she might hit overload at any second. "We have yet to find a suitable replacement for Mrs. Haga. With the wedding preparations and Mrs. Ayer's current schedule, there just hasn't been time for interviews or even applications."

Maggie was twisting through the situation as much as Patty Ann was. Then a thought occurred to her. "You know, there's a girl that helps out at the stables. Jamie something. She's Tanner's girlfriend."

Patty Ann stared at her clearly having no idea who she was talking about.

However, Maggie knew for her own sanity that solution was better than hiring someone she didn't know. "Jamie was really good with the kids when we were down there. Maybe she would be interested in babysitting."

"Under normal circumstances I would have to check this Jamie person out, but..."

The phone rang. Patty Ann looked at it and then glanced at Maggie. "If you can get her, do it."

The house was quiet. Blessedly, thankfully quiet. Knowing he needed more than his own wisdom for this one, Keith had spent 30 minutes when he got off work reading the Bible. All day long his mind had been twining through the possibility that he was right, but while he was reading, it was as if the rest of life dropped away. There was something so comforting about reading those words.

If he could just stay here and never go back to the real world, he would have. However, there were answers he needed, and so at just after seven, he put the Bible in the little compartment and went to the office where he clicked on his computer and set to the task at hand.

With everything in her Maggie fought calling him to find out about Jamie. She didn't want to disturb him. Moreover, she didn't want to get Dallas and have to explain why she needed to talk to Keith. Something in her told her that if she didn't keep her distance, Dallas would figure out what Maggie wouldn't even let herself admit. So, one excuse after another she whittled away the evening, hoping the world would mercifully come to an end and she wouldn't have to make that call.

Three Dead in Two-Car Crash. Dateline: Midland, Texas

It had taken almost two hours of searching, but when Keith read the headline, he knew this was it. Just before he could read into the story, however, the phone rang at his elbow, and he picked it up. "Hello?"

"Keith. Hi. This is Maggie."

Breath slid from his lungs, and he turned his chair from the computer's glare. "Maggie? What's wrong?"

"Oh, uh. Nothing. Really. Umm. I was just calling to see if you might have Tanner's phone number."

Nothing in him liked how strained her voice sounded. "Tanner's? What do you need his number for?"

"Oh, well. Umm. We're needing a babysitter for the kids for tomorrow, and I mentioned Jamie might be interested…"

"Why do you need a babysitter?" The thought of her leaving and never coming back smashed into him.

"Well, Greg and I were talking, and I realized I don't have a dress or anything for the wedding, and…"

The sentence continued, but Keith's brain had stuck at the words *Greg and I*. After a moment, he realized she had stopped talking.

"I'm sorry," she said. "I shouldn't have called. I know you're busy."

"No!" The word jumped from him. "No. That's fine. I've got his number. Hang on." Keith stood on shaky legs and walked out to the kitchen. The fading twilight was not enough to read by so he snapped on the light. "So how's everything up there?"

"Okay. Good," she said. The words sounded rushed and thrown into the silence between them. "How are the stables?"

"Pretty rough. The whole Saturday thing really threw everybody for a loop."

"I bet."

"But they had insurance on him, so I guess it wasn't a total loss."

She didn't say anything for a long moment. "Insurance doesn't bring him back."

Keith wasn't at all sure if it was the softness of the words or the words themselves that ripped the façade of Keith Ayer from his guard atop his heart, but in one breath he was gone. He sat down heavily on the barstool. "I know, but they all make it sound like it should."

"They all?"

The name hacked through his heart. "My dad. He said it was pointless to save Dragnet because he'd never race again, and what was the point of having a loser around?"

"He said that?"

"In so many words." Keith exhaled as all the heartache from the last week surfaced. "He's so smart in business, how can he be so clueless about life?"

Maggie didn't answer right away. "How about you?"

"What about me?"

"Do you buy into the idea that if there's insurance, life doesn't really matter all that much?"

His spirit sunk. "I don't want to, but everybody else makes it sound like that's the only way to think. What am I supposed to do, swim upstream my whole life?"

"Well, I think that depends on if you want to look rich or to be rich."

"Huh?"

Maggie laughed softly. "Oh, it's something Mrs. Malowinski

used to tell me. 'Maggie, there are people in this world who look really rich, but they are so poor you should feel sorry for them because they are poor where it counts—in the heart, in the places only God and love can fill. And then there are those who don't look rich on the outside, but they are because they know what's important, and they center their entire lives on it.'

"So I guess the question is: Do you want to look rich or to be rich?"

No one had ever asked Keith that question, and although he knew what he wanted the answer to be, he couldn't let himself believe that was the one that could be. "I've got Tanner's number here."

"Oh, okay. I'm ready."

When she hung up with Keith, Maggie placed the call to Tanner and then to Jamie. In a matter of minutes, she had Jamie lined up, and the world itself seemed to line up right behind her.

In the dark room Keith didn't bother to turn the light on. He sat down in the office chair and spun it slowly. The screen was black for having been neglected too long. He swept the mouse to the side, and the screen blinked to life. He closed his eyes, knowing and yet still hoping.

The story was still there when he opened his eyes, and one slow word at a time, he let it seep into him.

"A Midland couple and a Houston socialite were killed Friday night in a two car collision on Rural Route 72. James Montgomery and his wife, Christina, both of Midland, were pronounced dead at the scene. Bonnie Ayer, wife of Houston oilman, Conrad Ayer was airlifted to Midland Central where she later died of massive internal injuries.

"Conrad Ayer was also airlifted to Midland Central and remains in stable condition."

The chair back caught Keith as his hand went to his mouth. His father was there? His father was there. Somehow, in every single thought he had ever had about the accident, he had never once had his father in that car.

"The cause of the crash remains under investigation although authorities said that alcohol was a factor."

Disbelief, shock, horror doused Keith's spirit, dragging it down, pushing it down, scratching huge holes all the way through it. That's why they wouldn't tell him what happened. They were protecting his father. Anger flashed through all the other emotions. Ike knew. All these years, Ike knew, and he had never said anything. Inez knew too. The names slashed one after another through his consciousness. It was possible everyone in the world knew—except him.

And then one name crowded the others out. It was a face so gentle, it brought a moan of anguish up with it. "Maggie..."

Twenty-Four

The barn door was much easier to open now that she knew the secret. Carefully, Maggie drove the little Chevette out into the sunlight, threw it into park, and climbed out to close the door. Patty Ann had added a few items to her list—a "decent outfit for the rehearsal and shoes that don't look like they're from the dollar store." Where she was going to find anything like that, she had no idea.

Just as she made it back to her car, she heard the unmistakable rumble of the Dodge. Her gaze went to the trees. The pickup didn't break through, so she got in her car and drove up to them. At the trees she stopped, noticing the pickup sitting in the garage parking place. The garage was opened, but no one was around.

Next to the pickup sat the pewter Jaguar, and Maggie knew what that meant. She turned her gaze to the drive and purposely didn't look back.

"Who's that?" Dallas asked as the navy car went by the front window.

Keith looked up from his sandwich, and his heart fell into his shoes. "Probably Ike." He didn't want to think about who it really was. He didn't want to say her name or hear her voice or so much as see her face even in his dreams—although it was there in every one. As much as that hurt, Maggie Montgomery was better off without Keith Ayer or anyone else in his disgustingly wretched family. They had wrecked her life, and now she was scraping by, trying to prove to them she deserved to work in their mansion.

If life was fair, it would've been the other way around.

Sunday morning Keith had a plan. Dallas might never want to go with him, but that didn't mean he couldn't go. He got up early, showered, and dressed. He wasn't out to impress anybody, but he needed some sanity in his increasingly insane existence. Easing out of the house lest he wake Dallas, Keith got into his pickup and made his way down the driveway and past the mansion. If he was lucky, Dallas would think he'd gone to work.

Work. The word itself was kind of funny in a parallel universe kind of way. He showed up every day, fed the horses, fixed what needed fixed, but he wasn't really a part of it anymore. Hodges had wiggled and strong-armed his way back into the feed contract, and although Ike ranted and raved about it, Keith knew it was he that had signed the final order.

The other side of work was the question of what he would do when all this was a memory. Dallas was pushing him to get a desk job. Mr. Henderson had offered him a job with his re-election campaign. His father's Galveston branch had called three days before requesting an interview. However, nothing in Keith wanted anything to do with any of them. His heart said they were all wrong, and so he did nothing about them.

The Dodge rounded the last corner in Pine Hill and slid up into a parking space outside the little church. This was it. If God couldn't help him make sense of this, no one could.

Maggie's thoughts traveled down the little trail to the beautiful guesthouse beyond. Dallas was the luckiest girl in all of Texas if not the world. To be one week away from being Keith's wife, it must be Heaven on earth.

"Gie. Gie," Isabella said as she fell into Maggie's arms.

"Oh, I love you, baby girl. You know that?" Maggie buried her face into the little curls, fighting not to cry. If it wasn't for the kids, she would've already turned in her resignation. This next week was sure to kill her. Watching them get married. A front row seat just in case she had any thoughts of skipping out. Why did Patty Ann and everyone else insist on smearing her face in the coming heartache? They with their schedules and their seating charts and their reminders about how important this is to the Ayer family's standing in the hierarchy of Texas and the nation.

As if she needed any more pressure.

"There is a hole in each and every one of us," the preacher said as Keith sat in their normal spot, feeling the emptiness of the space around him. "A hole that only God can fill." He paused. "I picture this hole as a kind of vertical pipe that goes from our head to our heart and all the way through us. This hole is not something we created but rather something God created in us.

"The purpose of life, the journey of life is meant to show us that nothing other than God can ever successfully fill that hole. Not money, not things, not ourselves, not our work or our accomplishments. Not our success or our awards. Nothing else can fill that hole.

"When we try to fill it with other things, we put them in the hole, but they slide right back out again, and we know we must fill it with something else. So we find another goal, another thing that's out there, and we think, 'Yeah, that's it. If I can just get *that,* then I'll be happy.' But it doesn't work that way. Because stuff is not what will fill the hole.

"It is just as Jesus says to the Samaritan woman at the well. 'He who drinks of this water will get thirsty again and again, but he who drinks from the water that I give will have a well-spring arising from his very being.'"

Keith knew that hole very well. He'd stood at its mouth and shouted into it, hearing the echoes of his own loneliness come back at him. Others more so than him had tried to fill his hole with other things—activities, work, chores, games, and when he was older, he had tried to fill it himself with parties and alcohol and women. But the truth was, it was still empty. In fact, it was emptier now than it ever had been.

"So how do you fill this hole, this vertical abyss that seems so unfathomably empty? You realize how inadequate you are to fill it on your own. Then you begin a quest to find the One who can. Jesus Christ came into our empty, wretched world to show us how to fill that hole. He came to show us how to be whole, and how to be holy. Filled and whole so that we are not condemned to live our lives scattered and empty.

"And how did Jesus say to fill the hole? By seeking to grow in love—love of God, love of our neighbor, and love of ourselves. When we grow in love, when we honestly want what's best for the other, then and only then can that hole begin to be filled.

"So we are called to go forth from this place and to seek God out in all situations, to bring His love to a fallen, dying world, to each of our worlds that need it so desperately. Find those who are hurting and show them God's love. Come to know His love, breathe it into your being so that you may then breathe it out upon others. In doing so, your hole will be filled.

"Let us stand."

Although he stood, Keith's mind was no longer on the service. It had traveled back in time to a day many years before as he and his mother sat under a tree watching the falls cascade over the hard rock.

"I thought Dad was going to come today," Keith said, his voice much higher pitched.

His mother looked at him softly. "He wanted to."

"Then why didn't he?"

"Because he's busy loving us." Her glance said she knew he didn't understand. "Your dad is a good man, Keith. It's just that sometimes he gets what's important and what's urgent mixed up." She knew this lesson was going over his head, yet she continued. "We all do that sometimes. We let the urgent things like meetings and making a living crowd out the important things like spending time together and loving each other. That doesn't make us bad, just confused."

"But can't you explain it to him? Make him understand?"

She smiled. "I've tried, Keith. I really have, but sometimes you have to let people be on their own journey, to find out what's important in their own time."

"But what if he never figures it out?"

In his memory, Keith could see her gaze fall, and he knew now she was struggling with that herself. Then her gaze met his. "We just have to pray that he does."

The ride home was the shortest of Keith's life, and before he knew it, he was turning in to the estate. However, he couldn't go back just yet, so he turned down the stable road and drove until he came to the rocky pass that led out to the falls. He needed them right now, their peace, their hope, so he turned that direction. When he'd gotten close enough, he got out and walked the last 100 yards.

There, he sat down by the tree and let his gaze drift out over the falls. He was alone now, and for the first time in ages, he gave himself the permission to let everything he had bottled up inside himself out. Disbelief was the first thing to punch through the numbness he had clamped over everything else.

"God, why did you let this happen? I don't understand. There was so much hurt and anger unleashed by my dad's selfishness. He hurt Mom and me and everyone else who got in his path." Then a vague memory of a wreck he had never even seen drifted through him. "He even ruined the lives of good people, people who loved You, people who trusted You. They didn't deserve to die like that. They were going to get their little girl, sleeping at a friend's house…"

The words trailed away from him as anger and pain smashed into him. "God, Maggie didn't deserve that! Why? Why did You let Dad live and take the other three? They deserved to live so much more. Why would You choose to take them and leave him? Why? I don't understand."

He sniffed and ran his wrist under his nose. "It's not fair, you know. It's not. You should've taken him. He should burn in hell for all the grief he's caused."

We have to pray that he figures it out, Keith. The words slid through him, but Keith fought them with a grip on both fists.

"I'm not praying for *him.*"

Find those who are hurting, and show them God's love.

His father's face crumpled with hurt the last time Keith walked out of his office traced through his consciousness. At that he yanked himself to his feet. Looking out over the falls, he let the anger take over. "You know what, God? He deserves to be hurting for all the heartache he's caused the rest of us. He deserves it. You hear me?" And with that, he went back to the life that was laid out before him.

Friday night Keith didn't know how he and Dallas would ever make it to Sunday in one piece. She was a basket case, and he wasn't much better. Her flowing white sheath dress hung perfectly around her lithe body, but she wasn't at all pleased with the fit.

She stood in the bedroom at the mirror, yanking and pulling and readjusting all the while muttering to herself. "Do you think we should show up together or separate?"

"Why wouldn't we go together?" Keith asked from where he was shaving in the bathroom. The razor took an unscheduled zag which left blood trailing behind it. "Crud."

"What's wrong?"

"I just cut myself." He examined the blood in the mirror. "Great. As if I needed one more thing to go wrong today."

"I knew I should've had the seamstress take these shoulders up. I look like a bag lady." Dallas appeared at the bathroom door looking anything but a bag lady.

Keith glanced over at her, trying to get gratefulness for his position in life to come over him. "You look beautiful."

She twisted her mouth. "You have to say that."

"Would you rather I said you look hideously awful?"

She smiled slightly. "At least you'd be honest."

Tenderness for how vulnerable she sounded went through him. Knowing they would only make it through this together, he turned and took her in his arms, oblivious to the remaining streaks of shaving cream still on his face. "You will have every guy jealous of me all night."

"Are you sure?" Her gaze spoke of genuine concern.

"Positive."

The shoes hurt, but Maggie couldn't worry about that. Too many other issues were more important, like the fact that Izzy's bow wouldn't stay in her hair, and Peter kept fidgeting with his tie. Her nerves hit the overload button when the limo rolled to the front of The Silver Rose. This place wasn't just fancy. It was lavish.

"Ma'am," the gentleman outside the restaurant said, offering her his hand. Maggie let him help her out, hoping she didn't look so out of place that he would notice. The once over his gaze did down her dress didn't help. Was it that bad? She helped the kids out and marched them up the stairs.

Choreographed to the second, the Ayers' limo pulled up just as she and the children got to the top step. With everything in her she wished she could reach down and fix her shoe, but she smiled like everything in life was wonderful as they waited for the Ayers to climb the steps and walk first into the restaurant.

The rehearsal at the mansion had been blessedly short, but this fiasco of a night threatened to be the longest of her life. Inside the restaurant Maggie found a quiet corner for her and the kids. She sat Izzy on her lap and put an arm around Peter.

"Why can't we just go home?" Peter whined. "I don't want to be here."

"Shh." Maggie leaned down to him. "I know, but Keith's coming. You want to see him, right?" She was at the end of her rope and fully intended on using every trick she knew—even those that might take her out permanently.

"Oh, don't you kids look so precious!" Jamie walked up, and Isabella squealed her delight. "Come here you." It took just that long for Jamie to be holding the little girl. Tanner walked up behind Jamie, and he smiled at Maggie.

"You made it, huh?" He extended his hand.

Maggie took it and stood. "Barely."

Greg stepped up to the little group. "Well, fancy meeting you all here."

Illogically he put his hand on Maggie's back, and trying to think of some way to steer the conversation so Tanner and Jamie wouldn't notice, she glanced around the room. "They sure do things up right, don't they?"

"You can say that again." Tanner pulled at the tie at his neck, and Maggie had to keep herself from laughing because he looked just like Peter. "If I'd have known about all this when Keith asked me, I'd have told him, 'No way!'"

"That makes two of us," Greg said.

They all laughed as Tanner's gaze slid past her. "Well, speak of the devil."

Without thinking, Maggie turned, and her heart lurched forward with a falling thud. White shirt, smoke-colored pants, no hat or bandana. Keith Ayer had arrived.

"They make such a good couple," Jamie breathed behind Maggie, and it hurt to agree.

Why it was so hard to play along, Keith would never be able to figure out, but he was exhausted from the effort. By the time dessert was over, his nerves were frayed to the point of snapping. All night the angel in the soft blue dress had played tag with his gaze. He was glad that Greg, Tanner and Jamie seemed to be keeping her company and helping with the kids, but it was all he could do not to trash everything and join them.

Twice he almost had. Once when his father cornered him with a sixty-second lecture on how he had to smooth things over with Mr. Henderson or else, and once when he saw Greg lean in so close to her that they might as well have been swapping air.

Finally Vivian announced to all that they had better get home so they could check on the final preparations. With his arm around Dallas, Keith watched Maggie make her way to the door. Isabella was asleep on her shoulder, and Peter was cradled in Greg's arm. It killed Keith not to go ask what their plans were. Was Greg going home with her too? Would they put the kids to bed and then pray over them?

"We're staying at the Crowne Plaza tomorrow night," Dallas said to the two bridesmaids that Keith didn't know all that well. From what he could tell, they were the giggle brigade. "Keith wanted our night to be special." Dallas's gaze slid over his face. "I'm the luckiest girl in the world."

When he looked back to the door, Maggie was gone.

The whole night Maggie had been dropping hints for Greg to leave her alone, but still was there. When they made it back to the mansion, he was right there to help her from the limo. He, of course, had driven his own car, insisting that he wanted to see her home even if they couldn't ride together.

"Here, I'll get him." Greg took Peter from Maggie, and Maggie gathered up Isabella. Up first one set of steps and then the others inside, Greg followed her. "This place always amazes me. It's like a museum with all the statues and stuff."

"Yeah," Maggie agreed. There was a blister on her heel that was taking up all the brain power she had left. She took Isabella and changed her, then put her to bed. Then she joined Greg in Peter's room to get Peter ready for bed. She felt Greg watching her as she worked, and it unnerved her. Her hands were shaking with the stress of the day and the trepidation of now.

In minutes Peter was sound asleep in bed. She kissed her fingers, said a soft prayer, and then pressed her fingers to Peter's forehead. "Good night, little prince." With that, she turned, and Greg followed her out. "These heels are killing me." She removed one, then the other. The process left her much shorter than she had ever seemed next to him. She glanced back at him. "You know, Greg. I'm really tired."

"You're so good with them." He sounded as if he wasn't really there. "I guess I've never really been around kids much before. They always kind of scared me."

"They're kids. What's so scary about them?" Kids were a snap compared with this. She wanted him to leave so she could go to bed, but he didn't leave.

Instead he stood there, looking at her. "Look, Maggie, I know I messed up, and I'm really sorry. Please give me another chance." His gaze was drilling through her although her head was down. "Please."

It took all the courage she had, but Maggie dragged her gaze up to his. "Greg, I like you. I really do. Just not like that."

His gaze dropped from hers to the carpet.

"It's not fair for me to let you think there's something there when there's not." She tried to look at him, but he wouldn't look up. "I'm really sorry."

Finally he nodded, and then he looked up with a tight smile. "Will you go with me to the wedding tomorrow?"

"Greg…"

"No. Not like that. Just as friends. Please?"

It took a breath, but finally she nodded.

"I can't believe Greg and Ike didn't take you out tonight," Dallas said as their limo rolled up to the guesthouse. "I figured they'd abscond with you at the first break in the action."

Considering that Ike wasn't talking to him these days and that Greg had left with the woman he really loved, Keith was kind of glad they didn't. "Yeah, well. It's okay."

"You know. I didn't pack all of my surprises for the honeymoon. Maybe I could get one out tonight for a little preview."

The thought made him want to throw up. He forced the air out of his lungs slowly. "I'm really beat, Dallas. Why don't you save it for tomorrow night when we're official?"

Official. The word sounded so very final.

She wrapped her arms around him like an anaconda. "Okay, but you don't know what you're missing."

The sun would be up in an hour, but Keith couldn't sleep. By this time tomorrow morning Dallas Henderson would be his wife, and there would be no going back. He sat in the recliner, letting scenes from his life flash before him. There were the turns he had taken and the ones that had been taken for him. There were decisions he made but more that had been made for him.

Although it knifed him to the core to think it, he knew that this marriage was the best thing for everyone save himself. It would make his father happy. Finally. It would make Mr. and Mrs. Henderson happy, although why that was, he wasn't really sure. It would make Dallas happy. But the one that kept him moving forward was the knowledge that if he just married Dallas, Maggie would be free to go on with her life.

Sooner or later she would certainly leave the mansion, and the Ayer family replete with all their curses and selfishness would be forever out of her life. She deserved that much. Of that and only that, Keith was perfectly sure.

Twenty-Five

"We need the children for pictures," Patty Ann said, appearing at the door of Isabella's room. It was only one o'clock. The wedding wouldn't start for four more hours. Whose brilliant idea it was to start with the children's pictures, Maggie wasn't at all sure, but whoever it was had no concept of how restless children got in dress clothes. "Mr. Ayer requested that they be brought to the waterfall for the pictures."

"The waterfall?" Maggie's heart sank through the thought. "Why can't we just do it here?"

Patty Ann's face fell into a scowl. "Really, Ms. Montgomery, you're not going to wear tennis shoes with that dress now, are you?"

Maggie looked down at her shoes beneath the soft satin of her formal peach dress. It was $25 at the thrift store, and it only had one small hole in the back hem. "Not for the wedding. Just for the keeping up with the kids for pictures and stuff. I got a horrendous blister from last night."

The secretary didn't look at all pleased. "Well, don't let anyone important see you in those things. We'll both be fired on the spot." She started to turn. "Oh, and Tanner is downstairs to take you to the falls. The wedding party is meeting down there."

"Okay." Maggie swept Isabella off the carpet and grabbed Peter's hand. At least Tanner would be there to keep her company. He and Jamie had been so nice the night before. They were a diversion, a distraction to keep her mind from thinking too far into the future or too much about the present. "Hi," she said at the bottom of the steps.

"Oh, look at you! You're so precious." Jamie squealed when she saw Isabella, and Isabella squealed back. "And Peter, my, aren't we handsome today?"

Peter smiled proudly.

"Well, let's just hope we are still precious and handsome four hours from now," Maggie said with a laugh.

The others would be descending on the place in no time. Keith knew that, so for one last moment, he stood at the edge of the falls and enjoyed the peacefulness. The wedding was edging inexorably closer, but standing here, he could pretend that he was again ten-years-old, with his mother and her wisdom.

"Mom, you know I only want what's best for everyone," he whispered, "even if it's not what I want."

The breeze whispered back to him, and then another sound hummed through that one. Keith turned, and his heart flipped over. Tanner's pickup parked next to the Dodge. Keith himself had sent Tanner on that errand, and so he knew better than anyone what his arrival meant. A door, another, and wedding attired people tumbled out. Tanner held Peter, and Jamie held Isabella. Then, behind them, Keith caught sight of the only one he'd been wanting to see since she'd walked out the night before.

"Looks like we even beat the photographer," Tanner said as he carefully descended the rocky path that was more fit for cowboy boots than a tuxedo. "Hey, Mr. Ayer. Sorry to keep you waiting."

Keith's gaze never left her as she picked her way down the path. "Don't worry about it. I'm just glad you made it."

With the way her luck was going, Maggie knew she would probably twist an ankle on the hard rocks and go crashing to the ground in a heap of peach and blood. It took only one glance at Keith to confirm how dangerous to her heart this situation really was. His white tuxedo set off the deep tan of his face and the dark hair that always made her ultra-aware that he wasn't just the estate handyman.

"I thought the photographer was supposed to be here," Jamie

said.

"Ike went to get him," Keith said, looking only at Maggie, and her nerves twisted over themselves.

"Where's Greg?" Tanner asked.

"Getting Dallas and the other bridesmaids." Keith looked at his watch. "They should all be here any minute."

"Keef!" Isabella squealed, tossing her arms out for him. He took her with a smile that ripped Maggie apart. She let her gaze drift out to the falls. It had always been so easy to be here with him. So deceptively easy.

"Hey there, little one. You look like a little princess." Keith turned for the tree, and the others followed him. "Come on. Let's get you out of the sun."

The heavens had had mercy on them. The weather was a cool 89 degrees, and for June, that was better than anyone could have hoped.

"This is so gorgeous," Jamie said. "I had no idea this was here."

Keith glanced at her. "Thanks." They reached the tree, and Keith put Isabella on the blanket he had already laid out. "Why don't you show her around, Tanner? There's some really nice views right over there."

Tanner nodded, and he and Jamie walked off hand-in-hand.

"They're a cute couple," Maggie said, trying desperately to ward off any serious conversation. He was so heart-stoppingly handsome today, she might well say something she would have to feel guilty for saying forever.

Peter sat down next to Izzy and started playing. The breeze caught a strand and sent it skittering across Maggie's face. She brushed it away, feeling Keith's gaze slide to her. Thinking she could just smile at him, she glanced his direction, but the intensity in his eyes jerked everything but her racing heart to a screeching halt.

"I'm sorry," he said softly, his eyes held a tender apology.

Concern slipped through her. "Sorry? For what?"

His gaze fell and then drifted back up to hers. "For how my family's treated you, for all the junk they've put you through."

She smiled and brushed the thought away. "It's no big deal."

The tenderness left. "No. It is a big deal... to me."

Her ears picked up the sound of a vehicle, but she couldn't

look away from him. He wouldn't let her.

"If I could make it all better, I would," he said, holding her gaze in a grip so tight, she couldn't breathe. The tree formed a barrier between them and whoever had gotten out of the vehicle up the path. "You deserve so much better. Don't ever let anyone tell you that you don't."

She wanted him to stop talking like this, like he was at somebody's funeral or something. "Keith…"

"No, Maggie." He reached out and took her hand. The warmth of his hand coupled with the gentleness of his touch sent tingles throughout her entire body. "I just want you to be happy. I just want what's best for you. No matter what that means. I…"

For the barest of moments Maggie was swept up in the completely illogical thought that he was about to kiss her. Then as quickly as the moment was there, it was gone.

"We made it," Ike said, stepping around the tree with an armload of camera equipment.

Maggie's hand dropped back to her side, and she half turned, some to get away from Keith, some to make sure Ike knew she was. She reached up and pushed the hair from her eyes, hoping the heat in her face wasn't evident to anyone other than her.

However, Ike took one look at them, and his smile fell into a frown. "There's more equipment in the truck. Why don't you go help him get it down here?"

"Oh, okay. Yeah," Keith said, and he walked around the tree away from her.

Maggie felt every step he took.

"Boy, you are some piece of something," Ike said, eyeing her from head to toe. "They're getting married today. Doesn't that mean anything to you?"

Words were smashing into one another in her head. "I…"

"You're here to watch the kids," Ike said with so much ice, Maggie almost shivered. "Don't forget it."

"I think we'll start right over here," the photographer said, lugging a camera and a tripod past the tree. "Will the bride be here soon?"

"She's on her way," Keith said, following him as if he had never so much as heard there was a tree by the falls. They went down to the rock shelf as Maggie fought to breathe. How she had gotten tagged Enemy Number One by Ike, she had no idea, but it was clear she had better steer clear or risk being roasted for dinner.

At that moment Keith's gaze snagged hers from where he stood with the photographer at the falls, and he smiled a sad, half smile at her. Maggie yanked her gaze from his. Behind her the roar of another approaching vehicle slid through the stillness. She whipped her head to the side to see who it was. From one door stepped Greg, from the back stepped three bridesmaids in celery green taffeta, and then from the other side stepped the real love of Keith's life. A goddess in the most beautiful dress ever created, and Maggie knew her heart would never be the same again.

Taking pictures was an ordeal. Had he known it would be this bad, Keith never would have suggested it. Dallas was in top form. She was either yelling at him or kissing him, and he couldn't decide which was worse. Throughout the nightmare of an hour of posing first here then there, he kept tabs on Maggie, and nothing in him liked the droop of her shoulders or the downcast of her eyes. She looked sadder than he had ever seen her, and he wondered if his bungling of the apology from before was what had upset her.

He hadn't meant to upset her, but trying to dance around the phrase I love you was harder than he'd ever expected it to be.

"Oh, joy," Tracy said as they stood waiting for the photographer to set the next shot of the entire wedding party sans ring bearer and flowergirl. "Greg, did you have to invite the dollar-store queen? I mean look at that dress. She probably fished it out of a dumpster somewhere."

Keith's heart slid through him at the luridly mean tone in Tracy's voice. Maggie Montgomery was ten times the woman Tracy would ever be, and yet beside him, Dallas laughed as if it was funny.

"She's the help," Dallas said spitefully. "You know Greg just can't help himself."

Greg stood next to Keith, and his tone was low and bitter. "You know, you two could be just a little more mean and maybe Satan would draft you for another tour in hell."

Dallas laughed at him. "Oh, come on, Greg. We're joking. You know that."

"Ha. Ha," he said, but he wasn't laughing and neither was

Keith.

"Okay, everyone look here and smile."

It was asking a lot.

"We've got more pictures to take at the mansion," Dallas instructed as the group made their way up the rocks. "So don't anyone get lost on the way back."

Lost sounded very good to Maggie. If she'd had her way, she would've gone the long route home, preferably through China. Carrying Isabella, she climbed up and up and up until she wouldn't have been surprised to have found herself in heaven at the top of the path.

"We should've all been smart and worn shoes like Maggie," Tracy said, and it was obvious it wasn't a compliment.

"Shut up, Tracy," Greg warned from his place just behind her.

"What? I didn't know we were going hiking."

Maggie pushed the words and the hurt from her. *Just get through this. Just keep moving and get through it.* At the top she put the kids in Tanner's truck without so much as looking at anyone. She was out of place here. They all knew it, and so did she.

"Maggie, Keith's taking Dallas back," Greg said, appearing at the door to Tanner's pickup. "You want to ride with me?"

"I… Oh." She glanced at Tracy, who was slinging arrows at her with her gaze just behind Greg. "Umm, no. I think I'll just ride with the kids."

"Are you sure?" Greg slid his hand over hers, which immediately pulled up memories of the last guy to hold her hand like that. Tears of helplessness stung her eyes as her heart turned over. She couldn't find a safe place to look. At the Dodge Keith turned and smiled softly at her, then with a glance back to the falls, he got into the pickup and drove off with Dallas in the passenger's seat. Maggie's gaze plummeted to the ground.

"Yeah, I'm sure."

Pictures of the wedding party at the mansion had given way to pictures of just Keith and Dallas, and from Isabella's room above the festivities, Maggie watched them below, holding hands, smiling at each other, and kissing. Every look, every kiss broke her heart into a few more pieces. She wrenched her arms over themselves to keep the pain away, but still it attacked her like warriors breaching barricades. He was getting married. Keith was getting married. This was real. It wasn't just some nightmare that she would wake up from. It was really happening. Tears slid out of her eyes as she watched them, so happy, so right together. Keith's arms were around Dallas just as Maggie had wished for so long they would be around her.

Dallas gazed up at him, and the look he gave her in return could hold no other meaning. Watching it was horrible. It was like being ripped apart from the inside out. The soft knock on the door smashed through her, and she swiped at the tears as she turned. "Yeah?"

"Maggie?" Jamie asked in instant concern when she saw her. "Maggie, what's wrong?"

Anguish crashed through the pain. "I... I can't do this."

Jamie's concern deepened. "Can't do what?"

Maggie raked her fingers through her hair. "I can't stay here. I've got to go."

"Go? But..."

An escape plan formed in her head as Maggie looked at the young lady. "You have to cover for me, Jamie. You're good with the kids. They'll be all right with you."

"Me? Maggie, what are you talking about?"

"Tell them I got a call from home. Tell them it was an emergency, and I had to go. Tell them I'm sorry." She stepped past Jamie and ran to her room, tears blinding her path. Nothing other than the overwhelming desire to run was getting through. If she could just leave, just get out of here before anyone knew she was gone, then surely her heart wouldn't crack in two.

As she dragged her suitcase from the closet, she heard the first strains of the violins downstairs. Guests were already arriving. She didn't have much time to make her getaway. In fistfuls she yanked her clothes from the closet and threw them into the suitcase just as the door to her room came open.

"Maggie? What're you doing?" Greg asked in horror. "Where are you going?"

"Back where I belong."

"Well, I guess you got what you wanted," Tanner said to Ike as Keith readjusted his tie at the mirror of the bedroom where they were getting ready. "Ms. Montgomery's leaving."

In one second the tie was forgotten as Keith spun. "Leaving?"

Tanner nodded. "Jamie just came and got Greg. She said Ms. Montgomery's real upset. She's packing to leave."

"What? No. She can't…" Keith was at the door in two steps, but before he could get through it, Ike stepped between him and his destination.

"Let her go, Keith. She's no better than the rest of them."

"The rest of…?" Keith wasn't comprehending. "Get out of my way, Ike."

But the old cowboy didn't budge, and with his foot anchored there, neither did the door.

Anger snapped into Keith. "Move, or I'll move you."

Ike stood for one more long moment, and then with a slow shake of his head he stepped to the side. Keith yanked the door open and raced into the hallway, through the upstairs, and right to the kids' wing.

At Maggie's door Greg stood pleading with her to stop. "You don't have to do this, Maggie. Really. It's not…"

Keith pushed past Greg, and the sight of Maggie standing at the bed, her back to the door, latching the suitcase slammed into him. "Maggie, what're you doing?"

In a breath she whirled around. The look in her eyes was hard and determined. "I know. I should stay for the kids' sake, but I just can't. Okay? Don't ask me why. I've just…" She reached back and swung the suitcase to her. "I've got to go."

"Maggie, wait." As she brushed by him, Keith snagged her wrist, and she stopped one inch from him. His gaze slid down her face to her lips and then traced back up again. "Please don't go. I don't want you to go."

She slammed her eyes closed, and he knew she was fighting as hard as he was. "I hope you and Dallas will be very happy together." With that she opened her eyes, and the look in them ripped his own helplessness wide open. One shake of her wrist, and she was free of him. "I've got to go."

Knocking into everyone she met on the way out, Maggie

headed for the stairs.

"It's time, everyone," Patty Ann said, climbing the stairs and meeting Maggie coming the other way down them. "Ms. Montgomery, where are you going?"

But Maggie never stopped. Keith followed her out of the room and stood with a whole audience behind him as he watched her go. He wanted to go after her, to stop her, and tell her that he loved her, but the truth was, he loved her too much to do that. She was better off without him.

"Would someone please tell me what's going on?" Patty Ann asked, her face livid.

"Greg." Keith turned to his best friend. He didn't even have to say the words, the look of sheer panic conveyed the message perfectly.

"Yeah, I'll go." Greg started down the stairs after Maggie, but Patty Ann stopped him.

"You're the best man. You can't leave."

"Oh, yeah? Watch me."

Glad for the tennis shoes, Maggie ran stumbling down the trail to the guesthouse. The suitcase banged into her leg, nearly tripping her, but she didn't care. She had to get away.

Knowing that the barn must be at an angle to her present location, she ducked into the trees and cut cross-country. "God, please, please, just get me out of here."

"The final guests have been seated!" Patty Ann exclaimed in horror as she climbed the main staircase into the emotional chaos above. "Your parents are walking down the aisle right now. You're supposed to be downstairs ready to go. What are you all doing standing around for? We've got a wedding to put on."

The others seemed to scatter to their rightful posts, but Keith couldn't move. He stood there at the balcony railing gazing down into nothing. He couldn't move, not a finger, not a toe. If Greg didn't find her, she might be gone forever. It was what he said he wanted for her, but watching it happen was killing him.

"Mr. Ayer," Patty Ann said, reappearing at the bottom of the steps. "Now!"

In her headlong dash to leave, Maggie had almost forgotten the secret of getting the barn door open. Finally with a bang of her body into it, the bolt came free, and the door swung open. Motion after motion she made until she and the suitcase were in the car, and it was running. She spun out of the barn and urged the little car up the path to the trees.

Details like closing the barn door were lost in the haze of numbness. She drove past the garage without looking at it and turned on the pavement. In less than a minute she was at the mansion and in less than another she was out the front gate. Swiping at the tears she forced herself not to think about what time it was, about what was happening, about life itself. Where she was going, she had no idea. Anywhere had to be better than here.

Six hundred pairs of eyes gazed at Keith as he walked out of the side room and took his place at the front of the assembled guests. He wasn't really breathing or thinking. It was more momentum carrying him forward than anything. Right up front his father smiled at him and nodded. There was something so spirit-sapping about that look, Keith had to look away. Yes, his father was proud of him because this wasn't him—it was some made-up, plastic replica of him that clinched him in its vice grip.

"Finally, you are rising to the occasion" his father's look seemed to say. Keith shook his head and replanted his gaze to the aisle beyond. Dallas, basking in the glow of having all eyes on her, walked gracefully beside her father. Mr. Henderson, too, was milking this walk for all it was worth. Flashbulbs went off ahead of them, and disgust clutched Keith's gut. In minutes he would be tied to that farce of a delusional display. It wasn't real. None of it.

"Do you want to be rich or to look rich?" Maggie's voice asked from deep inside him. Looking at them, Keith couldn't help but think how rich they looked but how terribly poor in morals and judgment and the things that really counted that they were.

When they made it to the end of the aisle, Mr. Henderson turned and kissed Dallas. Then he looked at Keith with a gaze that would've melted Everest. "Be good to her, you hear me?"

Keith swallowed and nodded. When Mr. Henderson stepped to the side, Keith offered her his arm. He wasn't going to make the mistake of taking her hand like he had at the rehearsal the night before. If he had learned anything, it was that this was important, and every detail had to be right.

"No!" Maggie wailed as the hissing sound increased sending the power in her car into a death spiral. When it rolled to a stop on the side of the road leading out of Pine Hill, she allowed herself to sit and wallow in her pathetic bad luck for one moment before she slammed her shoulder into the door to get it to open.

At the front of the car, she reached down to pop the hood, nearly scalding her hand in the process. When the hood was open, she waved the steam away. "I cannot believe this. What else could go wrong?"

Just then she heard the sound of a vehicle coming up behind her, and she turned and shielded her eyes from the late afternoon sun. Maybe if she was lucky, she could get a ride to a bus station. Del Rio sounded really nice right about now.

However, when she got a good look at the stopping car, annoyance jammed into her. In seconds it was stopped and the driver was out and striding toward her. In just as many she was buried in his arms.

"Maggie," Greg said. "Oh, thank God you're okay."

Twenty-Six

"Do you, Keith Warren Ayer take Dallas Celeste Henderson to be your lawfully wedded wife to have and to hold from this day forward 'til death do you part?"

The words seemed so simple. Two of them. Two little syllables in fact, but the questions and concerns smashing into each other in the middle of his gut wouldn't let them find the air.

The minister cleared his throat. "Umm. Mr. Ayer?"

"Huh?" Keith asked, looking up at him as if he had no idea why he was standing there.

"Do you take Dallas to be your wife?"

Keith's gaze slid to her, and one question trumped all the others. He glanced at the preacher and then at her. Finally his gaze settled on the preacher. "Hold that thought."

"I can call a tow truck," Greg said as they stood beside the road, examining the heap that used to be a car.

"I'm sorry." Maggie glanced at him. "You were supposed to be at the wedding. I didn't mean to drag you into this."

"Hey, don't sweat it. I'd rather be out here with you than at some pretentious showboat wedding anyway." He smiled at her. "Come on. Let's get out of here. I'll call a tow truck to come get this. We can go back to my place."

Panic seized her, but he just smiled. "Don't worry. I'll behave myself."

"Keith, what do you think you're you doing?" Dallas asked in a barely contained screech as he dragged her from the garden into the little side room. Once there, she yanked her wrist free of his grip. "This is not funny."

"I'm not laughing." He turned to her and put both hands on her arms which were bare owing to the strapless wedding gown. "Listen, I have to know something."

Her eyes were wild with frustration. "What? That you're insane?"

"No." Seriousness snapped through him. "Listen to me, Dallas. I have to know something before we do this."

"What? What in the world is so important that you humiliate me in front of six hundred people?"

Keith took a breath to settle the question in his heart. "Do you believe in God?"

At that, even her anger fell into incomprehension. "Wh...? Do I...? What kind of a question is that?"

"I have to know. It's important to me."

Dallas took that in, closed her eyes, and shook her head. "Keith, this is crazy. What difference does it make if I believe in God or not?"

"Just a simple yes or no, Dallas. That's all I need."

She thought a little longer. "Well, yeah. I guess so. I mean. What's not to believe?"

The answer wasn't really an answer, more of a question. "Do you have faith that He'll get you through life? I mean does He factor into your decisions at all?"

Her gaze turned decidedly skeptical. "God?"

His spirit was falling through her apathy toward the topic. "Yeah. Is He a real part of your life?"

"I..." She let out her breath. "I don't know. What do you want me to say?"

"The truth, Dallas. I want the truth."

The door swung open.

"What's going on in here?" his father hissed.

"Please, Dad. We're in the middle of something."

"Yeah, does the word *wedding* come to mind?" his father asked.

"Please, Dad, just give us a minute."

"You don't have a minute, Keith. You are embarrassing me in front of half the state of Texas. Now get out here."

"Is everything all right?" Vivian asked from outside.

His father ducked out. "Fine, Viv. Go sit down."

Then just before his father could rip into him again, Dallas turned knowing eyes on him. "This is about her. Isn't it?"

"Her? What her?" his father asked, coming back in.

"This is about that little tramp, that what's her name? Maggie." The name dripped like poison.

"Montgomery?" his father asked as his eyes widened, and too many pieces to count dropped into place behind them.

Keith let his hands drop. It really wasn't about Maggie, but he would never be able to convince them of that. He sat back on something he couldn't have named had he tried. "No, Dallas. This isn't about Maggie. It's about we're not right for each other, and we never have been. We want different things from life. You want the money and the stuff that comes from being an Ayer. And I..." He glanced at his father. "Wish I had never been born an Ayer."

"Keith Warren Ayer! Don't you even talk like that! You are privileged to be a part of this family," his father nearly yelled, only stopping himself because of the thousand ears outside no doubt listening for any sign of what was going on. "It's a wonder I haven't thrown you out before now!"

"Why, Dad? Because I wasn't good enough for you?" Keith dragged his gaze up to his father's, and hate and loathing were all he saw there. "Well, you know what? That's pretty remarkable coming from somebody who killed three people and walked away like it never happened."

The punch landed hard and true. The condescension in his father's eyes fell away. "What...? How...?"

"What? You didn't think I'd ever find out?" Keith asked. A haze of numbness so that he couldn't really feel anything fell over him. "And I'm sure you threatened the others so they wouldn't tell me, or did you just pay them off to keep them quiet?" His gaze came up and found Ike standing just behind his father.

The older cowboy couldn't meet his gaze, and he looked like he'd rather run than be there at that moment.

"Yeah, well. You almost covered your tracks good enough." His gaze dropped from Ike to his father. "Almost."

"Keith...," his father started.

Keith pulled himself to his feet and stepped over to Dallas. When his gaze came up, it was with true regret. "I'm really sorry you got mixed up in all this, but us getting married isn't right, and it's a lie I'm not willing to try to live." He started to step past her.

"Keith, wait," Dallas said, her dress whooshing as she turned. "Can't we get married now, just... just so these people won't know? We can always go down to city hall and get a divorce tomorrow."

It was so hard to believe he'd almost forced himself to say, "I do" to her. "No, Dallas. Lying's not my style." With that, he turned instead to the inside door. A twist of the knob and he walked away from the whole, ugly horde of them forever.

"Can I get you something?" Greg asked as Maggie sat on his couch, trying to get everything that had just happened to line up in her head.

"No, thanks."

"I've got Sprite," he said, a teasing quality edging the statement.

She smiled up at him sadly and shook her head. Greg stood there, looking down at her for the longest time. Then he spun and sat on the couch, a full cushion away.

"Okay. Here's what I don't understand. Why didn't you just go for it with Keith? Dallas wasn't here. No one would ever have known."

Maggie shook her head, the dreams she hadn't let herself acknowledge were there flowed through her even now. "Keith isn't like that."

Greg turned to her. "That's just it. Keith is like that, or at least he was. All through high school and college even after he met Dallas. Women were never an issue for him. He'd take what he wanted and never look back."

Again Maggie shook her head. "That's not the Keith I know. He's sweet and kind, and he cares about people—not just on the outside but about how they really are in here." She put her hand to her heart and then let it slide up her neck. "At least that's who I thought he was."

With a twist, Greg took his jacket off and laid it on the couch arm, smoothing the fabric with his hand. However, halfway down it, he stopped.

"What?" she asked, seeing his hesitation.

Slowly Greg reached into the folds and pulled out a little box. "Hmm. Something tells me they'll be wondering where these are." At that moment Greg's cell phone on the counter beeped, and both gazes went to it. He stood, went to it, and answered it. "Hello? Oh. Hi."

His gaze traced to hers, and Maggie caught the implication. Panic surged through her as she shook her head. "No," she whispered. "Don't tell them I'm here."

Greg turned to the phone call. "No, man. I looked. I don't know where she went."

Keith considered leaving the guesthouse. Dallas already had amidst a hail of curses from both her and her parents. He stood there, absorbing them all as they gathered her things and left. They were right. He was good-for-nothing. He had led her on in hopes of making everyone believe he was something he was not. And he had let her down in the worst way imaginable. The only thing that could conceivably have been worse would have been if he'd actually married her.

When they were gone, he sat down in the chair and pulled the Bible from the little compartment. Something about the fact that it didn't have to be hidden anymore lifted his spirit from the muck ever-so-slightly. He let it fall open to no particular page. At 2 Peter, he started reading.

He is patient with you, not wanting anyone to perish, but everyone to come to repentance.

Keith groaned with the reading and let his head fall back on the recliner. "God, how could You be patient with me? Me, of all people. I've done such horrible things. I was so hurt, I didn't care who got hurt because of me." The pain of a life poorly lived knifed through him. "Why don't You just put me out of my misery and get it over with?"

His hand slid the pages to the side as the anguish gushed over him. "I'm not worthy of You, Lord. Can't You see that?" His gaze fell to the words even as tears blinded them from his sight.

Because of His great love for us, God, who is rich in mercy, made us alive with Christ even when we were dead in transgressions—it is by grace you have been saved.

Keith breathed in those words, read them again, and breathed some more. It was like inhaling God for the first time. "I don't understand, God. I don't understand why You won't just let me drop. That's what I deserve." Again his hands worked the pages and his gaze fell to the words there.

Where can I go from Thy Spirit? Or where can I flee from Thy presence? If I ascend to heaven, Thou art there; if I make my bed in Sheol, behold, Thou art there.

He didn't know where Sheol was, but he had a sneaking suspicion that God had been there and every other place Keith had ever been. God, for some inexplicable reason, seemed to be dogging his every step. Exhaustion was beginning to take over, but he let his fingers trace through the pages one last time. The red attracted his gaze.

If any man is thirsty, let him come to Me and drink. He who believes in Me, as the Scripture said, 'From his innermost being shall flow rivers of living water.'

Living water. What had the preacher said about filling that place, that hole with anything other than God? That's what Keith felt like he'd been doing for all of 30 years—filling and filling and filling, and always finding the hole empty. First it was spending his father's money—cars, women, wine—the world made it look so easy. Yet, at the end of the day, at the end of every party, when he woke up in the morning in someone else's bed, the emptiness was always right there with him.

It was just like that verse said, "Where can I run from it?" It followed him. No. It didn't just follow him. It was a part of him. No, not even just that. It was him. He was the empty hole, waiting, hoping, wishing, pleading for something or someone to fill it. And still it was empty until a young lady with funny glasses and shoes two sizes too big had stumbled into his life.

He closed the Bible and ran his hand over it. The others had all given him themselves—for an hour, for a night, but she had given him something better, something he had been searching for his whole life. She had given him the answer to filling the hole.

As if compelled by some force he didn't recognize, Keith got up and went to the phone. He dialed information, and in minutes he had the number for Del Rio. Home. Yes, Maggie would have gone home.

The shower had felt good. It calmed her and warmed her—at least it had tried. True to his word, Greg had been nothing but kind. She knew he was still trying to sort everything out, but then again, so was she. Her hair still dripping she walked into the living room, toweling it out.

Greg was sitting on the couch. He only glanced up when she entered. "Keith called again. He's really worried about you."

"Huh. I can't believe he's not halfway to Hawaii by now."

The deep concern of the brown eyes gathered her in. "They didn't go through with it."

The towel dropped three inches. "What...? Why not?"

Greg smiled. "Same reason you took off. Keith's a basket case with worry." His gaze questioned her. "Do you love him?"

There was no real way around the truth. "Yeah, but it would never work between us."

"Why not? He loves you. You love him."

"Because, Greg. He's Keith Ayer. He's worth a gazillion dollars. He rides around in limousines and trains million dollar racehorses. I'm some vagrant from the sticks who doesn't know a salad fork from a shrimp skewer."

Slowly Greg shook his head. "Do you really think he cares about that?"

"His family does."

"His family is not him."

Maggie's gaze fell to the carpet as the drying continued.

"He really is worried about you."

Panic seized her. "You won't tell him where I am, will you?"

It took a minute, but Greg finally shook his head. "No. Not if you don't want me to."

Twenty-Seven

Keith went to church on Sunday, but it didn't feel right without her there. Afterward, he went to the gravesite and put a dozen daisies in the little flower holder. They were his mom's favorites. Then he went home and buried himself in the Bible and prayed for two more hours. Finally when he could take the quiet no longer, he got in his truck and headed out for the falls.

Under the tree his mind traced back to that last magical moment with Maggie, holding her hand and gazing into her eyes. If only it could have been different. If only he could've done what he so wanted to do and taken her in his arms. What her lips must feel like. What she must feel like. As he let his thoughts float, other thoughts—darker ones overtook him. She would never forgive him if she knew what his father had done to her family. He couldn't bring himself to forgive. How could she?

You have to let people be on their own journey, to find out what's important in their own time. His mother's voice soft and graciousness drifted through him, and he let his head fall back on the scratchy bark. *Mercy is shown to those who show mercy.*

Mercy. Keith breathed that word through the hard rock at the top of his chest. Mercy? To a man who had dragged him and so many others through a hell they didn't deserve? Mercy to one who bought and sold people's loyalty like it was on an auction block? Mercy to the man who had taken life itself as if he was God? How could he ever show his father mercy?

"Because he is where you are." Keith spoke the words as if he knew them for himself. Out loud, in his own voice, there was no denying it. His father was empty, lonely, sad, and hurting. He closed his eyes and shook his head. "God, help me. He needs You more than he knows, but I don't even know enough to help him find You."

Softly the answer came. *Trust, and walk through the doors I open.*

Maggie walked to the nearest church on Monday. It was locked, so she sat on the steps and prayed as the morning rush passed by. How long she sat there, she wasn't sure, but she prayed in depth for every one she could think of. When her mind wound round to Peter and Izzy, her heart twisted in on itself. It was pure selfishness to leave them like she had. That hurt to acknowledge, but it was true. She prayed that God would be with them even when she couldn't.

Then her mind traced to Keith. "God, please be with him. Help him find what he needs the most."

"Dad, can I talk to you?" Keith pushed the door to his father's office open and found him not at his desk but standing at the window, staring out into the yard beyond as the wedding scene was dismantled before him. "Dad?"

His father glanced over his shoulder, but his gaze went immediately back to the window. "I didn't mean for it to happen, you know? Any of it. I really wanted you and Dallas to be happy— just like your mother and I were."

Slowly, carefully, Keith joined his father at the window. "Will you tell me about it? The accident, I mean?"

The pause stretched between them, widening with each passing second. "I'd been to a conference all week. Bonnie didn't want to come, but they were having a big party on Saturday night, and I talked her into coming anyway. I told her it was important for my work. She didn't want to. She wanted to stay... with you. It was some... I don't know. Something at school."

"The Star Parade." Keith hadn't thought of that in years, but he remembered how disappointed he was that not even his mom was there. Thinking back now, he didn't really remember who had taken him, just that he was on stage with no one who loved him in

311

the audience.

"She thought it was important. I told her there would be others. Besides, she didn't have to go to every single one. Of course, she didn't like that much. You know your mom."

That didn't surprise Keith. She was always there. Always. Even if his dad wasn't.

The tone in his father's voice grew more somber. "I'd been drinking at the party. I always drank at parties back then. It was what you did. It was what everybody did. But then we left, and I took a wrong turn. Bonnie kept telling me I was going the wrong direction and to turn around. She was all panicked and telling me we would never find our way back because it was dark, and we had no idea where we were. But I thought I knew best. I always knew best, and I was going to show her I didn't need her help or anybody else's."

In Keith's mind the car careened through the darkness barreling down on the stop sign Keith knew was at the end of that road. He braced himself for the impact as if he was there.

"They said there was a stop sign. I guess there was. I never saw it." A pause slid through the story. "The next thing I remember is holding Bonnie. There was blood everywhere and lights and people. I don't know where they all came from. They were telling me I had to let her go, that they'd take care of her, but I knew... I knew even then she was gone."

The other car, twisted and gnarled, crept into Keith's consciousness. "What about the others?"

That brought his father's memories to a halt. "Others?"

"In the other car."

The pause lasted much longer than Keith had expected. "How did you know about that?"

"James and Christina Montgomery." Keith let the names seep into the dismal air between them. "Maggie's parents."

Everything stopped, and then his father turned to him almost without moving. "Maggie? Are you sure?"

"May 7th. They were going to pick her up."

"But how...? How long have you known?"

"Couple of weeks."

"And you didn't say anything?"

"I didn't know how."

"Does Maggie know?"

"No, and now she's gone." Keith let that go through him, and it unleashed the pain in every cell it met. He pushed it back, knowing that even the hurt wouldn't bring her back. "It's probably for the best. She deserved better than me anyway."

His father's gaze drifted over to him. "I don't know about that. I think you'd be as good for her as she is for you."

Incomprehension smashed through Keith, and his gaze went to his father's. "What does that mean?"

The older man's gaze went back to the yard. "It means I'm proud of you."

The word cracked over him. "Proud? Of me? Why?"

"Because you know who you are, you know what you want. Heck, you stood up to Lee Ferrell who's eaten my lunch more than once." His father's smile was filled with sadness. "You are who I always wanted to be."

Keith wasn't following. He kept hitting brick walls of how he'd always thought things were. "But you always wanted me to be you."

The laugh was barely there. "That was the problem. You *were* me. The drinking, the partying, the living on the edge. I was never really sure you weren't going to blunder it all just like I did until..."

"Until?"

His smile was thoughtful. "You hadn't been to church since she died, had you?"

Keith's gaze fled out the window to the relative safety it provided. "No. Had you?"

Soft enveloped the answer. "I couldn't. I couldn't face Him with what I'd done to her... and to you."

So many days Keith had spent believing his father hated him when in fact he loved him too much to trust himself to do it right. "Well, maybe we could go sometime. You and me."

There was surprise in the glance. "You think they wouldn't throw me out?"

"Hey, they didn't throw me out."

They stood like that then—father and son looking out on a world they had created as it was dismantled.

"Have you talked to Maggie?"

The thought knifed through Keith. "I don't even know where she is. I called her foster mom, but she hasn't heard from her since she left for here. I called Greg. He doesn't know where she is either."

His father thought for a long moment. "I'm sorry to hear that... for you and for the kids."

The kids. The pain ached deeper. He'd messed things up for them too. "Who's with them?"

"The little girl who had them at the wedding."

"Jamie?"

"Is that her name?"

Keith nodded. It was crazy how badly he missed them. "Do you mind if I go see them? Just to say hi."

"I'm sure they would love it."

"So we're good?" Keith held out his hand.

With a nod, his father shook his hand. "Yes. We're good."

When Keith got to the kids' door upstairs, he had to steel himself to face the scene on the other side. He knew even before he got there that seeing them without Maggie would be visual verification of just how stupid he had been. He pushed the door open, and Isabella was the first one to see him.

"Keef!" She scrambled to her feet and toddled over to him with her arms out the whole way.

He dropped to his knees and wrapped her into himself. "Hey, baby girl." He stood with her in his arms, and on the other side of the room, Jamie stood as well.

She pulled her jersey down over her jeans nervously. "Hi, Mr. Ayer. Umm have you heard from Maggie?"

Keith put his nose into Isabella's hair and breathed in the baby smell. "No. Unfortunately not."

"I'm sorry."

He tried to smile, but it hurt.

Peter walked to Keith, rubbing his eyes. "Where's Maggie?"

He knelt and put his arm around Peter. "Well, buddy. I'm not real sure."

"Is she coming back?"

Keith looked at Jamie. "I don't know."

"But I need her to come pray with me. I don't know how."

As much as he wanted to, he didn't have a good answer for that. "Well, I'll tell you what, I'll come up and pray with you later… if you want me to."

Peter looked unsure. "Really?"

"Really."

Sunday night, true to his word, Keith knelt beside Peter's bed. He'd told Jamie he would put the child to bed, so she had left them alone. He took Peter's hand, and the large eyes stared at him, afraid but trusting.

"Dear Lord, we know that You know things we can't, so we're going to trust that You have a plan all worked out for this. But Lord, we're really worried about Maggie. We don't know where she is, or how she is, so please if there is a way, bring her back to us because we need her, Lord. We really do. Please bless everyone that we love and hold them in Your hands tonight."

The prayer stopped, and he looked down at Peter.

"What about the boys and girls part?" Peter asked.

Fear nudged into Keith. "I don't know that part."

So Peter took over. "Please be with all the boys and girls in the world who are hurting or alone. Let them know that You love them as much as You love us. Amen."

"Amen," Keith echoed. He stood and reached down with his fingers to touch the boy. "Good night, slugger."

"'Night, Keith. Thanks." And Peter rolled over and closed his eyes.

Monday morning Keith was saying prayer after prayer as he drove to the stables. There was no telling what havoc his impromptu decision on Saturday had unleashed. Worse, he wasn't even sure he still had a job. After all, it was now June 5th, and he was supposed to have left for good on the third. His only defense was to act like nothing had happened and hope for the best.

In the stables he grabbed the hay and started his morning chores.

"No," Tanner said, coming out of the office. "I just checked, and it's only half of what we ordered."

"I do not believe this…" But the sentence trailed off when Ike joined Tanner in staring at the cowboy currently feeding the horses. "Keith. What…? When did you get here?"

"Just made it." He threw the hay to Buck and rubbed the horse's soft, cream head. "I thought I'd check into getting some new tires for the trailers today. Those ones you're running are death traps."

"I…" Ike looked at Tanner who caught the message to give them some time.

"I'll just be checking the water by the track," Tanner said, and Ike nodded.

Keith continued to throw hay, liking how it felt to do physical labor again. Two stalls and then three, and he was even with where Ike was standing.

"So is that it then?" Ike asked, putting his hands on his waist over the brown belt. "You're just going to pick up where you left off like nothing happened?"

Another two slabs of hay and Keith wiped off his hands. "You got a better idea?"

"Well, one. You might tell me what happened, why you went off the deep end like that."

"I just came to my senses. That's all."

"Yeah? Well, it looked to me like you lost your mind… again."

Peace overtook Keith. "It must've been hard all those years trying to keep me in line." Slowly he began to see the past as it really was. Keith making stupid decisions, and Ike trying desperately to keep them from killing him. Keith shook his head. "I know you've put yourself on the line for me more than once. And I know there are things you didn't tell my dad so he wouldn't know how lost I really was. I get that now. But I'm not a little kid any more, Ike. I need to make some decisions for myself."

Ike snorted. "I've seen how you make decisions, and that doesn't inspire confidence."

"That's because I was the one making the decisions back then. I'm not anymore."

The leather-tanned face fell in incomprehension, and Keith laughed.

"Trust me, I know. I've made more rotten decisions than a guy should get to make in ten lifetimes, but I'm not that guy anymore. I don't need the dumb decisions to fill the hole."

"Hole?" Ike's expression was getting more worried by the second. "I don't…"

Keith shook his head. "It's something I'm learning… about

filling the emptiness with the One it was meant to be filled by."

"And who's that?"

"God." It seemed so very simple, but it had been so very hard to find.

"God? I didn't know you were religious."

Keith laughed. "Neither did I." His mind traced back. "Years ago, when Mom was here, we went to church a lot, not that I ever really liked it much back then, but I see now the stuff she was trying to teach me, the stuff she knew I needed for when things got rocky. Unfortunately I was a little too pigheaded to understand the gift she was giving me at the time, and when things got rough, it never occurred to me that God could help."

"And now you do?" The question was skeptical in every syllable.

"Yeah. I see now that God was with me every step—even when I was being a complete idiot about everything. He was leading me here, letting me see that none of those things would ever bring me real happiness. I get that now, and to tell you the truth, I can't wait to see where we're going next."

"And your dad?"

A smile touched Keith's heart. "We're learning. We see the mistakes we've made, and we're learning to forgive ourselves and each other."

Ike didn't look wholly convinced. "What about Maggie? I'm sure she was thrilled when you told her the thing with Dallas fell through."

That sent Keith's gaze crashing to the boards at his feet in a hail of hurt. "She left. I don't know where she is."

"Well, I can't say that I'm surprised. Why would she be any different than all the rest of them?"

It wasn't anger so much as a need to get Ike to understand that went through Keith. "That's just it. She was way different than the others. Maggie let me be me. She wasn't impressed with the money or the cars. She could've cared less about a fancy house or a job with the right company. She had peace, and considering what she had been through… that was saying a lot."

"What she had been through? What does that mean?" The questions were harsh and full of judgment and condemnation.

However, there was no reason to keep it a secret any longer. It had been hidden far too long. "The wreck my dad had, the one that killed Mom? Maggie's parents were in the other car. They were killed instantly."

Ike's arms unwound as he stared in disbelief. "Wh...? Keith, are you sure?"

"I read the newspaper articles myself. All of them." Keith exhaled the long night spent reading. "She grew up in the foster system because of that night and my dad's stupid decisions." Then Keith knew he had to say it, but he wasn't sure he could. He took a deep breath to settle the words. "That's why I need to say thanks, Ike. Thanks for every lecture you ever gave me about drinking and driving, thanks for every time you came and got me when I was stoned-out in some corner, thanks for every second you spent worrying about me and trying to make sure I didn't end up like him. I know it wasn't easy, and I didn't make it any easier. But I also know without you, I'd probably be rotting away in some jail cell somewhere... or dead. So thanks."

Ike scratched his sideburn. "You know, if I didn't know better, I'd think you've gone and grown up on me."

Keith smiled. "Hey, it had to happen sooner or later."

Just after Keith got home from praying with Peter the next night, his cell phone beeped. His pulse leaped into his ears when he caught sight of the ID number. He clicked it on. "Have you heard from her?"

"Well, hello to you too," Greg said. "No. No more news."

"Crud. I was really hoping she'd call you."

"We were just friends. I'd think she'd call you before she called me." Greg didn't sound exactly jovial. "Listen, I called to tell you I've still got your rings from Saturday."

The rings. Keith hadn't even thought of them, and they were the last thing he cared to think about now. "Can't you just put them in the mail to me?"

"The mail? They're mega-bucks rings, Keith. You really want me to mail them to you?"

Truth was he didn't want them at all. "Well, then maybe you can bring them over some night."

"No, I don't think so. I'm really swamped right now. I was wondering if you could come get them though. I don't want the responsibility. You know where the key is, right?"

"Same place as always."

"Yep. It's still there. Anyway. I'll leave them on the kitchen cabinet if you want to swing by sometime and get them."

"Oh, okay." The thought was less than appealing. "I'll try."

Twenty-Eight

"Are you sure you don't want to come with us?" Keith's father asked Vivian who stood, glaring at them from the staircase.

"To church? Why would I want to go to church?"

Peter who stood with his hand in his father's looked up at her. "Because Jesus loves you, and He wants you to come see Him."

Keith could have kissed the child, but instead he let his gaze trail up to Vivian who looked positively dumbfounded.

"Oh. I… Are…?" She couldn't get a full thought out.

"You're welcome to come with us," his father said, and Keith could hardly contain the hope. "But you don't have to if you don't want to."

"Well, I guess… I'm not doing anything else." She looked down at her outfit. "I should go change."

"You look beautiful." His father held his hand out to her. "Come on. Come with us. We want you to go."

The only person missing was Maggie, but for her, the family picture would have been complete. Keith let Vivian hold Isabella although in truth that made his arms feel awfully empty. He said a silent prayer for Maggie's safety and then sat to listen to the sermon.

"The Lord is my shepherd, I shall not want," the preacher intoned. "*I shall not want.* We say them, but do we ever really hear those words? They imply something our society doesn't understand, something we don't really believe because if we did, it would change everything about how we live. The fact is that when you put your life in God's hands, you don't have to want anything anymore because you already have everything that you really need.

"I shall not want.

"Samuel 1 tells us that the Lord does not look at the things man looks at. 'Man looks at the outward appearance, but the Lord looks at the heart.' That means, God isn't impressed with your cars, your house, or your bank account. He's impressed only with what's in your heart. In fact, in a very real way, your stuff only serves to chain you to the world—a world that will tell you that you must want everything, that you can only be happy if you get *this* toy or *that* thing. If we let it, the world will convince us to look to others for their acceptance and approval, for them to tell us how we're doing, but God doesn't work like that.

"God looks only at what's real, and the only thing that's real is the love in your heart. Everything else means nothing. The great and terrifying secret of the world is that you can work your whole life to accumulate things, pushing what is really important to the side. Only to realize at the end that you missed the only thing God will ever care about when He looks at us.

"There is only one thing we can take with us from this life to the next, only one thing that will define us as we stand before the seat of judgment. It isn't our money or our stuff. It is the love we have given away." He stopped to let that sink all the way in. "All we take with us, all we will have to show for this life when we stand before the throne of the Most High God is the love we have given away. Not the love we have attained, not the respect we've gained, not even the good works we've done to gain the applause of those around us, but only the love we have given away.

"That love can and should be manifested to the world at large, but it starts when it takes root deep in each and every heart. Then it grows outward from there, touching lives, changing lives, changing hearts. It holds out forgiveness to those downtrodden by sin. It heals. It helps. It loves—at all times, in all ways.

"Let that kind of love take root in you today. Let it permeate your life so that your every act is borne out of it. Because when you root yourself in the love of God, you already have everything you will ever need, and Heaven itself is within your grasp—not some day but right now. This very minute.

"The Lord is my shepherd. I shall not want." He paused. "Let us stand."

Keith stood as the unbelievable peace of God's love flowed around him. *Love,* he thought, *and life will take care of itself.* As scary as that sounded, he was ready to take the step from the world's way of doing things into God's. "Okay, God, You got it. My life is Yours. Take me where we're going."

"Would you like to join us tonight for dinner?" his father said as they stood in the bright sunlight outside the church.

"Dinner?" Keith asked in shock. "Tonight?"

There was mist in his father's eyes, and he looked older and much more fragile than Keith remembered. "We'd love to have you."

For some inexplicable reason he wanted nothing more than to hug the old man. "I'd love to, Dad." And with that, he walked through the door God had opened between them as he stepped forward and wrapped his father in his arms. They had missed so much time in the hurt and anger, but Keith was determined from this moment forward, they would be defined by the love between them rather than the animosity.

He backed up, and the tears in his father's eyes shimmered.

Keith nodded. "I have a couple errands to run first, and I'll be there. What? About 5:30?"

"Whatever time you get there, you will have a place."

It was time to start looking for a new job and a new life. Maggie was grateful for Greg's generosity the past week, but she couldn't live here forever. First and last month's rent, a car that ran, even money for groceries. She was at the bottom of the bottom again, and how she would ever get up from here, she had no idea. "God, please, You're going to have to do this one because I sure can't."

As she sat down on Greg's couch, she shook her head at the irony. She didn't even have a reference from her last job. She laughed at the thought of calling them. "Yes, I realize I messed up your son's life forever, could you tell them I'm punctual?" If it wasn't so funny, she would have cried. She had just slid to the floor with the classifieds and a red pen when the doorknob jiggled.

Her attention snapped to it, and instantly fear traipsed through her. Greg wasn't supposed to be back until later tonight. She scrambled to her feet, grabbed the vase from the end table, and took a step toward the door. The door opened, and a man stepped in, his head down as he worked the key back out of the lock. It was only when he looked up and came to full height that she realized who was standing there.

The second Keith caught the unbelievable image of Maggie standing there with the vase poised to strike, his heart slammed forward. "Maggie! What…?"

"Keith?" She sounded almost as surprised as he was. "What're you doing here?"

"Me? What're *you* doing here?"

"I… I'm…" The vase lowered and then clattered to the glass table. She pulled her white tank top down around her old tan pants. "I'm… Umm, Greg didn't tell me you were coming."

Yeah, Greg didn't tell me a lot of things. "Well, he didn't tell me you were here either."

She anchored her arms across her middle as her gaze fell. "I told him not to."

"You…?" He could hardly make it all the way through the questions jamming his head. "What? Why?"

"Because." She turned for the window on the other side of the room, leaving Keith to close the door so the whole world wouldn't hear.

He slid it closed and stepped into the room behind her.

"I didn't want to mess things up for you." Her words sounded like she was being strangled. "I'm… really sorry… about Saturday."

He watched her for a second, standing there, apologizing. "I'm not."

She glanced back at him, and he heard the sniff.

"That wasn't your fault, Maggie. Look, Dallas and I were a disaster waiting to happen."

"But you loved her. You were going to get married." And when she turned, there were in fact tears coursing down her cheeks.

His heart fell at the sight. "Her idea of love and my idea of love were two different things. We just waited a little long to figure that out." Keith couldn't bear even the sight of Maggie in tears, so he stepped over to her and put his arms around her. "I'm so sorry I hurt you. You'll never know how sorry I am for that."

Maggie couldn't take how nice he was being especially after everything she had done. She didn't want them to be, but Ike's words were never far away from her consciousness when she was with Keith. Even if Dallas was no longer in the picture, that didn't mean she had any better chance with him. She wasn't good enough for Keith Ayer, and she never would be. Pulling herself from him his embrace, she stepped in the direction she least wanted to go— away from him. "Well, I'm sure your family was glad to be rid of me."

"Rid of you?" His face fell in concern as he stood watching her go. "Are you kidding me? They're as worried about you as I am. In fact, Peter and I've been praying every night that you were safe and that we'd find you again."

The pull of the words turned her to him. "You've been praying?"

He laughed. "That's about all I've been doing. Man, Maggie. It's been so incredible. Dad and Vivian went with me and the kids to church today."

Incredulous dropped across her face. "To church? What did you do, hog-tie them and drag them there?"

"No. They came because they wanted to." He let out a breath, walked to the couch, and sat down. "It's been so long since Dad and I've really connected... maybe for forever. But he's coming around. He even put Pete on his lap at church today."

Maggie had to sit down before she collapsed from the shock. She went to the couch as well but made sure to put plenty of distance between them when she sat. "Your dad?"

"Yeah." Keith looked over at her, and there was an almost smile on his lips. "Who would've believed that?"

"What in the world? Did he get a brain transplant or something?"

"More like a heart transplant." Keith's gaze plummeted to his hands, and the laughter fell away from him.

A moment and then another and Maggie began to realize something wasn't right. "Keith? What is it? What's wrong?"

He glanced at her, took a breath, and closed his eyes to gather his courage. She didn't like anything about how long it was taking him to tell her. Finally he turned his full gaze on her.

"Look, Maggie, I have to tell you something, something that..." He closed his eyes again and shook his head. The battle to get the words out was clear. When he looked at her again, his eyes pleaded with her to not trash everything over whatever he was about to say. After a moment, he turned and took her hands in his, holding them gently as the storm gathered in his eyes. "Maggie, I don't know how to tell you this, so I'm just going to say it." He let out a long breath. "My dad was the one. In the wreck. With your parents."

She was having trouble getting everything her senses were telling her in. It was too much, and in the overwhelm, she wasn't understanding what he was telling her. "What... what do you mean—the one?"

Keith took another breath to settle the words. "My dad. He was the one driving the other car. He killed your parents."

"My...? What?" Without really realizing it, Maggie pulled her hands from his, stood, and walked to the window. Words and memories swam in front of her eyes.

"It was too big of a coincidence," Keith said, following her with his words only. "When I found out they were in Midland when Mom was killed, I had to know."

Maggie absorbed that and then turned slowly, only able to concentrate on one thing at a time. "And he told you?"

"I looked it up first. He didn't have much choice after that." Keith let his gaze fall to his empty hands. "I'm really sorry, Maggie. If I could bring them back, I would."

In fistfuls the pieces snapped into place in her heart. "That's when your mom died."

Pain etched across his face as he nodded. "Yeah. I didn't know... I didn't even know Dad was with her until the other day. They never told me."

For as bad as this was, when Maggie looked at him, she couldn't leave him alone in his grief. She stepped over to the couch, sat down carefully, and reached one hand over to his shoulder. "I'm so sorry, Keith. For your loss. For everything."

"I hate this. I hate what it did to you."

Her gaze dropped as the words brushed her heart. "I'm okay. I've learned to forgive and to love in ways I might never have if it hadn't happened."

He nodded, and then anguish washed through his eyes as his gaze found hers. "I spent so many nights being mad at her for leaving, mad at God for taking her, and now I realize how much time I wasted wallowing in all of that."

"It wasn't wasted," Maggie said softly. "It led you here. It made you who you are today, and who you are today is someone that I'm very glad to call my friend."

Questioning misery went through his eyes. "Friends? Is that what we are?"

The questions pushed her backward. "I… I don't know. Isn't that what you want us to be?"

Answer upon answer went through his eyes. Finally he shook his head. "No. I can't just be friends with you." He exhaled, and her heart plummeted. However, when his gaze grabbed hers, there was a glimmer of peace and hope. "The truth is I've fallen in love with you, Maggie. I think about you every second. I count the minutes until we can be together again. When I thought I'd lost you, it was killing me to think I'd never see you again. I know this is sudden, and I know it makes no sense, but I love you, Maggie. I do. I have ever since you fell down those stupid stairs."

Joy, happiness, and disbelief danced through her. "And I've loved you ever since you wouldn't let me carry my own suitcase. I thought you were completely crazy."

"I was… about you." Levity dissipated as his eyes grew serious. And then, as if life itself had never stood in their way, he leaned toward her and tilted his head so that his lips met hers in a burst of light and awe. One kiss and he slid closer to her so his arms could gather her into them.

Maggie felt weightless, taken up by his kisses and the feel of the strength of his arms around her. How many nights she had dreamt of this, and how many moments had she told herself it would never happen? And now, suddenly, beyond anything she could even have let herself wish, she was here with him, and it was better even than she had let herself ever believe it could be.

Breathless from the kiss, she let his strength hold her as he backed away. Her eyes slid open still lost in the dream.

"And now I have to ask you something that you're probably going to run screaming from the hills when I say," Keith said, but he never let her go. "My parents are having dinner tonight, and I've been invited." His gaze drilled into her spirit. "Will you come with me?"

Surprise jumped through her. "To dinner with your parents?"

He nodded.

No invitation to meet the parents had ever carried the weight that one did. "I... Umm..." She sat up, took a breath, and looked down at herself. Her hand went to her hair, and she knew she must look a mess. "I don't have anything to wear."

Keith laughed. "Then what do you say we go do a little shopping?"

Hand-in-hand they walked up the steps to Greg's apartment. The three mall bags in Keith's other hand dangled there as if they belonged nowhere else. At the top of the stairs he opened the door for her. "Why don't you go get ready, get your other stuff, and we'll take off?"

"Okay." She took the bags from him with a shy smile.

He watched her walk down the hallway, and the truth was he would be happy to watch that walk forever. He'd waited only a few minutes next to the couch when noise at the door drew his attention there. A second and he was standing face-to-face with the best friend a guy could ever have.

"Keith," Greg said in surprise. His gaze slid down the hallway. "Hey, man. What's up?"

"What's up. Yeah... You say that like you don't know."

Fear traced across Greg's face.

Keith laughed. "Well, I came by to get the rings, which to be honest I didn't even really care about, but it's the funniest thing. You never told me you got a new roommate."

Greg ducked his head and stepped past Keith to the kitchen. He grabbed a glass from the cabinet and filled it with water before he faced Keith. "She didn't want me to tell you."

Keith smiled. "You didn't."

"Hi, everyone," Keith said, stepping into the dining room. Maggie was behind him, her hand firmly held by his so she couldn't run. "I brought you a surprise."

Around the table all gazes came up to him. He pulled Maggie around him, and questions turned to chaos.

"Maggie!" Peter exclaimed, jumping from his chair and running to her. She caught him in a hug that brought tears to Keith's eyes.

"Gie! Gie! Gie! Gie!" Isabella yelled, bouncing in her high chair until it practically tipped over.

"Hang on." Keith laughed as he tried to free the excited, kicking little girl. "You're stuck." His fingers worked the lever. "There we go." He lifted her out, stood her on the floor, and she toddled to Maggie and Peter who were having a tear-filled reunion on the floor of the dining room.

"Come here, you," Maggie said as she gathered Isabella in too. "Oh, I missed you so much, baby girl." She kissed the little girl soundly on the top of the head as she gathered her into her embrace.

Keith's gaze went from her to the head of the table, and he snagged his father's attention. Keith nodded in answer to the question in his father's eyes. It was all right. His father just didn't know it yet.

"Oh, Maggie," Inez said, nearly tripping over her when she came in with dinner. "What're you doing here?"

Happiness radiated from Maggie's face. "I couldn't stay away."

Dinner was wonderful. It was almost like being a part of a real family, Maggie thought. The kids were so happy, it was hard not to be, but then there were the times she chanced a glance at Mr. Ayer, and she knew this was anything but easy for him. When dinner was over, Maggie was less than sure what came next. Was she here as a nanny again or as Keith's date, and where did one end and the other begin?

"Keith," Mr. Ayer said as they exited the dining room, "I'd like to talk Ms. Montgomery... Maggie for a minute, if you don't mind. Can you handle the kids?"

"Handle them?" Keith asked wickedly. "I'll handle them all right." He swung Peter up and over his shoulder. Then he reached down and took Isabella's hand. Bouncing so that Peter made uh, uh, uh sounds, Keith climbed the stairs. At the bend he stopped and looked right at Maggie. "We'll be up here when you're finished."

"Okay," she said, wondering how she even got those two syllables out.

"Come with me," Mr. Ayer said.

Maggie swallowed half of her trepidation, leaving the other half to suffocate whatever confidence she'd managed to acquire during the meal. She followed the man who held her future in his hands all the way to his office. If this could've been any more nerve-wracking, she wouldn't have known how.

Instead of sitting at the desk as she had expected him to, Mr. Ayer went all the way to the huge window behind it. He stood there, hands clasped behind his back, staring out into the twilight beyond for the longest minute of her life.

By the time he started talking, she wasn't even breathing anymore.

"You know, Ms. Montgomery, I had pretty much given up on what I always thought were my dreams ever making me happy. I had managed to acquire everything I'd ever wanted—money, fame, prestige, a family, this house and estate. I had businesses and clients and employees. But I knew something was missing."

He glanced back at her. "A long time ago I made a huge mistake. One I've never forgotten about even for a single second. I knew it at the time, but I thought if I just covered it up good enough, no one would ever see me for what I knew I really was. So, instead of going away, it festered, and the harder I tried to pretend it wasn't there, the worse it got. That night, all my behavior before it and after it just dug me in deeper and deeper until I didn't think there was any way back out. And then you came along."

The words pushed Maggie backward. "Me, Sir?"

He smiled at her sadly. "I didn't just lose my wife the night you lost your parents. I lost my son and my self. I lost what it was to be happy, to love someone else." He exhaled. "Keith took the brunt of my stupidity as I'm sure you well know, but I'm afraid it wasn't just him who suffered. I believe you did as well."

Maggie tried to wave it off. "I'm…"

"No, Ms. Montgomery, you have shown grace and courage in the face of great difficulty. I find that awe-inspiring. You have held your own in this house, and let me just say, I know that hasn't been easy." With that he faced her. "I guess what I'm trying to say is that you, my dear, are my role model. I cannot tell you how impressed I've been with how you have guided Keith to something better than he ever was before. It reminds me very much of another young lady much like yourself who tried to get a head-strong young businessman to see how badly he was missing what's really important."

"I wasn't trying…"

"No, you didn't have to try because that's who you were. That's who you are." He smiled. "I want my children to learn from that. In fact, I want to learn that as well."

"Sir…?"

He stopped her with a raise of his hand. "Now, I want it made perfectly clear that when Keith asks you to marry him…"

Maggie's eyes went wide as her heart jerked forward. But he stopped her before she could protest.

"Which he will. However, I do not want Peter and Isabella to grow up without your influence. I know after my track record, and I have no right to demand anything, so I'm asking you. Will you stay and teach my children what I cannot?"

For as irrational as that sounded, Maggie's heart went out to him. His humility in the face of everything that had happened overwhelmed the last traces of her anger toward him. She stepped around the desk and over to him. The hesitation lasted only a second before she put her arms around him. At first he was taken aback by her actions, but then he let her hug truly embrace him. Gently he patted her arm without returning the gesture. When she backed up, she looked at him squarely. "And just so you never have to wonder, I forgive you. God and I hashed that out a long time ago. I know you didn't mean to hurt them."

"Oh, I didn't. I really didn't. If I could go back…"

"No," she said, stopping him firmly. "We can't go back, but we can go forward."

His smile was slow and hopeful. "I'd like that."

"Are they asleep?" Maggie asked as she treaded down the hallway, lit only by the glow of the nightlight. She felt like she'd missed so many nights with them already.

"They're down," Keith said as he closed Isabella's door. "But I think Peter's waiting for his angel to come and pray with him."

Maggie's heart cracked open as joy surged through her. She stepped past Keith then turned. "You coming?"

He put his hand over hers. "I wouldn't miss it."

She pushed into the room, and Peter looked over at her. "Maggie!"

"Shh." She put her finger to her lips although she really wasn't mad. "Izzy's sleeping." Softly she crept over to the bed, and she was momentarily sad when Keith dropped her hand. However, in seconds he was on the other side of the bed, reaching out for her once again, and something in her sensed how his spirit had been doing that to hers from the very beginning.

With no reservation she laid her hand in his and bent her head. "Dear Heavenly Father… Huh." She had to shake her hair back away from her face at the amazement of it all. "Thank You so very much. Every good thing comes from You, and we thank You for all the blessings You have given us. For Peter and Isabella, for the Ayers, and Inez and Patty Ann, Tanner, Jamie, and Ike. We thank You Father for all of them. Thank You for keeping them safe for us. We ask that You keep those who You have already drawn back to Yourself in Your loving embrace until we can see them again.

"Most of all, God, we thank You for the gift of love." She squeezed Keith's hand lest he not understand the depths of her gratefulness. "We know it is a gift from You, and we give thanks that You have chosen to share it with us." The prayer was winding to the end. "We ask that You keep all boys and girls in the world safe tonight. If they are lonely, give them comfort. If they are hungry, send someone to feed them. If they are in danger, protect them, O God. Keep us all safe in Your love this night and every night. Amen." Her eyes stayed closed as she let the prayer and the peace settle into the deepest recesses of her being.

"And please, dear God," Keith said, startling Maggie out of her reverie, "let Maggie say, 'Yes.'"

Her gaze slid to his in incomprehension. He smiled at her. "Amen."

"Amen," Peter echoed, and Maggie could hardly get her gaze off of Keith long enough to remember Peter was still in the room.

She pushed herself to her feet, wobbling on the weight she found standing. Her two fingers knew what to do, which was a lucky thing because no rational signals were getting from her brain to her body. She kissed them and pressed them softly to Peter's forehead. "Good night, sweet prince." With that, she turned and headed for the door.

"Night, slugger."

Her heart flipped over at how natural this all felt. In the hallway she waited for him, and she had to steel her breath when he joined her. Those arms, that presence—if anything it had gotten stronger since they'd last stood here.

When the door was closed, Keith turned to her. He narrowed his eyes at her and shook his head. "Man, I hope God was listening." He stopped for only one moment, and then he knelt on a single knee. "Maggie…"

Astonishment swept over her, and she put her hand to her mouth. Gently he reached up, took it from her mouth, and pulled it down into his. "Maggie Montgomery, I don't ever want to spend another day away from you. Please make me the happiest man in the world. Say you'll marry me."

Breath was her only answer for a long moment. "I… Yes. I'll marry you."

He stood, swept her into his arms, and kissed her like she'd never been kissed before. Then holding her in the safety of his embrace, he backed up and smiled at her. "I'm sure glad God was listening."

Epilogue

"I thought you said you wanted a simple ceremony," Keith's father said as he picked his way down the rocky path. "Haven't you ever heard of an aisle?"

"It gets better over there," Keith said, pointing to the tree as he helped his dad and Vivian down the steep slope. However, even the happiness in him snagged when he caught sight of Maggie, standing with the children under the tree waiting for them. The falls beyond sang with the fresh rain that had fallen the night before. Washed clean the scene was so perfect the fact that God had created it was the only logical conclusion anyone could have surmised.

The ground leveled out, and Keith let them go to travel on their own.

"Oh, Conrad. This is beautiful," Vivian exclaimed. "I didn't even know this was here."

His father was equally stunned. "I'd forgotten that it was."

Stepping from their presence, Keith walked over to Maggie. With Peter and Isabella gazing up at them from her side, he put his arms around her. "I didn't know it was possible to feel like this," he whispered to her. His smile shone from the depths of his heart as he took in the soft gaze, the gentle face, yes, even the new gold-toned glasses that he'd accepted so reluctantly—he loved them all because he loved her.

"You ready?" she asked, gazing up at him.

"More than."

Maggie's hand stayed in Keith's as they turned to the preacher. If there was an ounce more joy in her, she felt like she would burst right open.

"Keith and Maggie, have you come here freely and without reservation to declare your love before God and man?"

"We have." Her voice mingled right into his, harmony personified.

The preacher motioned for them to look at each other, and Maggie had the feeling that she was falling more in love with each passing second as he held her with his gaze. As the preacher said the words, Keith said them to her, and his voice blended with the melody of the falls.

"I, Keith, take you, Maggie to be my lawful wedded wife. I promise to be true to you in good times and in bad, in sickness and in health, for richer or for poorer. I will love you and honor you all the days of my life."

Her smile drifted through her heart to her eyes and right to him. "I, Maggie, take you, Keith to be my lawful wedded husband. I promise to be true to you in good times and in bad, in sickness and in health, for richer or for poorer. I will love you and honor you all the days of my life."

"The rings please."

Keith let her hand go to reach into his pocket. He gave the rings to the preacher and took not a second more to have her hands in his once again. The preacher blessed the rings and gave Keith the simple gold band.

"Maggie, take and wear my ring as a sign of my love and fidelity. In the name of the Father and of the Son and of the Holy Spirit."

Her hands were shaking so badly, Maggie was afraid she would drop his. But she managed to get it from the preacher's hand onto Keith's finger. However, even when it was on, the emotion gripped her, and she wasn't at all sure she could get the words out. However, she looked at him, and his smile flowed through her spirit.

"Keith, take and wear my ring as a sign of my love and fidelity. In the name of the Father and of the Son and of the Holy Spirit." She slid the ring to his knuckle, and he slid it all the way on without ever dropping her gaze from his. A breath and his hands were once again supporting hers.

"Now, by the powers vested in me by the State of Texas," the preacher said. "I now pronounce you man and wife. Keith, you may kiss your bride."

Maggie's heart filled to overflowing as he took her in his arms and brushed his lips to hers. One kiss and then one more. He backed up and then with a laugh swept her up once more and kissed her soundly. One thing was for sure, being with him would never be boring. When he finally let her go enough to put air between them, wonder was in his eyes.

"May I present to you Mr. and Mrs. Keith Ayer."

With his arm securely around her, Keith hugged the moment to them. The others clapped, and then his father stepped up to them.

"Maggie, Keith, I probably should wait until the reception later, but..." He looked out to the falls, and when he looked back to them there were tears in his eyes. "I want you to know I have taken the liberty of setting up two foundations to be run by the two of you. One, run by Maggie for the benefit of the foster care system, is to be called the James and Christina Montgomery Foundation. It will be seeded with ten million dollars and will no doubt benefit many of the children Peter prays for every night."

Speechless, Maggie looked at Keith, who was equally stunned.

"And Keith." His father looked at him. "I do not know who you are meant to help in this world, so I have left the exact mission of the Bonnie Ayer foundation open-ended. I do know, however, that you'll do the right thing with it."

Tears flowed down the old man's cheeks as he pulled them into a hug. "God bless you both."

"Keith!" The voice from the rocks crashed through the celebration. "Keith... Keith... Maggie..." Stumbling down the path came Jamie with Tanner right behind her. She had a cell phone up in the air. "I know. I know, but this call just came in, and I knew you would want to take it."

Maggie's gaze went to Keith as he took the cell phone from Jamie. "Hello?" His gaze traced down to her. "Yes, this is Keith Ayer." The pause set her pulse racing as she tried to figure out what was going on. "Already?"

He looked at her, and she read every word. Stunned disbelief smashed into her. "Already?

"Yes. Yes, ma'am. We can be there tomorrow morning. Yes.

Thank you. Yes, thank you, Ma'am." He squeezed Maggie to him as he beeped the phone off. Love surged through her like a gigantic fountain. After a moment for just the two of them to enjoy the news, his gaze swept over the others and then down to Maggie in confirmation. "Well, we were going to wait to tell you this, but I guess it's kind of late now."

Her gaze stayed on him as love so strong it swept the rest of the world from her gushed through her.

"We applied to be foster parents, and well..." He looked down at her again. "They have a little girl they want to place with us in the morning."

Ohs and gasps criss-crossed the little group.

"It was a little unconventional," Keith said, gazing at Maggie who was lost in his words and his eyes, "but they pulled some strings, and it's for real. Elisa Marie will be with us by tomorrow night."

She let out a long breath as Keith turned to her once again and pulled her into his embrace. Never could Maggie have guessed she could feel for another person what she felt for him at that moment. They were together. They were a team, and deep in her heart she knew this moment had been in God's plan from the very beginning. God had taken everything life had thrown at them and stitched something very, very good from it. She now had a husband and a family, and tomorrow she would be the bridge for a little girl to learn that even life's trials aren't the end of the story if you trust God to open the doors you were meant to walk through.

Somehow, she had always known that to be true, and as Keith hugged her to him once again, any questions that had remained on that count faded away forever.

For it is by grace you have been saved, through faith, and this is not from yourselves, it is the gift of God.
--Ephesians 2:8

For more about becoming foster parents, please visit:
The Bair Foundation
http://www.bair.org/

Chapter 1

"Don't give me that, bro. Come on. We want details. Lots of details."

At the stainless steel refrigerator in the kitchen, Ben Warren grabbed the handle as he smiled. "Oh, no. I don't kiss and tell." He reached in, snagged three cold ones, and headed back for the large round table currently taking up a good portion of his living room. Setting the other two beers on the table, he sat down and twisted the cap off his before taking a long drink.

Friday night and the living was good.

"Since when?" one of the guys called.

"Yeah, come on, Ben," Kelly Zandavol, Ben's best friend since high school said as he nailed Ben with an I-don't-believe-that-for-a-minute look. "You can't leave us hanging like that. What's she like?"

"No. Uh-huh." Ben shook his head even as he took another drink. "You ain't getting any more."

"Dude," Logan Murphy said, surveying his cards although there was only sparse attention to the actual game, "you know that you're our in with the ladies. Now you're gonna freeze us out just when it's getting good? What's up with that?" He rearranged the cards in his hand though presumably that didn't help. God Himself couldn't help Logan with cards or with the ladies as he called them. "If I can't live through you, I'm doomed."

"Not to mention the shape Kelly'll be in," Todd Rundell added. "You know what that marriage thing can do to a guy."

"Hey. Hey." Kelly lifted his chin. "Speak for yourself there. Me and my lady are doing just fine."

"Uh-huh." Todd put down his beer, picked up his cards, and shuffled them back and forth in his hand. "That's why you're over here at nearly midnight on a Friday night."

"That's better than you turkeys," Kelly retorted. "At least I've got a woman to go home to."

Logan laid three cards on the table. "Three." He waited for Kelly to deal him three new ones. "The man does have a point. Yes. Yes, he does."

Ben took one more drink of the beer before setting it down and getting down to the business of raking more of his friends' money to his side of the table. "Well, I'll take beer and cards over having some chick looking over my shoulder all the time an-y-day. Two." He waited and accepted the two cards Kelly gave him. He fought not to let the disappointment in the hand show, but it didn't work very well. "Dang, Kelly. I think you need to go back home to that lady of yours. This dealing thing is not your forte."

"Ha. Ha. Funny-man. You in or out?" Kelly nodded to the table, indicating the betting had begun.

A long breath that Ben exhaled very slowly. Finally he pushed his cards together. "I'm out. No sense playing trash like that." He stood to go back into the kitchen, figuring if no one was leaving, they might as well get some sustenance. Pushing the unbuttoned and rolled sleeves of his blue pin-striped work shirt up to his elbows, he reached into the cabinet and pulled out a bag of chips and another of pretzels. With two rips he had them open. He didn't bother with the dish. The guys didn't care about that kind of stuff anyway.

"Ah, dude! Aces? You're kidding me!" Logan exclaimed as Ben headed back.

"Hey, you play, you pay," Kelly said, raking all the money in the middle to his side of the table. "So, are you at least gonna tell us her name?"

Ben put the bags in the center of the table. He pulled a chip out and sat down, crunching loudly. Truly, truly, he wished they would stop the questioning. If they didn't, he might have to resort to making things up.

Unfortunately, Kelly had known him too long. He stopped gathering the cards and looked right at Ben who was crunching and drinking but not really looking up. "You don't know it, do you?"

"Know what?" Ben asked as if he had no clue what Kelly was talking about. Then he shrugged and grabbed another chip. "Of course I do. It was…" For one second too long, his brain went on vacation. "Cheris. Her name was Cheris." He bit into the chip and smiled widely. "See. I told you I knew it."

"Uh-huh." Kelly's look told Ben he wasn't at all sure if he believed that or not.

Truthfully, Ben wasn't completely sure whether to believe himself or not. That whole night after the company party was a little fuzzy. In fact, there were very few nights when he ended up in his bed or someone else's that weren't more than a little fuzzy. Of course, the guys didn't need to know that part, and they were on a need to know basis, if that.

The phone in the kitchen rang precluding anymore discussion of the subject.

"Speak of the devil," Logan said as Ben's gaze jumped at the sound.

Puzzled by who might be calling at midnight, other than Cheris—if that was her name—he got to his feet. Then again, he didn't think she had his phone number although she might. Those details weren't exactly clear. The thoughts swirled in his brain as he headed for the still ringing phone.

"Hi, honey," Logan said sweetly. "Oh, sure, you can come on over. I'll just chase the guys out..."

Ben wanted to deck him, but he was already to the phone. The guys all cracked up at the kissy noises Logan was making. For grown men who were all 30-something, they certainly could be childish sometimes. "Hello."

"Uh. Mr... Mr. Warren?"

In the background he could hear the too familiar sounds of a medical facility. Worry dropped on him as he spun and ducked next to the cabinet. "Yes, this is Ben Warren."

"Uh, Mr. Warren, I'm sorry to bother you so late, but this is St. Anthony's Hospital. Your father has just been admitted. You are listed as his next of kin..."

The rest of the words evaporated in a swirl of alarm and concern. "What? Is he okay?" He put his finger in his ear to block everything else out. "What happened?"

"I'm not really authorized to discuss it, but the doctors think it would be a good idea for you to get here as quickly as possible."

Ben ran his hand through and over his thick, dark hair. "Uh. Yeah. Yeah. Okay. I'll be there as soon as possible."

Somehow he ended the phone call, but it too was lost in the spinning of the world around him. He closed his eyes and fought to breathe, hoping to make it stop. However, when he opened his eyes, it was still tilting and shifting around him. Decisions. He had to make some decisions. First, he needed to get to the hospital to see what was going on. Pushing away from the cabinet, he stumbled through the myriad of possibilities as he headed through the living room.

Three surprised and very concerned faces gazed up at him.

"Something wrong?" Kelly asked.

"Uh. Yeah. I guess. I don't know. It's my dad." None of the words seemed to even correlate with reality. "I don't know. Something happened."

At the little closet, he pulled out the first jacket his hand found, and he yanked it on. "You guys just lock up when you're done."

"You want me to go with you?" Kelly asked, standing. His dark face was ash-washed with concern.

"No." Ben tried to shake the looks on his friends' faces from his consciousness. "No. Of course not. I'm... I'm sure it's nothing." *Do they call you from the hospital at midnight if it's nothing?* He couldn't answer that question, and he didn't even want to try. "I'll just..." The words were jamming together in his brain in no distinct pattern. "Um... Just let yourselves out when you're finished. And be sure to lock up."

Remembering he would have to drive, he patted his pockets and then looked around. "Keys? Where are my keys?"

"By the front door where they always are?" Kelly asked, clearly tipping toward legitimate concern for his friend.

"Oh, yeah. Right." Ben nodded, having no idea why.

"Are you sure you don't want me to go?"

"Yeah. Yeah. I'm sure. I'll let you know." Taking the keys from the little hook, Ben wrenched the doorknob and for one second, considered reconsidering his friend's offer. He didn't want to face whatever this was alone. Then he took his ego by the collar and gave it a good shake. He was Ben Warren, and Ben Warren didn't back down from any challenge. With that thought, he yanked the door open and headed to the hospital.

The final credits rolled up and off the screen as Kathryn Walker swiped at the tears streaming down her cheeks. The only good thing was that she was alone, no one here to witness this pitiful display of sap and desperation. She could hear Misty or Casey or her mother. Ugh. Her mother. That was enough to dry all the tears with one single sniff.

Her mother would count this as verifiable proof that being unmarried was the single worst disposition a woman could have on this earth. Especially a woman of 32 and three-quarter years. As Kathryn stood, she sniffed again and walked over to the DVD player to replace that disc in its proper case. It was strange how somewhere north of 28, she had started counting the months to and from her birthday like a ten-year-old.

"I'm still six months from being 30." "I'm only 30 and two months…" It was pathetic really—as if there would be something magical about the four months before she was 30 and six months, or 31 and six months, or 35, or whatever. At one time she had vehemently sworn to herself that by such-and-such an age, she would've found Mr. Right. But when such-and-such became six months ago and then a year ago, and then five years ago, she had given up that game and morphed into the newest incarnation of singlehood—the defiant, "I kind of like it this way. No, really, I do. It's easier…"

She wasn't sure if anyone believed her. She didn't even believe her. Especially on nights like tonight. The movie that was supposed to cheer her up had hardly done that. Instead, it had brought her face-to-face in vibrant color with the fact that everyone else found that perfectly perfect person for them through these neat, cute little coincidences that just, for whatever reason, never seemed to happen for her or to her. She couldn't quite tell which it was. She wondered for the millionth time if they knew some secret that she didn't. However, she was pretty sure it was all just one big, stinking luck of the draw thing. And she was about as unlucky in that department as anyone had ever been.

As she flipped off the light and gingerly made her way through her dark apartment toward her bedroom, she went through the inventory of herself once more. Weight—not bad, could be better, but not bad. Looks—above average but definitely not model territory. Financial standing—quite good actually. Good job— check. Moral with values—check. Although honestly, she wasn't sure if that one counted for her or against her.

Certainly she could have bedded many in the past if she had

been into that existence, which she most definitely was not. No. Even snagging a guy wasn't worth giving up her self-worth. Besides, she knew quite a few who had done just that only to find divorce papers on the other side of the marriage certificate.

With a sigh, she climbed between the pressed cotton sheets and sighed. Nope, the hard truth was all the good guys were long gone. The only ones left had track records that read like rap sheets not to mention baggage from their several failed marriages and a couple of kids thrown in for good measure. Still, as she did every night, she closed her eyes, snuggled into the covers and thought about him. She had no real picture of him although she had seen him in her dreams on a couple of occasions—never his face, just vague pieces.

She snuggled deeper thinking about those pieces. Like his hands. She'd always liked his hands, with nice long fingers and a presence she couldn't quite put into words. And his dark hair. That one always made her heart snag. She would know that hair when she saw it. Of that, she was sure. She had seen it so many times in her dreams. Slowly sleep began to take over her senses, and as she drifted off, she let out a long sigh. "God, please be with him wherever he is. Keep him safe and guide him. And please let him know that I already love him. Amen."

The disorienting transition from the darkened parking lot and street lights into the blinding white light of St. Anthony's emergency room cut right through Ben's skull with the precision of a sharp scalpel. He blinked it back, hoping he wouldn't trip over something he couldn't see because he never even slowed down all the way to the counter. The nurse on the other side looked both bored and half-asleep.

"Excuse me, I need to know…" he started.

"Please get in line," she said with no feeling to her voice at all.

"What?" He glanced around in confusion. "There is no line."

"All patients must get in line behind that sign." She pointed to the ceiling without so much as looking at it.

Ben looked around and up at the sign. *For privacy, please remain behind this line until you are called forward.* The same was written again in Spanish and then in some language he neither spoke nor could decode.

"Please step behind the line and wait to be called."

Man, he wanted to argue. More than he'd ever wanted to do anything in his life, he wanted to argue, but he sensed from Ms. No-Nonsense that doing so would only prolong this nightmare. Tilting his head at that understanding, he nodded. "Okay." He pushed back from the counter and took the four steps to the front of the non-existent line. After a moment, he put his hands out to his side to indicate that he had fully complied with the request.

The nurse took her own sweet time as she finished up whatever she was doing. Then, looking like she was bored to tears, she looked up. "Next."

Finally. Ben rushed forward.

"Name?" she asked.

"Um, it's for my father."

"Name?"

Frustration growled through him. "Mine or his?"

She checked him with a condescending scowl. "Are you the patient or is he?"

"He is. They said they brought him in..." Composure slipped away from him as he looked at his watch. "Like an hour ago or something like that."

"Okay. His name?" She put her fingers on the keyboard.

"Ron... uh, Ronald Warren."

"Ronald F. Warren?"

"Yes."

She nodded but didn't continue. As panic set into his heart, he arched forward, straining to see what was on that screen. With a deepening scowl, she looked at him and turned the screen from his line of vision as he backed off.

"Sorry."

You should be went through her eyes. "Mr. Warren has been taken to the 8th Floor, Neurology."

"Neurology?" Ben repeated the word, trying to understand the horrors it hid in its depths.

"Yes." The nurse glanced behind him. "Next."

It was a fight to keep his balance on an even keel as he turned from the desk and hurried to the elevators at the far end of the room. This part he knew. This part he had memorized. The riding the elevator part—up to see doctors, down to see administrators—working to incorporate his company's newest line of life-saving drugs into the hospital's current regimen of patient care.

At the elevator, he hit the button and stepped back, putting his hand on the beltline of his jeans. He arched first his gaze and then his neck to watch the numbers above the elevator slowly slide downward. Part of him wanted them to speed up. Part of him wanted them to stop altogether. If they just stopped, then he wouldn't have to deal with whatever came next. He tried to think about what that might be—what neurology meant, what he should do if this was truly serious.

He let out a quick I'm-being-stupid breath and fought to tamp down the clutch of fear around his chest. His father was fine. Of course, he was fine. He was, after all, only 66. That was hardly old. With the back of his hand, Ben scratched the side of his face as indiscriminant nerves attacked him.

The elevator dinged, yanking his attention upward. He stepped back as those on the elevator disembarked, and then raking in a breath, he got on and hit the round number 8 button. So many things. So many memories and thoughts of the past and future criss-crossed in his brain as the little box slid upward. Should he call his mother? She would probably want to know. Especially if it was serious.

What about Jason? Surely his mother knew where his brother was. She should make that call. Ben certainly didn't want to— even if he knew the number, which he didn't. Truth be known, he didn't want to do any of this. If he could somehow just skipped over the next hours or days or whatever this turned out to be, he would with no questions. He didn't do serious or responsibility very well. How had the universe not gotten that memo? Or maybe it had, and this would in fact turn out to be nothing. False alarm. Nothing to worry about.

The bell dinged, and he forced all the other thoughts and worries down into himself. First, he would find out how bad it was. Then he would figure out how best to proceed.

It wasn't like there was a barking dog or even traffic noises this high up, so there was really no excuse for not being able to sleep.

However, Kathryn had endured more than one night like this, and she knew there was no forcing sleep. In frustration, she flipped the covers off her legs and swung herself to the edge of the bed.

"Ugh." Why did life have to be so impossible? She stood carefully and got her balance before turning her steps for the kitchen.

Over the sink, she turned on the little light and squinted into it. Two blinks and her eyes began to accept the invasion of the light. On auto-pilot and with a yawn, she went first to one cabinet, then to the other, gathering what she needed for chamomile tea. It was her first line of defense on nights such as these. If this didn't work, she'd be back for hot chocolate in an hour. Then melatonin if all else failed.

She filled the little cup with hot water from the tap. It would give the tea that funny after-taste she hated, but it was quicker than going the kettle route, and since she'd read that stupid email about not heating water in the microwave, she'd been too much of a coward to try that again. Instead, she took her mostly lukewarm water to the counter and put in the teabag.

In no time the clear water had turned to a dull brownish-yellow. With one half teaspoon of sugar, she lifted it to her lips. "Ugh." Terrible as she figured it would be. Not caring, she lifted it again, switch off the light, and headed back for her bedroom.

"Mr. Warren, your father has suffered a massive stroke." The doctor in the white coat that Ben had never met before gave the news softly but with noted firmness.

The little consultation room seemed to close in on Ben as he shifted in the chair. He swallowed that feeling down. "Okay."

"As next of kin, where we go from here is pretty much up to you and the good Lord," the doctor continued obviously assuming Ben had some connection to the Creator that he really didn't.

Ben narrowed his focus, trying to find the answers the doctor seemed to think he had. "I... Okay. Um. What are our options?"

"Well, we've stabilized him as much as we can. At this point, we could try surgery although with his heart history and his present condition, I can't guarantee anything."

Ben absorbed the news with another swallow, a nod, and a

small shift backward. "Heart. Yeah... Okay. So..."

"We have an MRI scheduled for the morning to determine the exact extent of the damage. Once we get those results, we will probably know more about how to proceed."

"Okay. Good." It was incomprehensible that he should know what to say. "Um, can I see him?"

"He's in ICU right now. They're getting him settled. You can have a seat in the waiting area. ICU visits don't really start until 8 a.m., but for you, I'll make an exception. Your father and I played many rounds of golf together. I know he would want you to have this time if..." The words stopped. "Well, he would want you to have this time."

Although Ben tried to wrap his mind around all of this and think it through, the truth was he was lost, like being in a forest with no trail and only brambles and briars for as far as the eye could see. How or why he had gotten dropped here, he had no idea. Where he was supposed to go from here was even vaguer. "Um, do you... do you think I should call my mother and... well, should I let everyone know?"

The pause was almost imperceptible, and then the doctor nodded. "I think that would be wise."

Read more about the #1 Religious Fiction @ Amazon book "Coming Undone" at Ebook Romance Stories:

http://ebookromancestories.com/2012/02/10/the-story-coming-undone/